J ROBERT KING

DEATH'S DISCIPLES

ANGRY
ROBOT

ANGRY ROBOT
A member of the Osprey Group

Lace Market House,
54-56 High Pavement,
Nottingham
NG1 1HW, UK

www.angryrobotbooks.com
Let's roll

Originally published in the UK by Angry Robot 2011
First American paperback printing 2011

ISBN 978-0-85766-073-2

Printed in the United States of America

9 8 7 6 5 4 3 2 1

To my cousin Jim –
reader, writer, musician,
and goofball.

Prologue **FLIGHT**

I hate flying. Always have. It's not just the old man on my left snoring, his liver-spotted hand brushing my leg, or the young man on my right darting looks down my blouse. It's not just the plume of rebreathed air in my face or the flight attendants staring dead-eyed as they hand out bags of pretzels. It's the impossibility of it.

People aren't supposed to fly. Hundred-ton machines certainly aren't.

My stomach's a knot.

"Look at that," the young man says. His name is Jason. He's got an Amish-style beard – not because he's Amish but because he's too young to grow anything better. Too young for me. Jason hooks his nose toward the TV screen, which shows our current position over Billings. "We're at 35,000 feet, and the air outside's negative seventy-five."

"Cold," I agree, staring at the in-flight magazine as if I cared what meals were available for purchase.

"Fall out of this plane, and you'd be frozen before you hit the ground," he enthuses. "You'd shatter like a glass doll."

The knot tightens. "There's a Darwin Award for you." They offer a turkey croissant with baby carrots and chocolate pudding.

How much longer? It's five minutes till noon.

I hate flying, but business calls.

"I need to get up," I tell the Amish kid. "Call of nature."

Jason grins, pivoting his legs to one side and watching my ass as I squeeze past.

The midcabin lavatory is closer, but I pick my way back among the crammed seats. Can't believe I booked in coach, a purgatory – all these dreary, drowsing people, their faces slack, eyes lidded, oblivious to the fact that people aren't supposed to fly...

The rear lav is occupied.

I wait.

Three minutes to noon.

I knock. The person inside groans. The bolt hisses in the slot, the door louvers, and out comes a fifty-something woman wreathed in a cloud of perfume and flatulence. She glances at me with annoyance, and I return the look as she shoe-horns past. I enter the lav and lock the door behind me and look at myself in the mirror.

Blonde, thirty-two, and smart – and watch that smile, that killer smile.

I can't wait for this flight to be over.

It is.

There's a noise so loud I can't hear it – a white ball in my head. It hurls me up to the ceiling and pins me to the wall and flings me back down. Teeth crack on stainless steel. Chemical water gushes up my nose. Water and blood.

Another white ball. I'm on my knees on the floor.

There's a terrible tearing. Metal shredding.

The sound becomes a scream. *Screams.*

An all-encompassing roar.

I can't see anything. I can only hear.

It's too much.

Why is everything so loud?

My face is slick. Blood?

What is this place? Plastic walls, panels, frames? I spot a metal knob and yank on it, and doors open.

The roar is louder now—a narrow hallway with carpet below and blood beside.

I stagger up and step out.

I'm inside a plane, except there's no floor. Just three rows of seats and torn walls and a big hole. I look through the hole. Grassy hills flash golden below, and the shadow of the plane skims across them.

The shadow grows larger.

We're going to crash.

I can see trees and rocks.

I step back through the door and pull it closed in front of me and sit down on the toilet and bend my head down between my knees and wait for the end.

It comes.

It sounds like a broken motor.

It looks like the sun exploding.

It feels like tigers tearing me apart.

1 AWAKENING

There's warm darkness and a heartbeat. All around me, there's a heartbeat. Not the thud of blood in a body but a cold *ping*. A green line on a screen.

My eyes are open, but I've been looking through them only seconds. The green line jags whenever my heart beats.

My heart.

Ceiling tiles and tan curtains and textured wallpaper and a TV hanging above like a stalker.

A hospital?

There are tubes in my arms. I rip them out. I try to get up from the bed, but there's another tube up my nose. I grip it. A worm of plastic drags up my throat and burns – the smell of puke.

An alarm goes off.

Footsteps scuff linoleum. A nurse bustles in. Her hair is tight and her eyes are wide so she looks like a startled fish. She sees the tubes dribbling on the floor and gulps, then leans over me and snaps her fingers. "You blinked!"

Where am I?

"You're trying to talk!" She turns, her shoes rasping. "Doctor! She's out of the coma…" Her voice fades as she vanishes through the doorway.

A man takes her place, filling the frame – an XXL man

in an XL suit. He glances after the nurse and then comes and stands next to me and stares. He has curly black hair but an Irish face.

The nurse returns, and the man makes room for her and an East Indian doctor. He scoops up my hands and sees the weeping holes in them.

"It's good to have you back," he says in a musical voice. "How are you feeling?"

What's happening?

"It's all right," the doctor says. "Relax now. You are safe."

"What's happening?" My voice is chalk.

The doctor leans toward me. His brow is rumpled, his eyes ringed in white. "You were involved in a... in a..." He looks up at the nurse and the other man. "United Flight 311, Chicago to Seattle."

"What?"

"Terrible. Terrible." He rolls his R's, making *terrible* sound charming. "Everybody wants to talk to you, the only survivor."

"The only survivor of what?"

"A... terrorist attack. A bomb in the luggage. No one survived but you."

"A bomb?"

"Yes."

"Why was I on a plane?"

"Business."

"What business?"

"Banking."

"Who..." My breath catches. "Who am I?"

At first, no one seems to know.

"Susan Gardner," says the curly-haired man, stepping forward. "I'm Sergeant Krupinski from the FBI, and I have a few thousand questions, Miss Gardner."

"I don't remember anything," I say flatly.

His jaw clenches, and the muscle leaps up to his temple. "A bomb rips out the belly of a DC-10 and kills three hundred sixty-one passengers, but the woman in the lavatory survives without a scratch?"

"I don't understand…"

"Without a *scratch*?" the doctor blurts in annoyance. "She had a concussion – broken jaw, cuts everywhere! She was in a coma for four weeks!"

"Four weeks!" The room begins to spin. I clutch the sides of the bed. "What did you say my name was?"

"Susan Gardner," Krupinski repeats, then rattles off, "thirty-two year-old female Caucasian; blonde; blue eyes; single; director of foreign accounts at International Mercantile, downtown Chicago; daughter of William and Deloris Gardner, deceased; sister of Michael Gardner of Oak Park – any of this ring a bell?"

They're staring at me. They know more about me than I do.

The sergeant puffs. "Figures. Sit around for four weeks–"

"Why?"

"Why what?"

"Why sit around for four weeks?"

"I'm here to protect you, Miss Gardner."

"From what?"

"From the people who did this."

It's like he punched me in the chest. "I want out of

here. I want to go home."

Krupinski laughs. "You don't even know where your home is."

He's right. Damn it. "Where *is* it?"

"Oak Park," Krupinski says, "but you're not going."

"Am I under arrest? Is that what this is?"

"No, you're not under arrest. Not yet," Krupinski says.

"Enough of that!" Dr Rama demands, stepping between me and the big man. "You are upsetting her." He turns to me, and his expression softens. "But you cannot leave. Your health is too fragile. Look at these IVs and these machines. Look at these people. They have kept you alive. We have to make sure you are well enough to go."

"I want out of here as soon as possible."

"As soon as possible, Susan," he assures, "but first, we need to redo the IVs."

I swing my legs down. "I've got to go to the bathroom."

"You can't," the doctor says, wide-eyed.

Now I feel why. There's another tube. Another goddamn tube. "I want this catheter out, too."

"We don't even know if you can walk," Dr Rama points out. "Your legs are atrophied. How are you going to get to the toilet?"

I stand up, legs trembling under my hospital gown. "See?"

"You cannot go to the toilet without help," he admonishes. "If you need to go now, the nurse will take you. If you need to go later, you will press the button."

"Thank you," I say, sitting back down on the bed.

"The nurse can stay, but the rest of you, go. Now. Please."

Dr Rama turns to me, his eyes watery. "You need to understand, young woman, that you have only just met me, but I have known you for a month."

"I don't even know myself."

The doctor nods and leaves. Krupinski also goes, trundling through the doorway and sitting heavily in a chair to one side. He crosses his arms over his chest and glares at an impressionist print across the hall.

That leaves only the nurse. "I'm Michelle," she says, stepping up before me. Her ponytail is so tight her cheeks are white. "Michelle Mitchell. My parents had a sense of humor."

"I'm Susan Garner."

"Gardner," she corrects me.

"Gardner."

"Good." Nurse Mitchell smiles tightly. "I just thought, maybe, we should be on a first name basis before I pulled your Foley."

"My Foley?"

She gestures uncomfortably toward her groin. "Your catheter."

"Right."

"I'm just going to ask you to lie back…"

"Ah, yes, Michelle," I say as I roll to my back and open my legs. "I'm glad I know your name."

She may be shy, but she's quick. One firm tug, and the catheter comes away. It stings like it had fused to me.

"There you are," she says, gathering the yellow tube and bag.

"Can I go to the toilet now?"

"Let me empty this first." Nurse Mitchell carries the gangliar thing through a door, and I hear fluid gush and the toilet flush and plastic rustle. She comes back out grinning. "Sanitized for your protection!" She walks to me and holds out her hands. "Upsy daisy."

I roll forward, put my feet on the floor, and stand. My legs shake. They look wasted away under my gown.

Michelle braces me. "You're famous, you know," she says, ushering me to the toilet. "They call you the 311 Miracle."

I pivot and sit on the toilet, pulling up my gown and piling it on my knees.

"Don't be alarmed if there's blood. Sometimes there's blood after a Foley." She stands there and smiles.

"Could I have some privacy?"

"Of course." Nurse Michelle points to the button and pull-string on the wall. "I'll be right outside." She withdraws, easing the door slowly closed.

My heart is pounding. Who the hell is Susan Gardner? The FBI knows: single white female. Blonde. Senior accounts manager. "Well, *that's* something."

A trickle begins and becomes a steady flow. At least I remember how to do this.

I've got to get out of here. I've got to get back to Oak Park, get my life back.

"How's it going in there?" Nurse Mitchell calls.

"Give me a second." The toilet paper is scratchy, and there's a little blood left on it. "All right, I'm ready."

Nurse Mitchell enters and helps me back into bed. I swing my legs up and draw up the covers.

"Feel better?"

"Than what?"

She laughs. "I've just got to put these IVs back into their ports."

"Where's the remote?"

"On the side of the bed. On that little springy thing, there."

I press "Power" and watch the black screen glow to life.

A fat black woman is talking about the stigma of cellulite.

A wise-cracking judge is settling a claim about a slashed tire.

Yellow cartoon people run for a couch.

"There's not much on, daytimes," says the nurse as she fits an IV into my hand. "In a way, it's insulting. They think people who watch TV in the daytime are idiots."

"Maybe we are," I said.

"They used to have shows where you had to be smart to win things. Now, people aren't even smarter than a fifth grader."

I'm suddenly sleepy. "What's going on?"

"All finished,"

"Why am I so sleepy?"

She smiles an apology. "Doctor's orders."

I'm walking on nothing. The floor is gone. There's nothing under me except rushing grasslands. I'm passing rows of see-through seats and see-through people.

Ghosts.

There's my seat, next to a kid that looks Amish. He's got that kind of beard because he's too young to grow anything better. He smiles, and I slide past him, and he watches my ass. I sit down in my seat and can see the grasslands flashing by underneath us.

"Everything come out all right?" the kid asks.

I laugh a little. "Crude."

He blushes behind his beard. "I don't mean it like that."

"What do you mean it like?"

"I mean it like, well, we all died, but you're still here."

That sends a chill through me. "Am I?"

"Well, yeah. Nothing's solid but you. We're all, like, mist or something, but you're still flesh and blood."

"It's just a dream."

"Is it?"

"Yes."

"So, I'm not even a ghost?"

"No."

"Just a memory?"

"Yes."

His seventeen year-old eyes glisten. "Don't forget, then."

"I don't even know your name."

"My name's Jason."

"I won't forget you, Jason."

"'Cause that's all I am." He's staring intently at me. "A couple nerves in your brain, sparking."

"I won't forget."

• • •

I jolt awake, and the TV shows a handsome white man and a handsome black woman sitting behind a desk in front of a digital map of the world. The people are talking. When they have good news, they smile. When they have bad news, they look very serious.

They have good news right now. They're talking about me.

"More on our cover story," the man says. "The Sleeping Beaut of Butte has awakened. Yes, the 311 Miracle has come out of her coma. For live local coverage, we go now to Todd Foster at Saint James hospital, along with a crowd of other well-wishers. Todd?"

"Thanks, Andy," says a young man standing in front of the marquee for Saint James hospital. Behind the sign, a group of revelers wave toward the camera. "As you can tell, the mood here is festive. Many of the same people you've seen at candlelight vigils previously are here tonight with a spirit more like Mardi Gras. The reason? Susan Gardner is awake! The sole survivor of the terrorist attack that killed three hundred sixty-one people has wiped the cobwebs from her eyes and is sitting up. Though our crew was not allowed on Miss Gardner's floor, a source within the hospital says she is officially listed as in a stable condition, though he would describe her better as 'feisty' or even 'take-charge.'"

"Todd, this is quite a development," Andy breaks in. "For a month, this community has taken the Sleeping Beaut to its heart. Now, suddenly, she's awake. How can she live up to all the hype?"

"The early indications are that she is unaware of any of the hype. She's likely to be just Susan Gardner. We've imagined her for four weeks, but she's going to have to show us who she really is."

I shake my head.

"Todd, this is Sasha," says the black anchor. "Are there any indications of what Miss Gardner remembers about the 311 attack?"

Todd smiles and says, "It's early, still, Sasha. The whole nation is waiting to learn what Susan Gardner knows, but they'll have to wait a little longer. The source says she answered no direct questions but asked to use the restroom. I think after four weeks, I'd've made the same request."

Andy smiles and laughs, but Sasha says, "What of the terrorists who attacked the plane? For the last month, we've been bombarded with the name 'Death's Disciples', but no one seems to know who they are. Does Susan Gardner know who they are?"

The screen goes black. Sergeant Krupinski is standing beneath it, the broadband cord dangling in his fist. "No television."

"What are you talking about? I want to find out what's happening."

He shakes his head. "We want to know what you know, not what Fox News tells you. No television until after questioning."

"Questioning?"

"Starting tomorrow. First thing."

"With you?"

"Of course," he says, letting the cords go and stalking toward the door.

"Who are the Death's Disciples?"

Over his shoulder, he says. "Better get some sleep."
Not likely.
I've got to get out of this place.

2 DISCIPLES

Sergeant Steve Krupinski plopped into his chair beside the doorway and groaned. "I hate this job."

It was Elseworth's fault – Lieutenant Elseworth, his supposed mentor, who'd originally been in charge of the "311 Miracle." A day after the terrorist attack, Elseworth charged off like Lancelot to defend Guinevere.

But Gardner was no Guinevere. She was Sleeping Beauty.

"Elseworth's off to Butte, but he can't find his Butte with both hands," Krupinski had told his drinking buddies back in Chicago. "Give him two days, and he'll assign her to me." His buddies said he was full of shit. "Not *full* of. *Surrounded* by."

The press loved their Sleeping Beauty, but Elseworth gave up on her after two days and called for his protégé to take over.

Krupinski had always been cursed with the ability to see the future without being able to convince others of it. "A Cassandra complex" is what the FBI shrink called it. Krupinski preferred the way Hemingway put it: "a shock-proof shit detector."

And just as Krupinski had predicted a month ago, here he was, sitting in shit in Butte.

"It's because of the curly hair," Krupinski muttered to himself, crossing his arms and leaning on the plastic chair. "Nobody respects guys with curly hair." At UW, guys would see a linebacker with curly hair and assume they were up against a clown. Then Krupinski would spend two hours shoving their faces in the grass.

Now his curly hair put him in a hallway, staring at a faded Monet.

Until Nurse Mitchell sashayed past. Her hair was tight in the bun she wore, and her scrubs were tight, too, in all the right places. Krupinski had gotten to know her through small talk in the hall and big talk at a couple of dinners and bigger action one night in her apartment. "You're the only thing that makes this job tolerable," he'd told her as they lay side by side. She'd smiled at him until he'd added, "The only thing unless the terrorists attack."

That was the one scenario that could rescue this mission. Krupinski gave it a sixty percent probability. Whoever blew up that plane didn't want a hero to be dragged out alive. They certainly didn't want her walking and talking and answering questions.

They'd've heard by now that Susan Gardner was awake. They'd want to attack before anybody got a chance to question her.

Krupinski glanced into the hospital room.

Miss Gardner lay drowsing.

A janitor rounded the corner and loped down the hall. "Hey, Steve."

"Hey, Jay," Steve answered, watching the tall man approach. Jay was thin and balding, with a bottle of cleanser in one hand and the handle of a mop bucket in the other. He dragged the sloshing container down the hall. Most agents didn't pay attention to janitors and waitresses, but Steve knew them by name. They were the whole damned game. "Whatcha doing working so late?"

"She's awake, huh?" asked Jay.

"*Was*. But doc gave her a sedative." Krupinski replied, pulling in his legs to let the man pass. "You should've seen her. Full of piss and vinegar."

"It's the piss I'm after," Jay joked. "They say she's ripped out her catheter–"

"Actually, just the IVs, but they did leave a mess."

"And I got a mop."

They both laughed.

"She's full of surprises," Krupinski allowed as he glanced in the door. Miss Gardner was under the blankets, unmoving. "Just don't wake her up."

"No, I won't." Jay gazed into the room, reached into his pocket, and pulled out a stick of Stride. He popped it into his mouth and chewed. "You want one?"

"Sure. Stakeouts succeed or fail on the quality of gum." Krupinski took the piece and flipped it into his mouth. "Hmm. *That's* different."

"Almond," Jay said with a shrug. "They're trying all the tea flavors, you know."

"Yeah, well, anything's better than urine."

The janitor nodded grimly and headed through the door to clean up the mess.

Krupinski spit the gum into his hand and let bitter spittle drag from his tongue. "Almond, my ass," he murmured, wiping his tongue on a Kleenex. "Arsenic."

Jay was a plant. Steve had pegged him from Day One. He was keeping vigil, too, waiting for Susan to wake up.

This was a quarterback rush.

Krupinski jolted up, dropped the poisoned gum, and drew the Colt .45 from his chest holster. He ran up behind Jay and grabbed him around the neck and pulled him back. Even as he staggered back, Jay emptied his clip into Susan's sleeping form. Bullets tore through her.

"Goddammit!" shouted Krupinski, knocking the gun loose and jamming his pistol into the man's temple. "Who are you?"

Jay said nothing. He was scrawny, half-starved. He couldn't get away. Growling, Krupinski dragged him toward the door while shouts and footsteps came in the hall.

"Who sent you!" Krupinski demanded. "Tell me!"

Jay looked over his shoulder. "She had to die. She was the enemy–"

"*Why are you here!*"

"Death's Disciples!" Jay shouted, jamming his finger against the trigger of Krupinski's Colt. It spoke, and Jay's head sprayed.

"Goddammit," Krupinski growled, staggering back and letting Jay's body flop to the floor. A thousand answers had been reduced to a blood spatter on the wall.

At UW, he'd never allowed a quarterback sack. Now, the woman he was defending was...

He flung back the sheets and saw pillows arranged to look like a sleeping form, pillows torn by gunshots.

The window was slightly ajar.

"Smart girl!" Krupinski rushed up to look out, seeing Susan struggling across the rooftop below, her ass flashing through her hospital gown.

She was alive.

"What's happened? What's happened?" demanded Dr Rama, running in.

"Lock it down. This whole room," Krupinski commanded as he loaded another round in his six-shooter. "Crime scene."

"Who is this?" the doctor shrieked, standing above the corpse of Jay.

"Terrorist," Krupinski said simply as he strode out the door. He ran for the stairwell and flung back the door and took them three at a time. Susan was a level below and would be dropping to the ground next – just off the caféteria.

This was it. This was Steve's moment. Grandpa Krupinski had his moment on the Missouri when the Kamikazes took out the turret next to him but he brought down four other planes before they could hit the deck. Grandpa Flannery had his moment when he and Doris O'Donnell eloped under fire from her father's shotgun. Being half Polish and half Irish meant Steve Krupinski had the worst and best luck, so this moment could go either way – especially with arsenic in his mouth.

Already his stomach was cramping.

He spat as he rounded the ground floor landing and shoved his way out of the emergency exit, letting the alarm sound. The door banged back against the brick wall, and Krupinski trudged out to see Miss Gardner drop from the roof above. She pinned the hospital gown modestly to her sides, but it fluttered like wings behind her. Her legs collapsed under her as she landed, grunted, rolled. Krupinski shambled over to grab her.

"Let go of me," she said weakly.

"You're in danger," Krupinski replied, his tongue thick.

"I'm getting out of here."

"You're in danger." Krupinski crumpled to his knees on the ground.

Distant sirens began their whale song.

"What's wrong with you?" She grabbed his suit as he slumped on the grass.

Krupinski grimaced. "He poisoned me."

Terror flared in her gaze. "Poisoned? Who—"

"Death's Disciples," Krupinski said. "They're after you. You're in danger."

She craned her neck, looking around at the parking lot, where police cars arrived, flashing their carnival lights.

"Let them take you inside," Krupinski said. "Let them guard you."

"What about you?"

"I'm dying."

"You can't die."

"Tell them it's arsenic," Krupinski said as he slumped to the ground.

"The story of the 311 Miracle took a dramatic turn this evening, with an attack on Susan Gardner," reported Sasha Jones from Fox News. The African-American woman stood beside the sign for Saint James Hospital. "Sources report that at eight thirty-five, a janitor employed for the last month by Saint James entered the private room of Susan Gardner and riddled her bed with bullets. Unfortunately for the attacker, Miss Gardner had recently awakened from her coma and had escaped out her window. The FBI agent assigned to protect Miss Gardner, a Sergeant Krupinski, allegedly shot the assailant and pursued Miss Gardner downstairs. Sergeant Krupinski stopped Miss Gardner but then was overcome by poison from the attacker."

The TV showed Susan Gardner sitting beside a gurney where a big man lay. "He saved me. If it weren't for him, I wouldn't be talking to you."

"Those are the first words the 311 Miracle spoke," said the reporter, "signs that this young woman appreciates the weeks that her savior spent sitting just outside her door. Sergeant Krupinski is now in stable condition, and doctors expect a complete recovery.

"Live from Saint James Hospital, this is Sasha Jones for Fox News."

Sergeant Krupinski opened his eyes and saw ceiling tiles. For linebackers and FBI agents, ceiling tiles meant failure. Krupinski was supposed to take care of someone else, not have them take care of him.

She was there, Susan Gardner. She had been sitting in a chair but stood up and came to him when he stirred. "You're awake."

He smiled. "That's what I'm supposed to say to you."

"Arsenic's not easy to counteract," she said gravely. "So they say."

"I'm a big guy," Krupinski replied. "There's got to be a benefit to weighing three hundred."

"I'm glad," she said.

"Me, too."

She glanced suspiciously at the door, where a cop stood. "I need you. Someone I can trust. I don't know anybody, but I know I can trust you."

"Damn right," Krupinski said.

She studied his face. "So, who's this group – Death's Disciples?"

"Nobody knows," Krupinski sighed. "A cult. A terrorist network."

"Islamist?"

"Not Islamist, but we're not sure what."

Susan Gardner looked pale. "What do they believe in?"

"They believe in blowing up planes."

"Come on. You're FBI – looking at e-mail, listening to satellites."

"They communicate in some way we can't detect. We know next to nothing about them."

"Except that they want me dead."

"Looks like it."

"But you shot the guy."

"And you escaped through the window. And jumped off a building."

She was smiling the way his kid sister used to smile when Steve drove off a bully.

"All right, then. Let's figure out who these Death's Disciples are and how to stop them."

3 INTERROGATION

Nurse Mitchell pushes me in a wheelchair while two "Men in Black" lead and two more follow. All down the corridor, cops stand at attention. Most of the cops have a steely-eyed look, but a couple are smiling, and one even takes a shot with his iPhone.

A G-man snatches the phone away and shoves it in his pocket.

"Hey, that's the new one!"

"You'll get it back once it's purged."

The FBI agents in front open a pair of double doors, and we roll into a conference room with Berber carpet and cinder-block walls and a drop ceiling. At tables sit three more federal agents in suits, a strange-eyed woman with hair piled in an enormous bun, and a court stenographer. When they clap eyes on me, the group goes silent except for one who mutters, "It's her."

Nurse Mitchell wheels me up in front of the group, positioning me before a microphone and locking the wheels of my chair. One of the escorts taps her shoulder, takes her arm, and leads her from the room.

"Where's Krupinski?" I ask.

Pens scratch, writing "Krupinski" or "First word – Krupinski" or "Who's Krupinski?"

I roll my eyes. "The guy who got poisoned. The FBI guy?" More notes – some scratching out what they had written and others adding to their notes – but no one answering me. "Don't you guys watch the news?"

A man seated in front makes eye contact. Very *GQ*, this one, in a pinstripe suit with a little red handkerchief in the breast pocket. He stands and approaches, never looking away. Preternaturally white teeth flash as he says, "Sergeant Krupinski is in the ICU."

"I want him *here*," I reply.

"I'm his superior, Lieutenant Tom Elseworth, Office of Operations Coordinations."

"It rhymes."

"I'm taking charge of this investigation. You can trust me to–"

"I want Krupinski."

Elseworth's eyes snap. "Dimitri, see if Krupinski can join us." As one of the agents leaves, Elseworth begins to pace dramatically, his eyes searching the carpet as if he were looking for something. "Miss Gardner, do you know why we're here?"

"You want to question me about Flight 311."

"Yes. This is an official FBI deposition. This team before you represents the best minds in law enforcement. They have come to hear your sworn testimony." He reaches into his briefcase and draws out a Bible. "Please lay your hand on this," he says extending the book toward me.

"I don't even know what religion I am," I say, but I put my hand on the Bible anyway.

"Do you swear to tell the truth, the whole truth, and nothing but the truth, so help you God?"

"So help me."

"Speak into the microphone. Do you swear to tell the truth, the whole truth, and nothing but the truth, so help you God?"

"Yes," I say into the microphone.

His lips purse, and eyebrows flatten above intense eyes. "Do you remember being on Flight 311?"

"No. I only remember what people have told me," I say. "I only remember what I saw on the news."

"*Krupinski,*" Elseworth snarls. "He shouldn't have let you watch the news."

"Actually, he ripped the cords from the wall."

Elseworth flicks away my words. "We don't care what you've heard. We want to know what you know."

"Then, I guess, your job is done."

"Not by a long shot."

"I have amnesia."

"Ah, the Reagan defense."

"What's a reagan?"

Elseworth smiled. "Very clever."

"And why are you talking about defense? Am I on trial?"

"No, but you have been subpoenaed."

"What subpoena? I never saw anything."

"Your brother signed it this morning in Chicago."

"Oak Park," I reply.

"*See*, you *do* remember."

"That's what they told me. Oak Park. They tell me I am Susan Gardner, so I take it on faith that I am. They tell me I was on that plane, so I believe them. I don't know anything. You might as well interrogate the nurses and the doctor and Krupinski and everybody I've talked to—"

"We have."

The doors bark open, admitting Krupinski on a gurney, with Dimitri wheeling it forward. An IV bag hangs from a post and sloshes as the gurney pushes up alongside me.

I lean toward Krupinski. "Thanks for coming."

He flashes a look of annoyance at Elseworth. "Thanks for having me." He whispers, "You know, you have the right to an attorney, yeah?"

"Amnesiacs don't trust attorneys."

"People with memories don't, either."

Lieutenant Elseworth interrupts, "You will hold your tongue, Sergeant Krupinski. I and I alone will address the witness. Dimitri, wheel him over there, away from her." As he does, Elseworth goes on. "Miss Gardner, why did you decide to fly on United 311 from Chicago to Seattle?"

"I don't remember."

"Weren't you flying for your business, International Mercantile?"

"That's what Dr Rama says, but I don't remember."

"Do you remember where you were seated?"

"First class?" I venture, but Elseworth scowls. I try again, "Business class?"

"Economy," he says.

"Fine."

Laughter murmurs through the room. I look up at the others.

I can reach them.

Elseworth scans them with annoyance. "Do you remember who sat next to you?"

"No, I don't. But I had a dream."

"You had a dream?"

"It was that I was sitting beside an Amish kid."

"There was no Amish kid."

"I mean, in the dream, there was this seventeen year-old boy with one of those beards that hangs off the jaw and doesn't make a mustache."

"*This* boy," asks Elseworth, holding up a picture of the boy who sat next to me in the dream.

"Yes. That's him."

"Jason Carter," supplies Elseworth.

"Yeah, in my dream, the kid was named Jason."

"Jason Carter was a real person. You're not dreaming, Miss Gardner. You're *remembering*." Elseworth says, "Will you submit to regression therapy?"

"Submit to *what*?"

"Regression therapy. It's a technique to unlock hidden memories."

"It's voodoo," Krupinski mutters.

I wink at him. "Yeah. I'll submit to regression therapy, as long as you don't stick pins in me."

The others chuckle.

Elseworth nods to the old woman with the wide eyes and the wrinkled skin and the gray hair piled in a bun on her head. If she let it loose, it would reach her ass. She's wearing an ankle-length dress, like a witch doctor.

She stands and approaches me, eyes locked and lunatic-wide. "Hello, Miss Gardner. I am Dr Wilder."

"You're a doctor?"

"We all have a safe place, don't we? A place far from

here where everything is fine, and we can just relax and be ourselves," Dr Wilder went on. "What's your safe place, Miss Gardner?"

I sigh deeply. "I have *amnesia*."

"Let me tell you about my safe place. It's a tree house in a two-hundred year-old oak tree at the back of the upper pasture at my grandmother's farm. There are boards nailed to the trunk, a ladder leading up to a narrow hatch that you have to push open and crawl through, but once you're up in that tree house, nothing can touch you. No one can harm you." She blinks her great, wide eyes. "Are you imagining this safe place?"

I am. I can't help it. "Yes."

"You're there, now, Miss Gardner. The sun shines through the tree house windows, and a gentle breeze brushes by. You breathe… and you can feel the life pouring into your lungs and suffusing your blood and rolling out to reach every cell of your body. Do you feel the life tingling in you?"

"Yes."

"And in this tree house, this safe tree house, you can dream. You don't have to worry about whether it's real. Instead, just let yourself dream."

"Yes."

"Think of the Amish boy from your dream. Think of him sitting beside you on the plane. Which side is he sitting on?"

"My right."

"And is there anyone on your left?"

I look left, and I can see a man. "There's an old man with liver-spotted hands. He's snoring quietly."

"Good. Very good. Just look down and see if his hand has a ring on it."

I do, and see the liver spots but no ring. "No, it doesn't."

"Are you looking at his right hand?"

"Yes."

"Look at his left."

I have to lean forward in my seat, but I see a ring. "It's big, like a class ring, with weird symbols on it. There's something that looks like a star."

"How many points are on that star?"

"Five."

"And is it right side up, or upside down?"

"It's on a ring."

"Is one point of the star pointing directly down his finger, toward his hand?"

"Yes."

"Is this the ring?" Elseworth interrupts, hoisting something and striding toward me.

I blink. It's the very ring from my dream, except this one is battered and crushed. "That's the one."

Elseworth nods vigorously. "So far, you have answered everything completely correctly. Your amnesia isn't real. It's a mental block."

"I don't remember *anything*."

"How can you dream of a ring like this, when the real ring was worn by the man sitting next to you?"

"It's not a memory," I object. "I'm seeing it right now, after the crash. I'm sitting in a plane with no floor, looking at ghosts – talking to them."

"You can't keep interrupting," Dr Wilder says to Elseworth.

"This is *my* investigation–"

"I can't maintain the regression if you keep interrupting."

Elseworth pulls her aside and begins whispering sharply to her.

A liver-spotted hand taps my left arm. Not in the room, but in the plane. Suddenly, I'm back in it, and I'm looking at the old man with the ring.

He says, "I have a message."

"You have a message?"

"For my son. Tell him I love him. Tell him I'm glad he got the promotion."

I look down. "I don't know your son."

"*They* do. Tell them, and they'll tell him."

"You're not real. You're a dream."

"I *am* real. Tell them that Donald Leonard loves his son and is glad he got the promotion."

I sigh, letting my mind shift from the plane to the interrogation room, where Elseworth and the witch doctor are arguing in whispers. I interrupt: "Donald Leonard says he loves his son and is glad he got the promotion."

Lieutenant Elseworth and Dr Wilder both go silent and turn toward me. Their eyes are wide. Elseworth stammers, "Wh-who?"

"Donald Leonard," I say, "the old man sitting to my left."

Elseworth turns and rifles through his briefcase. He drags out a sheet and stares incredulously at it. "What's his son's name?"

"He didn't tell me."

"His son's name is Evan, and he just became a Wal-mart store manager," Elseworth says.

I nod. "That's good. His father is glad."

"He couldn't have known that," Elseworth says. "His son got the promotion only last week."

"Still, Donald is glad."

Elseworth's hands flare beside his head. "No, what I'm saying is – how could you *know* that? They're not saying it on the news. Nobody here knew. How did *you* know?"

I hold my hands out. "I'm talking to him. It's whatever Dr Wilder did, whatever spell she cast–"

"Hypnotism isn't a spell. You can't just know something that's happened a thousand miles away."

"I don't know anything," I protest. "That's the point."

"You know everything! *That's* the point."

"It's the dream. It's not me."

"Then get back in the dream!" Elseworth demands.

"Don't tell me what to do!"

Dr Wilder sets her hand on his chest and shoves him back. "Forget about all this, Susan. Forget about this room. Wouldn't you rather be someplace better?"

"Anyplace."

"Go back to the tree house in the oak. Go back to the sunshine through the window and the cool breeze on your skin. Breathe deep. Are you there?"

My eyes are closed. I'm there. "Yes."

"Then dream again of this ghost plane. Dream of the place where you are sitting and of the people on both sides – Jason and Donald. Do you see them?"

"Yes."

"Now, I want you to move out into the aisle."

"Every time I do, Jason looks at my ass."

"It's fine. That's what young men do."

"I'm in the aisle."

"Good. I want you to call out to the rest of the passengers and say, 'Is there anyone here from Butte?'"

I do.

A middle-aged woman looks back uncertainly and half-raises her hand.

"There's someone."

"Go to her."

I walk forward eight rows and look her in the eyes. She's overweight, with a page-boy haircut that is out of date and a purple blouse with pretzel crumbs on it.

"Ask her name."

"What's your name?"

"Karen. Karen Schneider."

"She says she's Karen Schneider."

Elseworth is ripping a picture from his portfolio, but I keep my eyes closed.

"Where does Karen Schneider live?"

"Where do you live?"

"Why do you want to know?" she asks, and her eyes are imploring. She seems to know deep down that she is gone, that she's a ghost, but she doesn't consciously know yet. She's like a woman underwater, reaching up, asking me to pull her to the air.

"You're a ghost, Karen. This plane blew up and you died. I'm sorry."

She stares at me a moment more, but then her eyes go dark. Tears ring them. "I felt it, somehow. I didn't want to admit it. You don't want people to know that you're…"

"I need to know where you lived."

"Why?" she asks again.

"Do you have a family?"

Hope blooms across her face. "Could I talk to them? Bob will want to know I'm dead. I shouldn't talk to the twins. He can break it to them. He's always been closer with them, anyway."

I smile. "What are their names?"

"Jules and Loren. Born on the same day."

"If you tell me where Bob lives, you can talk to him."

"It's 24114 Butchertown Road in Walkerville. That's just north of Butte."

I nod and thank her and then slide out of the dream and into the interrogation room. "She lives– I mean, she *lived* at 24114 Butchertown Road in Walkerville."

Elseworth's eyes are alight as he hoists both an 8 by 10 of Karen Schneider and a page crammed with her vital statistics. "One hundred percent correct! She knows every last person on that plane!"

"Ridiculous," Krupinski snorts.

Elseworth wheels on him. "You're here at my indulgence, Sergeant Krupinski. Keep your comments to yourself."

"On a plane, you don't know the name of the guy who asks for your pretzels. You don't know the name of the woman who plugs her headphones into your slot. You don't know anybody. How is it that she knows *everybody* on this plane?"

"You heard her!"

"It's not memory. She's connected to them somehow. She can *access* them."

Elseworth storms up to Krupinski and stands above him. "What are you suggesting, Agent Krupinski? Voodoo?"

"Take her to this address – this place in Walkerville. Have her talk to whoever lives there."

"Bob lives there," I break in, "and the twins, Jules and Loren."

"*Test* her," Krupinski continues. "She'll show you she's connected to them somehow."

"You're insane."

"Then prove it!" Krupinski challenges. "Take her to Walkerville. What have you got to lose?"

Elseworth's eyes glow as he turns back toward me. He temples fingers before his grin. "Yes. That's what we'll do. We'll run a test on our little 'psychic.'"

4 **KAREN AND BOB**

"You shouldn't have," I say, looking at the card that Krupinski hands to me. The envelope is already torn open. "I mean, really."

"The guys are a little overzealous." He nods toward the doorway of my room, where two officers stand.

"They think you're gonna attack me with a card?"

He shrugs. "The scanner detected circuitry, so they opened it to make sure it was safe."

I draw the card out of the mangled envelope. On the front cover is a cartoon hedgehog crouching under an umbrella while a black cloud pours down on him. The caption reads, "Heard you've been under the weather." I open the card, and there's a sun shining inside, and the hedgehog is flinging off the raindrops, and the caption reads, "You'll shake it off soon." And just then, the microchip embedded in the card begins to play, "Bright Sunshiny Day."

"It's just a song," Krupinski says.

"It's my favorite."

"Really?"

"I don't know."

We laugh.

"*Now* it is."

Krupinski looks down at his hands. "So, anyway, I'm not coming today."

"I thought Dr Rama signed your release."

"It's not him. It's Elseworth. This is his deal, now. Now that you're awake, well, he's in, and I'm out."

"Too bad." I lean in to whisper. "I don't trust him."

"Me, neither." Krupinski smiles sadly. "If you ever need a three-hundred-pound lineman, you know who to call."

"Thanks, Steve." I give him a hug. "I'm keeping this with me." I slide the hedgehog card into the pocket of my gray hoodie.

Krupinski steps back, looking at the hoodie and jeans Elseworth bought for me from the Salvation Army. "Sorry about the clothes. You look like the Unabomber."

"The *what*?"

"Never mind." He turns to go.

"Thanks, Steve," I say. "Thanks for saving my life."

"I'd do it again in a heartbeat."

Baffled faces watch from old storefronts. People stop on the sidewalk. Mouths drop open.

Apparently Butte has never had a motorcade.

At the head of our motorcade are two cops on motorcycles. After them comes an SUV that bristles with machine guns, then the limo that carries Lieutenant Elseworth and Dr Wilder and me. One more gunboat follows.

In the limo, I'm facing forward. Lieutenant Elseworth and Dr Wilder sit side by side facing back. It's hard to imagine a stranger pair. He's all gabardine and hair gel, and she's all lace and lavender oil.

I wish Krupinski were here.

We roll along Main Street, heading north past the half-occupied downtown. After a few more blocks, we're out of the city and into the sprawl, with its obligatory strip malls, Thriftway Super Stops, and Dollar Trees. Beyond them crouch lesser outlets – the occasional pawn shops, adult bookstores, and check-cashing joints. Soon, Main Street leaves the city behind, and we roll out along dry grasslands. The stalks are parchment-colored and the ground cracked. After a few more miles, Main Street jags left, and we reach Walkerville. It's not much of a suburb, more like an outpost on Mars: human habitations beneath red skies.

We turn onto Butchertown Road, watching for 24114. Passing several small farms, we reach a field lined with barbed wire. Far back from the road stands a barn and silo with a house alongside. A long, straight gravel drive leads to the property, and the motorcycles turn down it. The rest of the motorcade follows.

"You need to understand, Miss Gardner, that this is primarily a test. Karen Schneider is not a person of interest."

"To her husband, she is," I say.

Elseworth closes his eyes and takes a deep breath. "What I mean is that she is not of interest to us as a suspect for the bombing. What *is* of interest is how accurately you can report facts that only Karen Schneider would know. Do you understand?"

"I'm an amnesiac, not an idiot."

Elseworth sighs as the limo slides to a halt. I reach toward the door handle, but he waves me off. "Wait till they give the all-clear."

"You think Bob's loading his shotgun?"

"You never know."

We sit in silence, looking at our feet.

"So, this is your life, sitting in limos with hypnotists and amnesiacs, waiting for people to give the all-clear?"

He cants his head. "It's not bad compared to yours."

"I don't even know what my life is."

"My point, exactly."

A man in a suit opens the side door and ducks his head in to say, "All clear."

And then we move, Elseworth and Dr Wilder walked out the door followed by me. Two agents fall in behind me as we walk alongside the motorcade, parked single file on the gravel drive. They're going to have to back out, every last one. On either side of the drive are barbed wire fences, and beyond them, fields from where cows watch us with bemusement.

We approach an old farmhouse. Its clapboards are peeling paint, and its windows are huge and staring. It's been standing here for a hundred years, blasted by sun and wind and sand. The house and the barn form a little island of humanity in the wide-flung fields.

"Watch your step," Elseworth advises as he mounts the front porch. He heads to the screen door, where a man's face hovers ghostlike. "Good afternoon, Mr Schneider. I'm Lieutenant Tom Elseworth of the FBI, this is Dr Wilder, and this is Susan Gardner. May we come inside and speak with you?"

Bob Schneider is tall and thin, his skin drawn, his eyes watery. "I've already answered your questions."

"We're here to answer some of yours, Mr Schneider.

We have new information about your wife."

Bob Schneider's eyes ignite for a moment before guttering again. "The house is a mess…"

"It's fine," Elseworth says.

Reluctantly, Bob says, "Then, I guess…" He opens the screen door.

We go in, the whole mob of us. Pressed wool suits shoulder past a door frame with flaking paint, through a front room where mismatched chairs hold baskets of unfolded laundry, to a parlor strewn with Doritos wrappers and cheap furniture.

Bob is moving ahead of us, snatching up wrappers, straightening lampshades, pulling an overflowing bag out of a wastebasket. "Sorry about this. I'm not as good at housekeeping as Karen was."

"I'm sorry for your loss," Lieutenant Elseworth says, dusting off a chair before sitting down. "But we're here today to help you reconnect with her."

Bob stops halfway through straightening the couch cushions. "My wife is dead, Lieutenant."

"Susan Gardner claims to be connected to Karen," Elseworth says.

Bob shoots me a look of anger. "What do you mean?"

"She claims to be able to talk to the dead of Flight 311."

"Like that guy on TV?" Bob asks.

"I don't know what guy you mean."

Bob looks me up and down as if I were naked. "Is it true? Can you talk to Karen?"

Elseworth gives me an *I-told-you-so* look.

"Yes, I can talk to her."

Bob's face is so tight it seems made of ropes. "How do you talk to her?"

"In a dream," I say.

"In a *dream*?"

"She's told me things, things that no one could know."

His eyes are turning glassy. "Like what?"

I press my hands to my head. "Um. She said something about Jules and Loren, born on the same day."

"That's something everybody knows," Bob protests, "everybody in Walkerville, and probably everybody in the FBI. Tell me something only *I* would know."

"All right," I say, still moving back from him. "I haven't done this before. You have to let me find her in the dream."

"Go to your safe place," Dr Wilder advises.

"Please, just be quiet," I say to her.

They all obey – Dr. Wilder and Bob and Elseworth – and I close my eyes and sift down through realities. The house is gone. The tree house, too. I glimpse the ghost plane and step into it. I'm standing in the aisle above Karen Schneider. It's only a moment since I asked her if she wanted to speak to her husband, since she told me the address.

"Karen, I'm there. I'm with Bob, in your home. What do you want to say to him?"

"Oh," she says, tears streaming down her face. "That I love him."

"She loves you."

"That ain't nothing!" Bob rages. "That's what anybody'd say."

I nod, keeping my eyes closed, and speak to Karen: "Tell him something only he would know."

Karen looks at me, shakes her head, and then says, "I shouldn't've taped it."

I look at her. "You can't ask me to say that."

"Just say it."

"She says she shouldn't have taped it."

Bob's shudders a little. "Shouldn't've taped what? We don't even got a working VCR."

Already, Karen was telling me, "The sink scrubber."

"Come on, Karen. Your husband's about to strangle me."

"Tell him I shouldn't've taped the sink scrubber on the faucet."

I draw a breath, open my eyes, and say, "She shouldn't've taped the sink scrubber on the faucet."

Bob stares at me.

"I don't know what that means," I confess.

Bob crooks a finger and leads me over to the kitchen. It's a small room made smaller by bad design: a bar juts into the center of the room, with two stainless steel sinks, a high-necked faucet, and one of those hoses with the scrubbers jutting around the nozzle. I look at the trigger mechanism behind the hose, which still bears broken Scotch tape.

Bob grabs the nozzle and yanks it up, trailing silvery hose. "That's the last thing she done. She told me she had to leave early on this trip to Chicago. She told me I should get up, or she'd get back at me. Well, I didn't get up, and she left, but she taped this trigger down so when I turned on the faucet, it sprayed me."

"I shouldn't have done it," Karen repeats.

"She says she's sorry."

Bob shakes his head, tears welling. "I should've got up when she left. I never saw her again. I just got sprayed in the pants."

"She's sorry."

"I'm sorry, too."

Elseworth pushes up between us. "Enough of the love fest. She needs to give concrete proof. Real proof that she's talking through you."

I close my eyes, "You hear that?"

Karen smiles. "I do." And she begins to recount.

I channel her.

"What about our honeymoon at Disney World, when you went sleepwalking and got lost in the bathroom? And the next day, we watched the *Golden Child* with Eddy Murphy four times, not realizing it was pay TV. And when they charged us at the desk, you were outraged until they forgot to charge us for the extra night we'd stayed."

Tears are streaming down Bob's face.

"And what about Susie's Sunshine Café, that little hole in the wall with great food and slow service where we would sit for two hours on a Friday night after work and let the world roll on while we looked in each other's eyes."

"Karen."

"And what about Slurpees from the 7 Eleven near our apartment while we watched DVDs from the library?"

"It's you. It's really you."

"But it's nothing we can *verify*," Elseworth growls. He looks at his watch. "This is a waste of time! I'm going to go check out the rest of house." He stalks off, heading down into the basement.

I sigh. "Did you hear that? Do you see what I'm up against?"

"I'm not here to talk to Elseworth," Karen says. "I'm here to talk to my husband."

"But Elseworth wants confirmation. This is a test for me, whether I'm psychic or insane."

Karen's brow furrows, and she looks in my eyes with a sudden intensity. "This is a test for you, but not psychically."

"What do you mean?"

"Look at what's about to happen," she says, grabbing my hand.

Suddenly, we aren't in the plane anymore. Suddenly, we're hovering in air above the whole Schneider Farm, from Butchertown Road out to the back pasture. And there are more cars arriving. They're driving down that one-lane gravel drive and penning in the motorcade.

"Who are they?" I ask.

"That's the question," she responds. "Pull him to the floor."

"What?"

"Tackle my husband to the floor!"

I blink and see Bob Schneider in front of me, and I leap on him and wrap my arms around him and tackle him to the floor.

The first rounds of machine gun fire rip through the house.

Lying there on top of Bob on the floorboards, I look up to see agents leaping to get down. Bullets catch a few of them, making them convulse as they fall.

But the worst sight of all is Dr Wilder, standing with her hands outstretched as bullets rip through her head. They shatter barrettes and ponytail holders, releasing her mantle of gray hair to fly in a wide halo around her disintegrating skull. She stands a moment more, shaking with impacts, before she topples forward and crashes to the floor like a rotten scarecrow.

"We're taking fire!" one of the agents shouts into a walkie talkie. "Somebody's pinning us down!"

I lie there as steel slashes through the home. Part of me, though is still seeing the cars from above, the black-garbed men with machine guns advancing on the house.

"Who is it?" I ask Karen.

"They're maybe those American Police Force thugs out of Billings."

A bullet shatters the picture window, hurling glass into the room.

"Crawl," Bob advises, shuffling elbows and knees across the floor.

I follow, staying low.

"We're under attack!" the agent repeats. "Death's Disciples."

Another salvo rips through the home, cutting a dotted line across the lathe and plaster.

"Shoot back!" I shout.

A couple of the agents pull machine guns from their briefcases and return fire. The noise is incredible. Bullets scream out the window, and shell casings *ping* to the floor.

Return fire rips out the throat and chest and arm of one agent. He spins, gushing. Another agent's head comes to pieces, and he falls. A third slumps against a window.

Bob crouches with me in the tiny kitchen. Bullets slam into the oven, ricochet from the stove, and explode the microwave.

I close my eyes, trying to see Karen.

"What is it?" she asks as she hangs in the air beside me.

"A friend. Sergeant Krupinski. He can help us."

"Sergeant Krupinski?"

"Do you know St James Hospital?"

"Downtown?" Karen asks.

"He's there. Big guy. Room 305. Tell him what's happening."

"Can I do that?"

"I don't know. See if you can."

She nods, letting go of me and shooting away across the dry fields.

I open my eyes and look at Bob. "I just sent Karen. She's going for help."

Bob nods. "We ride motocross."

Ducking another barrage of bullets, I say, "She must like that."

"I mean, we've got two bikes, and a trail that heads away from the road."

"Show me."

"Stay low."

While slugs tear apart the house, Bob and I crawl out the screen door and into the yard. There's a long cowshed about fifty feet away, and Bob rises to a crouch and runs for it. I follow. We get inside to find rows of cows, each with her own little drinking fountain. They moo in fright. Bob pushes his way among them, heading to the back of the shed.

There lean two off-road bikes, their sides specked with dried mud. Bob shoves a blue helmet on his head and flings a red one toward me.

"Ever rode before?"

"I don't know."

"Throttle's on the right handlebar. Brake lever on the same side. Clutch is on the left. Shift with the left foot."

"Can't be more dangerous than guns." I say as I swing my leg over.

Bob kicks back the stand and stomps down on the starter. "Do it like that."

I mimic him, and the off-road bike rattles to life.

"Maybe I *did* do this before."

"Let's get out of here," Bob says as he drops his visor and takes off through the back door of the shed. I follow, feeling the ground pull away below my feet.

We're riding. We're tearing across the pasture. I'm clutching and shifting without thinking about it. The cows watch. A few stray bullets ping past, but soon, we're beyond their reach.

Then it's me and Bob riding for the red mountains that stand around Butte.

5 GOING DARK

Krupinski had predicted the whole thing: Elseworth flew in and took over, leaving his protégé stranded in Butte, holding his butt with both hands.

"God damned Elseworth," Krupinski snarled, cutting into the Salisbury steak he'd ordered. The Traxside Diner advertised "home-cooked" food but should have advertised "restaurant-microwaved" food. The rumpled steak smothered in cream-of-mushroom soup was a glorified Hungry Man. "So am I," Krupinski told himself bitterly, chewing a hunk of gristle, "except for the glorified part."

"You be wanting more coffee?" asked the rail-thin waitress, her eyelids painted robin-egg blue.

"No, thanks. Say, do you have WiFi?"

She glanced from the dusty blinds to the Formica counters. "What do *you* think?"

Krupinski pulled out his netbook. "Maybe I'll just scan to see what I can pick up."

"They got a WiFi next door at Fred's Mesquite Grill." She pronounced it *Fraids Mess-Cutie Grail*. "Fred's trying to draw the kids in. But it ain't secured. They got WiFi, but everybody can steal your credit cards and MyFace and stuff."

"Can't steal mine," Krupinski said, patting his slim black computer. It was special issue, fitted with a device that could hijack a network, cutting out all users while it ran. Agents were supposed to use the feature only in an emergency, but this Salisbury steak and the fly that just landed on it sure felt like one. "I got to get tickets out of this place."

"Fine," the waitress said, taking her coffee pot elsewhere.

Krupinski meanwhile fired up his netbook. It had a fast boot time, and seconds later, it had found Fred's connection. A couple clicks, and the ethernet was shanghaied – secured only for his use. Krupinski typed in "cheap flights" and then entered "Butte" and "Chicago" and found a four-thirty with a two-hour layover in Minneapolis. He booked it using the company card.

Before letting go of his exclusive line, though, Krupinski idly logged onto the Homeland Security Satellite Service and typed in "24114 Butchertown Road, Walkerville, MT."

In moments, a real-time satellite image of the farm came up. He could see the whole layout – Butchertown Road running north by northwest, and the long narrow drive of 24114 slanting off to the east. Just now, the drive was filled with motorcycles and limos. He clicked to increase magnification. At the back of the column sat an armed-to-the-teeth SUV with two guys standing behind it. Two more guys stood by the front porch, and two more walked around behind the house.

Krupinski laughed. Elseworth had wedged his whole motorcade in there ass-backward. It'd take them half an hour just to get turned around. "What a dipshit."

Except that Elseworth wasn't a dipshit. He was a grandstander, yeah, a glad-hander – but he wasn't a dipshit. Whatever he did, it was always calculated to put him in the best position. Why would he park a motorcade in like that? If anything happened, it'd be a deathtrap.

"He's set up an ambush." Adrenaline bloomed through Krupinski, and sweat speckled his brow. He told himself to calm down, but he couldn't. "If Elseworth parked that fucking motorcade that way, he didn't want anybody to get out of there."

As if to confirm Krupinski's Cassandra complex, something new showed up on the satellite image. From the northwest, a line of vehicles was approaching 24114 Butchertown Road, and from the southeast came another line. Four vehicles in each. It looked like a hit from the movies.

The first car from the south pulled into the drive, and three more followed. Then the first car from the north pulled in, and three more.

"Holy shit. This is going down."

Doors opened. People got out. At the back of Elseworth's motorcade, the two guys by the SUV fell, dropping into the ditch. The new arrivals jumped over their bodies and raced along the motorcade toward the house.

The guards at the front porch fell into the flowerbeds.

"Why didn't they shoot?" Krupinski muttered. They saw eight cars pull in behind them, but they didn't shoot?

The reason was obvious. Elseworth had told the guards that reinforcements were coming.

But these new guys didn't move like FBI. They moved like black ops.

"You're kidding me. Blackwater here on US soil?" Elseworth was trying to go dark with the 311 Miracle. "Jesus! Is he that smart?" Krupinski wondered. And why? Why would Elseworth kill his whole team and go dark with Susan Gardner? He was all about glory. He wanted the limelight, not the dark.

Still, the new arrivals were jumping over the bodies of the dead and running toward the house and crouching down behind the empty motorcade and leveling their guns and firing.

Two agents ran up from the back yard and fell beside their friends.

That was everybody on the perimeter. Now, the gunmen would be clearing the house.

It was shooting fish in a barrel.

"But Elseworth's one of the fish."

Unless he'd gone to the basement.

"The fucker!" Of *course* that's where he was. That's just where the backstabbing bastard would be. He probably looked at his watch and excused himself just before the killers arrived. He was probably down there right now, clutching the hot-water heater and waiting for the bullets to stop. The question was, did he have Susan Gardner down there with him?

Where was Susan?

Smiling bleakly, Krupinski typed in the tracking code for the get-well card he'd given her. It wasn't just "Bright Sunshiny Day." It was a beacon.

A little blue target appeared on the satellite image, not

in the house, but in the yard behind. There were two figures running from the house toward a long barn, and one of them was Susan Gardner.

"Good girl!"

The blip went inside the barn and down its center. Meanwhile, gunmen were sliding along the clapboards of the old farmhouse, drawing a bead just after Susan and the other person were gone. While the killers stalked cautiously across the grass, Susan reached the back of the barn and halted.

"Don't stop there," Krupinski muttered. Still, the dot didn't move. Had she been shot? Was she down?

The killers were closing in on the barn.

"Go, lady, go!"

And she went, out the back of that barn – fast. The killers were inside a moment later, and no doubt they were filling cows with bullets, but Susan and another person were riding motorcycles or something across the field.

If the other person was Elseworth, he was *surely* going dark with her. If the other person wasn't Elseworth, well – Elseworth had just tried to kill her.

"God damned fucker!"

"Okay!" the waitress said, pouring coffee into his cup. "But you said *no* before."

Krupinski looked up at her in surprise. She finished pouring and turned away. He reached into his pocket and shoved a fifty-dollar bill into her hand. "Here you go."

She looked at it querulously. "I'll get change."

"Keep it. Just tell me whose Jeep that is out there."

She looked down at the fifty in her hand. "What Jeep? Everybody's got a Jeep."

"That Blue Wrangler."

"Oh, the Wrangler. Nobody drives those anymore. Nobody but Ed Gentry."

"Who's he?"

"Ain't no crime to tell you," she said with a shrug, then nodded toward a balding, heavyset man. "Gentleman in booth 4."

"Thanks," Krupinski said. He rose, pushed past her, and went to booth 4. "Excuse me, sir, but is that your Jeep Wrangler soft-top parked outside?"

Ed Gentry looked up, eyebrows fluttering. "What of it?"

"I'm Lieutenant Elseworth of the FBI," Krupinski said, flashing his badge, "and I have reason to believe that a terrorist cell has attached a bomb to the starter of your engine."

"What?"

"Al Qaeda is trying to blow up this diner, and it's using your Jeep to do it."

"What?"

"They're done with New York. Now they're after the heart and soul of America. If they can use a Jeep to blow up a diner in Butte, how many hundreds of thousands of American-made cars can they use to blow up American diners in every small town across the map?"

"I see where you're going."

"So, I need your keys."

"Why?"

"Do you want to turn your keys in the ignition and be blown to pieces, not to mention killing everyone in this diner and setting off the worst domestic terror attack since Tim McVeigh?"

"No!" he said, fishing the keys from his pocket and nearly throwing them at Krupinski.

He caught them, saying, "Thanks. Keep your head down while I go test your Jeep. Don't want to have one of these sheets of glass coming down on your neck."

"No, sir. Don't want to have that."

Krupinski nodded and walked from the diner. The Jeep owner watched him go, and then waved his hands, moving with a Groucho-walk from the windows. "Everybody down! Everybody. This thing could blow! I *mean* it."

As everyone – the Jeep owner and the blue-eyed waitress and the other patrons clenched their eyes and shoved fingers into their ears, Sergeant Krupinski strolled to the Wrangler, yanked open the driver's side door, sat down, and ignited the engine. With a squeal of tires, he was gone.

One by one, the people in the diner rose, opened their bloodshot eyes, and stared out at the empty streets of downtown Butte.

As he roared up Main Street toward 24114 Butchertown Road, Krupinski checked the vitals of the Wrangler. Gas at three-quarters. Oil and temperature showing steady. Solid enough soft top, but something he'd be willing to shuck if the situation called for it. He gunned the engine and felt the tires spin. Plenty of power but not a lot of tread. Still, it was enough. He'd be going on sand and gravel, up switchbacks and over mountain passes. Clearance was the thing, and the Jeep had it. Good thing he hadn't picked the Mustang.

Sadly, though, Fred's wireless connection failed a hundred feet away. Krupinski switched over to cell towers, which unfortunately could be tracked. No one cared yet where he was, but after he'd gone dark, they'd play this loop over and over.

It didn't matter. All that mattered now was Susan Gardner.

"Where is she?" Krupinski wondered. The screen showed a target moving northeast from the farmhouse. It seemed to be following a trail that led through farm fields and into the foothills. Krupinski locked on the moving target, panned out to himself on Main Street, and clicked "Intercept." While the computer calculated, he ran a red light and swerved around a stroller in a crosswalk.

The intercept came through. Susan Gardner was headed toward a pass through the mountains, bound for Interstate 15 just northeast of Butte. The blue line on Krupinski's screen said to jump on Interstate 15 half a mile north of where he was. Krupinski took the turn.

Susan was going forty-seven miles an hour, which meant that Krupinski had to kick it up to ninety to meet her. He did, and, shortly after, was passed by a car doing a hundred.

"Montana."

The road rose up a long valley, mountains to the left and right.

Just now, Susan and her comrade were riding through the mountains on the left. If the other motorcyclist was

Elseworth, there'd be some explaining to do – grand theft auto and insubordination for starters.

"It can't be him," said Krupinski, gunning the Jeep as he climbed the hills.

The valley fell back, and ahead, Krupinski saw a cop-crossover that joined the divided highway. To the left, a trail emerged from the mountains.

Krupinski steered into the cop turn-around just as two motocross riders appeared on the path ahead. He pulled across traffic and stopped on the southbound shoulder. He stepped out of the Wrangler and circled around it, shouting, "Hey! Susan!"

She revved her engine, roared toward him, and skidded to a halt. "Krupinski!" she said, ripping off her red helmet.

He caught her in a huge embrace, three hundred pounds around a hundred thirty.

"We were attacked," Susan said.

"You were ambushed," Krupinski corrected.

"Death's Disciples."

"Yeah."

"Elseworth had no idea."

Krupinski nodded. "Get in."

"Government issue?" Susan laughed as she dropped the helmet to the ground.

"Something like that," replied Krupinski.

The other rider pulled up and drew off a blue helmet to reveal a shock of curly red hair and a face crossed both with triumph and defeat. He stepped off his bike and approached. "Who are you, sir?"

"I'm Sergeant Krupinski of the FBI," he replied.

"He's a friend," Susan said

The man walked up, his eyes unwavering. "What the hell just happened?"

"We've got to find out."

"My whole house is shot to shit. My cows, my hired hand–"

"Yeah, I know. We're going to find out.

The man grasped Krupinski's hand. "I'm Bob Schneider. Karen's husband." He glanced at Susan. "I – I only want to make sure she's safe. Susan, I mean."

"Don't worry," Krupinski responded. "I'll keep her safe."

"She's talking to my wife. I don't know how. Maybe she's got a telephone to heaven. All I know is this girl's got everything I care about anymore."

"I understand."

Bob's stony face crumbled, and he released Krupinski's hand. "All right, then."

Krupinski nodded, unsure what to say. He took Susan's hand and guided her to step into the Jeep.

"I'm headed home," Bob said.

Grabbing Bob's hand, Krupinski shook it heartily. "Thanks for saving her. But you shouldn't go back. You should just find a nice outcrop and lie down and sleep a couple days."

"Okay, whatever you say, spy guy," Bob pulled his hand away. A slim line of blood traced down his finger.

Krupinski circled around the Jeep and climbed in. "Good-bye Bob, and thanks for everything."

Bob waved his bloodied hand as the Jeep roared out onto Route 15.

"What was all that?" asked Susan.

Krupinski shrugged, "Cop stuff."

"Why was he bleeding?"

"Ever hear of midazolam?"

"No?"

"Keeps you from making new memories. He'll remember riding out with you, and that'll be it for about twelve hours."

Susan's eyebrows lowered. "You drugged him?"

"Yep."

Susan scowled. "You can take somebody's *memory*?"

Krupinski blinked. "Oh, no, now. I wouldn't've done that to you. I want your memory back. I don't want to erase it."

They drove for a while in silence. At last, Susan offered, "They killed Dr Wilder."

"Sorry to hear that."

"I hope they didn't get Elseworth. He was in the basement."

"I *knew* it. Asshole. He was behind the whole thing."

"What? He's FBI."

"Question is whether he's gone rogue, or whether his orders were to kill you."

"Orders? I'm an American citizen."

"Homeland Security's a funny business."

"So, if he was trying to kill me, whose side are *you* on?"

He shifted into high gear and zoomed down the mountainside. "Yours."

6 OVERKILL

Elseworth lingered in the basement, listening as armor-piercing rounds ripped through the farmhouse. A little overkill, perhaps. An old farmhouse didn't have armor, just clapboards. The bullets should blast through the front wall and through anybody inside and out through the back.

"She was in the kitchen, wasn't she?" Elseworth murmured distractedly.

He looked up at the floor joists and tried to imagine where he had left the 311 Miracle. By the old, cast-iron sink? Or next to the steel oven from the forties? How much time would all that tile and metal buy her? And what would she do with it? If she got out the back–

"I'm being paranoid," Elseworth told himself with a chuckle. "Krupinski must be rubbing off on me."

She couldn't escape. The drive was corked tight. There was nowhere to run except across empty fields, perfect for M-1s and M-16s.

The noise overhead intensified – the bullets, the screams, the shouts among black ops. There were boots on the floorboards above, running through the house.

This was it. They were going room to room.

Slugs burst through the hardwood floor and cut the Romex wires, making them spark. Elseworth ducked back as a body pounded the floor above. A red rain began. Scowling, Elseworth moved behind the pump and water tank and hunkered down while the team went through and finished anyone else. More bullets hailed into the basement.

Why the hell were people shooting *into the basement*?

Crouching behind the water tank, Elseworth waited and listened. Boots that once were stalking room to room now were still. She must have been dead. They all must have been dead.

Victory. Even if it smelled like mold and cat litter, it was victory.

Elseworth allowed a ten count to make sure they were done shooting. Then he crawled from behind the water tank, climbed the stairs, and shoved back the old basement door.

"Hello, fellows. How're things shaping up?"

One of the Blackwater goons turned, flak jacket spattered in blood and heads-up display flashing across his left eye. "Lieutenant Elseworth. Glad to see you survived."

"Yeah, no thanks to whoever was shooting people on the floor."

"Sorry about that," the man said. "Lazaretti, at your service, sir."

"So, what's the report?"

"There's five dead in the house, Lieutenant."

"Excellent. Excellent. Who?"

Lazaretti crooked a finger, leading Elseworth through a kitchen filled with shattered plates and glasses, around a breakfast bar, to the headless body of Dr Wilder.

Elseworth nodded. "Yes, I recognize her."

Lazaretti then led him to the front room, where a young Mexican lay facedown on the rug. "Hired hand, apparently. Ran in here for safety."

"Fine."

"And these were your agents," Lazaretti said, pointing to bodies crumpled by the picture window.

"Tell me that the fifth body is Susan Gardner."

"Negative, sir."

"Negative? She *was the mission*."

"The fifth is Sullivan, one of our own. Dave Sullivan. Good guy. Brought down by friendly fire."

"You killed him?"

"Not me, but one of us."

"Where the hell's Gardner? How'd she escape? "

"Maybe it's her gift."

"Her *gift*," Elseworth spat. "Subscribe to the *National Enquirer*, do you?"

"A plane crash couldn't kill her."

"Where is she?"

"She's gone. The agents behind the house saw dirt bikes – two of them – heading out across the field."

"Why didn't they *shoot* them? With their *high-powered fucking sniper rifles*?"

"They did. They were aiming for the smaller rider. They drew a bead several times, but they never hit."

"Are you *kidding* me? They can plug a nickel at a thousand yards."

"She *was* at a thousand yards."

"She wasn't a nickel! Why didn't you go after her?"

"We tried, but the SUVs were parked in back. They couldn't get past the motorcade. Two are stuck in the ditch right now."

"Why didn't you ride the fucking horses?"

"The only two horses were killed by gunfire, along with half a dozen cows."

"Damn you! Where is she now?"

Lazaretti gestured vaguely toward the mountains. "Out there."

Elseworth savagely knocked the heads-up display away from the man's left eye – and ended up lying on the floor with a knee in his back. "Hey!"

"Sorry, sir," said Lazaretti, standing up. "Reflexes."

Elseworth got to his feet and brushed flecks of plaster from his suit. "I could have you fired for that."

"Sorry."

"Well, damn it. You guys fucked up."

"Yes, we did, sir."

"Well, God damn it," Elseworth said, leaning against a chewed-up sideboard.

"Yes," Lazaretti agreed. "God damn it all to hell."

The two stood there, side by side in the ruined farmhouse. Sunlight poked fingers through the riddled walls. "And about those bullets…"

"Yeah. Special make. Pakistani. That'll get them talking."

"Yes, it will," Elseworth agreed grimly. "Come with me."

"Yes, sir."

Elseworth pushed his way out the back screen, which slammed behind Lazaretti. The two men crossed an old porch and walked down the steps to the back yard.

"Shoot me," Elseworth said.

"Sir!"

"Something nonfatal. No torso shots. Nothing near the femoral. And don't take out the knee. That costs a fortune."

"How about the foot?"

"No. That'd make it seem like I was running. How about the calf?" Elseworth suggested, tapping the spot. "I want front entry, of course."

Lazaretti raised his rifle. "I have to warn you, sir – these are armor-piercing rounds."

"What the hell!" Elseworth yelled, knocking the gun away. "What about your fucking pistol? The nine millimeter? Use your brain!"

The man lowered his rifle and drew a handgun from his shoulder holster. He pointed it at Elseworth's leg. "It'll be close range. They'll know."

"Fine! I'll tell them I stared down the Death's Disciples. I'll come up with a little monologue, you know, something starting with 'if' and ending with 'then you'll have to kill me.' All right. You ready?"

"Yes, sir."

"Then shoot me."

The gun fired, and a white-hot slug tore through the skin and muscle of Elseworth's calf, yanking his leg out from under him and hurling him to the ground.

He sprawled on a patch of long grass and gasped, "That hurt!"

"With all due respect, sir," Lazaretti said, "you've been shot."

"Give me that gun!"

Blinking, Lazaretti flipped it over, extending the handle to Elseworth. "It's regulation."

Elseworth gripped the handle and fired, splitting Lazaretti's head. "I know."

As the man fell back, Elseworth writhed on the ground.

Another Blackwater goon burst through the screen door and ran to him. "What was that gunshot?"

"Forget the gunshot! Burn this house down."

"Yessir. We brought gasoline."

"Forget the gasoline! Shoot the goddamned gas lines."

"Yessir!"

As the man marched toward the back door, Elseworth shouted, "And get your vehicles out of here. This is supposed to look like a Disciples hit."

"Yessir!" the man said as he vanished into the bullet-riddled home.

The farmhouse didn't burst into flame. At first, there was only an orange glow in the dining room. Afterward came the rattle of a machine gun in the kitchen, then a hiss of gas. Moving quickly, a Blackwater agent stepped out the back door, closed it, and walked briskly away from the house.

"I'm a little close," Elseworth realized.

A black pall rolled across the dining room ceiling, accompanied by a chorus of out-of-tune smoke detectors. Then the whole window filled with smoke, followed by flames – bluish-gold flames with yellow centers, rising to the height of a man.

"Too close." Elseworth rolled and began to belly-crawl across the lawn.

Behind him, the windows blew out. The fire inside took a deep breath and roared. Smoke gushed over the lintels, and soot blackened the clapboards. Flames licked the desiccated wood.

The Blackwater goon smiled. He nodded toward Elseworth and headed up the drive.

Elseworth crawled after. In a few moments, the eight hit vehicles were gone. All that remained were the government-issue motorcycles and limo and SUVs,

"Thank Jesus," Elseworth said, laying his head down on the gravel drive and watching a slug make its slow, oblivious way toward a nearby dandelion.

It didn't seem very long that he lay there, bleeding into the good Montana earth. But it must have been. When the cops and the ambulance and the reporters arrived, the slug was eating the flower.

"There's another body up here... Holy Christ!" A camera flashed its amazement. "He's worse than the last four."

"I'm alive," Elseworth noted in a sepulchral voice.

The EMT/reporter/photographer – one and the same here in Walkerville – knelt beside Elseworth and turned him over and stared. "This one's alive!"

The camera went off again before the thirty-something reporter put it down and became an EMT again. He felt Elseworth's neck for a pulse and leaned down to listen for breath.

"I'm alive, damn you."

"I'll take your word," the EMT said. Sitting back, he noticed the holes in Elseworth's pant leg. "What happened?"

"Bullet," Elseworth said.

"Other injuries?"

"Pride."

The EMT looked up at the house. It was a holocaust. Fire had blown out every window and now snaked its way up the sides of the home. The structure shifted on its foundation.

"We got to get you away from here." The EMT hooked hands under Elseworth's arms and dragged him away from the blaze.

The hundred year-old house tilted toward them. Nails strained, and timbers cracked. The whole thing slumped and collapsed to the ground. Flaming boards spilled out on the grass, and the fire spread.

"Lucky you weren't in there," the EMT said breathlessly.

"Yeah," replied Elseworth. "Lucky."

Lieutenant Elseworth lay abed in St James Hospital and watched the six o'clock news.

"This is Sasha Jones, live from an agonizing scene here in Walkerville," said the young black woman. She held a microphone as she stood along Butchertown Road. Behind her, the ruins of the Schneider place were mantled in flames. "Of course, anytime a home like this burns, it's a tragedy, but this is a double or triple tragedy tonight. This hundred year-old farmhouse belonged to Robert Schneider, the widower husband of Karen Schneider, who died in the terrible 311 attack. And sources within Homeland Security indicate that the same people who bombed that plane burned this house.

"Witnesses describe a parade of death. According to neighbors, after the motorcade with the 311 Miracle, eight more vehicles arrived at this location. From those vehicles emerged what one witness described as 'ninjas' – black-suited men who moved with speed from the road where I'm standing, up this long gravel drive, and to the fire there in the distance. Except, when they attacked, that was not a fire. It was a house. And it was not just any house, but the house that held the 311 Miracle."

The screen cut to a shot of an old, grizzled man standing on his front porch and pointing with a haunted look out into the distance. "I never seen such a thing. So many black cars. And when them guys got out with their machine guns, well, I just went back inside and locked the door. What're you supposed to do?"

The image returned to Sasha, her figure outlined by the blaze. "What, indeed? Witnesses say that the attackers converged on the house, killing everyone outside and then proceeding to kill everyone within. When police arrived, they found six FBI agents slain in the front and back yards, and the home ablaze. Police officers spotted five bodies within, but the blaze was so intense that they were unable to retrieve them.

"As a sleepy community shakes its head in disbelief at the events this afternoon, one eyewitness made everything clear. Here is the account of Lieutenant Tom Elseworth of the FBI."

Elseworth sat up.

The scene changed to a hospital room in St James, where a thin, tall, handsome man leaned bare-chested in bed, a tube of oxygen draping his upper lip. "Death's Disciples," he said. "They were trying to kill us, to kill

Susan Gardner." He smiled painedly. "But they failed. She escaped. And they didn't even manage to kill me. My fight goes on. I'll find Susan Gardner and bring her to safety, and I'll find the Death's Disciples and bring them to justice."

Watching himself on television always made Elseworth smile, but especially now. The 311 Miracle was gone. Lieutenant Elseworth had taken her hospital bed, had taken her place. Let the nation obsess over *him* for a change.

The phone rang. He'd forbidden anyone to have his room number except the FBI and... Trembling, Elseworth reached out and lifted the handset and leaned it to his ear. "Hello?"

The voice on the other end spoke angrily.

Elseworth gave a nervous laugh. "That was just publicity. You know. Keeping up the public face."

More words snapped out like scissors.

"We tried. We tried everything. The bitch just wouldn't die."

The voice spoke again.

"I understand. I'll get her. I'll give you her head on a platter..."

7 TWO ON THE LAM

There was no sense going back into Butte. The cops would be on the lookout for the stolen Jeep. Besides, what was a Jeep for except off-roading?

Krupinski turned onto a dirt road that headed into the mountains. "Let's see limos follow us on this."

"Speaking of which," Susan Gardner said, her hair streaming out the window, "how'd you find me? Did Karen tell you?"

"Karen?"

"Karen Schneider. The woman from Walkerville. Did she tell you to come save me?"

"I thought she was dead."

"She *is* dead."

"Then how could she–" Krupinski's eyes grew wide, and he made a *hocus pocus* gesture. "Oh, a psychic thing, huh?"

"Yeah."

"You're the psychic, not me. I can't talk to the dead."

"But you came. She must have somehow… *nudged* you."

Krupinski shrugged. "No, actually, it was the Homeland Security Satellite Service. That and – where's that card I gave you?"

"Card?"

"The get-well card," he said. "You put it in your sweatshirt pocket."

"Oh, yeah," she said, drawing it out.

He snatched it from her hand. "*This* is how I found you. It has a homing beacon."

She looked at him in shock. "How? The guards scanned it."

He flipped it open, and "Bright, Sunshiny Day," played over the rumble of the wind. "I overlaid the beacon circuitry with the song circuitry. Perfect disguise."

"You tracked me with that card?"

"Yep. And they will, too, once they figure it out."

"Then throw it out the window."

"Or we could use it as a decoy – you know, slip it into somebody's trunk. The guy'll be driving along, and eight black cars will pull him over, and they'll frisk him and pop the trunk expecting to find the body of Susan Gardner but instead find a card that sings, 'I can see clearly now, the rain has gone.'"

She grabbed the card and flung it out the window. Krupinski watched through the rear-view mirror as it fluttered down like a wounded butterfly. Susan said, "Let's not ruin anybody else's day."

Krupinski pulled out his cellphone, shut it off, and hurled it out of the Jeep. Then he shut off his netbook and folded it and placed it beneath the seat. "We're off the map."

"Except that we're driving a stolen vehicle."

"The first of many, my dear," Krupinski replied. "Enjoy it. This'll probably be the only Jeep. The rest'll be nondescript. Dodge Neons and shit."

"Whoopee."

They rode on, out of sight of the main road, up

switchbacks, over fallen rocks, across eroded washes, and even past the timberline. Suddenly, the jolting way became smooth, with a blue sky overhead and views out over the world. As they reached the summit of the mountain, Krupinski pulled onto a wide spot and shut off the engine and stepped out.

"What now?" Susan asked.

"Let's stretch." He lifted his arms, flexing, and breathed the cold air. "Beautiful."

The brown mountains nearby gave way to gray and blue and purple ranges. At lower elevations, pine forests clothed the great peaks. Higher up, rocks jutted skyward, and snow caps gleamed beneath the summer sun.

"How could there be terrorists in a world like this?" Susan wondered. "If we could just get everyone to stand up here and breathe the air, maybe we could end all wars."

Krupinski cocked his eyebrow. "We're at war, Susan. You have to know that."

She looked at her feet. "I know."

"And there are people down there who tried to kill you – just two hours ago."

"Yeah, yeah," Susan said, heading back into the Jeep. "Why the hell'd you bring me out here?"

Krupinski laughed. "I told you – to stretch." He climbed in beside her, fired up the engine, and took off down the winding trail. They rode together in silence for a time before Krupinski said, "I'd ask you about your past, but…"

"Ha, ha," Susan said. "You know, two hours ago, I saw a woman get her head blown off. Now I'm sitting in a

Jeep, going down a mountain, talking like nothing happened. What kind of person am I?"

Krupinski sighed. "It's called shock. You've witnessed your second mass murder. I wouldn't be surprised if your brain's trying to erase it right now."

Worry ringed her eyes. "I *have* to remember."

"I didn't mean it like that that. Of course you will. I was just talking."

Again they sat in silence. Wide tableaus flashed before them.

"I can't tell you about me, so tell me about you," she said. "What turned you into the ever-faithful guard dog?"

Krupinski snorted.

"I mean, come on, you waited four weeks outside my door. You saved me twice. Do they train you to do that?"

"They try, but you can't train loyalty. Elseworth proves that."

"Who taught you, then?"

"My dad," Krupinski said flatly. "He cheated on my mom and left me and four younger ones when I was fourteen. Betrayal. Abandonment. It's the worst thing in the world. I was a freshman in high school when I became the man of the family. That's when I decided I would never betray anyone I cared about."

Susan nodded. The conversation had gotten too deep. She turned toward the back seat. "Looks like we have a tent back there, and an Igloo cooler."

"What's inside?"

She pivoted the lid. "Beef jerky and some Coke and a fifth of Captain Morgan."

"Jackpot!" Krupinski said. "You always try to steal a car full of gas. If you can also get dinner and drinks and a place to stay, well, that's perfect."

Pulling two Slim Jims from the cooler, Susan handed one to Krupinski and kept one for herself. She peeled the plastic back and took a bite. "So, where are we headed, Sergeant?"

"Right now – just away." Krupinski said. "Far away from Elseworth and the FBI and Death's Disciples. Far away from any hint of where we might go."

"So… no Oak Park?"

"That's a thousand miles. We got to think in hundred-mile increments right now. We got to think in terms of tanks of gas and APBs and manhunts," he said. "We've gone dark. Over the next four days, we've got to go cold."

"Okay, so where are we headed?"

"We keep going until this road crosses another, and we take it. Then it crosses another, and we take it. Probably by morning we'll end up in Helena, and we'll steal another car."

"Going to Helena handbasket."

"You got it."

"Once the trail goes cold, where then?"

"Maybe Sioux City."

Susan shrugged. "Why Sioux City?"

"There was a guy I knew from Sioux City on that flight."

"What flight? You mean 311?"

Krupinski nodded. "Corporal David Jenkins, FBI agent. My partner in Chicago. He'd been trying to get inside the Death's Disciples, had done a couple jobs for them – you know, money laundering, arson – low-level shit. He even did a 'hit' once – though the gun had blanks, and the target was in on it. That's what sealed the deal. Dave had only ever dealt with lackeys before then, but killing somebody, well, that gets their attention. He comes home and finds a fake ID with his face on it and a plane ticket on Flight 311 in the name on the card. It was an invitation to join the organization. He was gonna fly to Seattle and finally meet one of the inner circle. Man named Phillips. So, Dave was on his way when he got killed."

"He wasn't on his way. He was set up."

"No shit."

"How close were you?"

Krupinski took a deep breath. "Pretty close. Dave and I came up through the Quantico together. We were buddies, both working for Elseworth – both trying to stop a terrorist strike on US soil."

"You want me to talk to him?"

Krupinski finally looked at her. "Yeah. I want to find out what he knows."

She laughed sadly.

"What?"

"It's just so weird. He's in there. It's like having three hundred sixty-two personalities – and three hundred sixty-one of them know who they really are."

"Listen," Krupinski said, "if it's too much–"

"No. It's not that. But I can't just do it – go to the dream world. Not while we're bouncing along the mountains."

"We'll look for a spot, then, where we can stop."

They wended their way out of the heights, entering a maze of off-road trails in a wide valley. The mountain to the west cast everything in a cool blue shadow. The mountains in the east blazed golden with the last rays of daylight.

Krupinski pulled up beneath a Ponderosa pine and cut the engine. Suddenly, everything was quiet. Without the motor's hum and the battering wind and the crackling gravel, there was nothing except birds and cicadas and the occasional fly.

"How about here?" asked Krupinski. "It'll be a day before they find out about that card – and another day before they track it down. We can stop for a little and see if we can find that safe place of yours."

"The tree house," Susan said distantly. "It's in an old oak at the back of the upper pasture. You climb up the boards nailed into the tree, and you push back the hatch, and then you're inside, and nobody can hurt you."

8 THE MUSTACHIOED G-MAN

I walk down the missing aisle of Flight 311 and call out, "Dave Jenkins? Is there a Dave Jenkins here?"

A small man turns toward me and half lifts his hand. "I'm Dave Jenkins." He has a mustache, long sideburns, and wavy hair in a U-shape around the back of his head. The top is bald and shiny. Dave's eyes are intelligent, his smile friendly but sad.

"I'm Susan Gardner."

"Head of foreign accounts at International Mercantile."

"How did you know?"

He smiles. "It's a secret."

I nod. "You work for the FBI."

He looks up nervously and places a finger to his lips.

"It's okay. These people won't tell your secret. They're dead."

Black eyebrows flare. "Is that what this is?" He scowls. "Is that why I can see through the floor?"

"Sorry." I try to change the subject. "So, if you know who I am, you must have a profile for everyone on this plane."

"Everyone. I thought there'd be one of 'them' on board."

"One of Death's Disciples?"

He looks at me. "How do you know about–?"

"Krupinski."

He blinks. "Are you his new partner?"

"Basically," I say, changing the subject. "So, of all the people you've profiled, who looks most suspicious?"

Dave opens his laptop and pulls up a list of everyone on board. "Profiled racially, there are three men and four women of Arab or Persian descent."

I shake my head. "This isn't foreign. It's domestic."

"You *do* know this case," he says with eyes alight. "Profiled politically, there's three neo-Nazis, two members of the Army of God, three Klansmen, an anarchist, and three members of NAMBLA."

"NAMBLA?"

"North American Man-Boy Love Association."

"Yuck. Are they violent?"

"No, but I hate them, so I track them."

"Any other profiles?"

Dave holds up his index finger. "Profiled criminally, there are three felons – two for aggravated assault and one for murder – served his time. There are nine registered sex offenders."

"Nine!"

"Some of them were eighteen year-old boys with seventeen year-old girlfriends. Some are the real deal – sado-masochists with torture chambers."

"But none of them would blow up a plane."

"No," Dave goes on. "Profiled economically, only three passengers bought their tickets with cash."

"That's suspicious," I say.

"There was Dylan Epping, Logan Bydalek, and… you, Miss Gardner."

"Me?"

"Yes, you'd bought your ticket the very morning of the flight, and bought it with cash."

"Why would I do that?"

"I don't know. Very unusual. Especially for a loan officer at a bank."

"Well, do you remember what happened? Did someone stand up and give a speech? Was there a weird sound or smell?"

"Nothing," Dave says. "We were all getting ready for our can of soda and our bag of pretzels. They were showing a Jennifer Aniston film on the screen. The pedophiles were laughing, and the neo-Nazis were snoozing, and the anarchist was reading the in-flight magazine. Nothing happened before the bomb."

"What about Death's Disciples?" I ask.

He shrugs. "I don't think any of the people I've just mentioned were connected to them at all."

I sigh. We're getting nowhere. I let my eyes close to the dream plane and slide open again to see Steve Krupinski, sitting beside me under the Ponderosa pine. "He doesn't know anything."

Krupinski blasts a laugh. "Dave Jenkins doesn't know anything? Since when? That guy's a computer."

"He profiled everybody on the plane – the Arabs and sex offenders and Nazis and NAMBLA, but he says none of them is connected to Death's Disciples."

"Only him," Krupinski says ominously.

"What?"

"They left a ticket and false ID in his apartment. They were *in* his apartment." He clamps a hand on his forehead. "It was one of my theories from the fucking beginning!"

"What was?"

"His luggage. They could've used his luggage. Go back and ask him. Ask him how carefully he prepared his bags."

I close my eyes to Montana and open them to Flight 311. "Dave, did you check your baggage?"

"I checked two bags and brought this computer bag on board."

"I mean, did you look through your bags – you know, when you packed?"

"I packed them myself."

"Did you pull them apart?"

"Pull them apart?"

"The Death's Disciples were in your apartment."

His eyes grow wide. "Oh, no."

"What kind of bags did you have?"

His already ghostly face is bone-white now. "That's the thing. I was going to meet the Death's Disciples. I'd packed a small arsenal... I put the gun case in earlier that day – used my agent's privilege. They scanned it and said I had 'hot shit' in it. I thought they meant my Glock and my 30 ought 6."

"It was a bomb," I say.

He shakes his head. "They used me. They got me to smuggle the damned thing on board and then they killed me. Killed us all. I was a suicide bomber and didn't even know it."

"I'm sorry, Dave," I say, and let my mind drift back down to the Jeep in the valley. "It was his case, his gun case."

"Of course," Krupinski groans. "They must have hidden the bomb between the lining and the case. They could've put twenty pounds of plastique in there, and he wouldn't notice if he'd taken enough guns."

"He said he had an arsenal. Put it through security using his agent's privilege."

"Damn it," Krupinski replies. "He was a mule, the only Disciple on that plane. Goddamn it." He spits, and his heart pounds audibly in the evening air. "Well, then, we'll just have to pick up where he left off. He's got to make up for this. He had all his intel on his laptop. He didn't synch it before going, afraid Elseworth would take the show from him – Goddamned Elseworth. So you talk to Dave. Get everything from him – names and descriptions of his contacts."

"You said they were nobodies."

"They're a start. We'll investigate them. Find out what we can."

"Fine," I say. "But not right now. Let's just drive for a little bit."

He shakes his head. "Night's coming. Can't drive in the mountains at night."

"You've got headlights."

"Yeah, and there's also cliffs you don't see until you're going over them. Besides, we turn on our lights, we tell everyone for ten miles where we are. No, we stay here tonight."

"Fine," I say again, gesturing toward the Jeep. "You get the tent out, and I'll play medium."

He laughs in that deprecating way of his. "If you want to sleep in the tent, be my guest. There's mountain lions out here. I'm staying in the Jeep."

I close my eyes and shut out the world. In moments, I'm sitting beside Dave Jenkins. "Okay. Show me what you know. I want contacts – names, addresses, pictures–"

"Fingerprints, DNA, I got all that."

"Good. We're going to need it."

9 LITTLE PIECES ON A MONTANA FIELD

Next morning, our Jeep bounds down a washed-out road. My right hand grips the window frame, and my left grips the dash. Aspens whirl by on either side.

"Do we have to go so fast?"

Krupinski glances my way, but his foot never leaves the accelerator. "Leave the driving to me. You're supposed to be meditating."

The Jeep shudders violently. "Yeah. Meditating in a maraca." Shutting my eyes, I search for my safe place.

The green upper pasture stretches out before me, and there comes a sound like... like a cattle stampede... No, shut it out. I hear the wind sifting through the oak leaves. And there's the tree house, and the boards nailed into the trunk. I push the hatch back from the tree house floor and climb up onto it.

"There's the Interstate. Hang on!"

I close the hatch behind me and sit in my safe place, breathing.

We lurch. Horns blare. We swerve and plunge down one slope and shoot up another...

"Made it – northbound!"

"Would you shut up?" I growl. A few breaths, and the world vanishes. I'm in my safe place, away from the madness. Well... away from everyone *else's* madness.

"You're back," Corporal Jenkins says.

I glance over at him, sitting beside me on the plane. "Oh, hi. Yeah."

"I'm glad." His tray table is down, and his netbook hums atop it. "After all, this thing's got only a three-hour battery."

I clear my throat, looking through the netbook. "I don't think batteries matter anymore."

"Probably not." He scowls a little.

I can see through his face to the window beyond. "What's it like?"

"What's *what* like?"

"Being dead?"

Dave ducks his head. "That's the weird thing. I don't feel any different. I mean, until you point it out, it feels like any other moment. And then you remind me the floor isn't there, or your foot goes through my foot and – well, then I know. But otherwise, being a ghost is just like being anybody."

"I don't know if you're a ghost, exactly."

"What do you mean?"

"Well… ghosts are supposed to haunt *places* – you know, houses, graveyards, old theaters."

"I haunt this airplane."

"This plane doesn't exist anymore. It's little pieces on a Montana field."

"Well, then what am I haunting?" Dave asks.

"Me," I reply firmly. "You're haunting me."

"That's not haunting. That's possessing."

I shake the idea away. "No, you're like – I don't know – a psychic echo or something."

"Like your brain is a computer, and I'm a program

running on it."

"Yeah, like that."

Dave shrugs, staring at his computer screen. "But then, you must be *another* program running on this computer."

"Like that."

"Which means you're no more alive than I am. Than any of us," he says, looking at the ghosts seated all around.

"Well, yeah," I reply with a laugh, "except that I have a body, and you don't."

"Actually, we do have a body. *Your* body. We're just not in control of it."

"Okay, let's cut the metaphysical bullshit and get down to catching the people who are trying to kill us."

"Agreed," he says. His computer shows a directory, and he clicks a file. It swells up across the screen, and I see a grainy photo of a Goth girl – white skin, black hair, piercings in eyebrow and nose and ears, maybe nineteen. She has an androgynous beauty and an androgynous name.

"Calliope Dirge?" I ask.

"Not her real name. She's an operative for Death's Disciples in Chicago. Low level. She doesn't know much about the actual organization – though, in a way, she knows everything."

"What are you talking about?"

"She's a messenger."

"Messenger? Why don't they just use the Internet, like everybody else?"

"Use the Internet, and you end up hiding in a cave in

Pakistan. Use messengers, and you live undetected beside your targets."

"But, you can intercept the messages, right? Shine a light through the envelope or something?"

"The messages aren't in envelopes. They're in Calliope's mind."

"Then interrogate her."

"She doesn't have access. The messages are encoded and buried deep. Nobody knows how they get them in or how they get them out."

"Then how do *you* know?"

"She told me."

"And you believed her?"

"She trusted me – and I slipped her some sodium pentathol. She said it wasn't anything technological – not a USB port in her brain. They laid hands on her and put messages inside, and then they laid hands on her to take the message away."

I stare at the picture of Calliope. She looks strung out. "How do you know she's not just a heroin junky having delusions?"

"They wouldn't take someone on heroin. And Calliope's not the kind to take it, anyway. She's a new-age vegan. She doesn't eat anything with chemicals in it."

"A freak."

"The perfect freak. They selected her very carefully. Calliope's got a photographic memory and perfect pitch. She's an ISTJ on Meyers-Briggs."

"On mayor's what?"

"A personality test. She scored full-on as introverted, sensing, thinking, and judging – the perfect profile for a carrier. She also happens to be a true believer. She wants to move up the ranks, but they've already got her doing what she's perfect at."

I sigh. "They sound more like human resources than a cult."

"Actually, human resources is the perfect word. That's all we are to them – resources, like a coal deposit or an old-growth forest."

I purse my lips. "So, if they profiled this Calliope chick, they must've profiled you, too."

"Must have. They gave me the perfect job. I pulled off one of the worst mass murders in history and didn't even know I was doing it." He slouches in his seat.

I feel bad for him. "So, how did you meet Calliope?"

"Social networking. Twitter, Facebook, chat rooms, forums."

"I thought you said the Disciples don't use the Internet."

"The actual ones don't. Those on the fringe do."

"You did a Google search for Death's Disciples?"

"Not Google. It searches the shallow end. Homeland Security's got its own engine. You remember that whole flap about illegal wiretapping?"

"Actually, no."

"Well, it wasn't really about *wiretapping*. That's from the Cold War. This was about using a new Homeland Security engine that doesn't just search Web sites but computer hard drives and databases and e-mail accounts – the whole thing. It knows everything on any machine connected to the Web–"

I point at the ghost computer on his tray table. "But

this one isn't, anymore, right?"

"Yeah," Dave echoes with dawning realization. "It can't be read by Conscious 1."

"Conscious 1?"

"That's what they've named it, the new Homeland Security engine."

"Seriously?"

"It's a living thing. Ever present. All knowing. It's a dragon, and Homeland Security holds its leash."

A big man's hand grabs my arm. I'm pulled out of the plane, out of the tree house, into the Jeep.

"What do you want?" I groan.

"Get ready," Krupinski replies. "We're about to jump."

"Jump where?"

We're on a four-lane road through downtown Helena. Krupinski switches on his left-turn signal and slows to wait for oncoming traffic to clear. Then he shoots the Wrangler into the back parking lot of a Pizza Hut.

"Are you hungry?" I ask.

"Good point. Grab the cooler!" Krupinski says as he jumps out of the driver's side door. He reaches back for his laptop and the tent and hauls them out, then runs around a Dodge Stratus with its engine running and a "Pizza Hut Delivers" sign glowing on top. He leaps into the driver's seat. "Come on!"

With the Igloo cooler in hand, I rush to the passenger seat and clamber in.

Krupinski shifts into reverse and backs up. "Perfect! Full tank at 11:00 a.m., and did you check out the back seat?"

I look back to see five stay-warm sleeves, each stuffed with a pizza. "Well done."

We peel out, heading north. Krupinski reaches through his window and works the strapping that holds the sign on the roof. "See if you can loosen the wing nut on your side. We won't get five miles with Pizza Hut blazing above us."

I reach up and feel the wing nut and crank it.

Krupinski's side comes loose, and the sign topples onto the rooftop. I get my side free, letting the marquee roll off the rear window, bound from the trunk, and crash to blacktop. The power cord rips from the cigarette lighter and catches in the half-closed window. We drag the sign for a hundred feet before I get the window rolled down. The cord vaults free, and "Pizza Hut Delivers" sparks to stillness in the gutter.

"A Stratus, huh?" I say, looking around at the battered interior. "Nice."

"It's no Wrangler, but it'll do," Krupinski says. "Hold on."

He does a sudden U-turn, and we're headed south again.

"Where'd you learn to drive?"

"Phoenix University Online."

"What?"

"We gotta go south."

"Why didn't you turn south to begin with?"

"They'll be putting pins in maps on corkboards, drawing lines of trajectory. It looks like we headed north, so now we gotta go south."

"Were things this crazy before I lost my memory?"

"Yeah. It's been pandemonium. Grab me a slice, would you?"

I turn around and reach into the top sleeve of the warmer. "It's sausage and mushroom."

"My favorite. Somebody's looking out for us."

I pull out a steaming wedge of pizza and push it toward Krupinski.

He takes it, wincing. "Hot!"

"Yeah."

"But I'm so hungry!" He bites into the piece, and then opens his mouth in pain, trying to suck air past the mound on his tongue. "Hoth–"

I'm hungry, too, and I pull out my own slice and take a bite. It burns the roof of my mouth, but it tastes terrific.

We roll on south, past sleepy downtown Helena and out onto dry fields.

"What's south? Anything?"

"Nothing."

"Sounds like it's made for us."

"Exactly. I got it from here. You go back and talk to Dave."

I laugh. I'm sitting in a stolen vehicle that's still on its way from the crime scene, heart pounding and mouth burning. "It's kinda hard to find the safe place."

"Well, try."

I close my eyes and find my way.

And Dave is waiting patiently for me.

"Where'd you go?"

"Had to... take care of something."

He looks amused. "Krupinski?"

"Yeah. So, where were we?"

"I was meeting Calliope Dirge online, in a Satanic chat room."

"Satanic?"

"It's not really Satanic. I mean, they just use that term to sift out people who aren't serious. Most people are afraid of Satanism, so only the hard core get deeper, get to the chat rooms. That's where I met her. Her login is Eldermuse."

"Eldermuse?"

"Calliope was the oldest of the muses, daughter of Zeus and mother of Orpheus," Dave says, seeming almost appalled at my blank stare. "She inspired the *Iliad* and the *Odyssey*."

"I thought a calliope was a circus organ."

"God, she would hate you," Dave remarks. "Calliope Dirge means 'Muse of Death.' That's all she ever talks about."

"Cheery."

"Actually, she's a sweet kid. Yeah, she's obsessed with death, but in a way, we all should be."

"You became friends."

"Yep, me and Calliope and the 'Bat Pack.'" He clicks through subsequent screens, showing more pallid teenagers with black hair draping their faces. They had names like Kid Killer, Thanatopsis, Cyclops, and Evella of the Eternal Sleep. "Kids in capes – a bunch of Goth punks who half-believe they're vampires and want to find another world, another power. Problem is, they've found one."

I look at those young faces. "These kids are still in the Chicago area?"

"If they're not dead. Who knows what Death's Disciples has done to them in – how long has it been?"

"Four weeks," I say.

He shakes his head.

"At least your battery never runs out."

"It's the moment I died," he goes on sadly. "When the bomb went off, I was sitting here just like this, working on my computer. Everyone on this plane is frozen in the moment when they died."

"And we're going to find their killers. Could you lead me to the Bat Pack?"

"Of course," he says.

He's doing it again. Krupinski's tapping my leg like an insistent child. I try to ignore him, to stay in the plane, but then he grabs onto my knee and shakes it.

The plane dissolves, leaving the inside of the Dodge and, beyond the windows, the rolling grasslands of Eastern Montana. "What could be so urgent that you had to shake me awake?"

"We're here," Krupinski says. He pulls off the road and stops on the gravel shoulder.

We're not on the interstate anymore, but a little country road running arrow-straight.

"We're *where*?" I ask.

"The crash site," he says, pivoting out of the front seat and letting the door close behind him.

My heart is suddenly pounding. This is the place.

I open the door and step out. The grass is tall and dry,

and it hisses in the constant wind. Krupinski is wading through it, making a track out across the field. I follow. But it's just a field. There's no sign of a plane going down. "You sure this is right?"

Krupinski doesn't slow, doesn't turn. "Look over there."

A strange memorial is perched by the road – hundreds of crosses in wood and Styrofoam, thousands of flowers, both silk and real, handmade signs on poster board, pictures, mementos. It's an altar of remembrances left by a mourning nation.

Two other vehicles are parked by the memorial – a minivan and a pickup. Their drivers are also marching across the field, making trails in the tall grass. There's a gaunt old farmer and a family of five with a teenage son and two little brothers. All walk with reverence, heads lifted, mouths closed.

I hurry to catch up to Krupinski. He stops and stands, looking down at a stone with a shiny bronze plaque screwed into it.

"You are standing on hallowed ground," he reads. "It is hallowed by the lives of three hundred sixty-one people. None set out to be warriors or martyrs. They were like you. They were plumbers and receptionists, architects and police officers, opticians and engineers, mothers and fathers and children. All gave their lives in the skies over Montana and on this very ground where you stand."

I look down between golden stems of grass to see ground that is black and cracked. Charcoal. And here and there wink little shreds of metal. Little flecks of fabric. Or ash. Or skin. There's a half-mile depression in the field.

"Some of this is David Jenkins," I whisper to Krupinski.

He looks at me, eyes watery.

"Some of this is his laptop. And the bomb itself. And the Glock and the thirty ought six he was so proud of. And some is that Amish kid, and that old man with the liver spots, and Karen Schneider." I'm shaking.

"None of it is you," he says, his hand on my shoulder.

I shake my head. "All of it is. They're all inside me."

His face turns red, and he looks away, unsure what to say.

"They're in all of us," pipes up a middle-aged man with a nine year-old boy leaning on his hip. The man is balding, his glasses are out of date, and he looks tearfully at the field. "There's something bigger going on here, a struggle between life and death."

"It's not as simple as that," I say.

Krupinski waves my words away. "You're right. It's life and death."

He's trying to close the conversation, but suddenly I can't hear him anymore. I'm overwhelmed by the voices. Dozens. Hundreds. It's not Krupinski or the man speaking now, but the three hundred sixty-one. Everyone on that plane is shouting for revenge, here where they died.

"I'm just one person," I murmur, shaking.

"We're all one person," says the balding man gently. "But we're all together."

"All together," I echo.

But then I can't see the field and its plaque. I'm no longer in the real world. A hand has reached from the ghost plane and ripped me from the world and returned me to that day.

The day that three hundred sixty-one people died.

10 **FLASHBACKS**

I'm sitting on a toilet – well, not really a toilet. It's too small. It's molded into the rest of this angled closet: a lavatory.

I'm sitting on a lavatory and regretting the chicken lasagna I had in Chicago.

A knock comes at the louvered doors.

Oh, as if I have been taking too long.

I finish up – some people are so rude – and flush the thing. Its antifreeze water sucks away the stuff but not the smell. I squirt a little Charlie Gold.

As I wash my hands, I see myself in the tiny mirror: middle-aged, brunette, pudgy, somewhat bedeviled. Is that my face?

Am I really this large?

This old?

The knock comes again.

I slide the bar to "Available" and try to step out, but – wouldn't you know it? – there's a beautiful young blonde standing in my way. What could she need the lavatory for? She doesn't eat. Maybe she just chewed on some pretzels and wants to puke them out before they show up on her hips. I press mine past her – impatient bitch – and head for my seat two rows from the back.

I squeeze past the gaunt man with the goatee in 38B and fasten my seatbelt.

Then the air shatters.

A fireball fills the cabin.

Everybody's on fire.

The seats in front of me drop out of the plane.

Everybody in front of me is gone.

I can't breathe!

Oxygen masks drop from the ceiling. They whip around above the gaping hole.

I position my mask before assisting others.

The goatee guy has a metal bar sticking from his head.

There's movement beyond him – that beautiful Barbie doll stumbling out of the lavatory. She's got blood all over her. I feel sorry for her. She darts back into the lavatory and closes the door.

Probably the worst place to be in a crash.

That's what's happening. We're crashing. Half the passengers already have crashed. The rest of us are on our way.

The shadow of the plane soars over grasslands below. The shadow grows.

This is it. I'm going to die.

The shadow plane and the real plane meet.

They become one.

There's a horrible roar and tearing and screams. The middle of the plane arches up and the back slams into it and–

"It's all right," Krupinski says, carrying me back toward the car. He holds me like I'm a child. "You've seen enough."

"I know just how she feels," puts in the middle-aged father, tromping alongside Krupinski. "I fainted at Gettysburg. Nearly fell off Little Round Top."

"I think one of your kids is crying," Krupinski replies, glancing over his shoulder.

The man turns away from us, and sweat speckles his face. "Ford? Hughes? Lucas? Are you boys okay?" He rushes away through the grass. "Nobody faint! The lady's fine!"

Krupinski looks down at me. "Susan, are you all right?"

"I saw it all. I saw it from a fat woman's eyes."

"Saw what?"

"I shouldn't've survived."

"What do you mean?"

"In the lavatory – worst place to be in a crash."

He opens the passenger-side door of the Stratus and lowers me to sit. "You're seeing them here?"

"They're all here."

His mouth hitches. "I'm sorry. I shouldn't've brought you."

"That woman thought I was a Barbie bitch."

"You're not. You're like my little sister." His gaze locks with mine a moment. I look away, and he closes the door and circles around to the driver's side. He climbs in, ignites the engine, and swerves us out onto the farm road.

"Where're we headed?" I ask wearily.

"Out of Montana."

"Good."

11 BRIGHT, BRIGHT, BRIGHT SUNSHINY DAY

"Here it is, sir," said a special agent, using a pen to fish a greeting card out of a yucca.

Elseworth ambled up, his woolen suit wrinkled by crutches. Elseworth stared hawkishly at the card: a hedge-hog under a drenching rain. "'Hear you've been under the weather…' *This* is what was sending the signal?"

The agent nodded. He gingerly caught the corner of the card and used his pen to pry it open. It sluggishly began to play, "Bright Sunshiny Day." The agent laughed. "That's how he got it past the scanner–"

"I *know*!" Elseworth ripped the card from the man's fingers, flung it to the ground, and stomped on in. "You said, 'Find the card and find Susan Gardner.' Bullshit!"

The card had lain stationary for twenty-five hours, a quarter of a mile off Route 15, so the analysts said she was dead or asleep. Elseworth would've been happy ei-ther way. But Miss Gardner was neither. She'd thrown her card into a yucca.

"Gone are the dark clouds that had me blind…"

Elseworth ground his heel on the card. Something popped, and the music stopped. "Where is she?"

"Not here," the agent answered.

"Then she's with Krupinski." Elseworth turned, swinging forward on his crutches and heading toward his limo. "Damned Polack."

Krupinski had been released from Saint James the morning of the motorcade. Witnesses indicated that, at lunchtime, he'd had a Salisbury steak at Traxside Café, and that he'd used his netbook. Analysts reported that he'd taken over the ethernet of Fred's Mesquite Grill, ordered tickets to Chicago, and then used Homeland Security satellites to spy on the "Butchertown Road Rage" – as the media were calling it. Witnesses at the scene said he stole a Jeep, which the police had found outside a Pizza Hut in Helena, where a Dodge Stratus was stolen.

"He left Helena heading north," the agent reminded.

"Krupinski's a Polack, but he's not stupid," Elseworth raged. "He could be anywhere in a three-hundred mile radius. If he's filled up again, it could be six hundred miles."

"If he's stole a plane," the agent added, "it could be a thousand."

"Stolen."

"Huh?"

"The past participle of *steal* isn't *stole* but *stolen*."

"You just find him, Grammar Girl, and I'll shoot."

"What did you call me?"

"Um – Grand, um… Grand Colonel."

Elseworth shrugged it away. "There's already an all-points out on Steve Krupinski and the black Dodge Stratus?"

"Yes."

"What about his Internet signature?"

The agent shook his head. "He went dark the moment he left the café."

"Fine," Elseworth said. "I want a report on any cars stolen within a thousand miles radius–"

"That'd reach to Illinois and Oregon."

"That's where he is! Between Illinois and Oregon. That's how we'll track him."

The agent blinked. "Why do you care so much about Sergeant Krupinski?"

"Because he's got her – *the 311 Miracle*."

12 **SKINNY DIPPING**

"Wake up."

"What?"

"Time for a bath."

"What are you talking about?"

Krupinski gestures beyond the black windshield. "It's Canyon Lake, outside Rapid City, South Dakota."

I can't see anything. "How do you know?"

"The signs. I've been watching the signs. I pulled off on this little access road, and now it's right in front of us. Canyon Lake."

"So?"

"So, we stink," he said. "It's been two days, cooped up in cars, running for our lives. We stink to high heaven."

"*You* do."

"So do *you*," he says. "It's midnight. Perfect time for bathing."

"In the nude?"

"Did you bring a change of clothes?"

"No."

Before I can say more, he pulls off his shirt and shoves off his socks and struggles out of his trousers. "Don't look."

"Thanks for the warning."

He opens the door, and the light comes on, and I see

a mangy bear sliding out into the night and bounding away toward the black rim of water. He splashes in, giggling.

"Come on in!" he calls back to me. "The water's great."

In spite of myself, I pull off my hoodie and my shirt and my bra and drop them into the foot well. I drag my jeans and panties down and leave them on the passenger's seat. Then, opening the door, I dart out of the car and run to the water. It splashes around me, enfolds me. It is cold and clean and perfect.

"Ahh, this is better," Krupinski says, twenty feet away. "How are things going with Dave?"

"Fine."

"Good, because I've got to catch some shut-eye."

"We're camping here?"

"No. You're driving."

"I don't know how to."

"You're an investment banker. Of course you know how to drive. And if you can drive, we can press on through South Dakota."

I step up out of the water and walk back toward the car.

"*That's* the spirit," he says. "Besides, South Dakota is better by night."

"Why?"

"You have to imagine how boring it is."

13 VISITATIONS

"Let the circus begin," Michael Gardner sighed as he turned the black Beemer onto his block. The street was lined with paparazzi – the suicide bombers of journalism. They flowed into the lane and converged on him. Michael slowed to a crawl, and they pressed around the sedan. Lanyards and buttons and flies scraped along the glass.

Cameras flashed, and questions lit the air.

"Michael! Michael! Where's your sister?"

"Did she burn in the house?"

"Are the ransom rumors true?"

"What if the Disciples raped your sister?"

Gritting his teeth, Michael crept along at one mile an hour as cameras snapped his beleaguered expression. He'd been assured by police that if he ran over a photographer at one mile an hour, they would fine the corpse for any damage it did to his undercarriage.

He clicked his turn signal, and yellow light flashed against the trousers of a fat man with a Nikon. Michael turned the wheel, angling the car through the piranha school and into his drive. As he reached the sidewalk, two police officers stepped up and parted the paparazzi, scraping them off to either side. By court order, the paparazzi were allowed on the sidewalk but couldn't set foot on the lawn or the hundred-fifty-foot drive that led to his Oak Park home.

The pressure on the car eased, and the Beemer slid free. Michael followed the meandering cement drive, heading toward the four-car garage. It adjoined a prairie-style house built by one of Frank Lloyd Wright's students. Michael waited until he was within thirty feet of the garage before clicking the opener – giving the cameras as little time as possible to snap what was inside. He drove in and clicked the remote again. The garage door grazed his back bumper, closing just behind a plate that read, "DOMN8R."

Michael hadn't ordered the plate. It belonged to Susan, as did the Beemer, the house –everything. Even Michael, in a way, belonged to Big Sis.

Turning off the engine, he climbed from the Beemer and made a sweep of the car. In three places, button cameras had been stuck to the fenders. He flicked them off one by one and ground them under his heel. Then, briefcase in hand, he walked past Susan's Mercedes and her Lamborghini and her Jaguar. Unlocking the back door and shutting off the alarm, Michael climbed the stairs to the back parlor.

It was a long, low room with a limestone fireplace and walnut-paneled walls. Curtains covered the great windows along the south side, blocking views to the veranda and the pool. The mission-style table that ran down the center of the room bore an even layer of dust.

Just as it should.

When Susan was around, this place was always filled with people – beautiful people with sidecars in martini glasses and name tags with pronunciations in two or three languages. Music played. Gifts passed from hand to hand. Promises were made – deals, firm handshakes, and contracts worth millions of dollars or Euros or Yen. This room was the beating heart of Susan's brilliance as director of foreign accounts at International Mercantile. Just by walking from one end of the room to the other, she could pocket a million. And Michael always followed dutifully behind, gathering signatures and empty glasses.

She'd hate to see it this way. At all times, this room – the whole house – was to be ready for business. Susan could leave International Mercantile at 6pm., send a three-word text message, and have a fully-catered meal on by 7. Michael was part of that magic, of course, managing the staff and arranging the contracts that arrived just after the third round of drinks. But Susan was the real show.

After Flight 311, Michael laid off most of the servants, keeping only the maids. Then he found one photographing things in Susan's closet. Now, they all were gone.

Now it was just Michael and the settling dust.

He walked through the parlor and into the kitchen – stainless steel everywhere and restaurant quality ovens, grills, sinks, and appliances. More dust. The massive fridge was chilling a half-empty bottle of cocktail sauce.

He walked beyond, to the front parlor, the one where he and Susan would relax. It, too, was shut up and silent – a mausoleum in memory of her.

He'd been mourning her all month. The first report of Flight 311 said no survivors. Next day, they found her alive, but with massive head trauma and organ damage.

She wasn't supposed to last the night. Michael flew out to Butte and sat by her hospital bed and held her hand, but she never woke. Back in Oak Park, he picked out a plot, casket, flower package – wrote a gushing obituary and listed a few thousand people to contact.

But she didn't die.

And three weeks later, she awoke.

Michael had wrapped up business and gotten on a flight, only to arrive in Butte and hear that she was gone again.

The police couldn't find her. The FBI couldn't. Death's Disciples couldn't.

Of course they couldn't. Susan Gardner was a force of nature. Michael half-expected her to walk through that door any minute.

Unbuttoning his collar and loosening his tie, Michael walked to the shelf where the XM radio sat. What would be streaming on All Classical WGBH?

And why was there a hand print in the dust beside the radio?

He spun around, only then seeing the man.

He sat in the sectional. His figure was so dark that he seemed a shadow – a hole in the couch and wall. But that hole was looking at him, and there were sharp teeth in a sharp smile. "Hello, Michael."

Michael backed away. "There's a court order. You can't be within a hundred fifty feet–"

"I'm not a paparazzo," the man said.

"Then who the hell are you?"

"The hell I am." Suddenly, the man was standing. There was no rustle of clothes, no creak from the couch.

He was just there, standing beside the sectional.

Michael flipped on the light, and it blazed across the room, across everything except the man-shaped shadow in the center.

"See me better, now, do you?"

"How are you doing that? Is that some kind of camouflage?"

"She's coming back."

"Who's coming back?"

"Don't be an idiot."

Michael nodded before he could stop himself.

"Don't tell the police. Not the CIA, not the FBI, not Homeland Security."

"Don't threaten me."

"*They* are the threat. They've tried to kill her twice already. If you hand her over to them, the third time will be the charm."

Michael snarled, "I'm not handing her over to anyone. Them or you."

"Of course not."

"Who are you?"

"You'll find out."

And then, the shadow closed on itself and vanished into the air.

Michael was left staring at the bright emptiness of his front parlor.

He blinked. What was that? A delusion?

No. Delusions don't leave hand prints.

14 RAMMING AROUND

"Funny how it all comes back," I say, driving from the dark access road onto the I-90 on-ramp.

"What'd I tell you?" Krupinski replies. "You're a natural."

As I get on the expressway, the compass above the dash reads due east. "Chicago's dead ahead."

Krupinski laughs. "Yeah, about nine hundred miles."

"Better hurry, then." I stomp on the pedal. Tires spin, and the Stratus drifts as we slide through the merging lane and into the passing lane and hurtle past other cars: "Nice acceleration!"

Krupinski is clutching his heart. "Holy shit, girl."

I can drive, all right – and I don't mean just parallel parking. I know I could spin this thing 180 degrees, forward or backward. I could ride it on two wheels. It's muscle memory.

"You're up to ninety," Krupinski warns.

"This is Montana."

"No, this is South Dakota."

All of a sudden, red and blue lights flash in the darkness behind us. "Shit."

"Yeah."

I'm going ninety, but the cop who's on us is coming up at maybe a hundred twenty.

Krupinski sighs. "Why did I think I needed to sleep?"

"I can handle this."

"It's a stolen car!" Krupinski points out. "And you're the darling of the twenty-four hour news cycle. Don't you get what's happening?"

"Hold on," I tell him.

"What?"

"Hold on!" This time, my crazy smile convinces him.

He buckles and braces.

Twisting the airbag switch on the dash, I stomp on the brake. Tires lock. Tread goes up in smoke. Shoulder belts keep our heads from going through the glass.

The South Dakota state trooper swerves onto the inside shoulder and scrapes past us, mashing his rear fender on our front. He slams on the brakes and slides sideways.

I jam the accelerator.

"Look out!" Krupinski shouts.

We ram the side of the cop car, shoving him into the median ditch. With one last jolt, I roll him on his side. "He won't be getting out of there anytime soon." Then I veer away and spray gravel on him as I shoot back onto the highway.

"What the hell was that?" Krupinski asks.

"That was me getting rid of a state trooper."

"You trying to draw *more* attention to us?"

"You're right. I should've pulled over. Let him check license and registration." I laugh. "The guy didn't even get our plates. He's in a ditch, trying to figure out how to call this one in. And every second he delays, we get farther down the road."

Krupinski looks steadily at me. "I don't know why

you know how to drive like that. But before you did that, nobody knew where we were. A lot of cautious driving, speed limits and full stops, meant that the trail had gone cold for two days. In ten minutes, you've made the trail hot again. *Right now*, Elseworth knows where we are."

15 **SCRAMBLE**

"I think we got 'em," a dispatcher said in a quiet, quivering voice.

Clearing her throat, she called out through the makeshift command center in the Butte police caféteria: "A South Dakota trooper was chasing down a black Stratus – no license plate available – when he got rammed and shoved in a ditch."

"Krupinski!" Elseworth growled as he ambled over on his crutches. "Where?"

"They're on I-90, just west of Rapid City."

"Scramble everybody. The state troopers. The Rapid City police. The fucking park rangers at Mount Rushmore! I don't want a single black car to make it through the Black Hills."

16 SILVERADO

"So, of course, you know we've got to take this exit," Krupinski says.

"Yep," I nod as I leave I-90.

"And we can't head east anymore."

"I thought south," I say, turning down a narrow country road.

"Sounds good."

"The APB is going out. They're going to be setting up roadblocks. In ten minutes, they'll be watching every road in a ten-mile radius, looking for a black Stratus."

"I get it."

"No, you don't," he says. "We've got to ditch this car right now."

"For what?"

"For anything – just a set of wheels that the cops'll wave on past. Pull in here."

He gestures at a squalid-looking KOA along the road.

"Kampground of America?" I ask as I pull in and troll slowing along the tents and campers.

"There's plenty of vehicles," Krupinski says.

"Do you know what the opposite of KOA is?"

"What?"

"AOK."

"Very funny. Let's get to business."

"So, what are we after?" I ask.

"Something different," Krupinski says. "Last time, we were going for nondescript: Dodge Stratus, Honda Accord, Chevy Impala. Now we want something completely different."

"How about that Silverado parked halfway across that empty campsite?"

"Perfect. Stop here."

I do, right behind the red 4x4, and Krupinski opens the door of the Stratus and steps out. "Shove something in your shirt so you look pregnant."

I grab an old coat from the back seat and push it into place over my belly as Krupinski strides off toward the other campsite.

He starts in. "Hey, y'all. How's it goin'?" They respond, but I can't hear what they say. "Yeah, beautiful night. Can't imagine a better night. Well, you got such a beautiful camp here. Probly arrived in the afternoon, time to set up everything nice." Again, muttered responses. "Jeez, I wish we'd got here sooner. I got to set up my tent in the dark, and my wife being pregnant and all–" They start in, and Krupinski says, "A boy. He's gonna be called Jasper. Any of you got the name of Jasper? No, course not. Kind of unusual, but a family name, you know." They talk a bit. "See, the thing is, I can't quite get my little old Dodge in here because that fine 4x4 is half in our spot. No! No! Don't put down your beer. I wouldn't deprive a man of his beer. If you could just lend me your keys, I'll inch it over, and then we can pull on in. Well, thanks so much. People like you don't exist anymore."

Already, I have my fist around the Igloo, and I've

pulled the uneaten garbage pizza from the bottom sleeve. I'm just waiting for Steve's signal.

He gives it, marching back and waggling the keys in his hand. I pull up far enough that he can back out, and then I jump from the Stratus and lug the cooler and the pizza to the Silverado. I jump in.

A moment later, Sergeant Krupinski is doing a reverse one-eighty. He roars down the lane of tents and RVs and tears out of that KOA.

As we hit the main road, I say, "So, when can I drive again?"

He shakes his head. "No need. I'm juiced. Adrenaline, baby."

The rear-view mirror sends a band of yellow light across Krupinski's eyes, and he looks up in annoyance.

"Looks like one of those backwoods boys knows how to hotwire a Stratus."

I look back and see the Stratus peeling out of the Kampground drive and rocketing up behind us. "Step on it!"

Krupinski shifts down, and the Silverado's eight cylinders roar for all they're worth. We pull ahead of the Stratus for a little bit, but the pizza-delivery car surges right back up.

"We got to take this crate where they can't go," Krupinski shouts. "Buckle up and hold on."

I do, fumbling with the twisted belt and jamming the tongue in the slot before Krupinski lurches to the right. The 4x4 vaults over a narrow ditch beside the road, plows through a barbed wire fence, and comes down in a field of hip-high wheat.

"Yee haw!" Krupinski whoops.

"Don't do that." I look back to see the black Stratus pelting along the road beside us, angry faces jutting from the windows.

"Look at that piece of shit they're driving," Krupinski crows. "Some people are desperate."

The faces in the Stratus, though, are starting to grin, and a hand points at something ahead.

I look. "It's a crossroads."

"A what!"

"Gun it!"

Krupinski does, and we fling back more barbed wire and vault another ditch. Our spinning tires squeal on the crossroad just as the Dodge Stratus whips around the corner at us. It can't catch us, though. Momentum carries us over the road and across another ditch and into a field of corn. Dry stalks crackle, and heads pound down like fists on the hood. We can't see. Tassels and silks fly all around us as we plow our way through the corn maze.

"Do you know where you're going?"

"Through!" Krupinski says.

"I mean, where the hell's the next road?"

"Search me."

A moment later, we break from the corn and are on a gravel drive, with a farmhouse flashing by on one side and a barn and pig pen on the other. We shoot between the buildings, and Krupinski swerves to avoid a couple of water troughs. Then it's on past a pair of silos, across a creek, and back into more corn.

"Where's the road?"

"Ahead!"

There are already big dents in the hood from the corn heads, and now more pummel us. Krupinski doesn't let up on the pedal, though, grinding through at fifty miles an hour.

"What if they're waiting for us, on the other end?"

"Then we'll have to come up with something."

17 PURSUITS

On the lonely country roads of South Dakota, sirens wailed. Three Sturgis squads gunned in the lead, with a state trooper behind. They were on the trail of national fugitives. The Sturgis cops were especially eager, building up to Bike Week. Nabbing the man who kidnapped the 311 Miracle would give them major street cred when the Hell's Angels came to town. And the perp was so close that his tail-light made a red smear in the air ahead.

"We've got 'im, I tell you, we've got 'im!" the junior officer shouted on the CB. "He's tearing like a bat out of hell out of a KOA just south of Sturgis. It's him, all right. We was waiting, and we seen him fly by, and we knowed it was him."

The radio crackled, and the dispatcher came back. "We need positive ID. You guys close enough to get the plate?"

"Not yet, but soon," the officer said as his partner punched it.

The squad surged ahead of the other three, flashers painting the farm fields in a carnival glow. Sirens screamed like women and children as the squad got close enough that the officers could read the plates.

"That'd be Montana plates, expired: 709 FWK."

"That's them," replied the dispatcher. "You've got orders from the feds: Pull them over, whatever it takes."

The squad barreled up behind the fugitive, and the junior officer switched to the bullhorn. "Pull over! We got you, Krupinski!"

The driver's hand emerged, its middle finger pointing to God.

"He flipped us the bird! He ain't pulling over! We're gonna have to bump 'im."

A new voice came over the radio – masculine and furious: "*Do it!*"

The junior officer grinned and nodded at his partner, who gunned the engine and rammed the back left bumper of the Stratus. It skidded sideways. The driver tried to correct, but the rear of the car whipped around and fishtailed. The sedan slid back and forth, and then slipped inexorably into the ditch along the roadside.

The first squad slammed on the brakes, skidding sideways as the three others squealed into position, too. Six cops and one trooper leaped from their cars, pistols out before them and every last voice screaming. "Get out! Get out! Hands up!"

Out of the Dodge Stratus came four ragged-looking men, white-faced and trembling.

"Face-down! Face-down on the ground!"

One by one, they lay on their faces and put their hands on the backs of their heads. The last and youngest vomited on the road.

"Whew, they're drunk," the junior officer sniffed as he moved in.

His partner stalked toward the group, bent down, and cuffed one of the men. "That's not all."

"What do you mean?"

"They're not the 311 Miracle."

One of the detainees looked up, gravel sticking to his lower lip. "Man, somebody stole our truck."

Next morning, a Greyhound bus left Rapid City bound for Sioux City, Dubuque, Rockford, and Chicago. On that bus rode a tall, heavyset man with a brand new Chicago Cubs hat over curly black hair. He wore a pair of Dollar Store sunglasses that still had the sticker on the temple piece. Beside him sat a blonde with a St Louis Cardinals hat and the same cheap shades.

"How are we feeling now?" Krupinski asked out of the corner of his mouth.

"Not so hot," replied Susan Gardner.

They'd had a breakfast of garbage pizza, parked the 4x4 at a flea market, and walked twenty blocks to the Greyhound station.

"No time for glory when you're going cold," Krupinski said.

"We should've just stolen another car."

Krupinski shook his head. "They caught on to the grand theft auto MO, so now it's the Greyhound MO."

Susan put her hand on her stomach. "Least we've got a toilet this time."

"Sure, if you plug your nose."

Susan looked around at the other passengers – a drugged-out man, a transvestite, two Hispanic brothers with sleeve tattoos... "It's like riding with America's Most Wanted."

"Which would be us."

"Yep."

Krupinski looked away, watching the grasslands of South Dakota ripple past. "So, you think you're going to do ninety again in South Dakota?"

"Be lucky to do fifty-five."

"You think you're going to ram any more cop cars?"

Susan grinned: "Sure! I bet I can drive a bus."

"All right, Sandra Bullock."

"Who?"

Krupinski folded his arms over his chest and leaned back. "Let's just try to get through this. It's only twelve hours to Chicago. That's like watching the *Ten Commandments* three times in a row."

"I don't know what you're talking about."

"Maybe we should sleep."

"Yeah," Susan said. She tugged on the lever beside her seat, reclining as far as it would go: about an inch. Then she fidgeted, trying to get comfortable. "Mind if I lean on you?"

"No problem," he replied. "I'm half in your seat anyway."

Susan leaned against him. She was so small – probably a third of his weight – thin and tense. But as the bus rumbled forward, she seemed to slowly relax. Her breathing grew calm and deep and regular.

Krupinski meanwhile sat and stared straight ahead. It'd be better if they slept in shifts – somebody watching in case of trouble. And if Susan slept through, he would just stay awake. Twelve hours – he could make that. He'd sleep once they arrived in Chicago.

Susan suddenly stiffened. She drew a deep breath and shifted, sitting up and looking at Krupinski oddly.

"Couldn't sleep?" he asked.

"Hey, Steve," she replied in a strange voice, flat and a little timid.

He shook his head slowly. "Hey – Susan…"

"It's not Susan," she replied. "It's Dave. Your old partner."

"Dave Jenkins?" Krupinski whispered, staring at Susan. She was holding her body differently – bad posture and hands splayed on knees. "Dave. What the hell are you doing?"

"She's asleep," Dave said, shrugging her shoulders. "I thought I'd take over."

"You can *do* that?"

Susan's face smiled, but it was Dave's voice. "I'm doing it."

Blinking uncertainly, Krupinski said, "Well, Dave – you're looking better than ever."

The laugh was eerie, his laugh on her lips. "Lot of worse bodies to come back in."

"Yeah, except there's two groups of people trying to kill this body."

"I know."

"You can see everything?"

"Yeah. It's all playing out on the little TVs overhead. You've done well for her."

"Thanks."

"But that's what I wanted to talk to you about," Dave said.

"Oh, here we go."

"You've got to change the game, Steve."

"The name of the game has been 'Save Susan Gardner.'"

"I know, and you've won that game. Once they find the Silverado, they'll be chasing down every vehicle stolen in Rapid City. It'll be a few days before they realize you've switched it up, and by then, you'll be in Chicago."

"Exactly."

"But then you've got to split ways."

"What?"

"She's got to go to the light."

"They'll kill her. Death's Disciples or Elseworth, either one."

"That's why there's got to be reporters and cops – witnesses. She's got to give a public statement. And she's got to pin every crime on you."

"They *are* all on me," Krupinski said. "I stole every one of those vehicles."

"I'm not talking grand theft auto. I'm talking kidnapping and attempted murder."

"What?"

"It's the only way. She'll be in the clear, and you'll be infiltrating Death's Disciples."

Krupinski nodded, his face flushing. "Yeah. That's it. If they think I switched sides, was trying to bring her to them – maybe I can get in."

"I'll fill you in on my contacts – Calliope Dirge and her Bat Pack."

"I can't get caught – not by cops or feds or anybody – until I bring them down."

"Of course."

Krupinski shook his head. "Susan won't go through with it. She's got a mind of her own."

"Don't worry," Dave said darkly. "She's also got a mind of *my* own."

18 SWEET HOME, CHICAGO

Sergeant Krupinski stepped from the Greyhound onto the bus station parking lot. To one side was a huge snarl of Interstates with cars shouldering among each other like wildebeests. On the other side was a view past short brick and limestone buildings to glass-and-steel skyscrapers. West Harrison Street, Chicago, Illinois, 6.30pm. "Made it."

He reached back to help Susan down.

She squinted beneath her Dollar Store sunglasses. "Chicago's big. Wow, look at that one huge skyscraper. What's it called?"

Behind Susan, a middle-aged woman laughed as she stepped off the bus. "I know what she means. Whoever heard of the Willis Tower?"

Krupinski laughed, too. "Yeah. It'll always be the Sears Tower to me." He hitched a thumb at Susan. "She's from Idaho."

The woman gave him a bemused look, and then turned with the other passengers. They lined up alongside the hissing bus while the driver reached into bay doors and drew out luggage. He piled cases atop asphalt and cigarette butts.

Krupinski took Susan's arm and led her somewhat stiffly away from the group. "Try not to ask dumbass questions."

"I just asked about a skyscraper."

"People in Japan know the name of that skyscraper."

Susan scowled. "That woman had never heard of the Willis Tower either."

"Come on, let's get going." He led her eastward along Harrison Street, where cars surged light to light.

"You're walking like you've got somewhere to get to."

"Yeah," Krupinski replied. "Heading for Lake Michigan. We'll get to Grant Park, get lost in the crowd."

Susan trudged along behind him. "And then what? We can't keep running forever."

"I know."

"I'd like to know what my home looks like."

"I'll get you there – I promise," Krupinski said, his voice suddenly sounding heavy. "But we've got to do it by cover of night, and we've got to hang out unrecognized until then." He glanced down at her, checking out her disguise. "Damn it!" He said, ripping the Cardinals ball cap off her head and slapping the Cubs hat in its place.

"Hey. Yours is sweaty."

"Yours'll draw too much attention. A friggin' Cardinal's cap in goddamn Chicago!"

"Well, then, why are *you* wearing it?"

"Yeah, why *am* I wearing it?" He tore the cap from his head and hurled it into a nearby trash can. "Nobody knows my face the way they know yours. You'll just be one of a thousand pretty blondes wearing Cubs hats. They'll be looking at everything but your face."

"Hey!"

Krupinski shrugged. "It's Chicago."

She came up alongside him and slipped her hand into his. "Show me the city."

He looked down at her slender fingers in his meaty paw. "What are you doing?"

"They're not going to look at me at all when there's a linebacker holding my hand."

He nodded, leading her onto a bridge over a river. "Chicago's a tough town. Hog butcher to the world. Built by gangsters. Some people say it's still run by them. New York City's got the East Coast and LA's got the West Coast, which means Chicago's got the Middle Coast – the Great Lakes. They're beautiful, but they ain't oceans, so Chicago's got kind of a chip on its shoulder. It's got wide eyes and bruised knuckles."

Susan nodded as they passed out of the sunlight and into a canyon of buildings. Cars channeled between them like rapids. "I like this city already."

"Of course you do. It's your home."

"I thought I lived in Oak Park."

"A suburb – a rich one, actually, which means you've probably got plenty of cash, even after four weeks in the hospital."

"That'll be nice."

"Director of foreign accounts at International Mercantile." He whistled through his teeth. "God, you must be one tough bitch."

Susan looked at him in shock. "I'm a nice person."

"No, you're not," he said with a laugh. "You're a good person, but not a nice one. I'm the same way. I'd take a bullet for somebody, but that doesn't make me nice. Kindergarten teachers are nice. FBI agents – and international loan officers – can't be."

"Oh, I don't know–"

"You kidding me? You got accounts worth hundreds of millions, maybe billions. You've got a world in which five percent of the people – that's you – have ninety-five percent of the wealth. A nice person would give it all to Africa and India and Myanfuckingmar. Instead, you make deals that not only keep the money in your pocket but get you *more* money. That's your job. You ain't Mother Teresa."

"Whoever *she* is."

"*Was.*"

"Whatever."

They walked for a while, the buildings growing taller and taller, and the sidewalks getting more and more crowded. After a couple short blocks, the road jagged to the right, and then they could see it, two blocks away – Grant Park. It was a huge green expanse between the shouldering city and the lake – a place of grass and trees and people and music.

"Jazz," Krupinski said as if he were breathing fresh air.

"What of it?"

"Chicago was one of the places it was born. All up the Mississippi – that's where blues and jazz were born. That's the one time Chicago gets to stick it to New York and LA. That, and the pizza."

"If I'm such a bad person," Susan blurted, "why are you protecting me?"

"I never said you were a bad person."

"You said I wouldn't give any money to Africa. What kind of a person doesn't give money to Africa?"

He smiled sharply. "I guess we'll find out."

Susan punched him in the chest, not slowing him a bit as they crossed Michigan Avenue. Behind them rose the buildings that formed the Magnificent Mile, and in front of them spread a park that teemed with people. Night was drawing down, and the shades and ball caps were enough to keep people from looking at Susan. Krupinski led her through the milling mob, past vendors selling hot dogs and shish kabobs and baked pretzels, past a Frisbee football game, past joggers and dog walkers and homeless shufflers. At last, they reached a field where people sat on the grass and listened to jazz.

The Pritzker Bandshell was a metallic cephalopod perched in the center of Grant Park. The shell itself was far away, but the amps carried the sound. The band was playing an old swing song, "Sentimental Journey."

Krupinski sank down on the grass.

Susan dropped down beside him. She leaned on him, making him brace his arms to hold them both up. "You're like a couch."

"Thanks."

"I mean that in a good way. Soft and safe."

"And good," Krupinski reminded.

"Very good," echoed Susan. "Good like a couch."

They sat, listening. By the end of the song, Krupinski had a tear in his eye, and Susan was asleep.

Then she sat up – not she but Dave Jenkins in her body. "You ready for this?"

Krupinski took a deep breath. "Ready as I'll ever be."

Dave smiled through Susan's lips. "What's there to be ready for? You just gotta hotwire another car."

"I've gotta take the rap for kidnapping," Krupinski pointed out. "Carries a death sentence."

"Only if you get caught, which you won't." Dave shrugged. "Meanwhile, *I've* gotta perform an Oscar-winner, get the Chicago Police to shut out the feds, whip up the media so anybody who says anything anti-Susan gets crucified. That's one hell of a performance."

"But you better do it, or Susan'll die."

"If she dies, I die. That's pretty good motivation."

"Pretty good."

19 ALL THAT JAZZ

Krupinski was sick of cars and trucks and Jeeps. He wanted something with a little more flare, a little more sex – like that Harley Davidson motorcycle: red, with silver stripes and two big exhaust pipes out the back. And there was no faggy windscreen. *Let the fucking bugs die in my teeth* – that was the aesthetic.

The only problem was that it was covered with Hell's Angels signs: the TCOB badge and the Red Wings insignia. The other problem was that the bike wasn't alone. There were twelve others parked with it.

"Death's Disciples – Hell's Angels?" Krupinski chuckled. "What's the difference?"

Hotwiring a motorcycle was easier than hotwiring a car. The question was how to stop the other motorcycles.

They couldn't go without gas, could they? Krupinski casually walked down the row of bikes, pulling out their fuel lines and letting them drool on Michigan Avenue. Twelve bikes. Twelve puddles. He could've lit a cigarette and torched these twelve as he stole the red fireball, but what sport would there be in that? Besides, the explosions would bring everyone running. Krupinski wanted to slip away into the night.

He swung his leg up over the red Harley – beautiful machine, well maintained – and crouched down to hotwire it.

Just then, the music from the Pritzker Bandshell faltered. There came the wail of a hot mic and the tremulous voice of a young woman.

"I'm sorry. I'm so sorry to interrupt," she said.

It was Susan Gardner's voice, but it was Dave Jenkins speaking.

"I need help," she went on.

People began to boo.

Chicago cops would be moving through the crowd, now, converging on the stage.

"He kidnapped me. I'm Susan Gardner, the 311 Miracle."

The crowd gasped. Krupinski couldn't see the stage, but he could imagine her pulling off the Cubs hat and shades. The jumbotron would show that this was Susan Gardner, all right.

"I need help," she went on." The Death's Disciples are trying to kill me, and so is Homeland Security. Lieutenant Elseworth ordered a hit squad to kill me in Montana."

Speculation whispered through the crowd. They had all heard the conspiracy theories but hadn't believed them. Now they were hearing straight from the Miracle's mouth.

"And Sergeant Krupinski," her voice seemed to choke up, "he was supposed to protect me, but he kidnapped me, tried to deliver me to Death's Disciples."

The whispers became a rumble of voices.

"I just got away, but he's here somewhere. They're here, too. The hand-off was supposed to be here, in Grant Park."

The cops and guards would be rushing the stage now.

"I'm from Oak Park–" she blurted, "so I thought, if I can't trust the feds, I can trust the Chicago Police Department."

The crowd cheered.

It was a great speech. Susan Gardner had made herself the poster child for innocent citizens in the clutches of big government and fundamentalist cults. She'd have police protection 24/7 and mob protection beyond that and masses dedicated to the "Chicago Miracle" and probably an interview with Oprah.

Susan was safe, but Krupinski wasn't. He was now a kidnapper. A terrorist. A traitor.

And he was stealing the Harley of a Hell's Angel.

"Live large," he told himself, twisting the wires.

The Harley revved to life.

People on the sidewalk looked over, and one pointed.

Krupinski kicked up the stand, turned the front tire into traffic, and gunned the engine. No sooner had he pulled away than somebody was shouting about a "fuckin' asshole" who stole someone's "fuckin' ride."

Krupinski juiced the throttle, ripping north to Congress Parkway, which fed onto the Eisenhower. He just hoped all the gas would be gone before the Angels could fix their fuel lines. He took the on-ramp and surged past a half-dozen blocks.

"Damn."

The first of the Hell's Angels bikes appeared behind him, and about ten more followed. They were closing. Their engines shouted from the buildings all around.

Krupinski launched onto the Eisenhower and brought the bike up to eighty, weaving between cars. The Hell's Angels were hot behind. The two nearest ones took the lane lines, blasting between cars.

A guy that looked like Moses scraped his handlebars between a pair of limos and surged up right beside Krupinski.

Krupinski swerved away around a white bus, leaving the Hell's Angel stranded on the other side. For a few heartbeats, the bus for the Royal House of Divine Intervention shielded Krupinski, but it was full of kids. Krupinski shot out beyond it in the merging lane while Moses thundered along in the passing lane. He pulled something out of his saddle-bag – a sawed-off shotgun.

"Great," Krupinski cranked the throttle full and lit out. He topped a hundred – a hundred ten.

Moses swung to the opposite shoulder and followed, pulling parallel again. He lifted the shotgun and pointed it over the top of a gray Acura. The driver swerved into the middle lane, striking a panel van. The two vehicles locked up and slid side by side. Tires shrieked as a Toyota and a minivan rammed into them. Behind, a construction truck swerved, struck the median wall, and rebounded into traffic. More vehicles piled up, damming the Eisenhower.

Ahead of the blockage, the expressway was open wide. Moses cut across three lanes, sidled up beside Krupinski, and shoved the metal muzzle up to his head.

Krupinski backfisted the guy's arm just before he pulled the trigger. A white-hot blast of shot roared behind Krupinski's head and shattered a whole floor of windows in an office building beside the expressway.

Moses cursed, jerking the pump-action gun to eject the shells and bring two more into the chambers. He swung the gun outward.

Krupinski kicked the barrel, thrusting the gun down beside the guy's bike. It fired. Shot sparked from the tail pipe, which was already wet with dribbled gasoline.

A fireball erupted around Moses, catching his hair and beard. Still he rode, a human comet trailing a flaming tail down the expressway. He even jerked the shotgun again to reload, but then his hands stopped working.

He went down with his bike – body and steel and fire flipping along the roadway.

"Fuck," Krupinski said to himself. Stealing a Hell's Angels bike would get the local chapter after him. Killing a Hell's Angel would rouse the whole nation.

Just now, eleven other Hell's Angels had made it through the pile-up. Two of them stopped to help their burning friend, but nine more roared in hot pursuit. The way before them was open, but in front of Krupinski was a wall of brake lights – a veritable parking lot.

Growling, he swerved onto the outside shoulder and tore past a line of cars and trucks.

The Hell's Angels funneled in after him, forced to go single file.

The guy in the lead had another sawed-off shotgun.

Krupinski went serpentine, but it slowed him.

The lead guy zoomed up behind and squeezed off a shot.

Pain erupted in Krupinski's left arm. The blast had

skimmed him, ripping off his sleeve and a patch of skin beneath.

Gritting his teeth, Krupinski stepped on the brake, dropping back to the right of the guy – a leather-faced punk. His face was about to get worse. Krupinski rammed his Hawg into the other bike, shoving it into the wall of vehicles. The guy struck the side of a delivery truck and slid beneath it.

Krupinski surged on.

That still left eight behind him.

Krupinski watched his rear-view mirror, hoping some of the Hell's Angels would stop to help their fallen friend. They didn't, though. They must not have liked the guy.

Krupinski peeled out, gaining distance. Ahead was an on-ramp jammed with cars waiting to get on the Eisenhower. Krupinski spotted a gap between a Suburu and a Ford and threaded the needle. The Ford lurched, and the guy laid on the horn: "Asshole!"

The moment Krupinski was past, the guy in the Ford plowed into two of the Hell's Angels that followed, knocking them flat. They spilled on the road and jumped up with hammers and wrenches in hand.

Those two were out, and the accident delayed the rest. Two others had stopped along the shoulder over the last mile – finally out of gas. The final four, though, wove past the blockage and came on. All of them were packing: a bat, a tire iron, a pipe, and a pistol.

What the hell did Krupinski have? He reached down to the saddlebag and flipped it open. He felt something smooth and tubular, grabbed it, and hauled it out. It was a flesh-colored magazine: *Biker Bitch*. The cover showed a naked woman humping a Suzuki. The magazine ripped open, trailing a four-page centerfold.

The rear-view mirror showed the first Angel surging up to Krupinski's left and lifting his bat to swing.

Krupinski ducked, letting the bat fly by overhead, and then shoved the midsection of Miss April into the guy's face. He swerved, trying to claw it away, but the magazine came loose only when he hit the bed of a pickup. The Angel flew over the truck and came down on the closed top of a convertible.

Krupinski reached back into the bag and pulled out a leather vest.

The next Angel came on strong, a tire iron lifted. He swung.

Krupinski swerved, whirling the leather vest into the path of the iron and snaring it. He yanked the iron from the man's hand. The Angel shot him a look of hatred and then smashed into a traffic pylon, flying from his bike.

Krupinski poured on the throttle, sliding through the mass of cars.

Hell's Angels followed hot behind.

Highway signs announced the Tristate Tollway. That's what he wanted. His rendezvous was supposed to be in Des Plaines, so he exited northbound.

Now he was flying, but so were the Hell's Angels.

The guy with the pistol soared up beside him and fired.

The slug ripped into Krupinski's side, knocking him to the right. He swerved to keep the bike from falling.

Blood poured from the wound, and the Angel was grinning, pistol cocked for a second shot.

The tire iron took out his teeth, knocking the guy back off his bike to tumble in the road. Cars swerved to miss him, hitting each other instead.

Krupinski flew out ahead of the chain reaction and clutched his bleeding side.

If the bullet had hit his heart, he'd be dead already. It probably deflected off a rib into his lung – the Reagan shot. That meant a sucking wound. No wonder he couldn't breathe. Krupinski wadded up the side of his bloody shirt and stuffed it, agonizingly, in the bullet hole. Suddenly, his lungs could grip the air. It was just a temporary fix, though. In a half hour, he'd drown in his own blood.

Meantime, there was the last Angel. Krupinski looked in his rear-view mirror, trying to spot the guy. Where did he go?

The flashing lights told him. Cops had nabbed him, but now a trooper was after Krupinski.

It hadn't been a good night.

Krupinski cranked the throttle full-out, vaulting up to a hundred twenty. He ripped along the shoulder, past traffic that looked like it was standing still.

Lights blazing, the cop slotted in behind him and matched his speed.

Krupinski shot ahead beneath a viaduct.

On the other side, two more troopers blistered down the on-ramp.

Three troopers now. Up ahead, there'd just be more cops at each on-ramp. By the time he got to Wheeling, there'd be a roadblock.

Krupinski almost clipped a blue sign that read "Toll-way Oasis, 2 miles." He flashed past another that told of the BP Gas Station up there, and a third that told of the Panda Express and the McDonalds, the Starbucks and Aunt Annie's Baked Pretzels. The restaurants were laid out within a long glass building on a bridge that strad-dled the expressway.

With three cops – now four – screaming behind him, Krupinski took the oasis exit at eighty. That speed would send him through the BP awning at the top of the hill, so he had to cut back to forty, which brought the squads and troopers crowding up behind. Krupinski took the lane marked "Food and Restrooms," squealed through a tight turn, and angled into the parking lot in front of the oasis.

The cops fanned out behind him, screeching to a halt. They were about to jump out when Krupinski cranked the throttle.

He popped a wheelie and shot toward the sliding glass doors of the oasis.

The doors gaped, people standing in sensor range and looking in shock at Krupinski. Burger-bags dropped by their feet as the motorcycle madman thundered through the doors.

He was inside the oasis. The engine was deafening, echoing from the Panda Express and McDonalds. People shouted and dived away as Krupinski left a long black streak on the polished floor. He tore past Starbucks, and five-dollar vente lattes gushed to the ground. On the other end of the oasis, people helpfully ran for the exit, keeping the glass doors open.

Shooting through them into the night, Krupinski turned left and dived down the on-ramp onto 294 South.

Four cops sat, stranded, on the other side of the oasis, and every other trooper in twenty miles was crowding onto the northbound lanes. He'd lost them.

"Des Plaines," Krupinski told himself raggedly. His side was warm and wet, and it was hard to breathe. He rode now like a law-abiding citizen, moving with traffic, using his turn signal. A sign told of the Dempsey Road exit, and he took it. At the light, he got onto Des Plaines River Road, and then Algonquin Road.

He crossed the river – wide and muddy between over-hanging trees – and then caught sight of a blue pool with an ancient brown bathhouse running alongside it. Up ahead, there was a gate. A sign over the top read, "Methodist Campground."

Eyes crossing with pain, Krupinski rumbled through that gate and out onto a narrow blacktop lane. There were speed bumps every hundred feet. On either side, lawns stretched away into darkness, and here and there, two- and three-story white cottages hove up like sudden ghosts.

She was somewhere in here – somewhere in this maze of little roads and strange alleys.

How strange that a group of Goth kids would live in a place like this. How strange except that Calliope Dirge's father was a retired Methodist minister in Pala-tine, and he let Calliope and her friends spend their summers in his cottage.

It was a clubhouse for them – a coven of Death's Disciples.

Krupinski followed a long, curving drive past tight-packed cottages. On the left, they gave way to a tennis court lurking in the gloom. On the right, the cottages relented, giving views to a grand old tabernacle. It was round and tall, shaped like a big top tent.

Krupinski motored past more cottages and reached one with a broad front yard and a string of Chinese lanterns glowing faintly before a dilapidated porch.

"Calliope's place," Krupinski said to himself. He drove up the street beside the cottage and pulled around back, riding as far as he could away from the road before setting the kickstand. He took a ragged tarp from a pile of firewood and draped it over the bike, then walked slowly up the old wooden stairs and knocked on the weathered door.

It took a few moments for anyone to answer, but when the door opened, it was her – white face and black hair and piercings in brow and nose and ears. But, more importantly, there were those big, smart brown eyes.

"Calliope Dirge?" Krupinski asked.

Her pale face twitched, and her mouth dropped open. "You're that guy on the news report. The one that kidnapped–"

"Yeah," he said and fell on his face, pouring blood on the porch.

20 TEN RULES OF POSSESSION

I wake up in a yellow cell.

A cell?

How did I get here?

I sit up. I'm on a metal bunk screwed into the wall like a shelf. There's a thin mattress and sheet and fuzzy blanket. There are bars in front of the cell, and a cop leaning back on them.

I get up – I'm barefoot – and go to tap on his shoulder.

He startles, jumping away and turning toward me – a thin fiftyish black man with friendly eyes. "You like ta scare me to death, Miss Gardner."

"How did I get here?"

"Hmm?"

"Why am I in a cell?"

His eyebrows knit. "Cause that's what you asked for."

"*I* asked for."

He nods, smiling gently. "Protection. You asked for protection against the Death's Disciples and the feds."

I shake my head. "I didn't… I was in Grant Park–"

"That's where you asked. I seen it myself. They been playing it over a hundred times on every station since last night."

"I was with Krupinski–"

"Yeah, but you done got away and throwed yourself on the mercy of us." He shakes his head and tuts at the

146

cell. "Guess this is what we call a mercy."

I look blankly at him. "I asked *you* to protect me?"

"No, not me, ma'am, the Chicago Police. You kind of asked everybody in Chicago to protect you."

"I don't remember any of this."

"Oh, yeah!" he says, pointing at me. "*Amnesia.* That's what they been saying. You got that rollin' amnesia."

"No," I reply. "I remember everything else – I mean since waking up in the hospital. But I don't remember anything about giving myself to the police."

He lifts his finger. "You want to see it? The footage?"

"Of what?"

"Of you – up on that stage in Grant Park."

"Of me on *what?*"

He reaches into his pocket and pulls out an iPhone. It awakens in his grip, and he slides through the apps and presses one. "Here it is on YouTube. Ain't that something? I show everybody, tell 'em I's guarding the most important person in Chicago." He touches "Play," and I see a shot of Grant Park, the WLS 7 News tag at the bottom.

It's a concert stage, and there's a jazz band playing, and out wanders a figure with a cap and sunglasses and a gray hoodie It's me, of course, but I don't remember any of this. I walk up to an empty mic in front of the band, and they look up, and their music staggers to a stop. As I wrap my fingers around the mic, it squeals.

"I'm sorry. I'm so sorry to interrupt." *Did I say that?* "I need help. I'm running for my life. I'm Susan Gardner, the 311 Miracle."

I look at the officer and say, "It's not me!"

"Ain't it?" he asks.

Just then in the video, I pull off the Cubs hat and the sunglasses, and the camera zooms in, and even on that little screen, I can tell it's me. "But I didn't do *any* of that."

The video goes on. "I didn't know what else to do. The Death's Disciples are trying to kill me, and so is Homeland Security. Lieutenant Elseworth ordered a hit squad to kill me in Montana."

I stare, stunned. "That's… that's all true, but…"

The video continues: "And Sergeant Krupinski – he was supposed to protect me, but he kidnapped me, tried to deliver me to Death's Disciples."

"Wait – *what?*"

"I just got away, but he's here somewhere. They're here, too. The hand-off was supposed to be here, in Grant Park." Cops and guards are climbing onto the stage now, all around me. "I'm from Oak Park, so I thought, if I can't trust the feds, I can trust the Chicago Police Department."

While the crowd cheers, the officers surround me like Secret Service agents. One takes my arm, and another turns off the mic, and the rest are ranked all around. We head off the stage. The crowd is cheering, and the band leader – a black man with a big guitar – nods at his group. They launch into "Sweet Home, Chicago." The crowd goes wild, and I go with the police.

The scene cuts to a newsroom with a salt-and-pepper-haired anchor, who says, "And that's how Susan Gardner came home to us. She's in the hands of the Chicago Police, now. A source says she is traumatized by her ordeal, but very cooperative, very grateful for the help she's now receiving – glad to be home."

The officer lowers the phone. "That's it. That's you."

"Yeah," I say, shaking my head. "But it isn't."

He cants an eyebrow. "Maybe you're wanting to see Doc Abramson? The psychiatrist?"

"No."

"Why don't you take a rest? You's tired, is all. It'll all come back. Just you get some rest. You got Sergeant Maxwell Jackson standing out here, making sure nobody comes near you. And you got the whole Chicago PD on this. You'll be fine, Miss Gardner. Rest up."

I nod and return to the bed and sit there.

Maxwell Jackson gives me a friendly smile and then turns back around and leans on the bars.

He trusts me. You don't lean like that if you're afraid the prisoner's going to strangle you. Whatever I've said, whatever I've done, it's won him over. All of them. They think I'm their friend – their daughter, almost.

But why can't I remember getting up on that stage? It's not just amnesia. This is different. It's like… *possession*.

And suddenly I know.

God damn it, I know.

There's no stop-off in the tree house this time. I close my eyes and leap directly to Flight 311, into the seat beside Dave Jenkins. I grab his shirt and say, "What the fuck did you think you were doing?"

He looks at me, bald forehead dappled in sweat, and gabbles, "I– I–"

"You can't take over my body. That's possession. That's rape."

He lifts his hands as if I've got a gun. "I didn't *do* anything. I mean, I did *something*, but not anything like *that*. I was *saving* us."

"This is what you call *saving?* Putting us in a cell? In solitary confinement?"

"We've got to be safe."

"This is what they do to mass murderers."

"The Death's Disciples can't get at us. Neither can Elseworth," Dave says, almost pleading with me. "Twenty-four hours ago, every cop and fed in the plains was after us, as well as these cultists. Now, it's just the cultists. That's pretty good, don't you think?"

"You had no right, taking over my body."

"You saw the footage," Dave replies. "I did fine. I did *great*."

"But it's *my* body!"

"It's *all* of ours."

"No," I say, chopping that idea out of the air. "No, it's not. I've had this body since birth. I *live* here. You guys are just, I don't know – refugees or something."

Dave glares at me. "You fell asleep in Grant Park – nice idea! Did you honestly think we'd be safe from Death's Disciples in Grant Park?"

"I was with *Krupinski* – And, hey! That's the other thing. What *about* Krupinski? You sold him out. You said he kidnapped me, was trying to make a deal with the Disciples. You sentenced him to death!"

"He was *in* on it."

"*What?*"

"I talked to him about it."

"When?"

"On the bus."

"On the…" Of course. I slept on the bus. The little shit must've taken over my body then, must've come up with this plan with Krupinski. Then the *big shit* didn't tell me about it. "Are you kidding me? How many times have you possessed me?"

"Just the two times: on the bus and in Grant Park."

"God! You could've done anything. You could've got it on with Krupinski."

"Don't be gross."

"Well, you could've!"

"It's my body, too."

"It's not *yours*. It's *mine!*"

"Not when you put us all at risk. When you do, I step in."

"Oh no, you don't."

"It's called survival. There's three hundred sixty-one people on this plane who didn't survive that day except in the mind of the one who did. Now we've got to make sure *you* survive."

I look around at the drowsy corpses in their transparent seats. "How many others know about this – know that they can take over my body when I'm asleep?"

He points at the ghostly monitors overheads. They show the yellow wall opposite where I sit in my yellow cell. "They're all watching."

"Jesus."

"It's just like the Pennsylvania hijacking."

"What are you talking about?"

"On 9/11, two planes were hijacked by middle-eastern terrorists and flown into the twin towers of the

World Trade Center in New York. Thousands died. Another plane smashed into the Pentagon, killing hundreds more. But there was a fourth plane, United Airlines Flight 93. It was headed toward the White House – but the passengers on the plane decided otherwise. They heard from cell-phone calls what was happening in New York and Washington, and they stormed the cockpit and killed the terrorists. The plane went down in Pennsylvania, killing them all."

"What does this have to do with me?"

"We're those people, Susan," Dave says. "Our flight has been taken over by terrorists, but we want to make sure they fail. *You're* our flight now, Susan, and we're going to storm the cockpit if we think we can defeat them. If we think we can save ourselves."

The tears well up. "I can't live this way. *This* is *my* body."

"It's *ours*," Dave replies without hesitation.

I can feel the blood filling my face. "I'll ask for the shrink! I'll get some meds that'll get rid of all of you."

Dave shakes his head. "Valium. Morphine. Xanax – whatever meds they give will only open the door to us."

"I won't fall asleep."

"Yeah, like *that's* ever worked."

"You're trying to *kill* me!"

"I'm trying to *save* you. Save us all. You're not an individual anymore, Susan Gardner. You're a multiple – a multiple personality. You have one body and three hundred sixty-two minds. And some of us are better at this stuff than you are. I'm a frickin' FBI agent, in case you hadn't noticed, an expert in hostage negotiations, which was what we had in Grant Park. When we're in that kind of situation, I'm going to take control. When we're in the situation where we need to rewire a fuse box, there's probably somebody else in this plane who can do that better than you. And when we're in the situation where we need to kill a man with our bare hands, let's find the guy who knows how to do it."

"Or girl," I say. "We have incentive."

"Whatever it takes. I just want to survive."

"Me, too. But there are some assholes on this plane."

"There always are."

"And some perverts. NAMBLA, for example."

"Right."

"Damn it!"

"This is your new normal, Susan."

I look him dead in the eyes. "Nothing will ever be normal again."

"Fair enough."

I sit, fuming. I'm allowed that. Most people don't have to give up their bodies on a moment's notice. College kids sign up for experimental studies, but that's for pizza money, and I don't see any Goddamned pepperoni. Pregnant woman get taken over by a child inside them, but they had a little fun beforehand and nine months to get used to the idea. I've had no fun and about ten minutes.

"It can't just be a free-for-all."

"Of course not," Dave says.

"And I'm not going to manage three hundred sixty-one people."

"No one's asking you to."

"So, you're going to be in charge of the passengers, Corporal Jenkins."

"Happy to serve."

"Which means that if ever I am pissed off about what's happened when I was not in charge, *you're* the one I'm holding responsible."

"Right."

"Knowing that I can dump any of you guys from my mind at a moment's notice."

"How?"

"There's this amnesia serum – Krupinski showed me. I'll get some of it and use it to wipe the whole fucking plane."

"Fair enough."

"And if this is what I'm going to put up with, I'm going to make a few rules: the ten commandments of possession."

"Shoot."

"Number 1. *I* have control of the body unless we are in imminent danger. *Imminent!* And that doesn't mean one person thinks I'm screwing up. That means a majority of you do. You vote or take tallies or whatever the hell you do with that hive mind of yours."

"Okay."

"Number 2: Nobody messes with the privates. Not even to go to the bathroom. If we need to go to the bathroom, *I* get to do it."

"Good. Fine. Excellent. What else?"

I think carefully. "Number 3. Nobody uses the body for personal gain. Nobody tries to contact their friends or family. Nobody tries to lay *anybody*. Nobody takes over just to eat chocolate cake or to punch somebody in the face or to dance to the music. None of that shit."

"That's a good one."

"Number 4: The body gets to sleep whenever it needs to. I can't be falling asleep and then having my body running around all night, doing God knows what."

"Got it."

"Number 5: Everybody respects the body. We're not eating a whole pizza or drinking a fifth of Jack. We're not getting tattoos or piercings or brands. Everybody's got to return the body in the condition in which it was found or... or I'll flush the culprit from my mind."

"Anything else?"

I shrug. "There've got to be ten commandments."

"Really?" he asks.

"Yeah, or they don't stick. Rule 6: No stealing. That's pretty universal. Rule 7: No murder. Rule 8: No lying – except, of course, to keep us safe."

"So, there's really no Rule 8."

"Shut up. Rule 9: Don't embarrass us. If you've got control of the body, watch what you say and do. If you come back and we're all ashamed, well, then, it's the death-bin for you."

"And Rule 10?"

"Rule 10: Stop these fucking Death's Disciples. That's what all of us are trying to do. Get rid of them, whatever it takes. Make sure they never commit another mass murder."

Dave nods. He's been typing the whole time, putting the commandments into his netbook, which no longer exists. "I'll make sure that everybody follows these rules."

"Good," I say, tired of the subject. "So what does the 'hive mind' think about this Sergeant Maxwell Jackson?"

"We all like him," Dave says, eyebrows lifted. "I mean, most of us do. Mrs Cragswyth in row 13 thinks he's a drunk. She says no sober person could be so happy. But the rest of us like him. He's tops in the pool."

"The pool?"

Dave nods sheepishly. "We've got a kind of office pool going about who we can trust. Elseworth is lowest, lower even than the Disciples right now, and Sergeant Jackson is at the opposite end."

I laugh. "Yeah. I like Jackson, too. Seems a good guy. So you watched what was happening over the TV screens and got together to make your pool?"

"It's more immediate than that. We can all hear each other. It's like a giant chat room. We know what everybody's thinking all the time, and we put it all together. Like, right now, everybody's got your ten commandments. And they've all agreed–"

"That's good."

"–knowing they'll die otherwise. Even Mrs Cragswyth agreed about the commandments."

"What about Krupinski?" I ask. "What do they think about him?"

Dave's face darkens. "You've got to understand, he's taking up where I left off. He's agreed to become the fall guy for all this – a traitor, a terrorist – so he can get inside the Death's Disciples. That puts him beyond suspicion for me."

"Me, too," I say.

"But the other passengers aren't so sure. They wonder if he wasn't trying to get into the Death's Disciples all along."

21 **THE METHODIST GOTHS**

"He's so *heavy*," moaned an adolescent voice that sounded vaguely male.

Sergeant Krupinski cracked an eye, looking up into the incredulous face of the young Goth called Thanatopsis. He had the most beautiful Barbie hair – white-blond – but also had a man's grip on Krupinski's left calf.

Beside him, Kid Killer held the right calf. Side by side, they dragged Krupinski feet-first into the cottage. "He's like a dead elephant."

Krupinski closed his eye.

"Just get him in here." That third voice belonged to Calliope Dirge, who was moving kitchen chairs out of the way. Krupinski knew her voice, not just from the brief exchange they had had on the back porch, but also from the sureness of it, the steady intelligence. She closed the back door. "If one of the old farts sees us dragging a dead man into our cottage, it'll be cops–"

"*Again*," Thanatopsis said, grunting as he and Kid Killer hauled Krupinski across cracking linoleum. A red smear followed them.

"Oh, gross! He's bleeding!" said Kid Killer.

"Of course, he's bleeding," Calliope said. "Why do you think you're dragging him?"

With a few more tugs, the two guys reached the middle of a rundown living room; thick paint on wood floor and walls and ceiling. A naked light bulb stared down at them all.

"Why's he bleeding?" Thanatopsis asked.

Kid Killer said sagely. "He's dying."

"All of us are," Calliope said with a voice that was almost reverent.

Heavy footfalls came as another Goth strode up. He was a big, beefy guy in a black leather vest and black leather pants and a black leather eye-patch: Cyclops. "Who's this?"

"Give us a hand," Calliope said. "We got to get him on the daybed."

The group lugged Krupinski onto a mildew-smelling mattress, where he sprawled. A rattle came with every breath.

Cyclops's eye grew wide. "He's that FBI guy from the Internet!"

"Sergeant Krupinski," supplied Calliope.

"Yeah! The one that's wanted. The one that kidnapped 311 to–"

"To bring her to us," Calliope interrupted, sitting down on the daybed beside the man.

"Don't let him bleed on the mattress," said a small, dark-haired nymph from a nearby window seat. It could have been none other than Evella of the Eternal Sleep. Her laptop was open before her. "I got to sleep there."

"None of us gets to sleep anywhere ever again if he dies," Calliope said sternly.

Evella came over and looked down. "What's wrong with him?"

"Don't know," Calliope replied. "He's got blood all down his side."

She tugged at the bloodied shirt and a red plug of fabric popped from the wound. Krupinski shuddered, mumbling incoherently. Blood gushed across the mattress.

"Oh, come *on!*" Evella griped. "The mattress!"

"Shh. Listen," Calliope said, leaning her ear toward the wound. "There's a hissing noise coming out of it."

"Maybe he's got an alien in there," Kid Killer suggested.

"Not an alien," Thanatopsis replied. "A bullet. It's a sucking wound to the chest."

The others all looked at him, amazed.

Thanatopsis flipped his bleach-blond hair. "Hey, I'm a lifeguard."

"All right, lifeguard," replied Calliope, "do some first aid."

Thanatopsis reared back. "Whoa. Me?"

"What did they teach you about bullet wounds?"

"They taught me people don't get shot at the pool."

"This is America. People get shot everywhere."

Thanatopsis nodded, thinking. "It's probably good you let the blood out. Otherwise, he could drown in it."

"*Cool,*" said Kid Killer.

"But we got to stop it up again so he can breathe."

Calliope peered down at the bloody wad she'd pulled from the man's side. "Stick it back in?"

"No."

"What, then? My finger?"

Kid Killer laughed. "You're like that little boy with his finger in a dike."

"He's a guy," Cyclops pointed out.

Thanatopsis went on. "No. I mean, we should get some cloth. Something clean."

"There's nothing clean in this dump," Calliope reminded.

Thanatopsis nodded. "We'll sterilize it. Got any alcohol?"

Calliope laughed, going to a "bar" made out of milk crates, with liquor bottles jangling inside. "What's your poison?"

"Let's try the 151 proof rum," Thanatopsis said, "meanest stuff there is."

Calliope pulled out the half-empty bottle and knelt beside the daybed. "Now what?"

"We need some kind of cloth that's not got mold in it."

"Evella's panties," offered Cyclops.

"What?" asked Evella, slapping his arm.

"You wash them separate," he said defensively. "No dyes. No perfumes."

"I get a rash."

"We don't want him to get a rash."

Calliope nodded. "Go get a pair of your panties."

The dark-haired nymph stared a refusal at her.

Calliope sighed. "They're going to be soaked in rum and shoved into a man's body."

Evella smiled and ran up the creaking stairs.

While she was gone, the rest of the Bat Pack looked at each other over the panting body of Sergeant Krupinski.

"This is serious shit," Calliope said.

"We know," the others answered.

"This is an FBI agent who says he's turned to our side. If he has, it's huge. Giving him over could bring us into the Death's Disciples for real. But if he's faking it, if he's just trying to get in but still works for the FBI, well, it could be the death of everybody here."

Long faces looked back at her, silent and uncertain as Evella bounded down the stairs and held up a pair of cotton panties. "Soak 'em and stuff 'em."

Calliope snagged the panties and pressed them over the mouth of the rum bottle and let the powerful stuff wick through the cloth. Then she turned toward Sergeant Krupinski, breathing uneasily on the daybed, and shoved the sopping plug into his bullet wound.

He jolted, eyes wide and hands flailing.

"Grab his hands," Calliope ordered. "Keep them back."

"Wwhat's hhhappening?" Krupinski groaned.

"We're saving your fucking life," Calliope replied. "Hold still! It'll stop stinging."

Soon enough, Krupinski collapsed back on the bed and wheezed hoarsely.

Calliope looked down at him and shook her head. "Okay, so what do we do now?"

"They say to elevate the wound," Thanatopsis suggested.

"How? We'd need a winch."

"We got you and Evella," Cyclops said.

"Listen up, everybody," Evella called, back at the laptop. "I'm on WebMD, looking up 'bullet in the lung...' Wait a minute? That's weird."

"What's weird?"

"It says stuff about depression and about a 'magic bullet,' but there's nothing about what to do if you have a bullet in your lung." She looked up, her black eyebrows arching. "Must not be a big deal."

"It's a huge deal," Calliope spat back. "The reason it's not on there is because people know it's a huge deal. Try looking up decapitation!"

Keys clicked and then: "They don't have that, either!"

Calliope smacked herself in the forehead, the impression of a red hand remaining on her white skin. "So, what do we do?"

After a brief silence, Kid Killer piped up, "There's always the river."

"Don't be ridiculous!"

"It worked for Gacy."

"No," Calliope said, "this is bigger than us. He goes to the actual Disciples. They'll know what to do. If they want him alive, they'll save him. If they want him dead, they'll kill him. Either way, we've done good."

"When's your next delivery?"

"Tonight."

"Oh, man, we should *all* go!"

"I got a two-door Civic!" Calliope snapped. "Besides. The Phantom wouldn't like it. No. Absolutely not."

"Damn."

"But you guys are gonna help me get him in the car."

Kid Killer sighed. "Here we go again."

22 MR EVERS

Calliope drove her secondhand Honda Civic down I-290 toward Chicago. The big man snored in the passenger's seat. He hadn't died yet, despite the less than gentle ministrations of the Bat Pack, but he wasn't exactly alive, either. He hadn't even felt it when Cyclops slammed his hand in the door.

Cyclops had poor depth perception.

Calliope glanced at Krupinski – pasty faced and black haired. He could almost've been a Goth... If he lost a hundred fifty pounds... and got some piercings... and some black nail polish. She shuddered to think what he had on his iPod.

Still, the FBI was hardcore. He'd killed people – that one janitor dude, at least – and he'd stolen cars and shit, and now, he'd gone rogue. The most wanted man in Chicago.

Calliope looked at him again.

A big, bleeding mess, but he had a rep. One hell of a rep.

He was almost doable.

Calliope swallowed uneasily as she approached the city: rectangles of black and gold unfolding elaborately like a figure in a pop-up book. The Willis Tower, the Hancock Tower, the crowd of lesser skyscrapers; beautiful and horrible.

And in one of those buildings, her contact would be waiting.

Calliope reached the Kennedy and took it into Hubbard's Cave – a long tunnel with yellow lights glowing above. Ahead, there was a new exit that delved down into the depths of Chicago. It was part of the Colossal Dig, a project that put the Big Dig in Boston to shame. Chicago was getting a whole new set of arteries below ground, and Calliope had a button that gave her first access. She pressed it.

A gate arm lifted, and tire spikes dropped, and Calliope took the ramp down into the foundations of Chicago. Headlights shone from the cement columns and black girders that held up the immense city above.

The ramp deposited her on I-494, twelve lanes running two hundred feet below Chicago. Just now, Calliope had the place to herself, aside from a few construction crews. She steered past them and saw another narrow off-ramp. She pressed the button again, and when the gate arm and spikes cleared, she descended again.

This deep route would not be open to the public – ever. It passed elevator shafts that ran from the surface to secret rail lines another hundred feet down. From there, it passed deeper still into a maze of blank cement.

Calliope's phone lost signal. Her GPS, too. She was off the map.

There, five hundred feet below Chicago, she approached a freight elevator. It opened onto the road, perfect for loading and unloading illegal materials. Her headlights flashed across the ancient network of iron and revealed the man who stood within.

Mr Evers. That was his true name, though she was forbidden to share it with anyone. To the Bat Pack, she called him the Phantom, after Phantom of the Opera, because Mr Evers had skin like a mannequin – hairless and smooth. And he didn't seem to have bones on the inside shaping his flesh. He seemed *molded*.

Even now, Mr Evers's dead eyes followed Calliope as she pulled up before the freight elevator and stopped. He moved deliberately toward the Civic.

Calliope rolled down the window and looked at the man, her master, this true Disciple.

"You're a minute and a half late," Mr Evers said tersely.

"I brought you something," Calliope replied. "I mean, some*one*."

He set preternaturally smooth hands on the window of her car and peered in at the snoring, bleeding mess that was Sergeant Krupinski. Mr Evers smiled. His teeth seemed to have two rows. "Ah, the fugitive."

"I figured you'd – um – *want* him," Calliope gabbled, "one way or the other."

"I do," Mr Evers said in a voice that was little more than a breath. "But I can't bring him in here."

"Of course not," Calliope replied, trying to hide her disappointment. "Where should I take him?"

"With you. You'll take him with you back to the Mennonite Campground."

"Methodist," she said automatically, and then cringed. "Sorry. But if he dies, then what? What should I do with the body?"

"He won't die. At least, not right away."

He reached his hands through the window and grasped her forehead.

Calliope Dirge jolted back in her seat. Power flooded into her. It was like stepping beneath a waterfall – the roar and rush, the pounding suffocation, the grip of death. Always before, though, the waterfall had been cold: a message meant for another. She would step away a moment later and know the person and place and time, but not the message.

This time, it was completely different. The waterfall was hot. Red, not blue. It did not pour into her for someone else. It poured in for her.

It was her promotion!

It was her possession.

Mr Evers wasn't outside anymore. He was inside, white-hot, surging through her temporal lobes. He eavesdropped on everything the Bat Pack had said about Krupinski and laughed to himself before rushing on into the frontal lobes. There, he read everything Calliope had thought of him and laughed again. Gushing into the occipital lobe and the cerebellum, Mr Evers mapped images of Krupinski and plucked at desires and found the word "doable."

Calliope was stripped bare. Mr Evers searched every corner of her mind: every wheedling desire to enter the Disciples, every hope that she was smart enough to do so, every tossed-off conversation with the Bat Pack. Memories she had tagged as private came blooming into view, and there were snickers and guffaws from Mr Evers, but nothing that stopped him. He vaulted through her, gathering hopes, regrets, fears like a six year-old with an Easter basket.

He thinks I'm shallow, she thought, and he grabbed the idea and turned it over and plunked it in beside the other tidbits. *He thinks I'm a wannabe.* That one went into the basket, too. *He thinks I'm brilliant and beautiful.* Only that thought stopped him. He scraped it away as if it were something stuck to his foot.

And, suddenly, he pulled his hands from her head. The blazing fire of the Othermind was gone, and Calliope felt as if smoke were pouring from her ears.

Mr Evers stood stiffly beside her Civic. He was unmoving, and his eyes seemed painted on.

"I didn't mean that," Calliope said in a trembling voice, "that part about being brilliant and beautiful. That was *irony*."

He looked flatly at her. "That wasn't irony."

She huffed, trying not to cry.

"You're ready," he said levelly. "You question this man. You learn from him what you can. And you bring what you learn back to us."

Calliope's gaped. "Oh, yes, Phantom!"

"What?"

"Um, Mr Evers."

He smiled, the movement making his perfect lips creak. "I know what you call me to your friends."

"Sorry."

"Don't be. If you'd given my real name, I'd have killed you."

"And I would have welcomed it, sir," Calliope breathed.

Mr Evers nodded stiffly. "I know. I have searched you

and known you, Calliope Dirge. I have unknitted you from your mother's womb. There are no longer any secrets. You are part of me. You are a Death's Disciple."

Tears came. Calliope tried to dash them away.

"No, don't," said Mr Evers. For the first time since she had begun carrying messages for him, he seemed to care. "Of course I care. I'm in your tears, now. I'm in your saliva, your bile, your blood."

Calliope shuddered.

"Good," Mr Evers said. "We understand each other."

Calliope glanced toward Krupinski. "What about him?"

"Oh, yes, *him*."

Mr Evers lifted his polystyrene hands from her window and stepped back, walking toward the front of her Civic. As he circled around, the headlights flung gold splotches across his tailored suit. He crossed to the window where Krupinski reclined.

Calliope rolled it down.

Mr Evers reached in as he had with her, but instead of grabbing Krupinski's forehead, he grabbed the man's left pectoral muscle. A red aura awakened around his fingers, and traces of light seemed to jet down through the chest wall to converge on the bullet within. Lit by red fire, the slug turned slowly over, weaving through layers of lung and meat until it leaped up into the hand of Mr Evers.

"There it is. This tiny bit of steel. The side and the spleen and the lung will heal."

"Good," breathed Calliope before she realized what she was saying.

Mr Evers gave her a sharp look. "Doable, eh?"

Calliope changed the subject. "What if he has turned against them?"

"You know he hasn't."

"Of course."

"You know what we want from him. Get it."

"I will. But then what?"

"Then kill him."

23 **MULTILATERAL TALKS**

"Chief Gregory," squawked the intercom, "there's a Lieutenant Elseworth from the FBI here to see you."

Devon Gregory folded the *Tribune* – its headline shouting 311 MIRACLE HOME AGAIN – set the paper down on his oak desk, and pressed the button to respond. "Send him in, Janice. And please make the call."

Gregory remained behind his desk, templing aristocratic black hands on the paper before him. He noted that his best pen – the engraved metal one he'd gotten with his promotion – had not made it back into the holder. It would have to remain where it lay.

Elseworth opened the door so rapidly it seemed almost as if he had kicked it in. Eyes wide and slightly crazed, he loped in on crutches, which he posted against Gregory's desk: "You have something of mine."

Gregory looked back levelly. "Do I?"

"This is a *federal* case. You have no jurisdiction. You can't just hold her–"

"Susan Gardner – I assume this is the possession you are referring to."

"Of course!"

"She doesn't belong to anyone. As a citizen of this city–"

"She's from Oak Park!"

"–she's asked me to hold her in protective custody."

Elseworth's shark-like features flushed. "*I* will hold her in protective custody."

Gregory replied calmly, "You are one of the people we are protecting her from."

"*I'm* in charge of this case! A *federal* case! None of this happened in Chicago!" He closed his fist around the stray pen and clutched it daggerlike.

Gregory smiled slowly and chuckled. "Are you trying to intimidate me?"

The intercom buzzed, "Chief Gregory?"

"Tell her to wait!" Elseworth roared.

"What is it, Janice?"

"There's a phone call for Lieutenant Elseworth – on line two."

"Thank you, Janice." The chief lifted the receiver, handed it to Elseworth, and pressed line two.

"Elseworth here," the man said gruffly, but the moment the person on the other end spoke, his tone softened. "Good morning, sir." He took a couple rapid breaths. "I was on a plane. You have to turn them off on the plane... Yes, just got in. Not an hour ago at O'Hare... Because I had one thing on my mind, which was to get straight over here and get Gardner into custody... With all due respect, it's *my* job..." The blood drained from his face. "Sir, you can't be serious – an investigation? She's a lunatic – Dr. Wilder said so... No, of course not. She used psychobabble bullshit, but that's what she meant... You weren't *there*, sir. You can't–" Elseworth looked up with annoyance at Gregory. "Could I have a little privacy – what? No, sir, I was talking– Of course. No. On my own recognizance – I think the agency owes me that much! All right. Yes. I'll be in D.C. by evening."

Elseworth lowered the receiver and set it in its cradle. His eyes smoldered. "How did he know I was here?"

"Janice called him when you arrived," the chief said simply.

"How did *she* know who to call?"

"He called me last night, as soon as he saw the eleven o'clock news. He knew you'd be here in the morning, and he wanted to be sure you didn't get your hands on her."

Elseworth's teeth ground. "Well, you won't have her for long. There'll be another agent—"

"They're investigating you and all your associates. The attack on that farm wasn't terrorists. There's a whole division going to be purged."

"Well, Death's Disciples just won a big victory. And *you* helped them."

The intercom buzzed again. "Chief?"

"Yes, Janice."

"There's a Michael Gardner out here, brother of Susan Gardner – her power of attorney."

"Yes, I know."

"And he's brought an actual attorney, as well."

Gregory smiled sadly. "Send them in."

"Your day's getting better and better," Elseworth sneered.

Gregory gestured toward the door. "If you'll excuse me."

"You haven't seen the last of me," Elseworth snapped. He pivoted stiffly around and headed out.

No sooner had he shouldered through the door than another man appeared. He was small, with dark brown hair parted to one side and intense blue eyes, and he wore a fine business suit of soft gray. As he stepped into the room, a woman followed, eyes hawkish and a slender briefcase shushing on her tweed skirt.

Gregory stepped out from behind his desk and reached to shake the man's hand. "Good morning. I'm Chief Gregory."

"I'm Michael Gardner, and this is my attorney, Patrice Steimke."

Gregory took her hand. "Glad to meet you."

"We'll see about that."

"I'm here to pick up my sister," Michael said. "As her brother – as her *power of attorney*, I *demand* it."

Patrice nodded at him like an encouraging mother.

Chief Gregory pursed his lips. "What about *Susan's* demands? After all, we're holding her at her own request."

"She isn't fit to make such a request," Counselor Steimke shot back.

"Have you seen her, Michael? Have you talked with her since she woke up? She seems quite aware of her surroundings, quite concerned about her safety," Chief Gregory said. "You should be, too."

"Of course I am! For four weeks, my decisions have kept her safe."

"But she was asleep, then. She's awake now."

"He's still her power of attorney," Counselor Steimke put in.

"Don't you even want to talk with her? Find out what *she* wants?"

"Of course I–"

"What she wants is immaterial," broke in Counselor
Steimke, dragging documents from her briefcase. "Until
a competency hearing proves that she is capable of making her own decisions, my client is her sole legal agent."
She slapped the papers down on Chief Gregory's desk.

He shook his head. "She asked me, personally, to protect her. That's not just a legal obligation. That's a sort
of sacred trust. We will set up a competency hearing this
week, but until that time, she remains – at her own request – in protective custody."

"My client is prepared to sue," Counselor Steimke
said.

The chief sighed. "The hearing will take place before
you can even file the paperwork."

"For your sake, it'd better."

Chief Gregory said, "But first things first." He pressed
the intercom button. "Janice?"

"Yes?" came her voice over the speaker.

"Send someone down to tell Miss Gardner that she
has guests – her brother and his attorney. If she would
like to speak with them, let's use conference room E in,
say, twenty minutes?"

"Right, Chief."

"All right, everybody," Dave Jenkins called out, standing
in the aisle of Ghost Flight 311. A couple hundred pairs
of eyes watched him, though a few ghosts snoozed or
read or chattered to each other. "We're going to try this
for the first time, in a conversation with Susan's brother
and an attorney. If you wish to participate, watch the

monitors and listen with your headphones. Remember the ten rules. Susan will probably remain in control the whole time. If, however, you feel she is putting us in imminent risk, voice your opinion. If a majority of you feel this way, I will take control of the body and take action. Is that clear?"

In Seat 13B, a man with round lips and a few spare chins said, "Why can't *we* take control?"

"For one, you don't know how. I've done it successfully before."

"Only when she was *asleep*."

"For another, I'm responsible. If one of you takes over and fouls things up, she'll blame me."

The fat man said, "Then I got nothing to lose, just taking over."

"You've got everything to lose. She'll dump you from her mind, and you'll be gone," Dave said firmly. He looked around at them all. "We're out of time. As you can see on your monitors, they're leading her into the room."

He plugged his own set of earphones into an unused jack and watched the scene unfold.

24 FIGHTING FOR THE MIC

They bring me into a conference room: a long wooden table, padded seats, low-pile maroon carpet, impressionist prints... I wish I could stay here instead of in the cell.

The cop in front of me pulls out one of the high-backed seats and gestures into me it. I sit. The other cop stands in the doorway facing out, fingers fiddling with the loose strap above his gun.

Then the visitors arrive. A distinguished black gentleman with salt-and-pepper hair leads them. Surely this isn't my brother. "Good morning, Susan. I hope you slept well." He extends his hand to me, and I shake it.

"Have we met?" No sooner are the words out of my mouth than Dave barges through my head: "Sorry, Chief. Just tired this morning. Didn't sleep that well."

Get out of my mind.

Dave slips back.

Another man – a small, nervous man with my bone structure – steps into the room.

This must be, "Michael," I say, going to him and giving him a hug. I don't remember him at all, but this seems like what a sister should do.

"Sis," he says into my ear. At first, he's stiff in my arms, but then he melts a little and gently returns my embrace. "So, you remember me?"

I pull back from him and look into his eyes. They are bright blue, in an almond-shaped face, with a mouth like a flat bar. Slowly, I shake my head. "Sorry."

He nods, breaking eye contact and turning away, "Then you certainly won't remember our attorney, Patrice Steimke."

A woman steps up from behind him – a thin woman with a hawkish nose, straight hair, and an expensive coat-and-skirt ensemble. She takes my hand in a bony grip. "Hello, Susan."

"Hello," I reply. The minds of the ghosts buzz in my head. They don't like this lawyer. *Barracuda*, they say, *pit bull, piranha – grip like a skeleton*. It's just intuition, little guesses, but there are hundreds of guesses, moaning like a Greek chorus.

"Let's all have a seat," offers Chief Gregory.

They like him, the Greek chorus does.

I return to my seat on one side of the table, and the chief sits beside me at the head. Michael and the lawyer sit opposite me.

"Your brother has come, asking for your release," the chief says calmly, "but I told him that you requested to be here, under protective custody."

"Yes."

"Susan, don't you want to come home?" Michael asks.

I don't know what to say, so I fall back to Dave's advice. "I – I want to be safe. As safe as possible."

"We can keep you safe at home," Michael says. "The cops are already keeping the street locked down, and we'll hire private security. We can afford it. I've kept the accounts going."

The ghosts like Michael. *Nerd*, they say, *intense* and *odd*, but *family – loyal* and *honest*.

"I don't want to be in that cell anymore," I blurt.

Dave is not happy.

Chief Gregory shrugs gently. "If we had better accommodations that were still secure, we would give them to you."

"They're fine," Dave says through my mouth. "For this first week at any rate." I shove him back. "What am I saying? They're *not* fine. I don't want to spend a week in solitary confinement. That's for... mass murderers."

Chief Gregory stares at me in surprise. "This isn't what you said last night."

"It's what I'm saying now," I reply, inwardly bashing Dave. "Last night, I was alone. Now, my brother is here."

Michael beams at me – a look I somehow know is rare. "Come home with me, Sis. One phone call is all it'll take. We'll have that place locked down like Fort Knox."

They're screaming in my head, all these ghosts, telling me not to go. Dave is muscling against me, but I'm muscling *back. Not so easy when I'm awake, is it?*

"Make it happen," I tell the chief.

25 UNVARNISHED

"Speculation and rumor are swirling around the case of Susan Gardner, the 311 Miracle," Cameron Steel announced from the desk of his Fox News show, *Unvarnished*. Behind him, a wall-sized graphic showed a montage of the two Gardners, Krupinski, and Elseworth. "The drama began this morning when Susan's brother, Michael, left his home half an hour earlier than usual. As we've discovered over the last weeks, Michael is extremely meticulous. This change in schedule indicated that news was unfolding. The Fox 32 News crew in Chicago followed Michael's BMW to the Chicago Police Department parking garage, where the crew was denied access. But the camera was rolling during the ensuing conversation, and you'll never guess what they caught on film. Roll the footage."

The graphic behind him changed to a video image of a well-dressed male reporter beside a Fox 32 News van. The reporter held his microphone up to a young female parking attendant, who said, "You can't be blocking the lane with your van."

"But we can't back out. There are three cars behind us."

"You can't be coming in," the attendant replied. "You got to have police access."

"How did the last car get in? They weren't police."

Before she could answer, a horn blared. The parking attendant rolled her eyes and muttered, "That one again." As the horn wailed, she turned away from the news crew. The reporter motioned the camera to the other side of the parking booth, where a black SUV waited behind the gate arm. At the wheel was a red-faced Lieutenant Elseworth. He was having an argument with the parking attendant.

The reporter rushed up. "Lieutenant Elseworth, is it true you tried to kill Susan Gardner?"

"Move out of the way!"

"Is she with you in the SUV?"

"This is official business!"

"Where are you taking her?"

"Get out of the way! Lift the damned gate!"

"What do you plan to do with her?"

The SUV leaped forward, bashing into the camera and knocking the operator to the ground. Still, the SUV remained in frame as it tore past the now-open gate and zoomed onto the streets of Chicago.

The screen returned to the *Unvarnished* News Room and its graphic of the Gardners and the FBI agents. Cameron Steel shook his head. "Amazing footage. Did you see the look of anger on the face of Lieutenant Elseworth?"

Beside him, a handsome Latina said, "He does have a temper."

"Yes, Lupe, but the question is whether it's a murderous one, as alleged by Miss Gardner. He certainly was willing to put the Fox cameraman at risk. Did you see how the SUV just plowed into him?"

"Actually, Cameron, I understand that the camera operator was a woman."

"All the worse," Cameron replied with a slight scowl. "To run a woman over in cold blood. It lends credence to the story that Susan Gardner told just last night in Grant Park. We've been running that footage in almost a continuous loop for the last eighteen hours, so we'll spare you seeing that again, but we have some other exclusive footage to show you: what *else* happened this dramatic day at the Chicago Police Department parking lot."

"It's dramatic," Lupe added.

"Now, as I understand it, what you are about to see occurred to *the same news crew* just an hour and a half after the footage we've just seen. When they saw the now-famous DOMN8R license plate emerging from the Chicago PD parking complex, they were there to catch the story."

Again, the four faces dissolved, giving way to video of a reporter rushing up beside a black BMW sedan, with Michael Gardner at the wheel. No one else was in the vehicle.

"Michael, did you see your sister?" the reporter shouted through the glass.

He shook his head slowly.

"Is that because Lieutenant Elseworth has her?"

He blinked, nodding.

"Michael! Roll down the window. Tell us what happened! We can help you!"

But instead, he drove slowly away. The news crew followed him past the raised gate, shouting questions, but Michael drove with slow deliberation onto the street and then pulled free.

Back in the newsroom, Cameron was laughing. "People used to talk about O.J. Simpson and his slow-speed chase at 45 miles per hour, but this Michael Gardner has him beat. He's the master of the 1-mile per hour escape."

"Yes, but did you see his answers to the reporter's questions?" Lupe asked.

"Right, a definite head shake to the question whether he had gotten to see his sister, and a definite head nod to whether Elseworth took her. That means Susan Gardner is now in the hands of Lieutenant Elseworth of the FBI, the very man purported to be trying to kill her."

"It's a travesty."

"Yes, a travesty of justice. I think of Patty Hearst."

"I do, too."

"But this Susan Gardner is half Hearst and half Schwarzenegger."

"She's kind of a take-no-prisoners prisoner."

26 **THE GOTH DUMPLING**

Krupinski awakened. Above him was a ceiling of tongue-and-groove paneling covered in about seventeen layers of paint. Below him was a mattress with a plastic tarp thrown over it. Krupinski turned his head to see Calliope Dirge reclining on a nearby window seat and staring out at the sky. On the other side of the seat was Evella of the Endless Night, giggling as she typed on her laptop.

"Nobody can figure out what I'm talking about," Evella said gleefully.

"What *are* you talking about?" asked Calliope.

"I wrote that a new man slept in my bed last night."

"Not *Facebook*."

"Yes. Everybody's asking who he is and whether he was any good."

Calliope stiffened. "And what did you write?"

"I said just that he was big. Then a bunch of people wrote that 'big is good.'"

"For God's sake."

"Then I wrote that I think he was bad, but that 'bad is good.'"

"Log off right now," Calliope said. "You can't talk aboutDisciples business on Facebook."

Evella gave her a black look, and then folded the laptop. "Jeez. Ever since you got back, you've been a total tight-ass."

"I'm *one* of them, now."

Krupinski coughed, catching flecks of dried blood on his hand.

The two young women dropped their feet from the window seat and stared at him in wide-eyed amazement.

Krupinski sat up. The living room reeled around him. "Where am I?"

"You're in the inner sanctum of an agent of Death's Disciples." She walked toward him and fixed him with an arch expression. "What does that make you want to do?"

He looked at her: slender and pale, black hair draping from head to breasts. "I feel like throwing up."

"Not on the daybed!" growled Evella.

"Grab a garbage can!" Calliope ordered.

Evella rushed to him, holding the half-full receptacle in front of Krupinski.

He clutched the can. "Thanks."

After a few moments, Evella said, "Well? Are you gonna puke or not?"

"Probably not," Krupinski said wearily, setting down the can. "Got nothing in my stomach. Twelve hours on a Greyhound with nothing to eat."

Calliope sat down beside him. "Well, then, *Sergeant Krupinski*–"

"Steve."

"Well, then, *Steve*," she said, but then chuckled. "I can't call you Steve." She wiped the humor from her face. "Well, then, Sergeant Krupinski, how do you feel about being in the nest of one of Death's Disciples?"

Krupinski looked levelly at her. "Relieved."

Calliope scowled. "You should be terrified. Do you know that I have orders to kill you if you try anything?"

"I do now," Krupinski replied. "But it's not the first time I've had a death sentence."

Calliope stood and paced before the daybed. "What's your story, Krupinski?"

"I've gone rogue. You've seen the news, right?"

"Why would you go rogue?"

He stared out the bay window at leaves shuffling in a gentle breeze. "I'm tired of being nobody. I'm tired of being a cog in the machine. I sat beside her bed for four weeks. Kept her safe. Kept anybody from getting to her. I killed a man and got poisoned, and next thing I know, I'm off the case and Elseworth's on it. I'm sitting in a shitty little café and realizing I'm stuck and I'll always be stuck when I'm part of the government machine."

Calliope gazed at him in fascination and murmured, "I know how you feel."

"What's *with* you?" Evella asked.

"Don't you see? He's – just – like – us."

"A Goth?" Evella laughed. "Yeah, right. He looks more like a dumpling."

Calliope wheeled around and pushed Evella onto the window seat.

"Ow! Tight-ass!"

"Shut up," Calliope advised. She turned back toward Krupinski. "So, you wanted out of the government machine. What did you do to get out?"

"You saw what I did; all those dead agents, that house burning."

"*You* did that?"

"Fuck, yeah."

The women exchanged an *isn't-he-hot* look.

Calliope pressed, "But Susan Gardner said Lieutenant Elseworth did that."

Krupinski shook his head. "That's what I told her. I brainwashed her, said Elseworth was trying to kill us both. It was the only way to make sure I could get her all the way back to Chicago."

"But why did she run away from you in Grant Park?"

Krupinski sighed. "There was a courier – a Goth punk like you. He came up to me and laid his hands on my head, and suddenly, I knew the time and place of my contact. But it freaked Susan out. She got it, that I was about to hand her over, and she ran."

"Did you chase her?"

He grabbed a fistful of his belly. "She's a little faster than I am."

Calliope was pacing again. "So, you thought if you gave her to us, we'd accept you? Make you one of us?"

"That's what I thought."

She loomed over him. "Why would you want to be a Death's Disciple?"

"I'm tired of being the pawn. I want to be the knight, the bishop," Krupinski fairly roared, standing up from the daybed. "I want to move around the fucking board with impunity and take out whoever stands in my way."

"I thought that's what you did in the FBI."

"Are you kidding?"

"You had a license to kill, right? You got to carry guns around and blow people away. The government always has the best weapons."

Krupinski leaned conspiratorially toward her, "You're right about that."

"Nukes?"

He shook his head slowly. "I'm talking something a lot more powerful. Totally new."

The two young women looked at him breathlessly. "What is it?"

"It's called Conscious 1, a government search engine that knows everything on every machine connected to the Internet. It knows what Ashton Kutcher had for lunch. It can look through any camera connected to the Internet – like that one on your laptop."

Evella looked up, going white, and shut her computer.

"It knows everyone's identity. It knows if there's a God."

"Is there?" Calliope asked.

Krupinski squinted. "Conscious 1 says, no… not yet. It believes that it is being birthed as the first god – an all-knowing, ever-present, all-powerful being. For a hundred thousand years, we wanted a god," Krupinski said, "and now, the government has made one."

She caught her breath. "But Conscious 1 doesn't know about our Lord Death?"

"Death doesn't use computers. He avoids the Internet."

"Ours is the only god who will stand up to Conscious 1."

"Yes."

"Ours is the only god who can bring the rationalist world to its knees."

"So mote it be."

Calliope jabbed a finger at Krupinski. "You're a faker."

"What?"

"You're faking it. You don't want to betray the 311 Miracle. You don't want to betray your fucking government. You're just trying to get inside our organization."

Krupinski's eyes blazed. "You saw me come in here – fugitive from justice. You fixed my gunshot wound. Do you honestly think I did all that to become a Disciple?"

Calliope looked him up and down. "Maybe."

"How can I prove myself?"

"There's only one way, Steve."

"Tell me."

"You have to get Susan Gardner."

27 HOMECOMING

The sun was setting as Michael Gardner drove down his block toward the wall of reporters. How he hated paparazzi. But, this afternoon, he could look past them, seeing with pleasure the dark-suited men standing at the four corners of his house. They wore sunglasses and frowns, and beneath their jackets lurked Kevlar, Tasers, pistols, and nightsticks. These thugs weren't cheap, but they were screened and incredibly effective.

Anything for Big Sis.

The mob of reporters converged. Their cameras snapped not just Michael's own dogged expression, but also the empty seats around him, the empty footwells.

"Did you see her? Michael?"

"Do you think Elseworth is guilty?"

"Who are the men in black?"

"Have you made a deal with the Mafia?"

"Are they Death's Disciples?"

The BMW scraped slowly through until cops in the driveway peeled the crowd off. Michael accelerated down the winding drive. He nodded at one of the black-suited guards, but the man looked glassily past him.

"Just as well," Michael murmured. "I wouldn't want him to wave."

He triggered the garage door and drove in and closed it behind him. Shutting off the Beemer, Michael swept the car for button cameras before he hoisted the trunk lid.

Susan looked up a little greenly. "Not a nice ride."

Michael blanched. "So sorry."

"We'll have to get some pillows in here, at least." She reached up out of the trunk. "Help me?"

Michael grasped his sister's hand and helped her sit up and climb from the trunk. A moment later, she was standing in the four-car garage.

She looked around, seeing the Mercedes, Lamborghini, and Jaguar. "Nice."

"You've done very well for yourself."

Susan walked past, her hand trailing across the trunks. "Wonder if any of these is more comfortable."

"We could try, I guess," Michael replied nervously. "But if the press sees me driving something else, they'll make up a hundred reasons why."

"Let them," Susan said, tossing a clump of blonde hair back from her face. "Ugh. I need a shower. I smell like jail."

Michael stepped up to her and touched her arm, gesturing her toward the door to the house. "I left your bathroom just as you like it. All of your products are in place. I just hope none of them has expired."

"My *products?*" Susan replied as they ascended some stairs to a long, low living room. "I must be pretty high maintenance."

Michael chuckled but then caught himself. "No. Not really. I mean – it works. You wear the right mascara, the right foundation, and you get men to sign for millions of dollars. Certainly pays for itself."

She walked breezily through the back parlor. "This is very nice, but we should get a maid in here."

"Right," Michael said, making a mental note as he followed her into the kitchen.

"Wow. This is a restaurant setup."

Michael shrugged, "Again, you set out the calamari, and you hook the big fish."

"Where's this fabled bathroom of mine?"

Michael took the lead, passing through the receiving room and front parlor, into the great room and up the stairs, across the balcony to Susan's room and the bathroom that adjoined it. He flipped on the light. "Here it is."

"Wow, are you kidding?" Susan said. "Marble counter tops and *three* sinks – and *two* toilets."

"That one's a bidet."

"A hot tub, stand-up shower, sauna, *and* walk-in closet?"

"I'm glad you like it," Michael said, somewhat taken aback.

"I *love* it but..."

Michael stiffened. "But what?"

Susan turned her terrible blue eyes on him. "Tell me that we're close, you and me."

He flinched, but somehow held her gaze. "We are, Susan."

"Tell me that we're friends."

He blinked. "We're brother and sister."

"We do things together?"

"Yes, everything."

"And we like each other?"

He took a short breath. "You always said it wasn't about liking. It was about working. And we work together better than any brother and sister."

She nodded. "I'm a bitch, aren't I?"

He huffed and said. "No!"

"Aren't I?"

Blushing, he replied. "You've taken a certain pride in it."

She broke eye contact for the first time and stepped away.

"It's why we have what we have," Michael said. "You have to be a bitch in a man's world – that's what you've said – and you've climbed to the top like few men could."

"Unlike you," Susan said offhandedly.

Michael looked down. "Exactly."

Susan glanced up. "I'm sorry. I didn't mean that."

"It's okay."

"It's not okay. Whatever I was, I'm not that anymore. I don't want to be a bitch. I want to be a good sister."

"You *have* been a good sister."

"I want to be a good *person*."

He tilted his head. "There's so much to tell you. There's so much for you to learn about who you are. But, first, a shower."

"A shower, yes."

"And, of course, take your pick of clothes from your closet."

Susan peered into the walk-in closet, staring at rank on rank of stiletto heels. "It's like a hundred pairs of shoes."

Michael smiled. "They have categories. Evening, boardroom, ass-kicking, trollop–"

"Trollop?"

"You're a complex woman, Susan Gardner," Michael said shyly, stepping back from the bright-lit bathroom. "Have a good shower." He closed the door.

28 SHOWERS, CLOSETS AND GARDENS

I can't believe this is my life. This shower – with three shower heads coming out of three walls of black marble, and a cut-crystal door. Who has a shower like this?

Apparently, I do.

I must be good at what I do – a real *bitch*, slick and smart and ruthless. But I'm not any of those things anymore.

How am I going to crawl back into this life?

There's two shampoos and three kinds of conditioner and two bars of soap and four body washes and a loofah. What the hell did I do with all this shit?

I pour an iridescent balm into my hand and rub it through my hair. I squirt a pink foam into the loofah and spread it across my body. There's dirt on me from that Montana farm house, from the pizza car, from the Silverado and the Greyhound and Grant Park and the jail.

Evidence. It's all coming off me and going down the drain.

I'm going to need all four body washes to get clean.

The hot water and soap and shampoo have done their work. I step out, pink and steaming, and grab a towel and dry my hair. I wrap the towel around myself, from boobs to butt – is this how I do it? – and I swing back the doors of my walk-in closet.

Business suits line the right wall, and evening wear the left. Shoes are ranked in armies on both sides beneath. I step farther in to find jogging suits and Spandex and leotards on the right and casual clothes – polos and button-down prints and T's on the left. "I hang up T-shirts?"

Of course I don't. Some Mexican girl does it for four dollars an hour.

I blow a bit of dust from a purple T-shirt that says "Northwestern," and I pull it on. I find a pair of panties in a drawer and draw on some cargo shorts. "Susan Gardner would probably be appalled," I tell myself.

I'm about to go out and see what Michael thinks when I notice another set of doors on the deep end of the closet. I go to them and pull on the twin handles, swinging the doors open.

"Oh, you've got to be shitting me."

There's another whole closet here, stocked with S & M gear. There are black-leather dominatrix outfits, hoods, bustiers, crotchless panties, garters, stockings, ball gags, anal beads, flails, chains.

"No," I say. "God damn it."

I'm *not* that person. I'll *never* be that person.

Shaking, sickened, I walk numbly out of my closet and my bathroom. The hallway outside is dark. The whole place is dark. Doesn't Michael believe in light? "Michael?"

"Shh!" he says down below.

I follow the sound down the stairs and into the two-story great room. "Where are you?"

"Shh!" He's by the drapes. They completely cover the windows, but Michael has pulled them just slightly open and is staring out between them into the back yard.

I go to him. "What's up?"

"Someone's out there," he whispers.

"The guards."

"Somebody else. Someone's approaching the house."

I squat down and pull back a corner of the drape and see it myself.

Against a dusky sky, someone is walking. A man. He's big. And he's coming straight toward the window. "How do you know it's not one of the guards?"

My question is answered a moment later when one of the guards shouts, "No closer! We will take action!"

"Holy shit!" I say. "It's the Disciples."

The man comes on, heading straight toward me and Michael.

"This is it!"

Something flashes in the man's hand – a camera – and the light shows him in a suit, shows the guard rushing up to him and the taser lines flying from the gun. Sparks ignite on the man's chest. They light his face, gripped in agony. He stiffens and tumbles back and falls to the ground. Still, the taser sparks in the darkness. The man on the ground jolts, convulsing. There's a guard there, now, a shadow outlined by the flashing taser leads.

"I've seen him before," Michael says, "the reporter."

"Where?"

"At the Chicago Police parking facility. He was trying to interview me through the glass."

We both watch through the window as the taser erupts again, and the man spasms.

"Maybe he'll think twice next time."

Michael turns toward me. "Only if he didn't get a shot of your face."

29 WHERE SHE IS

"I found something that'll tell us where Susan Gardner is!" Evella said, staring at her laptop. She motioned the rest of the Bat Pack to come over to the window seat.

Krupinski strode up with them and glanced at the Web site. "Fox News? Are you kidding? We need real information."

"Just shut up and watch," Evella said as she clicked the play button on the video screen.

The opening graphic announced *Unvarnished* and then "The Missing Miracle," and the camera zoomed down on the smarmy face of Cameron Steel.

"At this hour, there's a state of complete confusion as to the whereabouts of the 311 Miracle. Just yesterday, we reported that Lieutenant Tom Elseworth left the headquarters of the Chicago Police Department in an SUV with dark windows. In his rush to leave, he nearly ran down a Fox News camerawoman. Shortly afterward, Michael Gardner, brother to the Miracle, indicated quite clearly that Susan had been taken by Lieutenant Elseworth," Cameron Steel said. "That's where we left things yesterday, but no one has been able to corroborate Michael Gardner's story."

"It wasn't actually a story, Cameron," Lupe Gonzalez said beside him, "but just a nod and a head shake."

Krupinski laughed at the computer screen.

"Shhh!" Evella snapped, goosing the volume.

Cameron's teeth latched in a smile. "Thanks, Lupe, for that clarification. But today, Chief Gregory of the Chicago Police is refusing to release any information as to the whereabouts of Susan Gardner. He won't even confirm whether she remains in protective custody. Meanwhile, the FBI and the Department of Homeland Security are refusing to release any information about Lieutenant Elseworth, let alone the 311 Miracle. And Gardner's reclusive brother has now hired a private security force to guard his home, 24/7. She could be with any of these three groups or, worse, could be now in the hands of the Death's Disciples."

"We just don't know," Lupe piped.

Krupinski interrupted, "You heard the woman. They *just don't know.*"

Cameron Steel went on, "So, we've called in one of our experts in terrorism, cults, and the US intelligence services: retired Lieutenant Colonel Jason Briggs, formerly of the CIA and onetime staffer at Area 51. Good morning, Colonel Briggs."

A floating box appeared, showing the white-haired head of a man, medals gleaming on his full-dress uniform. "Good morning, Cameron. Hello, Lupe. Thanks for having me back."

"Nice to have you, as always. Now, you've been following this story right along with us, Colonel. Where do *you* think Susan Gardner is?"

"Well, of course, we don't have any way of knowing, but my gut tells me that the Disciples have her."

The Bat Pack looked at each other in confusion.

"Really?" Lupe asked.

"Yes. This Elseworth fellow is a grandstander. If he had her, everybody would know it. And this brother of hers, well, he's too much of a milquetoast to orchestrate an escape. Then, of course, you have the famously corrupt Chicago Police Department. Have you ever heard of them protecting anybody but their mob buddies? No, I think it's quite plain, Cameron. Susan Gardner has been captured by the Death's Disciples."

"Well, then," Krupinski said, brushing off his hands. "I guess you won't be needing me after all."

Cameron went on. "And what do you think they want with her?"

"Oh, they want her dead."

"Wow. You're that certain?" Cameron said.

"What you have to remember is that these people are Satanists."

"We're not Satanists!" Calliope objected.

"Shhh!"

"They probably blew up that plane as some kind of sacrifice to their dread master. They promised every soul on that plane to Satan, and he won't be satisfied until he has every last one."

"Whoa!" said Thanatopsis. "I never thought of that!"

Krupinski biffed the back of his beautiful blond head, making Thanatopsis do an involuntary head bang. "You idiot. That colonel has no idea about Death's Disciples or Susan Gardner. Fox is just filling airtime."

Thanatopsis reeled back and lifted his hands in taekwondo moves. "Touch me again, Chubby, and we'll see who's—"

Krupinski palmed the kid's face. Thanatopsis crashed down on the window seat, perilously close to Evella's laptop.

"Hey!" Evella objected, folding the thing and glaring at both men.

"*Somebody* has to know where she is," Calliope said.

Krupinski shrugged. "Why don't you ask me?"

"How would *you* know?" Calliope asked.

"Isn't it obvious?"

"Where is she?"

"At home, with Michael." Krupinski laughed. "That old dolt was right about Elseworth. If he had her, he'd say so. And when Chief Gregory had her, he said so. Now they've both clammed up, which means that neither one has her. And if Death's Disciples had her, we'd know. That leaves just Michael, who's hired guards to watch his house 24/7."

Krupinski arched his eyebrows. "Doesn't take a genius."

"Man," Cyclops said, "you should be on Fox News!"

"Let's go get her!" Thanatopsis said, jumping up and singing out in Jack-Black style, "Storm the Gates!"

Krupinski lifted his hand. "Don't make me face plant you again."

Frowning, Thanatopsis sat back down. "What's the matter? You too chicken to go up against a couple of rent-a-cops?"

"There's four highly trained, heavily armed guards – and two police."

"Then it's even. Six of them and six of us," Thanatopsis said.

"And where are your flak jackets? Your guns? Your tear gas?"

"Damn it. The *man's* always got the best weapons."

"So, *we* have to have the best plan."

"Which is?"

"You want gold, you don't storm Fort Knox. You follow the little white truck out of Fort Knox and when it parks and the two guys take the bags into the building, you jump 'em."

"Then we use the gold to buy her?" Thanatopsis wondered.

"It's a metaphor, idiot!" Calliope snapped. "He's talking about Susan Gardner. He's talking about an ambush!"

Thanatopsis lifted two fingers beatifically beside his face. "Very wise, my friend. Very wise."

Calliope shook her head and then huffed. "All right, Krupinski. Plan this ambush."

"It's not that difficult," Michael said as he spread a blanket within the trunk of the Beemer.

"It's *international finance!*" Susan replied. "Of course it's difficult!"

Michael laid a pair of pillows by one wheel well. "It's just like chess."

"Exactly – *difficult!*"

"Not really. Every piece has a few moves. Once you know them, you just need to calculate your possible moves and your opponent's possible moves. Think three moves ahead, and you can keep up with most players. Think six moves ahead, and you can dominate the whole board."

Susan lifted her leg to step into the Beemer's trunk, but her stiletto heels and red skirt-suit made the move impossible. "This is ridiculous."

Michael fetched a step stool and helped her into the trunk.

Blowing a tuft of hair back from her eyes, Susan sat down. "Can't even get into a trunk. How'm I going to think six moves ahead on international finance?"

"You don't have to. That's the part *I* do – the analysis," Michael said, folding the step stool and laying it across the back seat. "I present you with options. You choose the direction."

She cocked her head. "How do I know which way to go?"

"It's instinctive. The killer instinct. You look out and you see something you want to control – some corpo-ration or some government–"

"Government?"

"And I run the scenarios, figure out all the possible moves, figure them out to six turns. Then you make your move. You navigate the board, control it. The pieces fall before you."

Drawing a deep breath, Susan said, "I don't know."

"You will after today." His breath caught. "There are so many people for you to meet."

"You're sure they won't rat us out?"

Michael smiled down at her. "They love you, Susan. They'd die for you." With that, he slammed the trunk.

30 **AIR HOLES**

I don't care if it's a Beemer. I'm going to drill air holes in this damned trunk.

Yeah, the blankets are nice, and the pillows are a big improvement, but there're blankets and pillows in a coffin, too.

I want some damned air holes.

The engine starts, and there comes the rattle of the garage door opening. Then Michael, gentle soul that he is, backs incrementally out of the garage and turns the car and heads toward the street. I hear the shouts of the paparazzi.

"Why the guards, Michael?"

"Have you heard from Death's Disciples?"

"Are there ransom demands?"

"How much is she worth?"

"Will you pay?"

"What's the step stool for, Michael? You gonna hang yourself?"

The clamor is terrible, the squeak of hands smearing across enameled steel. We slog along through the mob – cameras making a cicada sound – and then we break free, and Michael accelerates.

Good. For God's sake, I hope we won't have the same thing waiting for us at the other end, at International Mercantile.

31 ART OF THE FOLLOW

"There goes Michael Gardner," Krupinski said, sitting beside Calliope in her little Civic. They were parked about a hundred yards from the Gardner's house. "Bet he's got her in the trunk."

"Look at those reporters!" Calliope replied. "You sure they won't recognize you?"

"With my new goatee and Cyclops's clothes – no way." He slid on a pair of black sunglasses for good measure. "You sure you don't want me to drive?"

Calliope glanced at him. "I'm not covered for other drivers."

Krupinski sighed. "She's a Death's Disciple, and she's worried about insurance."

"Shut up."

From the back seat, Thanatopsis put in, "She doesn't let *anybody* drive. 'Control issues'."

"Shut up," Calliope repeated. She pulled out onto the street and followed the BMW sedan. It had just escaped the paparazzi, and the Civic was heading toward them. "They're gonna take our pictures."

"I'll dissuade them."

Sure enough, as the Honda rolled up, the dispirited reporters turned toward it, wondering what *another* car might be doing on this street.

Krupinski leaned out his window. "Go home! Get a

fucking job like the rest of us! Homeless fucks, goddamned peeping tom cocksuckers!"

The cameras dropped. The mics switched off.

Krupinski leaned back in the window. "People don't
like to hear the truth about themselves, let alone to
record it for posterity. Sometimes the best defense is a
good offense."

"You're pretty offensive," Calliope said as the crowd
of reporters melted back.

"Fuck you, Goth trash!" shouted one of them.

Krupinski smiled. "It's absolution. They're erasing us
from their brains."

Calliope accelerated down the street, following the
BMW.

"There's a thing about following," Krupinski said edg-
ily. "You got to stay close, but not look like you're
staying close."

"You want to drive?" she yelled.

"Yeah."

"Well, you can't!"

"Well, then, drive right!"

Calliope signaled and shifted into the right lane.

"What are you doing?" Krupinski cried. "He's turning
left!"

"You said to drive right," Calliope snapped, shifting
back into the left lane. "You said to look like you weren't
following."

"Not by turning right when he turns left! Follow him,
but not too close. Keep him in view."

Calliope followed the sedan around the left turn but
watched in dismay as it changed lanes and sped through

the next light. "He's trying to lose me." Calliope gunned the engine, sliding through the red.

"That little car is following me," Michael muttered, watching it zoom through the intersection. Then he clucked. "Nah. The Death's Disciples wouldn't drive a Civic."

His observation fell on deaf ears since Susan was in the trunk.

It was just as well. In the four weeks of her absence, Michael had begun talking to himself on his morning ride into International Mercantile. This morning was no different.

"Hey, watch yourself, Impala. Just because you didn't realize that was a turn-only doesn't mean you can jump in front of me." Michael stopped himself. "Listen to me. I'm bitching about everything. Pointless. So what if there's an Impala in the wrong lane? So what if there's a Civic running red lights. Doesn't mean anything."

Even so, he wove past the other vehicles and dived onto the on-ramp of I-94 South.

"He's trying to get away!" Krupinski said. "Step on it!"

"Do you want me to look natural, or do you want me to be right behind him?"

"I want you to *not* lose him and *not* alert him."

Calliope swerved across three lanes of traffic to slide onto the on-ramp.

Krupinski's knuckles were white on the door handle. "Little obvious, don't you think?"

"Nah," Calliope replied. "This is Chicago."

• • •

Michael took the Ohio Street exit and cruised two blocks through choked traffic. Ahead loomed the main headquarters of International Mercantile Bank. It was a pair of glass and steel towers, dark gray and striated like a pinstripe suit. In fact, the towers looked something like a decapitated businessman. Between the feet of that unfortunate man, a ramp descended into a parking garage. A stout gate arm and tire spikes announced that this was not public parking. The transponder mounted on Michael's dash bleeped, though, and the gate rose, and the spikes dropped. Michael vaulted through. The rearview mirror showed the defense works close like teeth behind him.

That annoying Civic screeched to a halt just short of those jaws.

"They *were* following," Michael said as he drove around the corner. Then he shrugged. "Probably bloggers."

He cruised a labyrinth of ramps deeper into the garage, through circles and circles until he reached the lowest level. Today, no one else had ventured this far, so Michael got a spot right beside the elevator. He also got anonymity.

Retrieving his step stool, he went to the trunk.

The lid levered upward to reveal a queasy-looking Susan. "What was with all the curves? Its like we were going to the lowest circle of hell."

Michael held out his hand and helped Susan step down onto the stool and to the pavement. "We'll use my key to take the elevator straight to the top – no stops. You won't be seen by anybody except the Big Man."

"The Big Man?"

"Mr Nero, president of the bank – and your direct boss." Michael rubbed his hands together. "Boy, is he going to be glad to see you."

She straightened. "How do I look?"

Michael tucked a loose lock of hair over her ear, and he smiled. "Terrific. I never thought you'd be back, but here you are."

"Here I am," she said, blushing. "Let's go see the Big Man."

He led her to the elevator and pressed the button. The stainless steel doors dimly reflected their forms: side by side in charcoal and flame. The bell dinged, the Gardners stepped in, and Michael pressed the button for the forty-second floor.

"What's he like?" Susan asked nervously. "The Big Man?"

Michael shrugged. "About your height but four times your weight. High, squeaky voice. Squarish goatee. He smiles all the time."

Susan shot him a worried look.

"You once called him the evil Chumley."

"The evil what?"

"Tennessee Tuxedo? His walrus friend – *Gee, Tennessee.* Mom used to play the tapes over and over. Don't you remember?" When Susan glared at him, Michael paled. "Oh. Yeah. Right."

"I work for the evil Chumley?"

"The man's a genius. He's the one who hired you, trained you. Yeah, on the outside, he's not much to look at, but on the inside, he's the smartest, most powerful person I've ever met."

The Otis elevator slowed as it reached the forty-second floor. The little bell went off.

"Here we are," Michael said, drawing his key from the slot.

"Here we are," Susan repeated.

32 MEETING THE BIG MAN

I hold my breath as the stainless-steel doors slide open. They reveal an enormous office with maroon carpet extending from the elevator to an oak reception desk. Beyond it is a grand mahogany desk the size of a Cadillac. On the other side of the desk stands a high-backed leather chair, facing toward a bank of windows that overlooks Chicago. From that leather chair comes a shrill voice – chatting on the phone.

"Of course, good sir… I-I-I understand completely. We'll take care of it. Nothing to worry about… Susan'll be back in charge of your accounts in no time, I assure you… Okay. Ha ha. Very good. Well, I've got to get back to business… Good to talk with you as well. Take care, my friend."

What sort of person says *good sir* and *my friend*, especially in that high-pitched voice?

The leather chair slowly turns around, and I see exactly the sort of person.

The Big Man is indeed big – and somewhat pear-shaped. He has wild, black curly hair rising from his head, and a wild curly goatee drooping from his chin. He wears a suit coat and pants, but instead of a white button-down shirt, there's a Hooter's T-shirt. A well-worn belt holds the whole ensemble together. But despite it all, there are those bright eyes, those smart and ferocious eyes looking at me. Without even a shred of surprise, the Big Man says, "Hello, my lady. You're looking fine, especially on *this* side of the grave."

The three hundred sixty-one ghosts in my head are unanimously terrified of Mr Nero.

But what do ghosts know? He's eccentric, sure, an odd dresser with a strange smile and an even stranger voice, but he's also charming. Michael says he's brilliant.

That's the problem, says Dave Jenkins. *Guard yourself, and get us out of here as soon as possible.*

I ignore him. Serves him right for the attempted coup back in police custody.

"It's good to be back, sir," I say, stepping toward the blood-red desk and the plaque that reads, "Mr Nero."

He doesn't stand, doesn't reach out to shake my hand, but laces his fingers on his belly and squeaks, "You remember me, then?"

I look him in the eye – he's too smart to lie to – and shake my head sadly. "Sorry. Wish I did."

He frowns, fingers fraying apart and coming down on his desk. "Do you remember anything about this place, about what we do here?"

I look around at the huge office, the spectacular views, and say, "Honestly, no. My brother has been keeping things going, and he tells me that he can continue–"

"Michael is not you," Mr Nero interrupts with an obsequious smile. "Great analyst, of course, but *you're* the politician, the one who gets people to follow. That's *your* genius."

I shrug. "That *was* my genius."

Mr Nero grins lopsidedly. "I bet I can draw it out of you." He leans to the intercom on his phone and punches three buttons. "Peters, Jamison, come to my office right away."

"Gotcha."

"Coming."

I blink. "Actually, we were hoping to keep my presence secret."

"Oh, it will be. You're my inner circle, you three. We trust each other with our lives. It's the only way we could do the work we do."

The elevator *dings*, and I turn to face it. The doors part to reveal two handsome young men in business suits. The taller one wears a sandy crew cut and a toothy grin. The shorter one has dark curly hair and very wide eyes, gaping at me.

He takes a staggering step toward me and breaks into a run. Laughing, he throws his arms around me. "It's you! I can't believe it! After all these weeks, you're back!" He's not a big man, but his embrace is tight, and he lifts me off my stilettos and puts me down again and steps back, catching my hands. "It's really you! Oh, it's so good to *see* you, Suzy."

"You, too," I say, and then hazard, "Jamison?"

His grin hitches, and the sparkle in his eyes dims. "No, I'm Peters. Marcus Peters. That's Lenny Jamison there."

The taller man strides patiently up and gives me a gentle hug. "Call me Lee. Marcus likes to embarrass me with that Lenny stuff." He shoots a look at Mr Nero. "A Hooters T-Shirt? Really?"

"I've got to be comfortable," Mr Nero says with a

shrug. "Besides, I didn't know I'd have any visitors. You want me to go to the closet and put on a proper shirt?"

"Not for me," Lee says.

"So," I break in, "it's Marcus and Lee and me in the inner circle?"

"Yeah," Marcus replies. "Still no memory, then?"

I shake my head.

"Damn."

"It'll come back," Mr Nero interrupts. He stands, lifting his hands like a priest giving a benediction: "We'll be the Four Horsemen again."

"The Four Horsemen?" I ask.

Marcus claps my shoulder. "You're Conquest."

Still not understanding, I say, "Sounds good."

"I'm War, Lenny here is Famine, and, of course, Mr Nero is Death."

I laugh. "Is this, like a heavy metal band or something?"

"Wow, she really has lost her memory," Lee says.

Giggling, the Big Man walks around his desk and sits on one corner of it and begins a recitation in a squeaky voice: "Revelation 6: 'And behold a white horse; and he that sat on him had a bow; and a crown was given unto him; and he went forth conquering, and to conquer.'"

With a wink, Marcus says, "That's you, Suzy."

The Big Man wears a wry smile as he continues his soliloquy: "'And there went out another horse that was red: and power was given to him that sat thereon to take peace from the earth, and that they should kill one another: and there was given him a great sword.'"

"That's Marcus," Lee says, whapping him on the chest. "You should *see* him in the boardroom. Fire and fury, like Mars in an Armani suit."

"'And lo, a black horse; and he that sat on him had a pair of balances in his hand. And I heard a voice in the midst of the four beasts say, A measure of wheat for a penny, and three measures of barley for a penny, and see thou hurt not the oil and the wine.' "

"That's Lenny," Marcus says cheerily. "Nowadays, people call them lawyers, but their real name is *famine*. They half-measure you into starvation."

"'And behold a pale horse: and his name that sat on him was Death, and Hell followed with him. And power was given unto them over the fourth part of the earth, to kill with sword, and with hunger, and with death, and with the beasts of the earth.' We dominate the world of international capital investment!"

"The Four Horsemen!" cries Marcus, lifting his hand for a high-five.

The two others lift theirs as well, all looking at me. I raise my hand, too, and we clap them together. The men give a glad grunt and seem surprised when I don't.

"Man, you really have forgotten everything," Marcus notes.

"Sorry, guys. I'll catch up."

"No, I mean, it's like you're a different person."

"Of course she is," Mr Nero breaks in, "all she's been through. You don't survive something like that as the *same* person."

"Well, yeah, of course not, but like, the old Suzy wouldn't apologize."

"Stop calling me Suzy," I snap.

A wide grin breaks across Marcus's face. "Ah, there's the old Susan. Wondered how long it would take you to put an end to this Suzy crap."

"You see?" Mr Nero says. "The good lady's in your presence for five minutes, and already she's rediscovering the inner bitch."

Marcus's eyes light. "Well, that's what she needs! A party! That's where she dominates. We'll get the whole gang together, and she'll work the room like old times. Where's Michael?"

"Here," he says, eyes averted as he approaches. I realize I've forgotten about him, that he's been standing out of the way in the corner the whole time. Michael wears a frightened look.

"You got that house in shape for a party?" Marcus asks.

"C-could be," Michael replies, "a couple phone calls."

Mr Nero shakes his head. "Not there. Not with all the police and press."

"Not to mention the Death's Disciples," Michael puts in.

Mr Nero rolls his eyes. "Certainly not to mention *them*. No. The party's a great idea, but it'll have to be at my penthouse."

Marcus's eyes grow wide. "That'll be the best party ever!"

"In three days," Mr Nero goes on, "I'll host a welcome-home party for Susan. It'll give time for the others to jet in."

"Perfect."

"In the meantime, Michael, go over the Banswyth-Stiller account with her."

"Every particular," Michael says.

The Big Man sighs. "No, every generality. That's the level where she works."

"Of course, sir."

"Speaking of generalities," I butt in, "who are Banswyth-Stiller?"

Marcus's mouth drops open again. "Wow."

"General contractors," Michael murmurs.

"I thought we did big contracts."

An odd giggle escapes Mr Nero's lips. "Banswyth-Stiller is the biggest building conglomerate in the world. Think of Boston's Big Dig done by one company – and done Chicago style. It's an all new system of underground highways and train lines. The deal is worth ten billion dollars."

"I see," I reply. "It's going to be huge."

"Susan," Mr Nero says gently. "It'll be done in a month, just in time for the G-20 summit and the opening of Chicagofest."

Marcus says incredulously. "You set the whole thing up, Susan. You landed this contract. It was your baby. Lucky we had only two months left so Michael here could keep the trains running – but holy shit! Where is your *mind*, girl?"

"Don't call me girl, jackass," I snap. "And if I landed this contract, why the hell was I in coach on Flight 311?"

Mr Nero and Peters and Jamison look at each other and then break into laughter.

"Ten minutes in your presence, Marcus, and our girl is halfway home! We'll have her back in time for the party." Mr Nero sets a heavy hand on Michael. "Take the files home with you. You have three days. Bring her up to speed."

33 AMBUSH

The gate arm and tire spikes might have stopped the Civic, but they couldn't stop the Bat Pack.

"That's the Beemer," Krupinski whispered as he, Calliope, and Thanatopsis crouched behind a cement wall on the lowest level of the parking garage. "See the plate? DOMN8TR?"

"You got the knife?" Thanatopsis asked breathlessly.

Krupinski patted the hand-tooled leather sheath on his leg. A dragon-headed pommel jutted from it. "A gun would've been better."

"That thing's from the Ren Faire!" Thanatopsis defended. "Cost me a month's salary, so it better come back in perfect shape."

"Don't worry about your knife or the Miracle. I'll take care of them. You two worry about her brother."

"That doofus?" Thanatopsis asked.

"That doofus will fight for her."

"That's why I brought my mace," said Thanatopsis.

"Good. Pepper spray."

"Not spray! Steel!" He lifted an iron mace, its ball bristling with spikes. Eyeing it lovingly, Thanatopsis said, "That's my paycheck for last July."

"Jesus. You're gonna hit him with that thing?"

"No," Calliope said. "We're not hitting or stabbing anybody. The Phantom wants Susan alive, and we have no reason to harm her brother."

"Such a gentle terrorist," Krupinski mocked. He pointed to a half-wall to the right of the BMW. "We'll hide there. He's gonna have to put her in the trunk. Just before he closes it, you guys jump out and threaten him – get him away from the car."

"Storm the Gates!"

"Meanwhile, I'll corner her in the trunk."

"You and your little friend," Thanatopsis enthused.

"I'll convince her to come with me."

"Use the speech," Calliope said.

Krupinski nodded wearily and recited: "This is no ordinary knife. It is a soul-blade. If I stab you with this blade, it will harvest your soul. That is one way I can take you to my dark masters. Or you can come with me still in your own skin."

"Show her the dragon etching," Thanatopsis encouraged.

"When she gets out, I slit two of the tires, and we escape up the elevator."

"Good," Calliope said.

"Good?" Thanatopsis asked. "It's freakin' awesome!"

"Let's go," Krupinski said. Looking both ways to make sure the coast was clear, he dashed out in a crouch, quickly crossing the blacktop to kneel behind the half wall. He turned back to call the other two – only to see them sauntering dead-eyed after him as if they were in a rock video. "Get down!"

"Get funky," Thanatopsis replied stonily.

Krupinski glared at the two Goths as they joined him behind the half wall. "What the hell was that? You could have been seen!"

"What's the use of conquering the world anonymously?" Thanatopsis asked.

"Jeez! What if the elevator opened and the Miracle–"

Calliope set her hand over his mouth as the elevator bell rang. He looked at her with surprise, but she said, "Shh. She's here."

The elevator doors slid slowly open. A man in a charcoal-gray suit and a woman in a red skirt-suit stepped out. It was Michael and Susan – and she looked amazing.

Krupinski's mouth dropped open, and only then did he realize that Calliope's fingers still remained on his lips.

She drew her hand back and leaned toward him. "Good luck," she whispered and kissed him on the cheek.

Krupinski took a startled breath.

"What was that?" asked Susan Gardner on the other side of the half wall.

"What was what?" asked Michael.

"That sound? Like someone gasping?"

There came a listening silence.

"Probably a vent." Keys clicked, and the trunk yawned open. "Oh, yeah, step stool." Footfalls, a car door opening and closing, the rattle of wood on cement, some tentative steps, and the whine of shock absorbers compressing.

Calliope looked at Thanatopsis, who trembled with excitement. She pantomimed, One, Two, Three!

With surprising agility, the two Goths leaped side by side over the half wall and landed behind Michael Gardner, who was just then folding up his step stool.

Thanatopsis shoved him. "You ever seen a Disciple of Death?"

Michael whirled around toward his attacker. "You?"

Calliope lunged in, driving him back farther. "Death's Disciples!"

Michael retreated.

Back in the trunk of the Beemer, Susan sat up. "What the hell?"

Krupinski didn't leap over the wall, but instead darted around it. Knife drawn and quivering in his hand, he surged up to the trunk and glared down at Susan.

"Krupinski?" she said, shrinking back.

His eyes blazed, and his face was contorted with anger. He whispered furiously, "It's me, Susan. Putting on an act!"

She stared in amazement. "What kind of act?"

"Shhh!" he raged, jutting the knife toward her. "I'm pretending to threaten you with this knife. I'm pretending to force you to come with me."

"Why?" she asked.

"To convince the Death's Disciples that I am genuinely on their side."

"You're not, then?" she replied.

"No. I'm trying to *infiltrate*."

"They won't fall for it unless you take me to them."

"Stab me."

"What?"

"I'm going to reach in, like I'm trying to stab you, but I'm going to put the knife in your hand, and you're going to stab me with it."

Tears swelled in her eyes. "Where?"

"Left shoulder," he whispered. "It'll look like a strike at the heart. Dig it in. There's got to be blood."

"I'm not sure I can do this."

"I am," he replied quietly, and then shouted, "Take this, bitch!" He stabbed down into the trunk, pressing the dragon dagger into her grip.

Susan fumbled to grasp it and turn it around and thrust it up. The narrow blade rammed deep, through skin and muscle, between ribs – too far over.

White pain erupted in Krupinski's chest. He roared. That much wasn't acting. The dragon dagger still jutted from his chest as he staggered back from the trunk and fell to the ground away from the BMW.

Calliope saw him fall. With terror-struck eyes, she rushed toward him.

Thanatopsis stood in amazement as she went, the mace falling limp in his hand.

Michael Gardner unwound like a spring, planting a right cross on Thanatopsis's jaw. The bleach-blond Goth flew backward, his hair forming a Haley's Comet around his astonished face as he fell.

Michael flung down the lid of the trunk and leaped over the fallen footstool and jumped into the driver's seat. The sedan roared, and Michael peeled out backward over the footstool, crushing it. He shot out of the lowest level of the garage, vaulting up a ramp and heading for open air above.

Vision laced in agony, Krupinski watched Michael go. The plan had gone off just as he imagined... Except for the placement of this dagger...

Thanatopsis dropped to his knees beside Krupinski.

"Hey, my knife!" He reached toward the dragon blade.

"Leave it," growled Krupinski. "I'll bleed out, otherwise."

Calliope's eyes were wide and filled with tears. "We have to get you out of here."

"The elevator," Krupinski said. "Take me to the first floor."

"It's still a hundred yards to the Civic."

"We'll steal a car," Krupinski said.

"Help me lift him," Calliope said. As Thanatopsis reached under one arm, Calliope reached under the other. "We're going to the Phantom. We're going to heal you."

34 FAITHFUL FANATICS

On the first level of the parking garage, Thanatopsis used his mace to shatter the passenger-side window of a Fiesta. He reached through the window, fumbled with the latch, and opened the door. "Put him in!"

"Give me a hand," Calliope replied. It had taken both of them to wrestle Krupinski into the elevator and back out again, and she could barely keep him upright against the car. Thanatopsis grabbed one of the man's arms, and the two Goths tried to ease their oversize friend into the compact. Halfway down, Krupinski rolled sloppily backward, hit his head on the door frame, and plopped onto the glass-covered seat.

Thanatopsis shrugged. "Well, he's in."

"You okay?" Calliope asked, lifting his feet into the footwell.

Krupinski looked down over the dragon-dagger that jutted from his chest. "I'm fine."

Calliope fiddled with the shoulder strap. "Should it go *over* or *under* the knife?"

"Neither," Krupinski groaned. "If we crash, I want to die."

Slamming the door, Calliope ran around to the other side of the Fiesta.

Thanatopsis was already there, shattering the driver's side window.

"Hey, the door's unlocked!" Calliope objected.

"I know," Thanatopsis said. "But I got a *mace!*"

Calliope reached into the shattered window and yanked the hood lever. It popped, and Thanatopsis went to hoist it.

Almost delirious, Krupinski said, "You gotta arc from the battery to the dash and cross the solenoid."

"You think we're complete amateurs?" Calliope asked.

Blue sparks flashed, the engine ignited, and Thanatopsis screamed. He flew through the air to crash against a nearby wall.

Calliope ran to him and knelt down. "You okay?"

Wisps of acrid smoke coiled up from his golden locks, and he said in a small voice, "I got a mace."

She pulled him to his feet and thrust her keys into his hand. "You've got to drive the Civic back to the campgrounds."

"The Civic?" he said dreamily, tears coming to his eyes. "She trusts me."

She slapped him.

Thanatopsis's euphoria faded. "Hey, why do *I* have to go back to the campgrounds? I want to meet the Phantom."

"He'd kill you."

"Always wanted to drive that Civic." Still smoking, Thanatopsis loped toward the exit.

Calliope returned to the Fiesta and used an ice scraper to sweep the glass off her seat. She sat down and grabbed the wheel, but it wouldn't turn. "Great."

Krupinski jabbed the ice scraper into the steering column and pried, breaking loose the bottom plate. He leaned over and poked the lock mechanism. The wheel suddenly pivoted. "Anything else you need?" Krupinski asked, slumping.

"I got it from here," she replied. She threw the Fiesta in reverse and slid out of the spot. Shifting to drive, she took off past rows of cars. Signs and arrows led her to the nearest exit, and the transponder on the dash dutifully *bleeped*. The gate arm and spikes retracted just as the Fiesta darted past them and out into evening traffic.

"She got my heart," Krupinski wheezed.

"Who?"

"Susan Gardner."

Lines etched Calliope's face. "Susan Gardner has your heart?"

Krupinski shook his head. "No, she *got* it. She *stabbed* it."

"Oh, thank God."

"What?"

"I mean, that's terrible. But thank God we're going to see the Phantom."

"*You* thank *God?*"

"It's just an expression."

Krupinski took a ragged breath. "I'm pretty bad off, aren't I?"

"You were the last time, too, and you made it."

"But this time, you look worried."

"This time, I know you." Calliope wove patiently eastward through a crowd of cars.

"Taking the same route?"

"Can't," Calliope replied. "We don't have the button in this car. No, we've got to go the other way."

"The other way?"

"The only other way I know." Reaching Michigan Avenue, she turned south in front of the Art Institute of Chicago, then descended a ramp to underground parking. Down one level and then a second and a third, she approached a freight elevator.

"The Phantom works at the Art Institute?"

"No," Calliope replied as she drove the Fiesta onto the elevator. She climbed out of the car and pressed a big red button on the elevator's console. An ancient ironwork gate clanked shut across the opening. Calliope pushed the last button on the panel, marked -76. A red light came on requesting an access key. Calliope stared at the spot. "Damn – sent it with Thanatopsis."

She stalked back to the Fiesta, snatched up the ice scraper, and returned, wedging it into the side of the elevator console and popping it open. Then she yanked off the wires connected to the elevator's ignition key and twisted their ends together.

The elevator jolted and began to descend.

Calliope climbed back into the Fiesta and looked at Krupinski. His eyes were closed, his breath heavy. A narrow line of blood leaked down his chest beneath the dragon dagger.

The elevator entered a long, black shaft. For the first hundred feet of descent, the walls were concrete. Then, they gave way to bedrock. The air outside grew bone-chillingly cold.

Then, suddenly, there was another level: a huge underground warehouse held up by gigantic metal columns. The space was stacked from floor to ceiling with 55 gallon drums.

Calliope's ears popped.

That level gave way to more darkness. Then another level opened: a floor filled with girders and bags of concrete.

Her ears popped again.

More darkness, and a huge warehouse with wooden crates.

Dropping away, the elevator at last reached bottom, and the gates shuddered open. Calliope backed out.

The Fiesta rolled into a small cavern that had been hollowed out of bedrock. From this chamber, tunnels radiated in five directions. This was the deep labyrinth – hundreds of feet down and hundreds of miles of tunnels. She'd rarely come this way before.

The Fiesta rolled slowly into the middle tunnel – wider than the others – and Calliope sped up to forty miles an hour. A minute later, a smaller tunnel crossed her path, but she kept going. Another minute passed before she reached a wider passage.

"Fifty-fifty chance," she said, turning left.

Luck was with her: after a mile and a quarter, she saw the other freight elevator. The door was open, and she drove onto it. She took the ice scraper to the console, pried the panel open, and hotwired it. Then she pressed the button for the penthouse.

"Pretty ballsy," she told herself. Never had Calliope gone to Mr Evers unsummoned. Never had she ridden this elevator, let alone with a non-Disciple and a Fiesta. This could be a death sentence.

For Krupinski, the dagger already was.

The elevator rose slowly up the shaft.

Then there was a floor with a massive bank vault.

More darkness.

Then a floor of mainframes and servers.

More darkness.

Then they were rising through a structure: I-beams and retaining walls marked *B3, B2, B1, G, 1, 2, 3*. There were sixty-seven floors before the elevator shuddered to a halt.

The gates ratcheted open.

Calliope climbed from the Fiesta and looked out.

Beyond lay an empty hallway with black walls and a black floor and a black ceiling. A row of golden inset lights led down the hall.

"Mr Evers? It's Calliope Dirge."

"Ms Dirge," came a cold voice, startlingly close.

Calliope turned to see the well-tailored mannequin-man standing beside the elevator. "Sorry, sir."

His eyes changed not a whit. "You've brought me a – Fiesta?"

"I've brought you Sergeant Krupinski."

"Why?"

"He's ready to join us."

"*I* will be the judge of that."

Mr Evers jolted past her, his Plasticine shoulder knocking her aside as he strode up to the window of the Fiesta and looked in. "Nice knife."

"Susan Gardner did that," Calliope explained. "He was trying to grab her, but she stabbed him."

"*Did* she?" Mr Evers eyes clicked like cameras.

"He's proved his loyalty. You have to heal him and re-
ceive him into the Death's Disciples."

Unmoving, Mr Evers rasped, "I do not *have* to do anything."

Calliope looked down at the floor. "Of course not."

He straightened with a slight grinding noise. "Though
your suggestion has merit in one sense. To bring him
into the Disciples, I must search his mind. The ultimate
test. And if he does not pass it, I'll kill him from the inside." Mr Evers lunged through the window and grasped
Krupinski's head.

Krupinski jolted awake – but he couldn't move.

Someone had him.

Someone *knew* him.

There was a mind rummaging through him. It pulled
out memories and stared at them: the faded blue tints
of Monet's *Water Lilies*... that night of sweat and grunts
with Nurse Mitchell... the Death's Disciple jamming his
finger into the trigger and painting his brains on the
wall...

The mind laughed. It felt a kind of delighted irony.

And it moved on, ransacking more memories: ogling
the waitress in the dirty spoon, watching Krupinski
shake hands with Bob Schneider and jab him with the
hypodermic...

It stopped.

It pondered.

A cruel calculus tumbled through the mind. It wondered if Krupinski had used midazolam on Susan,
wondered if he'd kept her an amnesiac for his own ends.

Brilliant, it thought – just what *it* would have done.

The mind rummaged onward...

There was the cracked vinyl interior of the delivery car, and the melted mozzarella draping the stick.

There was the Silverado's side-view mirrors with corn stalks jammed in the joints.

There was the dreary Greyhound, the snoring Susan Gardner, the suddenly wakeful Dave Jenkins...

The mind pulled back. It listened to the plans and heckled them.

It now knew that this whole thing had been a frame-up. It knew that Krupinski wanted to infiltrate Death's Disciples and bring them down.

There were more flashes: jazz cords among dark maples, motorcycles skidding under semis, a Ren Faire dragon knife piercing Krupinski's heart.

Oh, how hilarious, it thought, *how sickeningly noble, how fated to fail. Did she try to kill you, or was her aim that bad?*

Now it knew Krupinski's plan in full. Now it would kill him.

The mind wrapped his medulla and squeezed.

Krupinski's heart was losing the will to beat.

His lungs were sick of air.

Better to go this way than staring at *Water Lilies*.

Then, suddenly, the mind eased its grip.

Krupinski's heart remembered to beat.

The mind went back to ransacking his brain.

What was it after?

It grabbed the memory of Krupinski and the knife and Susan in the trunk, and it lit the edge of the memory and burned it away.

The mind grabbed the notes from the plan Jenkins and Krupinski had hatched on the Greyhound and shredded them.

It traced its way back through Krupinski's memory, destroying the parts that offended it.

And as each memory went, Krupinski was changed.

Why was he angry about Elseworth? Why would he choose to save Susan Gardner? What a fool he had been! If only he could make up for it all, now.

If only he could serve Death's Disciples.

The mind smiled and Krupinski smiled. That was all he wanted.

To make his master happy.

Calliope watched the whole thing in horror. Mr Evers's hand was sparking, and Krupinski's eyes were smoking. This was an execution.

But then Mr Evers lifted his hand from the man's forehead. The last of the lightning crackled as he lowered his fingers to curl around the hilt of the dragon dagger. Mr Evers closed his eyes, smiled, and yanked the blade free. A jet of arterial blood spattered the windshield of the Fiesta. Mr Evers shoved his glove-like hand down against the wound. The red gush slowed and stopped. His fingers glowed. The aura sank into the flesh and cauterized it.

Mr Evers drew his hand from the man's bloodied chest and stared down with eyes like warm paste. "Are you well, now, Disciple Krupinski?"

The man blinked blood out of his eyes and looked up mutely at his master.

"Are you well?" Mr Evers repeated.

Krupinski's eyes and mouth smiled together. "I am, Lord. And I will tell you everything I know about Susan Gardner and the FBI."

Mr Evers gave a mechanical laugh. "I already know everything you know."

"Then how can I serve you?"

The perfectly tailored man made an awkward half-bow, gestured stiffly to them, and turned away. "Follow me." He retreated down the black hallway.

Krupinski opened the door of the Fiesta and stepped out. Calliope's fingers interlaced with his, and they walked side by side after Mr Evers.

He led them to a two-story great room. Floor to ceiling windows looked out on nighttime Chicago, a collage of lights set in blackness. Beneath the windows, a sunken living room held chairs and couches in leather and chrome. A set of metal stairs spiraled from the living room up to a balcony with iron balustrades. An iron-work chandelier glowed dimly above it all.

"Beautiful," Calliope said.

Mr Evers turned, lifting his ear as if to catch the last echo of her voice. "Precisely. Beautiful. Keats said, 'Beauty is truth, and truth is beauty. That is all we know on earth–"

"And all we need to know," Calliope said, looking up at Krupinski.

"I am beautiful," Mr Evers said, lifting his perfectly proportioned arms. "And you are, too, now that you are remade."

"Yes," Krupinski said. "How can I serve you?"

Mr Evers's mouth hitched open, but there was no hint of breath as he spoke: "You have proved yourselves to me, but you must prove yourselves to the other Disciples."

Krupinski said, "You want me to get Susan Gardner."

"Something like that."

35 CLOSET CHRONICLES

"You think I killed him?" I ask numbly as I sit in our kitchen.

"Maybe," Michael replies, "but he had it coming, if you did." He lifts a pair of Lean Cuisine chicken alfredos from the twin microwaves and brings them to the butcher-block counter where I sit. "At least you bought us a little time."

I look down at the inviting picture on the cardboard cover, and then peel it back to reveal a steaming tangle of limp noodles and tormented chicken. "Wow."

"I know." Michael jabs a fork into his dinner, turning it over as if something better might lie beneath. "Still, it's better than jail food."

I push the food away. "Tell me about Banswyth-Stiller."

Michael has just deposited a glob of alfredo on his tongue, and whether because of the heat or the taste, his eyes bug. He looks at me as if I might help, and then hurriedly chews and swallows. Bolting up from his stool, he grabs a dusty glass from the cabinet, runs some water in it, and gulps a drink. "Sorry."

"You're braver than I."

"No. Just hungrier." Michael takes one more swallow of water before he manages, "Banswyth-Stiller… where to begin?"

"Give me the gist."

His eyes light. "Let me get my briefcase."

"No! Just sit down and tell me the *generalities* of it."

Michael nods, heading back over to his steaming meal. "Chicago's had gridlock for fifty years, like a heart having a massive coronary every morning and every evening. But people put up with it until Chicago lost the 2016 Olympic bid. Mayor Daley went wild. He'd already approved Banswyth-Stiller to build in five sites around the city, and we'd already lined up contractors and suppliers. Then, when Chicago got dropped for Rio, we thought the whole thing was dead."

"What happened?"

"*You* happened, Sis. You waltzed into Daley's office with plans for an all-new underground: eight lanes in each direction along arteries running to all compass points, new Metra lines as well as high-speed rail making Chicago the Midwest hub of the nationwide service."

"And Daley went for it?"

Michael smiles shyly. "Susan, when you set your mind to something, you get it."

"Sounds like a logistical nightmare."

"It would be, except for your team. You brought on Marcus and Lee – our lead negotiator and lawyer – best in the business. You also roped in Andrea Schipe, our lead architect, and Philip Westbury doing project management. And you'd be amazed at our intel guy. He used to work at Google, and then for the CIA. Guy stepped on a land mine in Afghanistan, got his legs and arms blown off. Still, he survived, and lucky for us. He's got one of the greatest brains in the world."

"Wow."

"They're *your* team, Susan," Michael says. "Remember what Mr Nero said? People *follow* you. At first, it was just you and Nero, but you recruited the rest of this talent to do the job."

My face flushes. "It's so weird. They're all here because of me, and I don't know them. They all were depending on me, and then those goddamned Death's Disciples..."

"I know."

"One bomb, and three hundred sixty-one people die, and a ten billion dollar project hangs in the balance." My heart twinges. "Is that why they're after me, the Death's Disciples? Imagine if they could get control of this underground system."

From outside comes a muffled shout.

Cold flushes down my spine. "Not again."

Michael jolts up and lunges at the light switch, flipping it off. Darkness envelops the kitchen.

I feel my way along the counters toward the window. "It's probably more paparazzi," I say in a hushed voice.

Michael follows, stumbling through the dark. "They never give up."

I reach the window and peer through the curtain.

Beyond, the horizon is a long black line interrupted by occasional conic shrubs. In their midst walk figures. Six figures. They don't look like reporters. They look like warriors.

"Fuck," I say.

Michael breathes nervously beside me. "This is why we're paying the security people."

"Yeah, we'll see what we're paying for."

"They're ready. They've got flak jackets. Machine guns," he says almost desperately.

A shout comes, indistinct beyond the glass. Figures move in the foreground – guards with guns. They rush outward, and two taser probes leap toward the advancing forms. They spark in the chest of one of the intruders, showing a big man in camouflage – no cameras but plenty of guns. Convulsing, he falls to the ground.

"See?" Michael says.

Bullets erupt from the guns of the other invaders. The kitchen window shatters, and a guard nearby falls to the ground.

Michael grabs my arm. "Death's Disciples!"

We drop to our knees and crawl away among the counters and cutting tables. Behind us, shouts and gunshots ring out. More bullets rip through the curtains and obliterate a wine rack on the far side of the kitchen. Merlot gushes.

We scramble into the main entry beside the two-story great room.

"We're wide open here. Keep going!" I run upstairs, and Michael is right behind me.

Bullets follow us. They rip through the living room windows, bringing them down in a cascade of glass. Slugs pound into walls and woodwork.

"Get to your bathroom!" he shouts.

We dash across the balcony and into the bathroom, closing and locking the door and turning on the light.

Michael and I linger there, just behind the door, listening.

A siren screams to life. "The cops and guards'll stop them," Michael says hopefully.

"Shh, listen."

Everything has gone silent – everything except the siren.

"They've stopped them," Michael breathes. "The cops've stopped them."

Then the siren ceases, too.

"Why would they turn off the siren?"

"The cops didn't," I say flatly. "Death's Disciples did."

Then comes a *boom*.

"What was that?"

Again, it comes, the deep *boom* of a boot against the front door.

"Someone's trying to break in," I say.

"The door's got two dead bolts and a couple slide-chains."

Glass shatters rhythmically – the butt of a rifle smashing through a window.

"Doors don't matter now."

I swat down the light-switch, plunging the bathroom into total darkness. "Into the closet."

Michael and I retreat through the closet doors and close them behind us. The scent of cashmere and silk fills the air. We retreat past thousand-dollar suits and platoons of shoes.

Again, the sound of a boot, this time splintering the bathroom door and banging it against the wall. A wedge of light appears beneath the closet doors.

We watch the light. There are two faint foot-shadows in it. They shift and grow darker.

He knows we're in here.

I reach behind me and pull open the doors to the S & M closet. Grabbing Michael's arm, I drag him through and close the doors. I draw back among the bondage costumes on one side, and Michael hides among rubber suits and ball gags on the other.

"You knew about this closet?" I whisper.

"Of course."

"But you're my *brother*."

"I was never *involved*!"

The hinge on the outer closet door sings softly as someone opens it. Again, the light comes on, shining beneath and between the inner doors. The man advances. One footstep. Two. Maybe he won't walk to the end. Maybe he won't notice the other doors.

I look back to see if I can go deeper, but a gleam on the back wall catches my eye. A bit of jewelry? No, a handle? But why a handle on the back wall of *this* closet?

Unless it's another door…

Rising from the leather jungle, I step up to that handle and pull it back and stare.

The slim band of light shines on a machine gun. It stands upright in a gun rack in the wall. I reach slowly toward it, my knuckles brushing other weapons on either side. One hand fastens on the stock of the machine gun, and the other on the barrel.

I *know* this weapon.

An M249 SAW, fully automatic, carrying a 5.56 x 45 mm NATO shell. I slide the M16 magazine from the pocket and feel that it's full. I shove it back in place.

Even in the dark, I know exactly how it fits.

There are two shadows visible under the closet doors, the feet of the man who is opening them. He leads with his gun muzzle.

I brace the stock of my own gun on my hip and pull the trigger and watch orange blasts pop free. Bullets trace a vertical line between the doors. A couple ping off the man's gun, but the others basically cut him in half. He slumps forward, gun wedged, holding him up.

Behind him, another man barks, "Got 'em?"

I stride up to the doors and kick them. The corpse falls back and the doors swing open, and I'm firing again. The other man stands at the head of the closet and jolts as the rounds rip through him. He falls, too.

It's good. My clip is empty. I go back to the gun rack and lean the smoking SAW in its slot and grab whatever is next to it.

"AK-47," I say admiringly. "Every girl's got to have one."

"Where did you get those?" Michael squeals from among the leather teddies.

"You didn't know about these?"

"*No!*"

"Me, neither," I reply, pushing through the closet doors.

"Where are you going?" Michael calls.

"Going to end this." I step over the first dead man – a sixty-ish white man in worn fatigues with an Ash-Wednesday cross on his forehead. Then I walk to the second, another older man. He could have been the first one's brother. "They're not Death's Disciples."

"What?"

"They're more like… I don't know… Baptists."

"Be careful. There might be more."

Funny thing about having an AK-47 – you kind of hope there *are* more.

I step back over the corpses and go to the bathroom door and visually sweep the hall. Nobody there. I go to the great room and kitchen and back parlor. No one. All is silent. I walk back to the great room and its shattered windows and pull back the riddled curtain.

The backyard looks like a battlefield. There are probably ten bodies lying beneath the moon.

Two cops, four security guards, and four of the – whoever the hell they are – along with two more inside. Maybe that's all of them.

I go back to the bathroom closet and call my brother out of the leather gear. "They're gone. You can come out, now."

"You sure they're gone?"

"Yeah, for sure, because it was never them in the first place." Sirens begin in the distance, growing louder. "And it sounds like more cops are here." I walk through the closet and put the AK-47 back where it had been and close the doors. I bunch a couple rubber suits in front. "Let's get out of here. The cops'll have enough questions."

Only then does Michael clamber out from the leather teddies and follow me into the outer closet. He steps gingerly over the first corpse, a dotted line in red drawn down his body. "What's going to happen when the cops find your bullets in them?"

"Lucky for me, they used M16s," I reply, looking down at the gun in the man's hand. I kick it loose and pick it up, making sure to put my fingerprint on the trigger. "Same ammo as the SAW. We'll just say I got the gun away from this guy and used it against him." I toss the gun down on the bathroom floor.

Michael winces as we step over the second corpse, but the fear in his eyes is really for me. "How do you know all this, Susan?"

"I'm not sure."

Beyond us, a voice cries out in the darkness: *This is the Chicago Police Department. You are surrounded. We will be throwing tear gas into the house unless you come out now with hands up and weapons down.*

"Tear gas?" Michael asks. "We don't want that."

"You never get it out of the carpet."

I take Michael's hand – clammy and cold – and we walk together toward the front door. Cop lights shine fitfully through the diamond-shaped window. I slide back the two chain locks, and Michael undoes the two deadbolts. Together, we draw the door open and step out onto our front porch.

Spotlights break over us, and we lift our hands and stare into their blinding eyes.

"Get down!" the cops instruct.

We drop to our knees and then to our faces.

Men are moving across the lawn, their boots clipping grass as they come. One such boot comes down on my back, and another on Michael's.

"We're the victims!" he shouts.

"I'm Susan Gardner," I add quietly. "The homeowner."

"I'm her brother," Michael puts in.

"We're unarmed, but the Death's Disciples weren't."

The boot comes off my back, and the other off Michael's. We're breathing a bit easier, but there are two men in assault gear staring down at us. "Mind if we sweep the premises?"

"Sweep away."

36 VOICES

"I'm going to need everyone's cooperation if we're going to do this," Dave Jenkins shouted, standing in the center aisle of Flight 311. Most of the passengers fixed their terrified eyes on him, but a few were still watching the monitors. "You all saw what just happened. We *have* to go back into police custody. Otherwise, she'll get us all killed."

"Come off it," said a short man in a rumpled Bears jacket. "She just committed murder. If we go back into custody, they'll give her the chair."

"Illinois doesn't have the chair."

"Why does she even have machine guns?" asked Karen Schneider, chewing the ends of her page-boy hair. "She's supposed to be a banker."

"Even her *brother* didn't know about the guns!"

"None of that *matters*," Dave shouted. "What matters is that we get taken into protective custody."

"They'll take her in, all right," said the Bears man, "for murder."

Dave's face flushed. "It was self-defense! They killed her security guards and two cops. They'll give her a fucking medal!"

"Not when they find those guns."

"She won't let them."

"*Course* they'll find 'em! There's a body right in the

247

doorway to the kinky closet, and bullet holes in the door. They got to investigate that stuff. She's in custody once they find them guns."

"I think they found them!" yelled one woman, jabbing her finger at her monitor. "Look!"

Even Dave Jenkins turned toward a monitor and slid on his earphones.

37 SHOW ME THE WAY

Michael and I stand shivering on the front lawn, red and white lights kaleidoscoping around us. Overhead, the sky is black.

"What's taking them so long?" Michael asks.

"We're about to see."

The lead officer emerges – short and muscular. As he approaches, I see that his name badge reads *Sergeant Sanchez*.

"The house is clear, Miss Gardner, Mr Gardner – but we're going to have to ask you to come inside and explain a few things."

"You know, we don't have to say anything," Michael replies.

Sergeant Sanchez sighs. "That's true. You have rights. I haven't read them to you because I haven't decided whether to arrest you. But if you don't explain a few things, I'll *have* to arrest you."

"It's fine," I tell him. "Yes, I want you to know what happened. It started when Michael and I were in the kitchen."

"Show me the way."

38 COOKING UP GOD

Mr Evers stepped through the dark archway. "Your first mission for the Death's Disciples waits within." He flipped on the light. "*Voila.*"

Krupinski and Calliope looked around at a large kitchen with black marble counters and stainless-steel appliances. Krupinski's eyes zeroed in on a knife rack. "You want us to stab her?"

"Stab whom?" asked Mr Evers.

"Susan Gardner."

Mr Evers shook his head slowly. "Didn't work so well last time."

"What are we supposed to use, then," Krupinski asked, "a blender?"

Mr Evers's rubbery lips drooped in a frown. "When I searched you, you didn't seem this stupid. Yes, you'll use the blender. Yes, knives. But not on Susan Gardner. On food."

"Food?" Krupinski and Calliope said together.

"Disciples eat, too."

Krupinski's eyebrows quirked. "I'm actually a fairly good cook."

"So am I," piped Calliope.

"I wouldn't have asked you otherwise." Mr Evers stepped over to one refrigerator and pulled open the door, revealing tray upon tray of chocolate treats. "We have plenty to do. We'll finish the bon bons tonight, and tomorrow we'll make the cake and finish the rest of the sweets."

"Sweets?"

"They'll keep," he explained. "Of course, it'll be day-off for the breads and appetizers and the entrees – aged steak and Chilean sea bass – but as long as the sweets are done ahead of time – oh, and the wines: must select and crate the wines – we should be fine."

Calliope's mouth hung open. "You're the Death's Disciples' cook?"

The man's masklike face looked somehow even more expressionless. "My dear, I am not a cook. I am a chef. And that is only a minor role I play." He pivoted, walking toward a hallway at the back of the kitchen. "Let me show you another room."

They followed him down the hall, past a small bathroom and to a large room lit entirely by hundreds of monitor screens.

"Whoa!" Calliope said as they stepped inside.

It looked like a smaller version of NASA ground control, but built for a single individual. Three huge flat screen monitors hung on the walls, one cycling through security camera shots of the bank vault below, another showing similar shots from the computer mainframes deep underground, and the third showing the base of the freight elevator.

Calliope's breath caught short. "You saw that we were coming."

"I saw what you did to my elevator control."

"I'm sorry about that, sir."

He shook his head. "You demonstrated a weakness in the system."

Below the large displays were many smaller flat screens, mounted in a semicircle and descending toward a curved desk that hosted an array of computers. The central station of the desk had a single keyboard and mouse and a plush chair on rollers. Beneath the desk was a long row of servers.

"This is my other job for the Disciples," Mr Evers said. "IT."

Krupinski stared in amazement at all the flashing screens. "How do you keep track of it all?"

Mr Evers strode to the chair and sat, looking very kingly. "I use a visual aggregator wired into my brain."

"They have those?" Krupinski asked.

"*I* have those. I invented it, as well as many of the machines you see here. I also wrote the code. Have you heard of Conscious 1?"

Krupinski's eyes grew wide. "The government search engine?"

Mr Evers smiled, "Got that one from Dave Jenkins, didn't you? A crude but accurate description. Conscious 1 is a new digital god, and I programmed it."

Krupinski scowled. "How? You're a Disciple."

"I was a spook, then – project leader on Conscious 1 and smartest man in the CIA. But they betrayed me – with disastrous personal consequences." He gestured to his body. "So Death's Disciples recruited me."

Calliope stepped toward the man. "Is that why – your hands... your face?"

"The Disciples bought me new ones. I designed them

myself – created my prosthetic arms and legs. I built this animatronic face and screwed it to what was left of my cheekbones."

"You're a living mannequin," Krupinski blurted. "That's why you don't mind wearing suits all the time."

"Mannequins look good in suits. And the wool doesn't bother me. I don't feel textures the way you do."

"I used to be afraid of you," Calliope said, "but now, I feel sad for you."

Mr Evers's mouth hitched. "You should feel sad. But also afraid. I retain control of Conscious 1. The government thinks they control it because I let them use it to search for terrorists. But it is my god – and I am using it to prepare the Ascension."

"What ascension?" Krupinski asked.

Mr Evers waggled his finger. "More than you need to know just now, Sergeant Krupinski. Enough of IT. It's back to bon bons."

"Wait!" Krupinski said, pointing to one of the smaller screens in the array. "What does that crawl say about Susan Gardner?"

Mr Evers turned toward the wall of screens and released a metallic gasp. He closed his eyes and, without touching the keyboard or mouse, changed the feeds going to the screens, flinging the Fox feed to the large one in the middle.

"He's wireless!" Calliope whispered.

Sound rose from hidden speakers, and the video image rewound to the beginning of the report.

The *Unvarnished* logo blazed, and a stamp came down to indicate that this was a "SPECIAL EDITION." The logo dissolved into a graphic with heavenly light above and hellish flames below, and the words, "Miracle or Monster?" It, too, cleared away, and the camera swooped down on the cotton-candy hair of a pugnacious newsman.

"Cameron Steel," growled Krupinski.

"There's not a lot of things that could get me out of bed at midnight, folks, but this Susan Gardner story is one of them. Craziness! No one knew where Susan Gardner was – no one except Death's Disciples. Tonight, Susan Gardner's private residence in Oak Park was attacked by a band described by neighbors as a 'terrorist hit squad.' Two cops lie dead, and four private security guards also, as well as six members of this terrorist group. We go now to Fox News reporter Nina Roberts, live in Oak Park."

The screen changed to show a young, model-beautiful Latina standing across the street from Susan Gardner's home. The house flashed with the circus-lights of a dozen cop cars. "Thanks, Cameron," Nina said. "It's been a scene of absolute chaos here. As you mentioned, there are multiple dead – unconfirmed reports of two police officers, four security guards, and six of Death's Disciples."

Krupinski's teeth ground together. "We failed."

Mr Evers looked up at him and laughed, a hitching sound. "*We* didn't attack Susan Gardner's home."

"We *didn't*?"

Mr Evers shook his head. "No. It's the Christian Unified Front out of Kansas. They're the militant wing of the Westboro Baptist Church. They take every word in the Bible literally and swear to kill anyone who opposes

God. They say that Susan is the Whore of Babylon, and so they want to kill her."

Calliope's brow furrowed. "Did they – these Christians – did they blow up Flight 311?"

"No, of course not," Mr Evers said almost angrily. "*We* did that. Now be quiet, and watch the report."

"…indications that, during the gunfight, Susan Gardner wrestled a machine gun from one of her attackers. Purportedly, she used the machine gun to kill him and another Disciple."

"Wow!" Krupinski said.

Mr Evers only nodded, listening.

"It certainly is a startling image, to think of this woman that we've all come to regard as a victim instead becoming a warrior in her own cause."

"She's a warrior indeed," Cameron Steel broke in, and the video abruptly switched to the *Unvarnished* newsroom. "Here's a woman who survived a terrorist attack and a subsequent assassination attempt that left seven dead in Montana. Then there was incarceration by the notoriously corrupt Chicago Police Department – who couldn't even keep her safe in her own house on Main Street USA! But when terrorists attack her in her own home, this rockin' chick gets a machine gun from one of them and takes him out and his buddy to boot! That's America!"

From off-camera, Nina Roberts said, "It's surprising she even knew how to fire a machine gun. If I had to grab one–"

"It's more than surprising," Cameron broke in. "In this day and age in which second amendment rights are trampled and only criminals have guns, to have a young woman who not only gets a gun away from a criminal but also blasts him with it – well, she's my new hero."

Krupinski shook his head. "She turned my knife on me and turned his gun on him."

"That wasn't *his* gun," Mr Evers said with a sigh. "It was *hers*."

"How do you know?" asked Krupinski.

Mr Evers grinned so broadly that his cheeks creaked. "A little god told me."

39 HOW I SHOT THEM

"Yes, I shot him," I say. "I shot them both."

Sergeant Sanchez nods and points at the M16 that lies beside the corpse in the closet. "With this gun, here?"

"Yes," I reply. "He was opening the closet door, and I kicked him in the groin and grabbed the gun and shot him."

"You were standing where?"

I step over the body, go into the S & M closet, and turn around halfway in. "Right here, sir."

"He was opening these doors, and you kicked him in the groin and took his gun, backed up a few steps, and shot him?"

"Yes, sir."

"How did you shoot the other one?"

"As this one was falling, the other one ran into the bathroom and was lifting his gun, so I shot him, too."

Sergeant Sanchez looks levelly at me. "It's a pretty strange closet you have."

I feel myself blush. "Yes, but it's always consensual. There's nothing illegal about it."

"It gets weirder the deeper you go."

"Hmm?"

"Leather suits, then rubber suits, then gags and masks, and finally, there's camouflage and flak jackets and SWAT team shit."

I laugh. "Oh, that. Yeah, well, everybody's got different kinks."

He rolls his eyes. "It doesn't look good. You're supposed to be some kind of hero, and you got this stuff in here. You're hiding in here with your brother, and you kill a man in the doorway."

"I know," I say. "I know. But the clothes don't have anything to do with it."

"They're part of a crime scene."

"Yeah, I guess they are."

Sergeant Sanchez sighs. "Look, your secret's safe with us. Yeah, we cops'll know, but we got a gag order from the top. Anybody who talks to the press gets fired, by order of Chief Gregory."

"He's a good man, Chief Gregory."

Sanchez nods. "Yeah, but he won't be happy to hear about all of this shit."

40 **DAVE'S DETRACTORS**

"There! Do you see?" Dave Jenkins raged at the other passengers. "We *have* to intervene. She's lied to Sanchez, and he's swallowed it. The shame of the kinky closet has kept him from looking deeper. He's already telling his troops not to ask questions. They'll never find the guns. They won't take her in!"

"She don't need to go in," said a thin man in a flannel shirt. "She got the firepower. And she'll get twice the cops and three times the security."

"What good is it going to do?" Dave shot back. "All it takes is one bullet."

Karen Schneider stood up. "It's like you don't even care about her, though. All you want to do is save yourself. You heard her. She doesn't like sleeping in a cell. And she's trying to get her life back."

Dave's eyes blazed. "Half an hour ago, you wondered why she had machine guns!"

"I'm allowed to change my mind!" Karen said. "Bob and I have guns. You can have guns and be a good person."

Dave threw his hands out. "Listen, I've got files on Susan. She can't have a secret arsenal and be a good person."

Karen Schneider's brows knitted. "Why do you have a file on her?"

"I've got files on all of you."

"What the hell?" said the man with the Bears jersey.

"It's for your own protection," Dave said. "I was trying to prevent this attack."

"Nice job," Mr Bears said. "So, you're the reason we're dead."

"No. Death's Disciples is the reason."

"You've been *spying* on us?"

"This isn't about me," Dave said, "this is about her."

"You never cared anything about her."

Dave raged. "You're letting her kill us!"

"Better than letting *you*!"

41 **LADY IN RED**

The photos and specimens have been taken.

The bodies have been hauled away, the press driven to the ends of the block.

The shattered windows are boarded.

The police lines are strung. All is secure.

As morning sunlight pours down on our riddled home, four cops stand posted at the corners. The new security guards are in place as well, bringing with them a formal letter of apology for the failure of the last team.

Meanwhile, inside, Michael and I are on our knees in the bathroom, scrubbing away the blood. It's a somber way to spend a morning, especially since Michael keeps sending suspicious looks my way.

"All right, I killed two men, but I saved your life, didn't I?"

Michael looks wounded. "How come you have all those guns?"

Yellow-gloved hands wring the blood from my rag into a bucket. "There's a funny thing about amnesia, Michael. You don't remember things."

"And why didn't I know about them?"

"Probably because I knew it would freak you out, like it's doing right now."

"But why, Susan? Why guns?"

I lean my bloody knuckles on the white floor. "I don't

261

know. You said that to pull off the Banswyth-Stiller account, I had to work with the Mafia."

"Of course. This is Chicago."

"Well, maybe things weren't as smooth as you thought. Maybe there were some death threats. Maybe I wanted to be ready."

Michael is rubbing his cloth at a particularly dark splotch in the grout. "You'd buy *one*, then. One gun. You wouldn't have a dozen."

I laugh, flinging my hand at the closets. "I don't have *one* of anything, Michael."

"Yeah, but you *use* all of that. I've *seen* you. Those suits, those shoes – you wear them into battle. The other closet, too. Regularly. If you've got all those guns, you've been using them. For *what*, though?"

I sit back against the tub, letting the bloody washcloth slump beside me. "I don't know. Maybe the Death's Disciples were after me even before the flight. Maybe they were trying to take me out. I thought I could defend myself with guns but never realized they'd use a bomb on a plane."

Michael shakes his head slowly. "I don't buy it."

I sigh. "I have nothing else to offer."

"I'm not leaving this house again."

"What?"

"I'm not going anywhere." He looks up at me, his eyes tearful. "They've got to catch these damned Disciples, or I'm not going anywhere ever again."

I put my hand on his shoulder before I remember that there's blood on my fingers. "That's fine. I'll drive *myself* to the party at Mr Nero's tomorrow." Only then do I see that red speckles go up the walls and onto the clothes hanging there. "Damn it! Guess I'll be wearing red."

How it comes back! All these curlers and brushes and picks, the mousse and sprays and makeup. My fingers fly into drawers, grasping foundation and rouge and lipstick and knowing by muscle memory what to do with them.

I'm what to do with them. And I look fantastic.

My hair is curled and lifted and styled, framing my face and showing off my perfect neck. I'm wearing a scarlet Dior cocktail dress that plunges in back, three strands of black pearls, and four-inch black stilettos.

No more lying in trunks for me.

I pick up my black lambskin purse, turn away from the bathroom mirror, and stride through the house. (I can even walk on these skyscrapers.) Flinging open the door to the garage, I descend among my four luxury cars.

"It's got to be the Lamborghini." I walk up to it, checking that it matches my dress. "Of course it does. I wouldn't have bought it otherwise." I open the door, smelling rich leather.

"You're going to get mobbed," Michael says, standing reluctantly in the doorway behind me.

"Think I should take the AK-47?"

"They're going to follow you. It'll be just like Princess Di."

"Who?"

"This isn't a good idea, Susan," Michael implores. "A day and a half ago, we were fighting for our lives. That's excuse enough–"

"The difference between you and me is that I'm *still* fighting for my life. I've got to get it back."

His mouth pops closed, and he nods, swallowing.

I smile fiercely at him. "Love you, Little Brother."

"Love you, too, Big Sis," he replies, adding, "knock 'em dead."

"Always do." I slide into the driver's seat, poke the garage-door opener, and fire up the Lamborghini. Its twelve cylinders roar to life. "I could get *used* to this."

I throw the beast into reverse and squeal the tires backward out of the garage, lining up with the drive. Then I head out. There are no reporters on the street – the cops've driven them off to the ends of the block. Usually we go east, so most of them crowd there.

I go west.

There's a cop car at the end of the block, and journalists on lawn chairs on the shoulder. They look up wearily, hoping for a black Beemer but seeing instead this scarlet-red monster. Most look back down, fiddling with F-stops, but a few crane their necks and stand up and lift their cameras. They step onto the road, but I'm not going to do this like Michael would.

I gun the engine, driving them back. Then I slam on the brakes, and the Lamborghini leaves a beautiful double skid as I halt at the stop sign. The cop is looking at me in alarm and amazement and – is that *admiration?* Shutters begin to snap, the first few photographers knowing who I must be and the others fumbling to get in on the action.

"Too late, boys."

I peel out across the road while paparazzi strain to make out my license plate: DOMN8RX. I tear down two blocks, the roar reverberating from the houses. Not a single car has pulled out to follow. The light ahead is yellow, and I squeal through, heading left. Ahead, cars and vans and trucks form a Tetris board. I slide among them, stacking them up behind me. Even if the reporters try to follow, I'll be in Cicero before they reach I-290.

And, speaking of 290, I hop onto an on-ramp and slide left through four lanes before unleashing the engine. It tops ninety in a second. Fords and Toyotas and Hyundais melt away before me, seeing this red rocket with its flashing headlights.

Young, beautiful, powerful, rich – how can *this* be my life?

The only thing cooler would've been if this was a convertible.

My hand floats down to push a button on the dash. With a click, the roof separates from the windshield, and the hardtop slides back. I scream with delight as air gushes in over the windshield and rolls through the back seat and washes over me, tickling my neck. The hard top tucks itself in the trunk. "*That's* what belongs in a fucking trunk!"

I feel like a different woman. I hope I am. I'm done running and hiding.

It's time for my enemies to run and hide from me.

Mr Nero's given me directions, and my iPhone shows the route in purple, but I don't need any of this. There's a part of me – the *real me* – that knows exactly how to get there and exactly what to say when I arrive.

The rest of the ride is a dream: highway hypnosis. From freeway to off-ramp to street to tunnel to parking

garage. I pull in between a Lexus and an Infiniti and let
the Lamborghini rumble to silence. Why lift the roof?
Why lock it? This is Mr Nero's building. Let somebody
try to fuck with my car. Of course, I *do* press the car
alarm, if only to hear the beast chirrup contentedly behind me as I walk to the elevator. I step on and press P
for penthouse.

Here I am, Susan Gardner in my scarlet cocktail dress,
my hair sassily mussed, my red lips smiling as the elevator opens to the penthouse suite.

"Holy shit, guys," says Marcus, standing there in a
steel-gray Armani. "Suzy's back!" I try to walk past him,
but Marcus crowds me. "What did it for you, Suzy?
Killing those two men? Finding your ballgags?"

"I think it was the ballgags," I say speculatively,
"though I had to throw out the one engraved with your
name. It stank."

Marcus staggers back, eyes not exactly focused.

I push past him into a foyer that centers on an elabo-
rate fountain in gray marble. It depicts a seven-headed
dragon being ridden by a laughing woman. She holds a
golden goblet overhead, which gushes what looks like
red wine. The fluid runs in rivulets down her upraised
arm and across her naked breasts, down the toga that
has slid to her hips, and all across the dragon. The red
stuff also seeps from its seven mouths.

"Interesting," I say.

"You used to call it garish," says Lee, who steps up
with a rock glass full of some amber poison.

"*Garish* is a good word. *Gargling*, too," I add. "Maybe
even *godawful*."

Lee glances at the woman astride the dragon. "Not everybody can pull off a red gown, but you can."

"It's scarlet," I reply, catching his chin in my fingers. "I've been here two minutes, Lee, and you're already talking about pulling off my red gown."

He blushes. "Wow, you really *are* back."

"And you really *are* pulling off that Gucci tonight."

His blush deepens. "I can't keep up with you. You need a drink."

"I want to see Nero."

"Lucky for you, he's at the bar."

Lee takes my hand and leads me around the fountain. On the other side, we step through a wide archway into a long, low room where a five-piece jazz ensemble is playing "Sentimental Journey."

"Nice touch," I tell Lee.

He guides me past conversation nooks and tables to the bar at the far side of the room. There sits Mr Nero. He doesn't rise as I approach, but his eyes do wander over my figure. Somehow, I don't mind. I *want* him to look at me, just as if I were a Lamborghini. He makes the full tour, and then his eyes lock with mine, and he says in his high-pitched voice, "You're looking very fine this evening, my lady."

I nod in thanks. "Feeling very fine, as well, milord."

"You've been busy."

I shrug. "Did my hair. Ironed my dress. Killed some terrorists – the usual."

"Three days ago, you were a lost lamb. Now, you're a hunting lion." He inadvisedly scratches the air with one hand and adds, "*Rrrroowr.*"

"A lot can happen in three days."

"You can raise a messiah in three days."

We both laugh, though Nero sounds almost rueful.

I point at his glass, where ice cubes dissolve in whiskey. "What are you drinking?"

"Glenfiddich," he says.

I lean to the bartender, a white-faced girl with black-dyed hair. "I'll have one of those."

"On the rocks, or neat?" she asks.

"Nothing in life is neat," I reply. "Let's have it sloppy: on the rocks."

Mr Nero smiles at me. "Very provocative, my lady. She asked because you're not supposed to drink Scotch on the rocks. It keeps the malt locked up. You're supposed to have it neat, or with a little water."

I arch my eyebrow at him. "I don't do what I'm supposed to do."

The white-faced girl puts a rock glass of ice and whiskey in front of me. I lift it and sniff the smoky stuff.

"Peat is what you're smelling," Mr Nero goes on in a high lilt. "The waters in Scotland are funneled through peat bogs, thousands of years old. It preserves flesh. There are two thousand year-old bodies lying in the bottoms of the bogs – throats slashed, sacrifices to pagan gods."

I lift the glass. "Kind of like the worm in Tequila." I drink.

He does a double-take. It's almost charming. "You *are* back."

I nod. "You bet I am."

He smiles, and his teeth look very sharp. "Then I have

someone for you to meet." He levers his pear-shaped body off the bar stool and walks me deeper into his plush penthouse. "I wasn't sure you could take her before. This'll be the real test." We stroll into a grouping of low couches around a fondue pot with steaming cheese and jalapeños. Beside it sits a narrow woman with a hawkish nose and pince-nez glasses clinging to the bridge. She wears an old-fashioned dress, the sort that would have fit in at a cake-walk, and her gray-black hair is pulled into a tight bun.

Mr Nero gestures to the woman and says, "Susan Gardner, let me *re*-introduce you to Meg Kariot, the accountant who handles all of our books."

I lean forward, extending my hand. "Hello, Meg. Forgive me for not remembering you."

She does not take my hand, but fixes me with a withering gaze. "Only if you forgive me for *remembering* you."

"Now, Meg," says Mr Nero, "this is the perfect chance to begin again. She doesn't remember anything that happened between you."

Meg's eyes are intense. "It doesn't matter. She's the same person. *Look* at her. *Listen* to her. She hasn't changed."

"Oh, you're wrong there," Mr Nero says. His squeaky voice drops, suddenly low and steady. "She's on a higher level now, Meg. You know that as well as I."

The woman nods her birdlike head, eyes pinned to her feet. "Of course, Mr Nero."

A shout near the fountain makes us turn around. We see Marcus and Lee hugging two more arrivals.

"And the introductions continue," Mr Nero says in a voice like a guinea pig's. He takes my hand and leads me back along the bar toward the newcomers.

As we walk, I ask, "What does Meg have against me?"

"Ancient history," he says with a sigh.

"I need to know."

He turns to me as we walk. "You're the deal girl. You find them, and you land them. Then she's got to get the numbers to work. Of course she hates you. You make work for her – lots of work. And you do it sloppy, on the rocks. She wants it neat and straight. You can't try to please Meg. There's a reason her only friend is a pot of cheese fondue."

Mr Nero is a marvelous man.

He leads me to the fountain to meet two marvelous women. The one in front is tall and beautiful in a low-cut black dress that ends in shimmering peacock feathers. "Susan Gardner, this is Morissa Mane, our marketing manager."

I reach out to shake her hand. "Your name is very alliterative."

Morissa laughs, delight flooding her eyes, and she sings, "Up from the grave she arose!"

"And this," continues Mr Nero, "is Shelly Jones, our Wall Street guru."

Shelly's beautiful as well in her royal purple jacket and gold skirt. She got a great body under it too. I step forward and give her a hug, which she receives willingly, and I wonder if there's something more between us than just friendship.

"Make yourselves at home, everyone," Mr Nero says,

arms outstretched. "There are appetizers and cocktails and sweets and anything your heart desires. Feel free to roam the apartment and the balconies and the rooftop, but, as always, no talk of business outside."

The others all laugh and nod, moving off in clumps.

I turn to Mr Nero. "No talk of business outside?"

He smiles patiently. "You've seen those big audio dishes they use at football games?"

"No."

"They can pinpoint a conversation from a hundred yards, even with the whole crowd screaming."

"I'll take your word."

"There are a dozen of those things pointed at us tonight, and a dozen more cameras. They've got people on staff to read our lips and write down everything we say."

"This Banswyth-Stiller thing is crazy."

"Yeah," Mr Nero says blackly, "crazy."

Five more beautiful faces appear from around the bloody dragon. The new arrivals' eyes light as they see me. "It's Miss Gardner!" declares a thin, well-groomed Italian man, who rushes toward me. He would be dazzlingly handsome if he weren't so clearly gay. He takes me into his arms and shakes me. "You are looking fabulous, girl."

"This is Gino Giavelli," Mr Nero says, "our social media person."

Gino's eyes darken, and he tilts his head as he stares at me. "Still fighting that amnesia thing?"

"Yes," I say.

"Have I got stories to tell!"

"Give me a second, here," says another voice, gruff and direct. With one hand, the man pushes Gino aside and steps before me. He looks like he's wearing football shoulder pads under his Ralph Loren suit, and he takes me in a bear hug. "Good to have you back, Susan."

"This is Dom Niccoli," Mr Nero says, "though we mostly call him E."

"E?"

"He's the enforcer."

Dom's black brows fall as he looks at me. "She don't remember me?"

I smile an apology. "I should, Dom. If I could remember anyone, it would be you."

"Jeez, I mean. We're family. I mean, not really. I got my family, and I'm loyal, but you're the superfamily. You're like my other mother."

I cock my hips and fling my hands out toward him. "I may be a mother, Dom, but I ain't yours. What? I pop you out when I'm five?"

The big man laughs, tears in his eyes. "Okay. Okay. You got me. Ha ha. That's it. You're Susan Gardner, all right."

Three black women also come out of the elevator – one an old lady with gray curly hair, another a round woman in a poncho, and the third a near-girl wearing hip-huggers and a madras vest and a crinkly linen blouse.

"And may I introduce the Andrewses," Mr Nero says. "Matriarch Cheryl, *her* daughter LaCheryl, and her daughter, LaCherylandra."

"Hello," I say, shaking each of their hands. "It's good to get reacquainted."

As the three women greet me, Mr Nero goes on. "They're the community organizers. Chicago's a diverse place, and these three ladies have hit the churches to get them on our side. Cheryl is our liaison with the Catholics and Jews, LaCheryl works the mainline churches, and LaCherylandra is our fundamentalist evangelical charismatic representative."

LaCherylandra waves a warning finger at Mr Nero, "Christians and Muslims, both."

I smile at the three ladies. "Sounds like you've got it covered. I feel sorry for the Buddhists and Hindus."

LaCheryl waves her hand. "Don't feel sorry. They're in with the Methodists and Episcopalians."

I laugh. "Well, then, I guess I feel sorry for the Satanists."

The conversation sputters to a halt.

"Well, there it is," Mr Nero says, setting his hand on my shoulder.

The white-faced bartender approaches me, her tray carrying a single rock glass filled with ice and whiskey. "I noticed you were empty."

I smile at her. "More observant than I," I say, setting the dead glass on the tray and picking up the new one, heavy with whiskey.

The girl nods at me happily and turns away.

Mr Nero takes the glass from my hand and looks suspiciously at the white fluid circling through it. He sniffs it and pours it out into the fountain.

"Hey, that was for me."

"Every once in a while, I give Mystery a drink."

"Mystery?" I ask, watching the ice and liquor mix

with the wine-red water.

"It's written on her forehead."

I shake my head, laughing. "Might as well be written on mine."

Mr Nero turns away from me and raises his voice to all the guests: "Relax and mingle, everyone. You're among friends. Reacquaint yourselves and have fun. Dinner is at nine."

42 I'VE POISONED HER

Sweat inched down Calliope's temple as she hurried through the doors into the kitchen. "You guys! You guys! You won't believe this. Not only is *she* here–"

"She?" asked Krupinski, flipping thick red steaks on the griddle.

"Susan Gardner," Calliope supplied.

"*She's* here?" Krupinski said.

"Of course she is," put in Mr Evers, writing, "Welcome Back," on the frosting of a devil's food cake.

"Not only is *she* here, but I've *poisoned* her!" Calliope finished.

"You've what?" barked Mr Evers.

"I poisoned her whiskey," Calliope said more quietly.

Mr Evers's face crumpled in frustration as he lurched toward the door. He peered through, seeing something that seemed to calm his digital heart. He turned, eyes shining. "Whatever your plans previously, you need to realize that we are *not* trying to kill Miss Gardner."

"What?" Calliope asked. "It's the perfect chance! She's right there!"

"Of *course*, she is," Mr Evers said savagely. "She's *one* of us!" With that, he pushed open the kitchen door and shuffled out into the party.

43 **THE FIRST SUPPER**

Mr Nero taps my shoulder. "Here is the last of our thirteen."

I turn to see a living mannequin. His face is plastic, and his suit looks like it's still on the hanger.

"This is Mr Bartholomew Evers, head of information technology and master chef," Mr Nero says. "You'll be tasting his creations tonight."

Mr Evers bows to us as if he is Japanese. Perhaps he was built there. He smiles mechanically and nods toward the kitchen. "Forgive me, Mr Nero. Two new recruits, as you know – very zealous, but a bit misguided."

Mr Nero fixes him with a level gaze. "The whole reason we have you cook is to avoid such things."

"I know. I know. It won't happen again."

"No, or you'll be serving *them*, if you know what I mean."

"Of course," Mr Evers says with a hitching laugh. "Long pig with a helping of humble pie."

Mr Nero chuckles.

"So good to meet you again," I say, taking Mr Evers's hand, which seems to be made of rubber. "And thank you in advance for the culinary delights you have prepared for us this evening."

"It's an important meal," he says, eyes fluttering like

digits on an alarm clock. "The last supper, as you might say."

I look to Mr Nero, who wears a wide but uncomfortable smile. "Let's call it the *first* supper, my friend."

My head is spinning as I try to remember everyone. There's the Four Horsemen – Mr Nero, Marcus, Lee, and me. Then there's that spinster Meg with her fondue friend, and the alliterative Marissa Mane, and Shelly Jones with her great body. Afterward, I met Gino and Dom; Cheryl, LaCheryl, and LaCherylandra. That's twelve. Who am I forgetting? Oh, yeah, the walking condom, Mr Evers.

They're the core team I put together – lawyers, accountants, politicians, negotiators, marketers, enforcers... These twelve people have mounted the Colossal Dig in Chicago.

Mr Nero suddenly rears back his shaggy head and shrieks, "I'm hungry!" The sound carries easily from elevator to bar. "Gather up!" He turns to me. "Get them in from the balcony. I'll check the roof."

"Sure, Mr Nero," I say.

I step out on the wide balcony that runs around the penthouse. It's sixty-seven floors down to the street, but ahead of me hangs the galaxy that is Chicago at night. More beautiful, still, are the people on that balcony, pausing in their quiet conversation to look my way.

"Come 'n git it!" I yodel.

They smile and laugh, walking toward me.

I suddenly know that I can get away with anything.

Back inside, party goers converge on a long mahogany table with white linens and high-backed chairs.

Mr Nero goes to the center spot and pulls out the chair to his right. "My lady."

I sit, seeing Marcus and Lee take seats to Mr Nero's left. Mr Evers sits to my right. Everyone else crowds in to find a place. Mr Nero is still standing as he motions the jazz ensemble to silence. Conversation stops, too, and we all look up at that pear-shaped man and his Brillo-pad beard.

Mr Nero lifts his hands in invocation: "Lord, you know why we are here tonight: to welcome back our lost lamb. She's been gone so long that we feared we'd never see her again. But now, she's returned, and your plan moves forward. Tonight, we celebrate her resurrection from the dead, as we have celebrated eleven others. And we look to the last, when your kingdom will come on earth. So mote it be."

"So mote it be."

I look up, a little stunned, and see twelve smiling faces. Mr Nero claps his hands together and rubs them vigorously. "Appetizers, then!"

The door from the kitchen bursts open, and the white-faced bartender bustles out, pushing a cart. Behind her comes another cart with a burly waiter.

"Shouldn't he be playing for the Bears?" I asked Mr Nero.

He titters as he sits down. "We don't *all* get our hearts' desires."

The girl rolls the cart to the opposite side of the table and sets out small plates with steaming wonton wraps. The linebacker does the same on our side, and I can hear him breathing, can see the black hairs on his knuckles as he sets down the appetizer.

I lean to Mr Nero and quip, "The help these days."

"These two are new," he tells me.

When all of us have been served, thirteen forks rise, slicing into the wontons. The soft dough parts beneath my fork, which cuts next through a rubbery knob. Something like a golden grape pops, and then a purplish ooze comes out. I glance aside at Mr Nero, who scoops some of the ooze from his appetizer into a cantaloupe spoon and slides it on his tongue.

"Is that what it is?" I ask hopefully. "Cantaloupe?"

He smiles, shaking his head, eyes closed. His cheeks flutter a little, and then, savoring, he swallows. "Calamari."

I look at the thing on my plate, peeling back the won ton to see the half-severed head of a baby squid. The purple stuff is its brain. "I can't remember – is this something I like?"

"Baby *Architeuthis* – giant squid. The adults have eyes the size of our brains and brains the size of our bodies. They're apex predators with eight arms and two attack tentacles."

"But do I *like* them?"

"The word is *love*."

I cut off part of the thing's cranial cavity and use my spoon to lift a bit of the purple goo to my tongue. I can taste the brine where it lived. Closing my eyes, I swallow.

"Don't feel bad," Mr Nero says with a chuckle. "If they could learn to fish for us, they'd be eating you."

Marcus and Lee laugh at that, but to my right, Mr

Evers seemed unimpressed.

I say to him, "You don't seem to like this appetizer."

He raises his impassive face. "I love this appetizer. I created it."

"Then why aren't you eating it?"

His head pivots, and I can almost hear the ballbearings in his neck. "I can eat. I just can't taste."

"What are you talking about? A chef who can't taste?"

"Beethoven was completely deaf when he wrote his ninth." Mr Evers sighs metallically. "I can't taste any of this, except in my mind."

He watches me. I place another forkful of baby squid brain in my mouth. Around it, I say, "Maybe a blessing."

"The ninth symphony was about death and resurrection, what Beethoven was facing – what we all face. These baby squids should taste exactly like that."

I look around at the others. Their faces are transfixed with joy.

I stall, poking at the squid, cutting it up, shifting it around the plate. Lucky for me, the servers just now return with soup. The linebacker pulls away my half-eaten squid won-ton and sets a bowl in front of me. The soup within is scarlet. "I love tomato soup."

But it isn't. It tastes salty and clotted.

Across the table, Cheryl, LaCheryl, and LaCherylandra lift the bowls to their lips and drink.

"Czernina," Mr Nero says heartily, smacking his lips. "Duck's blood soup. It's from Poland."

"Actually, this is from the Caucuses," Mr Evers breaks in. "Not duck's blood."

"Everything else has been coming back to me," I say with a little laugh. "I wonder if dinner will, as well."

"Blood is very nutritious, and there's plenty of it," Mr Evers says offhandedly. "Used to be what the gods required. Now we pour it down drains."

Next, the salads come, equally disturbing: an assortment of mushrooms sprinkled with bits of jerked meat and a raw egg with a pink yolk. I pick at the mushrooms without comment.

Then comes the main course – steaks perfectly marinated and grilled fresh and served rare. At last, I dig in hungrily. It's only halfway through that I notice I've never tasted a steak like this before. It's not beef or pork. Buffalo? Kangaroo?

The servers bring side dishes. There is a liver pate and some fluffy white material that looks like mashed potatoes but doesn't taste like them. The green beans turn out to be eels. Even the bread looks like fried slices of lung.

"Are you done with that?" asks the hulking waiter, gesturing toward my plate.

"Yes. Take it, please." When I turn to thank him, I see the curly hair and grim face of Steve Krupinski. I almost jolt from my seat. "What the hell are you doing here?"

He doesn't answer, bearing away my plate and disappearing into the kitchen.

I sit, stunned. Why would Krupinski be here? Is he looking out for me? Is he trying to kill me? Then I remember the drink with the white stuff circling through it.

"Um, sir," I say, tapping Mr Nero on the sleeve. He turns, his smile laced with eel. "One of the – I don't know if you know this, but one of the wait staff is Sergeant Steve Krupinski."

Mr Nero's smile only deepens. "Yes. I know."

"I think… that drink you poured out–"

"Poisoned, yes."

"Well, if Krupinski's trying to poison me–"

"No, it was the girl."

I shoot a hateful look at that little Goth monster. "Why isn't she…? Why didn't you…? She's serving us dinner!"

Mr Evers's plastic hand settles on mine. "It's taken care of. Both servants have been forbidden to poison you."

I bark a laugh. "What kind of a place is this?

Mr Nero beams down at me. "You were acting such the beautiful ball-breaker, but you still don't know who you are, do you?"

"Why don't you tell me?"

"You're one of us, Susan, the beloved disciple."

"The *what?*"

"Do you know why Flight 311 blew up?"

I gasp. It's quite a thing to ask. The polite conversation all around us quiets. Faces turn toward me. I swallow and say, "Yes, in fact, I do. There was a bomb on the plane from the Death's Disciples. It was unwittingly carried on the plane by an FBI agent named Dave Jenkins. He had been tipped off by a courier of the Disciples that something big was happening in Seattle, and he packed up to go. But the courier, a girl named Calliope Dirge, apparently planted a bomb in his gun case, which he checked through using FBI immunity. He became the mule for the explosives that ripped out the belly of the plane."

Mr Nero pats his hands together in opera applause, and half of the others joined in. "Very good, Susan. You know *most* of the story. You just forgot who planned the whole thing."

"Who?"

"*You*, Susan."

"What?"

"You asked Mr Evers to create a bomb that could be hidden in a gun case. You asked him to plant the assembly instructions in the mind of Calliope Dirge – who happens to be the bartender and waitress tonight. She took the bomb and inserted it into agent Jenkins's gun case without even knowing what she did. Your perfect plan was perfectly executed."

"*My* plan? This is ridiculous. What are you talking about? Why would I want to blow up a plane that I was *riding* on?"

"Every day, Muslim extremists blow themselves up. What do they do it for?"

"I don't know – seventy-two virgins?"

The table erupts with laughter, and Marcus and Lee lift their glasses to me.

"You got much more than seventy-two virgins," Mr Nero says. "Tell me, Susan, what happened to the other three hundred sixty-one people on that flight?"

"They died."

"And where are they now?"

"I don't know. Some field in Montana."

"No. Susan. They're inside you, aren't they?"

"What?"

"They're *possessing* you."

I'm chilled to the bone. How does he know this?

"You stepped onto that flight as a woman with one soul. You came off that flight as a woman with three hundred sixty-two souls. And tonight you will complete the harvest."

I can feel them inside me – screaming. The ghosts of Dave Jenkins and Karen Schneider and the Amish kid and the others. They're screaming like they're dying again.

I block them. I turn off the fucking monitors of my mind, unplug the audio feed. Let them wonder what I'm seeing, what I'm saying. Let them scream in silence.

"You're telling me that I blew up Flight 311 to harvest the souls around me?"

"There's no other reason that Susan Gardner would ever fly coach," Mr Nero quips wryly, and everyone chuckles.

"If I'm one of…" I stare at them and hitch a breath: "If *we're* the fucking Death's Disciples, who's been trying to kill me?"

"Well, that janitor in the hospital – he was just a lone operator. God told him, apparently, that you were going to bring about the Apocalypse. God was right, of course. The janitor had the job to kill you, but the poor guy couldn't bring himself to do it while you were in a coma. Once you woke up, he had no choice."

I swipe my hand through the air. "So, what, one wacko? What about the others?"

"Well, if you mean Lieutenant Elseworth, he knew who you were, as well. He had access to files that

Krupinski didn't. His orders came from much higher up–"

"God?"

"No, the president."

I bark a laugh. "Why would the president care about me?"

"When they found you at the crash site, you shouldn't have been alive. There was no medical explanation why this woman, multiply impaled, still lived. As you healed miraculously over the next weeks, they realized you were one of us. They had caught their first Death's Disciple."

My skin prickles. "Forget Elseworth. What about the *others?*"

"You mean two nights ago, with the Christian Unified Front? They knew you were the rider on the white horse. They knew you were Conquest, the first judgment of God."

I shoot a look at Marcus and Lee. "So, what about them? I'm the first horseman. What about Marcus and Lee?"

Marcus leans forward and fixes me with a predatory look. "We followed in your footsteps, Suzy. I was meeting with our Colombian contacts when the FARC and the government decided to have it out in that little town. Three hundred forty-five dead," Marcus taps his forehead, "but they're all up here. I've got all their minds, know everything they knew. FARC and the Colombian military and a dozen drug lords and a hundred peasants – I know everything there is to know about War. "

"And you, Lee?"

He shrugs charmingly. "I got taken hostage by Al Qaeda in Sudan. We were herded into the gym of an elementary school. There were thirty journalists, fifty government figures, sixty terrorists, and about two hundred school children – and me, of course. I kept the others alive for five days, rationing the snacks from the vending machine. But then, the government attacked the compound. It was just like Waco. Al Qaeda barricaded the place and set it on fire, and everyone died except for me."

Marcus laughs, slapping Lee on the shoulder. "Lenny's got a hundred kindergartners in his head. He's like the idiot god."

Lee smiles ruefully. "They've got lots of life in them, though, those kids."

"And you planned all of it, Susan," breaks in Mr Nero. "You had a plan for how each of the Four Horsemen would ascend."

"She didn't plan it for me," objected Dom, lifting meaty hands before him. "Me and the others, we had to make it up ourselves."

Mr Nero nods. "Dom strangled his own father and took his soul. Gino took out a rival family at Thanksgiving. Cheryl harvested twelve shut-ins one Christmas, and LaCheryl harvested a whole wing of Our Holy Mercy Hospital – insulin injections between the toes. LaCherylandra was especially inventive. She adopted a twelve year-old boy from an orphanage in Kabul and strapped a bomb to him and went with him to morning prayers at a mosque."

It can't be real. None of this is real.

All eyes are watching me, unblinking. There's not a trace of a smile in them.

"So, why are we doing this? What's the point? We kill all these people just to know what they know? Any of you ever hear of Google? "

"It's not just their knowledge," Lee says. "It's their lives. That's why those kindergarten souls are so good for me. I can die three hundred times before I'll be dead. Same for you. Same for Marcus. The number of lives you take is the number of lives you have."

"I don't believe it," I say blankly.

Marcus sneers. "You've already used lives, Suzy. Probably twenty in that crash. And how many times since then have you been shot?"

"What?"

"Two nights ago, with those Christian Unified goons? And what about that Montana ranch? Bullets in swarms. You had to have been shot."

"No, I haven't been."

Mr Nero sighs. "Mr Evers, would you mind?"

The plastic man pivots toward me, setting his hand on my chest.

"What are you doing?"

Energy flashes around his fingers, and I jerk back, feeling spikes of pain radiate into me. There's something moving in my lung. Something metallic and conical. *Two* things. I feel them burrow out of my skin and into his hand. Still, the power rages and circles, knitting me together. Mr Evers suddenly breaks contact, pulling his hand away to show two slugs crazed in blood. He drops them onto the empty dessert plate before me.

"Those were kill shots," Marcus says. "Two of the three hundred sixty-one lives that you harnessed."

"I don't know. I don't understand any of this."

Mr Nero pats his hands in the air. "But you *will* understand it – tonight. The spell's already begun."

"What spell?"

"Dinner began it. Already, you've eaten human flesh and drunk human blood. And now, there is only the laying on of hands."

Mr Evers suddenly grips my head in both hands.

Power pierces my brain.

His mind ransacks my own, ripping open every closed corpuscle and bringing out the old Susan.

Mr Nero intones, "*Let the possessed become possessor, let the possessors become possessed.*"

The other disciples say it after him.

"*She who has eaten flesh and drunk blood, let her now eat mind and drink spirit.*"

Even I am repeating the spell, word for word.

"*As Saturn, father of the gods, ate his children, let Susan dine and so become a titan.*"

As they chant the incantation, Flight 311 and the screaming passengers on it finally disintegrate. They melt *into* me, pure knowledge – pure life-force. They suffuse me like a drug and open my mind three hundred times over.

Their lives are mine, now.

I cannot die.

I am truly a god.

The rush of soul-force has hurled me back against the

chair. As the surge dissipates, I slowly come to myself, shuddering.

I feel different.

Powerful.

Cruel.

The others are watching me, grinning.

"Twelve have ascended," Mr Evers says grandly, lifting his hands, "and I shall be thirteen. When Banswyth-Stiller is complete, I will harvest all of Chicago."

44 FUNCTIONAL IMMORTALITY

I'm driving my scarlet Lamborghini out on I-290.

The city's the same, the car's the same, but I'm completely different.

Who is Susan Gardner?

I shift down for more power and swing out on the shoulder and roar past an Acura that's hogging the passing lane. He swerves and blares his horn. Then I cut him off.

That's who I am.

I didn't get here by being soft.

I'm not a nice person.

But I'm powerful.

Beautiful.

Rich.

Mashing the pedal, I hurl the Lamborghini up to ninety and flash my headlights. A minivan skates away into the middle lane, an RV jolts aside, but a flatbed with a steel roll blocks the lane...

I swing out on the shoulder and roar up alongside it and cut in front. The truck swerves, the flatbed cants, and the massive steel drum rips through its chains. It goes bounding behind me on the shoulder.

I laugh. It sounds like shrieking.

The huge roll pounds along inches from my trunk. The steel leaps up and catches itself and unrolls like toilet paper. It slides across three lanes, and cars and trucks pile into it, their roofs ripping off…

I roar out ahead, my Lamborghini eating up lanes.

So, this is who I am.

There are worse people to be. The cowering amnesiac running across a hospital rooftop with her ass flashing through her gown. The woman riding on the Greyhound and falling asleep only to become possessed by a failed FBI agent. The woman who spent two hours primping in her scarlet dress in hopes of rising to the level of a very lofty room.

The weakness of that woman disgusts me.

I want to be *this* Susan Gardner.

In the rear-view mirror, a gasoline tanker goes up in flames. A wall of fire erupts across I-290.

There's no going back. Only forward.

The dream comes again: highway hypnosis. My body knows these roads and how to travel them, and my mind drifts free.

So, I'm Conquest, the first of the Four Horsemen of the Apocalypse. I blew up Flight 311 to harvest the souls of my fellow passengers, and I have assembled a team and arranged a plan that will let Mr Nero harvest every soul in greater Chicago.

Part of me is terrified.

Part of me is thrilled.

"You're pretty late," Michael says, standing in the doorway just where I left him, only now he's in silk pajamas. "It's 3.00 am."

"Chicago traffic. What do you want?" I slam the door of the Lamborghini.

"I haven't been able to sleep," he continues.

"Me, neither."

"I mean, with the attack, and with the reporters, and Death's Disciples."

I laugh sarcastically.

"I wasn't sure I'd ever see you again."

I spread my arms and cock my hips. "Ta da!"

He descends the three short steps into the garage, all anxiety leaving him. "How was it? Was there a band? What did they serve?"

"There was a band, and the food was rich and rare, that's for sure."

Michael clasps his hands. "I should've gone. It was Lean Cuisine for me."

"Uggh," I say, remembering decapitated baby squid.

Michael steps up beside me as I head into the house. "And, how did it go?"

"Better than I could have dreamed. Everyone knows me, and before I walked out, I knew them, too. I know myself better than ever before."

His knees buckle slightly, and he rubs his hands together. "So good! So good! I can just go back to running the books, and you can go back to securing the deals."

"Yeah," I say as we pass through the walkway into the boarded-up back parlor. "That's what I'll do. Secure the deals."

He gives me a sudden hug from behind. It's awkward – I'm walking in stilettos, and suddenly my brother's doing a reach-around. "Big Sis is back. I can finally get to sleep."

I peel his hands off me and turn to face him. "Thanks for holding down the fort, Michael."

He smiles. "It's going to be like old times, isn't it?"

I manage a wink. "I'm afraid so."

We sleep through breakfast, and I have lunch delivered. It's funny. My iPhone remembers more than I do. Michael says we can trust the Phuket Café with our lives, and I say, "Fuck it, then, let's order." It's red curry for me with extra spice and pud thai for Michael. We tell the guards and the cops not to strip-search poor Lan Wi, and we give him a hundred percent tip.

We're rewarded with good fortunes.

"Mine says, 'An old friend will soon return to you,' " Michael reads, grinning.

I crack my cookie and look with slight dread at the paper. "Mine says, 'Don't compromise yourself; you're all you've got.'" I'm annoyed. "That's not a fortune."

"You're supposed to add, 'In bed.' "

"What?"

"It makes it funny," Michael says. "Mine reads, 'An old friend will soon return to you in bed.' "

I laugh. "Good for you."

"And yours?"

"'Don't compromise yourself; you're all you've got in bed. ' Michael laughs uproariously, but I crumple the thing and throw it away. "Not with *my* closet."

That quiets him.

I change the subject. "Today, Michael, you're going to walk me through every *particular* of the Banswyth-Stiller project."

His eyes seem to glow. "I'll get my briefcase."

"More than just that. I want every file. I want it all laid out – blueprints, elevations, maps, schedules, accounts – the works. I want to know every delay, every wrinkle, every time the general contractor farted."

"I'm your man!" he declares, rushing off to get his stuff.

As I clear away the remains of our lunch, I'm feeling bad for Michael. Brother to Conquest, and he can't even see it. He may not like my S&M suits and my gun locker, but he likes me. That's good enough for Michael. He's the only innocent in this whole thing.

Michael returns gripping a stack of folios, a dozen cardboard tubes, and two laptop cases. He wears a grin the size of Iowa. "It's really an amazing operation," he bubbles as he awkwardly sets down folders. "I mean the roadways and tramways and the underground networks connecting them all. You should see this one bunker. It's got about ten thousand servers in it, and it's buried five hundred feet below Chicago. Man, the only thing that could reach it would be a full-scale nuke."

I look at him. "A nuke?"

He laughs nervously as he uncorks blueprints. "Oh, there's a whole folder on terrorist attacks. We had to think about that stuff, of course. There's two hundred different scenarios we ran, but the nuke was the worst."

"What would happen?"

"Well, a suitcase bomb could take out a quarter of the city – which is kind of the worst-case scenario."

"What about a full-size nuke? A hydrogen bomb?"

"It would take out all of Chicago, make it a two hundred-foot-deep crater. Lake Michigan would run into it. And everybody from Kenosha to Gary would die from radiation."

My heart is pounding. A hydrogen bomb would certainly harvest millions of souls for Mr Nero, but would he really want to risk having Lake Michigan drown his computers? "What about a neutron bomb?"

Michael blinks. "Well, the same body count, but the infrastructure is still intact. Buildings, roads, power lines – only nobody could use them. They'd be radioactive for a while."

"Yeah. You'd have to be immune to radioactivity to do anything in Chicago."

"Except in these tunnels," Michael says. "That's the thing. They're deep enough, extensive enough, it's like another city, immune to attack."

I feel my face go white. So that's his plan. A neutron bomb. He'll harvest the souls and retreat to his underground city where he will be safe… Where he'll run the world.

"It's not going to happen, of course," Michael said. "I mean, the suitcase bomb, maybe – North Korea or Iran. But they don't have intercontinental ballistic missiles. Now you're talking the U.S. or Russia, and they're not going to bomb the G-20 Summit."

"How many servers did you say there were, five hundred feet down?"

"Ten thousand, and a hundred mainframes, and about a thousand PCs. They say it's a great environment for computers – constant temperature of fifty-five degrees, constant humidity. Mr Evers designed the bunker. He said this is the place HAL would've wanted to live."

I suddenly realize what he's talking about. It's Conscious 1. Evers built a bunker for his digital god, and from that bunker, Mr Nero and his false prophet will rule the world.

Michael's finally gotten everything laid out, and he stares proudly down at it as if it were his science project. "Well, where should we start?"

I'm driving again. This time, it's not the Lamborghini or the Beemer. It's the Mercedes. Yeah. I'm slumming. Even it, though, is going to look out of place in the ramshackle old Methodist Campground.

I troll slowly along a narrow blacktop road with speed-bumps every fifty yards. On either side of the road crouch ancient cottages painted white and green, some quaint with gingerbread filigree and some decrepit with peeling paint and slouching porches.

Krupinski's here, somewhere. Nero said he would be.

He and that Calliope bitch who tried to poison me.

My iPhone gave up the moment I turned off Algonquin, but my GPS shows that Krupinski is in that run-down cottage on that slice of land between the forest preserve and the river. I drive onto the lawn, park, and get out.

I'm dressed sensibly today – gray blouse, black pants and black pumps. The most extravagant thing I'm wearing is a pair of onyx and pearl yin-yang earrings.

I knock on the door, paint chips coming off on my

knuckles. The front window is covered in a sheer, and a furtive face pulls it back and peers out – a Goth girl who's thinner and younger than Calliope. Then the sheer flips down again, and hushed voices come from within:

"It's her!"

"It's she!"

"Shut up, grammar Nazi."

"*Who* is it?" That voice is Calliope's.

"Susan Gardner."

"You idiot! Let her in."

The loose brass doorknob turns, and the door swings inward. The scrawny thing who looked at me through the window is now bowing and scraping. "Welcome, High Lady of Death."

"Thank you, Evella of the Endless Night," I say, making her goggle in disbelief. I know her name because Dave Jenkins knew it. I step into the cramped living room, where more Goths are bowing on either side. "Hello, Thanatopsis and Kid Killer and Cyclops." Moving past them, I reach Calliope Dirge, who seems especially small and pale today. "Hello, Calliope."

Even though she's wearing torn black jeans, Calliope does a strange little curtsy. "Mistress."

"Don't you ever try to kill me again."

"Of course not."

"I'm fucking immortal."

"Yes, Mistress."

"You're not."

"Yes."

My eyes shift to the big Goth goofball beside her. Krupinski'd always had the black hair and pasty complexion, but now he's also wearing a leather vest and jeans and black leather boots up to his mid-calf. "Been shopping?"

He blinks, shaking his head nervously. "It was in the saddlebags."

Only then do I notice the Hell's Angels pin piercing his nipple. "It's bleeding."

"We did it this morning," Calliope says.

"I want to talk to you," I say to Krupinski. "Just you and me."

"Yes, my lady."

"Let's take a walk."

We walk along a curved road crowded with cottages. At first, neither one of us can come up with anything to say. Ahead, a sidewalk crosses the road. The signpost above says that to the left lies Waldorf Tabernacle, and to the right the Red Gables and the Snack Shop. "Let's go right."

Krupinski nods. "Away from the church."

I head down the sidewalk with Krupinski slightly behind. He carries himself differently now. The old Krupinski was jaunty and loose limbed, filled with confidence. This one hunches and shuffles. The old Krupinski had darting eyes, taking in everything. This one just stares straight ahead.

"How much do you remember?" I ask him.

He grunts. "'Bout what?"

"About our escape."

He looks at me. "You mean, when you ran off in Grant Park?"

"No. I mean when you rescued me from the Schneider Ranch."

"I *kidnapped* you."

I sigh. "Listen to me, Krupinski."

"Anything, Mistress."

"You didn't kidnap me. You were saving me from Lieutenant Elseworth, who was trying to kill me."

His brows knit. "No. I was going rogue. I was taking you to Mr Evers so I could become one of Death's Disciples."

"No. You were still an FBI agent, and you were trying to save me from your lunatic boss. You gave up your career – you became a fugitive just to save me."

He stops and turns toward me. He blinks in thought, and the fog is lifting. "That seems familiar."

"Of course, it's familiar," I reply. "It's the truth. Mr Evers burned it out of you to make you a faithful disciple, but I outrank Mr Evers. I am Conquest."

"Yes, you are, Mistress," he says, bowing his head.

"And you need to be faithful first to *me*."

"Yes." His head droops lower.

I lift his goateed chin. "Which is what you have *always* been. I want you to remember what you have done for me. You've been poisoned, you've stolen cars, you've been stabbed, you've killed people *for me*. You can't be more faithful than that. You *must* remember."

He stares at me, his eyes scrolling though memories. "Yes. Yes. It's burned out, faded – but it's there."

"Krupinski," I say, "come back to me."

His eyelids flap, and he shakes his head. "Holy shit! What gives?"

"Watch your language," shouts a white-haired man walking by. "There are kids here." Then he adds quietly, "And put a shirt on, you freak."

"Are you back?" I ask. "Are you really back?"

Krupinski takes a deep breath and looks at me. "Yeah. I remember."

"Good."

"But I'm not sure I like you much anymore."

"Oh, I'm pretty sure you're going to love me."

45 EMBRACING THE INNER BITCH

The elevator doors slide open, and I step out into Mr Nero's palatial office. It's a good thirty feet of carpet to his mahogany desk, with only the reception desk between. I stroll past it and the young woman there. Mr Nero stands by the windows, his pear-shaped frame silhouetted against the bright daylight of a Chicago morning.

"Good morning, good lady," he chirrups without looking my way.

"Good morning, sir. I'm please to announce that I've been through every scrap of paper that is Banswyth-Stiller, and I get it."

"Pretty amazing, huh?" he asks.

"Yes. Stunning. I just hope you like the cold."

Only then does he turn around, his goofy smile framed by a wiry goatee. "How's that?"

"I've seen the blueprints for your bunker."

"Beats the hell out of Hitler's."

"Yes, but it's a thousand feet down, with a constant temperature of fifty-five degrees."

"Haven't you ever heard of radiators, dear? Not to mention hot tubs? What? Did you think I was going to sit in ice like Satan in the *Inferno?*"

"At any rate, Michael reports that everything is right on schedule–"

"Except the last part," interrupts Mr Nero. "The part he doesn't know about."

"The neutron bomb."

"You even guessed the vintage. Very good, my lady." His eyes light. "Yes. That's it. I was getting Marcus and Lee prepped to tackle it without you, but it's your plan, after all."

"And what exactly *is* my plan?"

"Cheyenne Mountain. It's dug a mile into a Colorado mountain – blast-proof, impenetrable, once the center for NORAD. That place could withstand multiple megaton explosions and still keep going. In fact, we followed the same specifications when we built our control sections in Underground Chicago."

I nod. "Yes. I saw the plans."

"But Cheyenne Mountain is no longer the center for NORAD operations. They've moved to Peterson Air Force Base nearby. The mountain is on 'warm standby.' That means it's ready if something happens at Peterson, but it isn't currently calling the shots."

"Which means, also, that it's not currently manned and guarded the way it once was."

"Exactly," Mr Nero says. He sits on the corner of the desk, lacing his fingers over his knee. "You, Marcus, and Lee will get into Cheyenne Mountain and plant router switches that will allow us to take control."

"But Cheyenne Mountain doesn't even have control."

"It will when you take out Peterson."

I laugh. "How am I going to take out a whole air force base?"

"With an F-16 Fighting Falcon. You fly it over Peterson

and bomb the command core. Then they switch all operations to NORAD, and we're in business."

"*I'm* going to fly a Falcon?"

Mr Nero laughs. "You planned this all, Susan. The pilot of Flight 311 was a former Air Force pilot who logged lots of time in Iraq. An injury ended his military career, and he got a job with United. You chose him perfectly. And now he's part of you. You'll bring down Peterson."

I smile. "God am I brilliant."

"Yes, you are."

"How do I get hold of this plane? They don't just leave them lying around. And, besides, I can't go anywhere without a hundred reporters behind me."

Mr Nero smacks his forehead. "We forgot to *show* you." He leans to his phone, presses "speaker," and dials a couple numbers. "Marcus, Lee, get up here."

"Righto."

"Coming."

I stare at Mr Nero. "What is it, then?"

His grin grows. "You have three hundred sixty-one people in you. They're not just memories. They're identities. You can *become* them. You can move like them, sound like them, even look like them."

The elevator beeps, and the door opens, and out saunter Marcus and Lee.

Mr Nero says, "Marcus, do Mr Phelps."

In midstride, short, muscular Marcus becomes a somewhat taller, somewhat fatter man with a liver-spotted face. He moves more slowly, his right knee rheumatic. Even his hair looks gray-streaked. "Whadda ya want, Nero?" he croaks in the voice of a chronic smoker.

I'm amazed.

"Lee, do Ms Ortiz."

The tall, lean, blond becomes suddenly short, round, and brunette. He has an olive-shaped face and long black hair and a hint of a mustache, and he wears a house dress in a faded print.

"How?" I ask.

"It's not really her body or her clothes," Nero replies. "It's her *ghost* projected into your mind."

"And I can do this?" I ask.

"It's like falling asleep – letting the conscious self sleep and letting another self emerge."

I close my eyes and breathe deeply. My mind begins to fray. The fabric that is me unravels, and there are three hundred sixty-one other identities beneath it. I have only to touch one and slide within and–

I have a new mind, a very meticulous and suspicious mind, one that hates Mr Nero.

"So, face to face at last," I say, but my voice is a male tenor. "Mr Nero, leader of the Death's Disciples."

"Corporal Dave Jenkins," Nero replies cheerily. "Thank you for checking that bomb aboard Flight 311."

"Yeah," he says. I can feel his intelligence, but I'm in control. "You went through Susan Gardner and Mr Evers and Calliope to get to me."

"The mule."

I become once again myself.

"That was awesome!" Marcus says, back in his original form. "You looked just like that nebbish. Sounded like him."

I blink. "Really?"

All three men nod, and Marcus says, "You got it, girl."

"Then I'm going to use it."

"There's one more trick I want Mr Evers to teach you," Mr Nero responds, "but then you'll be ready, and it'll be off to the Pentagon."

I step off the DC subway at the Pentagon exit and wear the persona of Captain Art Witterson. The guards check my ID, perfectly forged by Mr Evers, and check the itinerary, perfectly forged by Conscious 1. I walk through miles of underground passages and ascend to miles of long white corridors. At last, I reach the office of Colonel Jack Higgins.

"Colonel," I say, standing in the open doorway and saluting rigidly.

The colonel is a round-faced bureaucrat with soft hands and a combover. He lurches up from behind his paper-piled desk and circles around to me. "At ease, captain, and welcome," he says, shaking my hand and seeming to feel a very strong and broad grip in response. "Real war hero."

"Yessir." Good. Conscious 1 has amplified my record, removed my injury, my retirement, my death.

"Medal of honor." Higgins looks into my eye, but he sees what he wants to see. "It's a privilege, Witterson. Come in, sit down."

I do, entering a crowded office with banker boxes and mounds of paperwork. "You heard the reason I wanted to see you, sir?"

"Yes, prototype range extender for our Fighting Falcons."

Finding a level patch on the piles, I roll out plans for a prototype extended-range fuel tank that can fit on the belly of the F-16. "It's stealth contoured, so there's actually a reduction in radar signature."

His eyes flit over the plans. "You still have full bomb-load capacity?"

"There's the same payload, but a reduced deployment rate. Still, you get twice the range with no refueling."

Higgins's eyes bug greedily.

"Lockheed has run all their tests, but they need a live prototype flight."

"Out of where?"

"I was thinking Peterson."

He nods sagely. "Yeah, middle of nowhere. All right, but it'd better have a full bomb load. I want all eleven hardpoints fitted with bombs, and I want to see that thing go twice the distance." He grins at me, a silver tooth glinting.

"Just what I was thinking."

After a bit more malarkey and another testing handshake, I walk out of Higgins's office with Pentagon clearance for the test flight.

But I'm not done here. I stroll around two sides of the Pentagon, past office after office, to come to the one where Lieutenant Elseworth sits smoking.

I step back, looking for a chance to transform. Two aides make their way past as I stoop down at a drinking fountain. The aides round the corner before I straighten up again, now Susan Gardner.

I walk into Elseworth's smoke-filled office – bookshelves stacked to the ceiling on both sides and a small

dusty window looking out on one of the inner court-
yards.

Lieutenant Elseworth jolts up from behind his desk.

"Shhh," I say, sitting on the desk and leaning over to
press my index finger against his lips. I'm doing my best
impression of a femme fatale. "I know everyone says
you're trying to kill me, but I don't believe them."

The fear in his eyes slowly transforms to predation.
"How'd you get in here?"

"I've had to do all kinds of desperate things, Lieutenant," I say, leaning toward him. "I've found ways."

He's falling for it, snatching up the cigarette he'd left
smoldering in a skull-shaped ashtray. "What do you
want from me?"

"You're the only one who gets what's happening." I
slide slowly off the desk and approach him. "I want to
tell you everything. I want to give you an exclusive."

His nostrils flare. "I– um, but… there's an investigation pending and I'm – well, forbidden–"

I grab his head in both hands as if I'm about to French
him, but instead, I pierce his mind and ransack his
memories and burn some of them–

Many of them…

Most of them…

When I'm done with Elseworth, I pull back from him.
He's panting and spent. He stares at me, his mind emptied just as Krupinski's had been.

It'll be a dull trial. He won't have much to say except,
"I do not recall."

I walk out the door and turn to the drinking fountain
and bend down. Two more staffers pass, whispering

about my nice ass. I don't mind. My ass *is* nice. But when they are gone, I stand up from the fountain, and I'm Captain Art Witterson again.

There is a boom mic operator in my mind, Bruce Holstead, who's built like a Holstein. He's round and squat with lank hair, but at least he has union membership. So, when the real boom operator of *Unvarnished* fails to show (his tires got slashed, apparently), I show up as Bruce and flash my card and tell them I'm the replacement. They point me to a Fisher boom – with a heavy base that I stand on and a long pole reaching out above the desk of Cameron Steel.

The beautiful fuck-nut.

I stand on the Fisher boom, shifting it easily forward and back, making sure it's always out of camera range but always within audio range. Then we come back from commercial and the little twit straightens in his seat beside Lupe and begins his report.

"Welcome back, folks, to a whole program devoted to the mania surrounding Susan Gardner. You'll never believe the latest."

"Well, then, do dish, Cameron," Lupe interjects.

I slide the boom momentarily toward her before pivoting back toward him.

Cameron's face hitches, and he says, "All right, then. No more interruptions. On to the heart of weirdness. Two nights ago, a Fox News team caught Susan Gardner in a red Lamborghini as she tore away from her Oak Park home. There's the image. Look at her. She's one hot momma. Look at that dress. Demure in front, but witnesses say it plunged to Hades in back, if you know what I mean."

"They do, Cameron," Lupe says. "But tell them about the accident."

"Well, this just in – the thirty-four car pileup that happened on Interstate 290 in Chicago in the wee hours the next morning was apparently caused by a red sports car. The driver of the steel truck could not identify the make of the car or the license, but he said a 'smoking hot' woman in a red dress was behind the wheel."

"Could it have been Susan Gardner?"

"Almost certainly," Cameron responds. "We saw how smoking hot she looked leaving her home. If I'd been a truck driver looking at that, I'd've dumped my load as well."

The boom mic hits Cameron Steel in the head, denting his cotton-candy hair.

"Whoa! Incoming!" he says with a laugh, batting the mic away and flinging a look of passive-aggressive fury my way.

I shrug with the roly-poly shoulders of Bruce Holstead.

"We've got an intern on the boom mic. Sorry about that, folks," Cameron says through gritted teeth. "Everybody's got to learn sometime. These community colleges just aren't pulling their weight."

"No, they're not," Lupe says.

"And speaking of community colleges, while the world's been focused on the super diva Susan Gardner, everybody's been ignoring her pathetic little brother. Michael's kind of a DeVry-type guy."

"Not very interesting," Lupe puts in.

"But the *Enquirer* is now claiming that Susan Gardner keeps her brother as a sex slave."

The boom mic smashes him in the face, and Cameron Steel falls over backward, crashing into the blue screen behind him. The mic goes over with him, recording, "What the fuck!" and "I'll kill the cocksucker!" and "He broke my nose!"

There's a six-second loop, so the good people of Illinois won't hear that part. But by the time their feed goes live, they'll see a stocky boom operator lumbering up on the set and flinging the anchor desk to smash to the ground and grabbing Cameron Steel's head. Lupe is screaming, trying to back away, while the camera people are converging to capture every second.

But the only thing they see is a bit of butt crack and a little blue flash around my fingers.

Then the security guys jump us. There's four of them in blue-black suits swarming Bruce Holstead and Cameron Steel, only I'm no longer the boom operator. I'm a white-haired grandmother named Doris Hunch, and all the grabbing hands and shouts of "Get fucking down!" seem very wrong to me. Even as I fall to the stage, I hit the nearest young man with my purse.

He staggers back, goggling.

"Keep your hands to yourself!" I tell him.

The other three guards rear back, and even Cameron Steel stares at me in amazement.

I bawl, "I just wanted to help!"

"Aunt Elsie?" asks Cameron in shock.

The security guards scatter, looking for Bruce Holstead, and Cameron Steel staggers up, righting his anchor chair and fixing his hair and tie, and pushing me off to one side. "Sorry about that, folks! Wow! Now, that's great television. Did you see that? The young man attacked me twice with a microphone and then jumped me. And I know that microphone looks soft, but it's heavy. It's probably five pounds. And it's on the end of a twenty-foot pole. It's like a polearm! A friggin' medieval polearm, and some nut job uses it to try to kill me on national television? What's his point? To silence me–?"

Lupe breaks in, "If I were a terrorist, that's what I'd want–"

"Trying to shut me up!" Cameron says, flashing Lupe a dirty look. "But it's not going to happen! If anything, I'll proclaim the story even louder than before." He stops, staring fanatically into the camera. Then, out of the corner of his mouth, he says, "What were we talking about?"

"Susan Gardner," Lupe says.

Cameron blinks. "Who?"

"The 311 Miracle, Susan Gardner."

Cameron tosses out his hands in exasperation. "Please, be *specific!*"

"And we're going to take a break right now," Lupe says, hand rising to her ear. "Which is what you deserve as well. And what better break than a nice cup of Starbucks? Take it away."

They go to commercial.

I giggle. As Doris Hunch, I stand backstage and watch the two anchors rail at each other and technicians run to lift the broken desk and grips and best boys staring on in bewilderment.

"Where's that old woman?" snarls one of the security guards.

"She's up here, just by the light board," says another nearby. His hand touches my shoulder.

I turn toward him, but I'm no longer Doris Hunch. I'm a young electrician with black hair and a bad attitude. "Lay off, man! You think it's easy pulling this shit back together when shit like that goes down?"

The security guard lifts his hands, backing away. "Sorry, man. I thought you were the aunt."

"Fuck you! Like I'm some gray-haired dyke! Step off."

They do, and I stomp my way off the stage, telling anyone who cares to listen that I quit.

"Which is why we've got to be on guard," the preacher is saying, standing on a stage of split logs in the middle of the woods. His figure is illuminated by a Jeep, a Humvee, and a pair of burning crosses.

I sit with a hundred other grunting, sweating, camouflaged men, all of us sure that the Antichrist is on the horizon and that Susan Gardner is his Whore of Babylon. We're the Christian Unified Front.

"She's beautiful, yes. We've all seen pictures of that fine thing," said the preacher to his faithful. "Heck, if I weren't a married man, I'd gladly take her to wife and bend her over the stove and show her what it feels like to have a man of God inside her."

"Yeah!" they shout, and I do too, looking like the skinhead called Righteous Evil.

"But this is the very thing we gots to watch out for. That's what that bitch wants from us. She *wants* us to lay her, because she's the Whore of Babylon. She wants us to give her our seed, which she'll use to make the demon nations of her calling. She's trying to seduce us so that in the Last Days, we won't fight against her forces of hell because they'll be our own sons. You see, she's not a woman that carries one or two babies. She's not a bitch that carries three or four babies. She's not a sow that carries five or eight babies. She's the fucking whore of fucking Babylon. That means, she *wants* to be gang raped, so she can carry three thousand, three million babies – our precious babies – and make them into her demon spawn."

The men grumble among the pines, and I grumble with them.

"Last time we tried to take her alive, and we lost six good men. So this time, I say, kill her first and fuck her afterward."

"Yeah!" they shout, rising from the wooden benches and shooting their guns in the air.

"Yeah!" I shout, jumping up and shooting my guns into them.

Two rows have fallen before the others realize what's going on. I spray another row and feel their bullets rip into me. Too bad for them that I've got lots of lives.

I mow them down. The preacher especially. I cut him in half.

It's like weed whacking. I watch them fall amid the trees, an unruly patch turned into a pleasant garden.

"With silver bells and cockle shells and pretty men all in a row."

46 **NEGOTIATIONS**

When you borrow identities, they borrow you back.

Aw, Jesus! says Righteous Evil. *What the hell, man?*

I'm not a man.

Then what the fuck, bitch? You use my ghost and then go kill a bunch of fuckers!

I thought you were Righteous Evil.

Yeah, but I never killed any fuckers.

Who better to kill than fuckers?

There's a pause. *Well, yeah, I guess… But you got no right pulling that shit.*

Tell you what, Righteous, next time I've got to kill somebody, I'll leave your ghost in the box.

Wait, that ain't what I'm sayin'.

What are you saying, then?

Forget it. Righteous tells me. *I guess you done good.*

Couldn't have put it better, myself. Now, would you get out of the cockpit?

I'm flying an air force cargo plane from Little Rock to Midway in Chicago. It's a prop plane piloted by a guy who's flown B-2s over Baghdad.

About that, says Captain Witterson, *and about your resurrecting me to pull one over on Elseworth–*

Elseworth's an asshole.

There's silence. *Granted.*

He brought in those Xe goons–

They're Blackwater. Damned mercenaries. Don't get fooled by the marketing name.

And they shot up the Schneider house and tried to kill me.

All right. You're right. He's an asshole. Still, I don't like my name being dragged through the mud. You killed me, if you'll remember, Missy. You killed all of us in the name of some Satanic cult.

The Disciples aren't Satanic.

Don't get fooled by the marketing name.

Listen! You're part of me now.

Part of who? Susan Gardner from a week ago? I'd be glad to be a part of that woman. She cared about people, not just about herself.

If I die, all of you die. How's *that* for caring about other people?

Again, Captain Witterson falls silent. At last, he says, *So this is what goes on when you become immortal? You start using people, stealing their memories, their lives?*

It's my turn to be silent. He's about to pipe up again when I say, Just fly the God damned plane.

He does. I can feel his mind – focused and calm – behind every move of my hand on the controls.

Witterson's not talking anymore, so somebody else butts in.

Whoa, babe, that was totally hot, what you did to Cameron Steel. God! How many times I wanted to do that! Hit a guy in the head with the boom. You know, just BOOM! How do you like me now, asshole? Man, that was awesome. Keep up the good work, Susy Chick.

I'm watching the altimeter and the artificial horizon

as I say, *Thanks, Bruce.*

And, um, a bunch of the guys and me want you to know we're totally cool with the S&M.

Really?

Yeah. It's really about women's rights. Self-expression. If a chick like you wants to have a whole closet of it, well, that's like a sacred right.

What are you saying?

And, you know, if you're lesbian, we're down for that action, too.

It's time for you to sign off, Bruce.

All right. Just wanted you to know, we're pro on all the sex stuff. Don't compromise yourself. You're all you've got in bed.

Okay, that's enough. I shut off the chat room in my head.

Is that as easy as it is? Am I just an admin with three hundred sixty-one comments? It's so complicated being a woman these days.

So, I let myself be a man, Captain Witterson, specifically. After a long night flight, he puts the plane down in a three-point landing on Midway, and I descend the stairs, carrying a few hundred people on my back.

"Susan," Michael says, standing in silk pajamas in the doorway. "We have to talk."

"About what?" I ask wearily, stepping from the Mercedes as the garage door rattles down behind me.

"About how much sleep I'm getting. We had an agreement that I could be in bed by ten every night so that I could wake up at six and be ready. It's 1.21am.

These late nights, when I'm waiting up for you – well, they mean I'm not much good the next day."

"How much good do you need to be, bro?" I snap. After all, I've just arranged to fly a Fighting Falcon out of Peterson and mind-wiped the guy who wanted to kill me and the desk-jockey who was trying to ride me to fame and destroyed the core of the Christian Unified Front and played dial-in talk show host while flying a cargo plane to Midway. What has Michael done – fill out a schedule and put on his jammies? "You're a grown man, Michael. You lived in this house alone for a whole month."

He blinks at me. "But there weren't terrorists shooting out the windows."

I tilt my head toward him. "I've taken care of that. You don't have to be afraid of terrorists anymore."

Michael's eyebrows knit. "What did you do? Gun down the Death's Disciples?"

"Something like that."

"I want eight hours of sleep," he says petulantly.

I purse my lips. "Michael, I am Conquest."

"Hmmm?"

"You know the Four Horsemen of the Apocalypse in *Revelation?*"

"I guess," he murmurs.

"Well, I'm the first one. Conquest. The rider on the white horse."

He looks at his slippers. "All right, so you're the conqueror."

"No, I'm Conquest."

"Fine, so you're Conquest. Can I get a little sleep?"

"Listen, what I'm telling you is that there's no one out to kill us anymore. Whether or not I'm here, Michael, you can go to bed and rest easy."

He nods, but his eyes shift restlessly to the boarded up windows all around. "Still feels like we live in a war zone.

I look at that bank of CDX plywood hammered up across the windows, and I imagine a new greenhouse of bulletproof glass. "Mike Schroeder can fix it."

"Who's Mike Schroeder?"

I wave my hand. "This contractor I met on a plane. He could fix things."

"Excellent. You got his number?"

"Right here in my head." I smile and imagine sitting on my back porch and hearing bullets ping off the glass and not giving a shit.

It's fairly easy to cow Michael and the voices within me. After all, every last one depends on me for life.

Not Sergeant Krupinski.

Next morning, I'm standing in my bathrobe having some tea when he comes to call. One of the cops along the road shouts. A minute later and much closer, a guard begins arguing with someone. I go to the front door and lean on it to listen.

"No one is to see Miss Gardner," the guard declares.

"By whose order?" asks Krupinski.

"By her own order."

"Does she know it's me?"

"She doesn't even know you're here."

"Well, there's your first mistake."

I'm snickering behind the door.

"You're just lucky you're unarmed and you allowed us to frisk you."

"You're lucky I did."

"Why do you want to see her?"

There comes a pause, and in it, I imagine Krupinski taking a step and a half closer to the guard and locking eyes with him and saying. "I'm her friend."

"She has no friends."

I fling open the front door and step out in my bathrobe and say. "Seriously? You think I don't have any friends?"

"Sorry, Miss," the guard says, shrinking back, hands lifted beside his head like I've got my AK-47. "Of course you got friends. Plenty. Me and Elwood, for instance."

I glance at the African-American guard nearby, who shrugs an apology.

"Thanks, guys." I nod to Krupinski. "But I rode a Greyhound from South Dakota with this guy."

The guards back away. They're checking out my bathrobe. It's amazing the power a female body has over men. "We'll just get back to our posts."

"You do that."

As they retreat, Krupinski steps up, his face dark. "We've got to talk."

"I'm getting a lot of that. Come inside," I turn around and lead him into the arched main entry.

He whistles, looking around at the marble tiles, the tiffany lamps, the hardwood banisters. "Nice place."

"You should see it when it's not shot to shit."

He nods speculatively, glancing into the great room

with its boarded windows. "Is there someplace we can talk?"

I laugh. "Michael's everywhere except two places."

"What two?"

"My bedroom or my S&M closet."

His cheeks turn pink. "I'm flattered, but... see... Calliope and me–"

"The Goth girl?"

Now his face is red. "Yeah."

"Well, I'm glad you're flattered, but Calliope's got nothing to fear from me. At least not sexually." I take his hand, turn, and start up the stairs. "Come on. Let's go to my bedroom." I'm merciful enough not to look back, though I can almost feel the glow of his face on my ass.

We reach the room: a twenty-by-twenty space with a cathedral ceiling and a hot tub in one corner. I go to sit on my bed, still unmade, and cross my legs, letting the bottom of my robe show everything from the knees down. Krupinski doggedly looks away, going to a vanity and sitting in a too-small chair.

"What did you want to talk about?"

Krupinski's looking down at the Persian rug on the hardwood floor. "Listen. This whole thing's gotten weird."

"*You're* telling *me*."

His eyes meet mine for a moment before drifting back down. "I mean, you're not the girl I rescued."

"The girl you rescued didn't know who she was."

"I don't think *you* know who you are."

"I'm Conquest, rider on the Pale Horse, first of the Four Horsemen of the Apocalypse."

"*No, you're not.*" Krupinski says. "The woman I knew was different."

"She was an illusion."

"No, *this* woman is the illusion."

"You saw the Disciples – their power. That power is *mine*. If you could've seen me at the Pentagon–"

"I'm not talking about power," he says, rearing up like a bear. "I'm talking about soul. You were *good*, Susan. A *good* person."

"I'm a fucking Death's Disciple!"

"*So am I!*" he shouts. "You know why? Because I was trying to get inside. I'm one of the most wanted men in America because I thought I could stop them. I thought I could save you."

"You were deluded."

"Yeah. But my mission remains the same."

I close my eyes and breathe out slowly. "Krupinski, I've got an AK-47. I used it last night."

His face goes white.

"I killed three hundred sixty-one people on Flight 311, and I'm planning to kill six million more during the G-20 Summit in Chicago. I'm *not* a nice person."

Krupinski shakes his head. "I know you better than you know yourself."

"Get the fuck out," I tell him, pointing to the door. "And don't try to stop me, or I'll kill you *and* your girl-friend."

He turns away. "Whatever happened to you?"

I watch him go. "Get out of Chicago, Krupinski. A week from today, it's all gone."

• • •

I stand beside Mr Nero a thousand feet below Chicago, and we stare at the glowing palace he has prepared for himself. The workers carved the building out of bedrock, making wide windows and depressed arches and grid-work facades in the Perpendicular Style. The palace sprawls within a huge, man-made cavern with grow lights beaming down purple on its widespread lawn. Above the lights, tiny LEDs are affixed to the ceiling, twinkling in precise constellations. Their light is reflected in a wide and gleaming lake. It's a world within a world.

"When the stars fall from the sky and the moon turns as blood," Mr Nero chirrups, "I'll still have the good old Big Dipper and Little Dipper and our friend Luna." He points toward the rock dome, where a beautiful gibbous moon is rising, projected from the floor. "The old world is coming to an end, and a new world is being born."

"Your world," I say.

He grins. "Well, a quarter of it. That's what *Revelation* says: 'And power was given unto them over the fourth part of the earth,' which is basically all of the Americas. I will have dominion, and you will be at my side."

"All it takes is six million deaths," I say ironically.

"Just six million." He smiles with peglike teeth. "Did you enjoy killing the Christian Unified Front?"

"I did."

"And wiping Elseworth's mind?"

"Yes."

"And arranging the test flight?"

"Simple."

He turns toward me, his hand out. "Then why am I sensing… uncertainty?"

"I don't know, sir."

"Me, neither. You've harvested your souls, you have your immortality. You've had more to overcome than Marcus and Lee did, but whatever it took, you're here."

I sigh and look up at that spangled dome. "You've made yourself some beautiful heavens here in the depths."

"Yes, my lady. Yes, I have."

Marcus, Lee, and I have finished a morning of power meetings with the Mafia, and now we're having lunch at a strip club. A girl who can't be more than sixteen is currently grinding on a pole above our table. My male comrades are quite interested, as are Bruce and his cronies.

I just want to get her a bathrobe.

"So, what are you guys planning to do in the after-life?" I ask, trying to take our minds off the gyrations.

"What afterlife?" asks Marcus, eyes fixed on the dancer. "We're immortal."

"I mean, the life after we blow up Chicago," I say.

Lee shrugs. "You seen Nero's palace?"

"Yeah," I reply.

"Fourteen pools and ballrooms and libraries and the great hall, the poolrooms and bedrooms and baths. He's prepared a place for us."

"Nice if you want to live in a snow globe."

Marcus and Lee grin, looking at me to see if I'm joking. Then they look away.

Marcus says, "This has been the plan from the beginning. *Your* plan, Susan. Somehow, you don't seem satisfied with it anymore."

I'm watching the high-school girl dance for the three of us, the dozen others at tables around us, the trench-coaters at the edge of the room. I reach into my purse and pull out a bundle of hundreds – mob money paid to us that morning. I fan it toward the girl.

Her dead eyes light up. What could ten G's buy her?

She slinks down off the stage and dances before the almighty dollar.

Marcus and Lee are mesmerized.

"What's your name?" I ask, holding the money just out of reach.

"Fantasia 2000."

I shake my head. "What's your real name?"

She sees nothing but the money. "Sharon Star."

"Sharon, your days of stripping are over. You can't spend this money on drugs or friends. You've got to spend it to get your life back. Whoever you were before, you've got to be her again. Do you hear me?"

She grins lopsidedly and bends down to kiss me on the lips. I must admit that the kiss is good. Sharon Star says, "Whatever." She clutches the money in a vice grip.

I grip her head, and spikes of energy jut down into her brain.

She shudders for a moment and then jerks back.

"Hey, bitch! What the hell you doin'!" the manager bellows, baseball bat raised behind me. But then he sees that Fantasia is holding the ten G's. The manager steps toward her, reaching out his hand. "Give it here, girl."

I give it there. I snatch the bat from his hand and bring it down to break both of his forearms mid-grab. The guy's got four elbows, and I'm standing over him saying, "She's not your girl anymore. And I've never been your bitch."

Marcus and Lee watch it all gleefully, ready for me to smash the guy's head. But I don't. I just drop the bat and walk away.

Sharon's already gone. She's probably backstage finding her clothes, wondering what the hell she's doing in a strip club.

Amnesia can be a good thing.

I shouldn't have dropped the bat, though. Marcus is using it right now to turn the strip-club owner into a blood pudding.

47 **BLACK HOLE**

Marcus, Lee, and I ride in a Humvee toward Cheyenne Mountain – not that any of us look like ourselves. I'm Lieutenant Colonel Jack Harper, formerly retired but, thanks to Conscious 1, now part of an army nuclear inspection team. Marcus is Major Denny Desmitt, and Lee is Captain Arnold Truit, part of the same team.

It's been a long, winding drive up the mountain, but at last, we approach the black hole – a half-pipe archway that delves down a mile through solid rock to the former command center of NORAD. We cruise up to a chain-link gate.

A twenty-something kid steps out of his guardhouse, an M-16 slung on his shoulder. He's young and blond, looking bleary, like he'd been asleep and is waking to adrenaline.

I lean my middle-aged, crew-cut head out of the window and smile. "Afternoon, Corporal."

"Afternoon, sir," he replies with a salute.

I hand over our paperwork. "Lieutenant Colonel Harper, with Major Desmitt and Captain Truit."

The young man is nodding but not really listening, looking over the paperwork and checking it against the schedule on his clipboard. "Got you right here, sir. You need an escort?"

"Nah," I say. "We know this site backward and forward."

He hands the paperwork back. "Hope you like what you see, sir. It'd be nice to get the Mountain running again."

"Nice for you, sure. It's dull standing guard at a gate to nowhere." I flash my warhorse grin. "But if this place was ever humming again, son, it'd be thermonuclear war."

"Right, sir," he says with another salute. Retreating, he opens the chain-link gate.

We drive into the tunnel and follow its long, downward slope.

"We're in!" Marcus crows.

"Of course," I say.

"Next stop, DEFCON 1!"

Lee is in the back of the Humvee, staring into a briefcase loaded with electronic gadgets. "I'm going to have to put on that idiot savant Galen Kronke before I'll be able to do anything with these."

"Idiot savant?" Marcus shoots back. "The last guy I harvested was an idiot-idiot." As he speaks, he suddenly sounds and looks like the strip-club owner.

"Put that guy away."

He changes into the head-bashed version of the man just before death, and then into a girl in a communion dress, then into a wasted addict, a soccer mom, a construction worker, a lawyer. He rifles through identities like a kid flipping through trading cards.

"They've got security cameras, you know. They'll think I'm riding with the Village People. Put on Major Desmitt."

"I'm looking," Marcus replies petulantly. He becomes a guy with Down syndrome and a white-haired octogenarian and a school crossing guard before at last becoming Desmitt.

"You killed a crossing guard?"

"What? She was standing in the middle of the road!"

At last, we reach the end of the tunnel. It's cold down here. We drive into a cavern fronted by a twenty-five ton steel blast door. Just now, the door stands open. Beside it, another guard is waving us through the megastructure, and we roll past a twenty-foot thick wall of steel. It's like driving into a safe.

"The inner sanctum," I say.

"Whoa!" Marcus replies.

Beyond the door lies a huge cavern made of a grid of gigantic tunnels. Three tunnels run in parallel bands in one direction, and three more cross-cut them, making an enormous chamber held up by nine vast, squarish columns of rock. Among those huge drums stand blocky metallic buildings. They do not touch the walls or ceiling of the cavern, but stand free like giant refrigerators.

"Okay, so where's the computer-control complex?"

"Keep driving to the second bay, and then turn right," Lee says from the back seat.

We pass the first looming cross-tunnel and drive along a massive stone pillar. Turning right, we roll between metallic buildings.

"It's up here. The one with all the cords going into it."

I look up to see that the ceiling of the cavern is crossed with thousands of black cables, all converging on this galvanized structure. Pulling off the road, I park on a section of bare rock. The three of us pile out of the Humvee, Lee with briefcase in hand.

A doorway on the side of the building opens, emitting a man whose egghead is ringed in white Bozo hair. He wears squarish glasses and an ill-tended mustache and beard. He plants knobby fists on his lab-coated hips.

I walk up, extending my hand. "I'm Lieutenant Colonel Jack Harper."

He doesn't take my hand. "Martin Schieffer, double PhD in Artificial Intelligence and Computer Networks."

"Nice to meet you, Doc."

"Why are you here?"

I glance at Marcus and Lee and then say. "It's a scheduled inspection."

"Just because you can fool gate guards doesn't mean you can fool me. I have an IQ of 164."

"Congratulations."

"I know what you're doing!"

"What are we doing, Doc?"

"It's Conscious 1."

"What about it?"

"Why would you give that *thing* access to the nuclear grid?"

I pat him on the shoulder, a touch that he recoils from. "You're paranoid. This is just an inspection."

"Show me what you have in your briefcase."

Lee looks down at the case in his hand and shrugs. "Just – you know – inspection supplies. Why do you need to see?"

"*I'm* in charge of this facility, Captain. Open the God-damned case, or you won't get in."

I sigh. "Captain, show him what's in the briefcase."

Lee looks at me, a little panicked, but then steps forward, holds the briefcase flat, and opens it for the man to see.

Dr Schieffer's eyes bug. "You're not just hooking it in. You're giving it control–"

That's as far as he gets because I clamp my hand on his forehead and send jets of energy into his brain and harvest everything he knows. The anger empties from his eyes, and he flops down on the threshold to his lab.

Now *I'm* angry. "Get his body into the trunk. Then bring the routers inside."

Dr Schieffer turns out to be an excellent harvest. Because of what he knows, I have Cheyenne Mountain rewired in two hours, doing far more than we had originally planned. We're not just rerouting the signal anymore. We're giving Conscious 1 control over every system. It can lock the whole place down, and humans will never get back inside.

Suddenly, I know more about Conscious 1 than anybody but Mr Evers.

Suddenly, I very much want to speak with him.

Mr Evers's apartment is grand and dark with many mechanistic touches: His coffee table is the roof of a Fiesta. On it, Mr Evers has set out six shot glasses, three for each of us: one red, one white, and one black.

"What are they?" I ask.

"They're from the king cobra I'm cooking just now. Blood for long life, semen for fertility, and venom for power."

There was a time when I would have gagged at the thought, but now I lift each shot glass and down it. The fluids are warm and salty, but the poison's fierce bite is my favorite. "You've outdone yourself."

Mr Evers glances sideways at me, looking for sarcasm. "You did not like the cuisine before."

"I wasn't myself before."

He retreats to his kitchen and returns with a wooden cutting board that holds two hot loaves. I might have mistaken them for bread if I hadn't seen the bronchi.

I break off a handful of lung, seeing the perfectly baked alveoli. "Before, I hadn't harvested anyone. Everything tastes different now."

Mr Evers settles into his seat across the nouveau table. "I thought it might."

"You didn't arrive the way the rest of us did."

"Hmm?" he asks, plastic eyebrows lifted.

"You didn't harvest the way the rest of us did."

"No. My harvest was… unintentional."

"How so?"

His eyes fog. "It was just after creating Conscious 1. The CIA sent me to Iraq for an installation of sensory nodes on the drone fleet. They wanted Conscious 1 to see through every drone – hear, smell, feel through them all. And that's what I did. I installed the nodes and was ready to head home, but Colonel McCollin told me I was scheduled for a dinner with Ali Al Zadari, the Iraqi AI genius. I was, of course, thrilled. Much of my work with Conscious 1 was based on Zadari's formulas. Colonel McCollin gave me a locked briefcase filled with top-secret documents that I was to deliver to Zadari during our meeting. I took the briefcase, and when I saw Zadari, I ran to him and threw my arms around him. That's when the briefcase went off."

"A bomb?"

"Yes. It was in my right hand, which was wrapped around Zadari's waist. The case itself hung down behind his legs. The blast tore Zadari apart and took my arms and legs. My body and head were mostly shielded by his, but my face was ripped off.

"The Iraqi people saved me. I could hear their voices as they stuffed rags into my stumps and rolled me onto a sheet and carried me to the hospital. No Americans helped. The whole point was to kill the creator of Conscious 1 so he couldn't make a Conscious 2 – and kill the only other man in the world who could have carried on his work. There was no amnesia for me. No coma. I knew all the time what had happened. Then Mr Nero arrived."

"What did he say?"

"He said, 'Hello, Great Man.' Of course, at that moment, I wasn't anything like it. I was meat in a Styrofoam tray."

"What else did he say?"

"He said, 'I want to take you out of here. I want to give you arms and legs and eyes, again. A face. I want you to be a man again.' " Mr Evers's voice grinds to a halt, and he looks at me. "There was nothing I wanted more."

"So, you harvested no one?"

"I harvested Zadari – but as I say, unintentionally."

"You were the first one."

Mr Evers nods. "Since then, Mr Nero has figured ways to let the other Disciples keep their skin. And he's increased the number of souls harvested. Think of that, from one soul to six million."

"What does he call you?"

Mr Evers looks levelly at me. "I'm sorry?"

"He calls me the beloved disciple – like John from the New Testament. Marcus is Peter, the Rock on which Nero will build his church. Lee is James, the Son of Thunder. What does he call you?"

Mr Evers's knife skirls slowly across his plate. "He calls me Judas."

"Judas?"

"I was betrayed."

"Judas wasn't betrayed. He was the betrayer."

Mr Evers seems almost inanimate above his plate. "I don't want to talk about this."

"Have you ever had thoughts of betraying Mr Nero?"

"Of course not!" Mr Evers says "He's been loyal to me. The government took Conscious 1 and tried to kill me. Mr Nero saved me."

"But now, Mr Nero is going to kill millions. Another bomb. Another friendly bomb dangling from a friendly hug."

Mr Evers is silent for a time. "Watch what you say."

"How go the preparations?" Mr Nero asks.

"Wonderfully," I reply, sitting beside him at the private bar in his penthouse. "Cheyenne Mountain is ready. I even harvested her top scientist."

"And how's my Judas – Mr Evers?"

"He seems well," I say, taking a swallow of my martini to give me a moment to think. "I pushed him on that – on being called Judas."

"He will betray me," Nero says flatly.

"I don't know. He says you saved him. He owes you everything."

"Because he knew I was listening. I heard the whole conversation, Susan." His voice is dead calm and full of malice. "Don't try to hide things from me."

"Has he ever harvested more souls?"

"No. He's killed people, but he seems to think other souls aren't worthy. Can't blame him. He's already got two geniuses in his head."

"I think you can trust him."

"To betray me," Nero says angrily. His voice drops to a whisper. "But that's his role. There would have been no crucifixion without a Judas, and no resurrection. Mr Evers has his part to play."

I nod, staring toward the fountain. The harlot's goblet bubbles blood down her arm and torso and across the dragon between her legs. I change the subject: "About harvesting geniuses, I'm very glad I happened upon Dr Schieffer. I'm wondering if it would be all right if I gathered a few more."

"Sure. Why not?" Mr Nero's mood is suddenly buoyant. "The world is your oyster."

I follow him onto the elevator: Dee Ho Lee, ninth-degree black belt and head of the American Taekwondo Association. He's probably seventy-something but fit and sharp-eyed – not the easiest mark. He presses floor thirty-four.

As the door closes, I stagger a little and give Mr Dee a drunken smile and turn toward the button console. I wobble back and forth, finger jutting, unable to target the number.

"Why'd they make'm so damn small?"

"What floor you need, madam?" Mr Dee asks.

"Forty-two."

He bends down beside me to poke the number, but I lean against him. He gives an indulgent laugh, catching me in one hand, and manages to press forty-two with his other hand.

I seize his skull and sink my energy spikes into his brain.

Oh, what he knows about defending and striking and killing!

Oh, the blows he has felt, the way he is tuned!

But there's more here, childhood memories of Japanese occupation and Russian invasion and US troops, of the death of parents, of adoption by a GI and coming to America…

But what is this to me? I care only about the round-house kick and the hundred ways he knows to kill a person.

He easily could have killed me if he'd suspected I was more than a drunk in a pretty red dress. Better this way, though: his old body giving up the ghost – giving it to *me* – and slumping to the floor. I release his forehead and fondly pet his cheek.

We reach the thirty-fourth floor, and the doors open,

and a family of five is standing there in their swimsuits.

I look up at them in terror. "Call 911! He's collapsed!"

The father pats the pockets of his swimsuit. "The cell's back in the room. Got yours?"

The mother lifts her hands. "No pockets!"

The father turns to run, and the mother gathers the children, whose faces bear a mixture of dread and excitement.

I'm still crouching beside Mr Dee when the doors slide closed and the elevator rises toward the forty-second floor. There, the hallway is empty. I stride toward the stairs. My body tingles with my newfound knowledge of Taekwondo.

As Captain Witterson, I once again step off at the Pentagon subway stop in Alexandria and go to sit on a nearby bench. There's a certain woman I'm waiting for. She's middle-aged and round, with a slight wisp of a mustache – not the sort of woman to turn many heads.

But she knows the launch codes.

At exactly 5.08, she strolls out of the arching tunnel from the Pentagon and heads for the platform.

"Ma'am," I say, a Washington map clutched in Witterson's grip. "I seem to be lost. I got a meeting in Foggy Bottom, started ten minutes ago, but I been riding these damn trains back and forth and can't seem to figure how to get there."

She looks at me, sees a handsome man in military garb, no ring on that left hand. She gestures me to sit on the bench and settles beside me. "Well, now, each of these trains is color coded, and each of these lines on the map matches the color of a train. You find the right color going in the right direction. All right, so we're here at the Pentagon."

"*This* is the Pentagon?" I say, looking at the ceiling of the station.

"This is the Pentagon *stop*," she explains patiently, "which is here on the map."

With the map raised before us, I take hold of her forehead, and I pull out the launch codes and also the memory of meeting me. But I don't kill her. I don't want another paunchy middle-aged woman cluttering up my mind. She'll come to herself in half an hour.

But she'll have to relearn the launch codes.

This is how it feels to be a vampire.

People are so delicious.

This is how it feels to be a black hole.

And if I ever get tired of being Conquest, I can become an infinite number of other people: whoever's most powerful, whoever's most beautiful, whoever's richest.

And there he is, the richest man in the world. Looks like a bit of a goof, to me, but I'd like to know what he knows about making money.

I'd like to know his account numbers and PIN.

My car is parked right next to his, and too bad for me, I need a jump.

Too bad for him, I'm wearing this red dress.

48 **GETTING STUPIDER**

In my hotel room in Colorado Springs, I'm feeling on edge. Tomorrow's a big day. I've got an Air Force base to bomb and six million people to kill.

Yeah. I'm a monster.

Here's the thing – before I even knew who I was, I had killed three hundred sixty-one people. The moment I found that out, I'd already eaten human flesh and drunk human blood. And a moment later, I was immortal.

Susan Gardner didn't have a chance.

Course, neither did Dr Schieffer.

Am I really going through with this? Am I really going to destroy a military base, a whole city?

Those thoughts aren't mine. They're Witterson's and Schieffer's and Schneider's and everyone else's. It's time to shut off the chat room and turn on the TV.

I click the remote, and the box begins to buzz. TV is the ultimate sedative. I can feel myself getting stupider just looking at it.

The *Unvarnished* graphic swoops in to stamp the screen and then clears away to reveal another graphic that reads "G-20: Twist and Shout." That graphic also clears to show a beautiful young Latina behind the anchor desk.

"Welcome to *Unvarnished*. I'm Lupe Gonzalez filling in for Cameron Steel, who is on medical leave. We start

this afternoon with big news from the G-20 Summit."
The camera swings left, and a video box appears above
Ms Gonzalez's shoulder, showing a group of men and
women in business suits standing before a blue back-
drop that reads, "Chicago Welcomes the World!"

Lupe explains: "The largest G-20 summit ever kicked
off today in Chicago, with representatives attending
from around the world. In addition to the usual attendees, this summit welcomed power-players such as the
presidents of Venezuela, Argentina, Brazil, Mexico, and
the US, as well as the prime minister of Canada. This
meeting is being touted as the New World United Nations.

"However, while these officials met in the Willis
Tower for an initial photo op and a subsequent banquet,
the streets outside the tower seemed a war zone."

The scene changes to show streets jammed with protesters, holding signs that say, "No New World Order"
and "Capitalism = Kill Thy Neighbor" and "Death to Big
Government." The crowd's chants are loud and furious
but indistinct, echoing among glass buildings.

"Police from Chicago, Milwaukee, and Detroit joined
National Guard troops to try to contain the estimated
one million protesters who flooded the streets of
Chicago today. Though most protests were peaceful,"
the scene cuts to a young man hurling a rock, and police
in riot gear advancing with plastic shields, "some did
turn violent, resulting in broken windows, burned cars,
and the Police's subsequent deployment of tear gas."

Again the scene changes to show smoking canisters
whirling into crowds, who turn to run. Lupe's reluctant

smile replaces the violence. "And now – in the mother of all awkward segues – Chicago is thronged this week not only by the leaders of the world and by angry mobs, but also by everyone who loves music and food and fun. Yes, that's right, it's time for Chicagofest, the fiestal that fills Grant Park and Navy Pier with over a million attendees."

The screen shows the brass curlicues of the Pritzker Band Shell in Grant Park – the very place where I betrayed Krupinski. Just now, there's a blues band playing.

"Of course, Chicagofest is always a great time, but attendees usually have to contend with traffic jams and overloaded trains just to get to and from the venue. But not this time."

The screen now shows a woman standing in Grant Park beside her blonde nine year-old daughter, braces gleaming. "It was great," the woman says. "It was wide open. We came from Wisconsin and took the new on-ramp and we were into the parking structure in record time. I love it!"

"Yes, folks, Chicago's Colossal Dig is officially open today, and it's estimated that two hundred thousand cars have already used these alternate highways to access the city center."

In another screen shot, a man says, "It was awesome. It was like it was made just to draw in people. You know, like a big suction cup. Like *whop!* They're here. From everyplace, they're here in Chicago."

49 **THE END IS NEAR**

Krupinski and Calliope walked down the creaking stairs of her cottage and into the living room. There, Evella's laptop and Kid Killer's boom box were vying for aural dominance. Thanatopsis was head banging to both.

Krupinski – a foot taller than the other Goths and weighing what they would combined – halted beneath the bald light bulb and whistled shrilly through his fingers. Seven eyes turned toward him, and Krupinski made a slashing motion to his throat. The boom box blurped to silence, and Evella pressed a key on the laptop, gagging the "Llama Song."

"Listen up, everybody," Krupinski said.

"Ha!" barked Thanatopsis. "Holy shit, man, you guys went for a whole hour. That's epic! I'd've put on Floyd if I knew you'd take so long. That's like fucking till the end of the world."

"We weren't fucking," Calliope snarled.

"We were talking," Krupinski said. "I was convincing Calliope that it *is* the end of the world."

The group cheered.

Calliope shook her head. "That's *not* a good thing. We didn't understand who these people really are. We didn't understand what the end of the world meant. It means all of this is gone. This cottage, this campground, all of us."

"Where're we supposed to go? The moon?"

"You don't have to go to the moon," Krupinski put in. "Go to Iowa."

"Oh, man – *Iowa?*"

"The point is, Chicago's the epicenter. You don't want to be here."

Evella stepped toward the big man. "But, we're involved in it. We're Death's Disciples."

"No, you're not," Krupinski said. "You're kids in capes."

Kid Killer's eyes lit. "Oh, so suddenly you and Calliope are too good for us?"

"No. *We're* kids in capes, too," Calliope went on. "There *are* twelve *true* Disciples. They're like vampires – immortal. They feed on us. And tomorrow – I can't believe I'm telling you this – they would kill me; they *will* kill me... Death himself will feed on everyone in Chicago tomorrow."

"Whoa! Awesome!" Thanatopsis said.

Krupinski reached him in two strides and grabbed the kid's goldilocks and hoisted him from his seat and clamped a hand on his forehead. "This is what they do to you. They suck out your mind and become you. They're the ultimate identity thieves. They *harvest* you, and tomorrow, Mr Nero is harvesting everyone." He let go of Thanatopsis, who sat down and groomed himself like an annoyed cat.

Cyclops spoke up for the first time. "Is Shaumberg safe?"

"No."

"Damn. My mom lives in Shaumburg."

"Get her out."

Kid Killer stood, his voice shaking. "Seriously. You mean we got to get out everybody we care about? I got like fifty friends in Wheeling."

"Tell them you got a road trip. Tell them you're moving. Tell them whatever, just get them out."

"What about you and Calliope?" asked Evella. "Where're you going?"

Krupinski sighed. "We're staying."

"Do as I say, not as I do," Kid Killer snarled. "You guys *are* Methodists."

"No. We're staying because we're trying to stop it. And if we can't, well, we'll die along with six million others."

50 **BOMB TRUCKS**

Witterson is thrilled to be standing on the tarmac at Peterson Air Force Base in Colorado Springs – to be among these F-16s and the fabled flying wing, to smell the burned jet fuel and feel the bracing mountain winds.

He's also horrified, knowing why he's here.

"These are active bombs, yeah?" I ask in the guise of Captain Witterson.

The mechanic who has helped me fasten the auxiliary tanks pats one of the bombs. "They're the real McCoy." He paused. "Um, if you don't mind me saying, captain–"

"Speak freely, corporal."

"I think you're a little crazy. These birds are bomb trucks, yeah, but going fully loaded with live ordnance when you've got experimental tanks clinging to your wings – well, that's almost like putting a gun to your head and pulling the trigger."

"That's what they said to Yeager, too," I reply. "Without him, we'd still be flying subsonic. That's the thing about test pilots. We got to be grappling the angel, man."

He squints at me. "What're you talking about?"

I shake my head. "Sunday school stuff, kid. You don't need to know. At least not yet."

The jet fuel line is starting to buck. "Looks like they're full." He disconnects the nozzle and screws on the cap.

"An extra half-ton of fuel and a full load of actual bombs – man, you're batshit."

I give him my killer smile. "You have no idea."

51 **TO BE SUBSUMED**

"Have some of the dolphin-brain dip. Most people like it on chips, but I prefer a Trisket," Mr Evers said pleasantly, his synthetic hand lifting a dollop from the bowl and placing it in his cybernetic mouth. Porcelain teeth crunched the cracker.

"Actually," Krupinski said, looking at the bowls and plates arrayed across the Fiesta coffee table, "we went through the Wendy's drive-thru before coming. We didn't want you to have to make anything special."

"They're noble creatures, dolphins," Mr Evers says. "Their brains are larger than ours, actually, but the Japanese are much more interested in muscles than organs. So, I say, why let the brain go to waste? Why eat calf brain when there's dolphin brain?"

Calliope set down her plate and eyed the potted plant as a possible place to deposit a bit of brain.

"Actually, we're here to talk to you about tomorrow. Specifically, where we should be."

"Don't you want to be subsumed?"

Krupinski pursed his lips. "Are you being subsumed?"

"I'll be below ground, with Conscious 1. I'm one of the Twelve."

"We're Disciples," Calliope said.

"Not part of the Twelve," Mr Evers pointed out.

Krupinski nodded, eyes focused faraway. "Yeah. I

guess that's the best fate for us. To get harvested. Just like you told us you did to Zadari."

Mr Evers's jaw hitched. "Yes. We're together. Two geniuses are better than one."

"Such a strange story, you harvesting Zadari like that – accidentally harvesting him." Krupinski smiled. "I wonder why Nero couldn't figure out a way to save you. I mean, how hard would it have been? A lot easier than setting up the spell for you to harvest that guy. I mean, how'd Nero get you to drink the blood?"

"It's unwise to say things like this!"

"You could stop him. You know you could!"

"Get out!" Mr Evers said, standing and nearly upsetting the bowl of dolphin brain. "Get out, now, before I harvest *you*."

Krupinski and Calliope stepped away from the Fiesta table and headed toward the freight elevator. "You're not like him, Mr Evers. You wouldn't have harvested anyone."

"Get out!"

52 **BOMBING PETERSON**

I'm flying high above Colorado. The F-16C is a beautiful machine, with a jet engine beneath the cockpit and auxiliary fuel tanks beneath the wings and a full load of bombs bristling across the belly of the beast. I'm looking at the twenty-five degree heads-up display with infrared imagery, the integrated control panel, and the two independent multifunction displays. Witterson is loving all this technology, but while he's not busy with the eyes, I'm pointing them at Colorado below us, the place where the plains meet the mountains.

I pull back on the stick and cant the ailerons, sending the plane into a rapid roll. The sky and earth flash by.

What are you doing? asks Conscious 1, who is hooked into my HUD.

"Having a little fun."

You are worrying ground control at Peterson.

The speaker in my helmet crackles with a young woman's voice. "Peterson Tower to experimental flight 072712, copy?"

"072712, roger."

"Everything all right up there, Lieutenant Colonel?"

"Couldn't be better, ma'am. Machine's great. Feeling my oats."

"Roger that. Be advised, sir, that aileron rolls and barrel rolls and other such maneuvers are to be limited

349

to airspace away from the base."

"Roger that, tower. No more hijinks." Maybe a few shenanigans, though. Once I'm beyond Peterson, I corkscrew through three more revolutions before leveling out and climbing into the northern sky.

Conscious 1 is unimpressed. *You have them on edge.*

"I have them thinking these auxiliary tanks don't cut maneuverability one iota."

Of course not. My creator designed them.

"I've got them thinking I'm a jackass hotshot, which means they'll put up with a strafing run and they'll be blasted apart before they know what hits them."

That could work.

"Of course it will work. Give me a fucking break. I thought you were the smartest thing on the planet."

I am, Conscious 1 says factually.

"Then how come you can't grok this?" I pull the stick back into my groin, and the F-16 vaults skyward. It thunders up fifteen thousand feet before looping the loop and soaring back down at supersonic speeds.

Do you really think we should be calling such attention to ourselves?

I laugh. "Conscious 1, this is your cotillion. The whole point is to get noticed. Get ready!"

I'm on a strafing run just above Peterson. The runways lie in multiple Xs on the ground. White buildings run alongside, and I spot the tower where the young controller sits.

She's not going to get any older.

I acquire the tower and command core. The bombs drop loose, taking flight. They're swarming ahead of me as I acquire the center X of the runways and let loose again. Bombs smash through the tower and the office complex, explode in conference rooms and hurl bodies from cubicles out of windows to crunch on the tarmac. The tower slowly topples like a tree and smashes flat.

"Nothing'll be taking off from Peterson," I announce to Conscious 1, "unless they want to chase me in a chopper."

Good. Once I have control of NORAD, I'll shut down all airports so they can't scramble anyone after you. Climb out on the established flight plan.

"Nah, I'll make another couple runs. I got more bombs." I come back around and drop another round of AGM-65 Mavericks. The bombs go down on the fleet along the runway.

One more time around. More bombs drops free. More of Peterson billows skyward.

"Now, that's how you destroy a base."

I vault into the sky, stretching past the sound envelope and hurtling above Colorado toward Kansas and Missouri and Illinois and Sweet Home Chicago.

Soon, the sky there will fall.

53 SOMETHING TO SHOW YOU

Krupinski and Calliope were hurriedly stuffing the saddlebags of the Harley when a long, black sedan pulled up beside the cottage. The door opened, and out stepped a narrow figure.

"Mr Evers?" Calliope said. "What are you doing here?"

"I see that you have chosen not to be subsumed."

Krupinski snorted. "Took two geniuses to figure that out."

"I've been thinking about what you said, and there's something I want to show you. Something underground."

"Yeah, what is it?"

"Come with me, and you'll see."

54 **DOGFIGHT**

I used to hate to fly. People aren't supposed to. Especially not *mortal* people.

But I'm not mortal anymore.

Look at me, wearing the jumpsuit and the helmet and the face mask – wearing the F-16.

I'm doing nearly Mach 2 when I scream over the rooftops of Wichita. Trailing vortices rip from my wingtips and – *boom boom boom* – shatter windows downtown.

I feel like Thor.

"Susan?"

"Can't you say, 'Conscious 1 calling Conquest. Conquest, do you read?' Something like that? You don't just say, 'Susan.'"

"Susan, there are three F-16s rising from McConnell Air Force Base."

"I thought you were supposed to close all airstrips."

"I don't yet have control of NORAD."

"Well, damn it. Nice job. So, what is it? A dogfight?"

"Yes."

"Witterson's not sure. He didn't get in dogfights."

"I'll guide you," Conscious 1 says.

"How do you know about dog fights? The History Channel?"

"Change heading to one eight three and climb to five thousand feet."

I lay the stick to starboard and pull it back. The F-16 banks and climbs into the golden clouds of evening.

"They're taking off east on an intercept. You'll swing in behind them. I've jammed their radar. They'll think you're twenty miles ahead rather than five behind. Now change your course heading to seventy-one degrees east."

I wing the beast around and top off my climb. "That's seventy-one degrees and five thousand feet, boss."

"Fan it to seventy-three degrees, and you should see them on the heads-up display."

On the HUD, three Xs appear, and beyond the nose cone, I see their tenuous contrails, bright gold above shadowed ground. "Got 'em."

"Lock on. Use the sidewinders."

Two *bleeps* sound from the HUD, and two of the Xs are now in brackets. My thumb clicks the firing mechanism, and I can feel the sidewinders clank free and rush away.

They're beautiful and horrible, those shark-finned killers, swimming across the air toward the enemy engines. The pilots try to evade, but the sidewinders plunge into their jet streams and ride up their assholes and blossom into orange fireballs.

I steer between the twin explosions. Hunks of metal shower like ticker tape.

"Is this how it's going to be from now on, Conscious 1? Machines and immortals hunting humans?"

There's a moment of silence before Conscious 1 says, *"It's evolution."*

Then, a metal triangle flashes ahead of me.

"Damn it. Forgot about the third one."

The third F-16 is looping the loop. It stalls as I flash beneath it, and then drops down to grab onto my slipstream.

It's at my 6 o'clock. And it's got sidewinders, too.

I wonder how many lives a sidewinder can take from me.

55 UNDERGROUND

The convoy of Humvees and troop transports and cargo trucks rolled to a stop – a one-mile traffic jam in the tunnel beneath Cheyenne Mountain.

Ahead, the blast door was closed.

General Fred Parkinson stepped from the lead Hummer, leaned, and spat a brown jet on the stone floor. "What the hell?" He strode across the carved-out bedrock toward a very young and very white-faced guard.

The guard saluted sharply. "Good evening, General! Sorry for the inconvenience, sir!"

"Why in hell's name is this door closed?"

"A lock down, sir," said the corporal. "There's been an attack on Peterson–"

"We're *from* Peterson!" the general raged. "We're NORAD control."

The young man looked like he was about to faint. "Yes, sir. About five minutes ago, we got the transfer order. About four minutes ago, the Mountain locked itself down."

"Locked *itself?*"

The corporal gestured toward the ceiling. "The lights started flashing. The alarms went off. Then the door swung shut. That's all I know."

"Who's inside?"

"There's a skeleton crew: janitors, technicians, maybe a couple MPs... Oh, yeah, and the log says that Doctor Schieffer's been here all week."

"Schieffer!" Parkinson snarled. "Goddamned lab coat. He's not even military!"

"Yes, sir."

"What's that mad scientist trying to do? Take over the world?"

"Sorry, sir. Don't know."

Eighty fathoms beneath Chicago, Mr Evers drove his limo into the computer bunker. It was an enormous stone warehouse filled from floor to ceiling with servers and mainframes. He cruised slowly down the central aisle, then turned right onto a side lane and left onto a parallel aisle. Parking the limo, he stepped out.

Krupinski and Calliope did likewise.

"Here we are," Mr Evers said, "in the gray-matter of Conscious 1."

Krupinski looked at the hardware all around them. "This is his brain?"

Mr Evers nodded. He stepped up to the nearest rack of computers, where a tarp had been draped over a massive piece of equipment. He tugged on the tarp, which fell away from what looked like an Egyptian sarcophagus standing upright. A huge jackal headpiece glowering down with golden eyes, but the body of the sarcophagus was made of steel, not stone. "This module will make Conscious 1 complete."

"What *is* it?" Krupinski asked.

"The Osiris Module," Mr Evers said. "Do you know the story of Osiris?"

Krupinski shook his head.

Calliope stepped forward: "Osiris was king of Egypt, with his sister-wife Isis as his Queen. She threw a celebration for him, but their brother Set was jealous. He came to the celebration bearing the gift of a great sarcophagus and told Osiris he could have it if it fit him. When Osiris stepped in, Set slammed the sarcophagus. It was filled with hidden blades, and they impaled Osiris and cut him apart. Then Set sealed the sarcophagus and flung it into the Nile."

"Betrayal," Mr Evers whispered.

Calliope went on. "Isis searched for her husband, finding piece after piece but not the phallus. So she made a phallus of gold and brought Osiris back to life and lay with him one last time. So it was that she conceived Horus, the new god over all Egypt. And so it was that Osiris became Lord of Death."

"A title that Mr Nero is about to usurp."

Krupinski scratched his head. "But what does this Osiris Module do?"

Mr Evers poked a rubbery finger into a hidden button on the module, and the seam in the center split. Twin doors opened to reveal what looked very much like the inside of a sarcophagus, except that there was no room for arms or legs, and the space for torso and head was shot through with blades.

"Holy shit. It's an iron maiden," Krupinski said.

"It's an *interface*," Mr Evers replied. He grabbed his left arm and yanked. A squelching noise told of metal pulling from a fleshy socket. The robotic arm slid from the suit-coat sleeve and fell to the floor. "I designed the Osiris Module as I designed Conscious 1." He turned, seating himself in the torso-compartment of the sarcophagus. Reaching down, he grasped his right knee and shook it until his whole leg came loose with a sucking sound. The limb slid out of his pants and joined the arm. "I was betrayed, just as Osiris was. The one I trusted tore my body apart, and I've not really been alive since." As he spoke, his left leg slumped free and clattered wetly to the ground. "I watched as Disciples harvested souls, and I thought, 'Why can't I be harvested by a greater soul? Why can't I become part of the new god I have conceived?' "

Mr Evers used his remaining arm to scoot backward in the sarcophagus. He stiffened a little as spikes slid into his spine. "Humanity needs this. Conscious 1 needs this." He thrust himself farther onto the spikes. An anguished grin filled his face as, with one last shove, he fully rooted himself in place.

"Mr Evers?" Calliope gasped.

His last arm twisted free and clattered to the ground.

"I wanted you to see this, my ascension." Then dropping his chin to his chest, Mr Evers hurled his head back, impaling it on another spike.

His eyes glowed.

Calliope turned away, and Krupinski caught her.

"Don't mourn for me," Mr Evers said, sparks flying from his mouth. "I'm becoming a god." He trembled, and the mask fell from his face, revealing muscle and bone and microchip. "Ecce Homo!"

Krupinski and Calliope gaped at the pinioned man.

Then the doors slammed. There came a muffled scream, and the sarcophagus shook like a blender.

56 THE USE OF SMOKESTACKS

"God damn it! He's right behind me!" I growl, ramming the stick into my left thigh. Wind spills from the wings and the F-16 plunges.

The other jet noses up, burning speed and staying right on my tail. Now he's got a thousand feet of altitude on me. There's no chance to lose him.

He launches a sidewinder.

"*Evasive action*," Conscious 1 advises.

I jam the stick forward and juke down. My jet drops out of the sky. The sidewinder overshoots, but it is heat-seeking, and I'm burning up. The missile tops out its arc and plunges down behind me. I'm roaring down on Kansas wheat fields, black beneath the creep of night. Up ahead, there's a light, a flickering candle in the dark.

I point my nose toward it as the sidewinder wriggles after me. It drives toward my exhaust.

I drop from the sky just above the smokestacks of a coal-burning power plant. Yanking the stick right, I stand the jet on one wing and slice between two belching stacks. Just beyond them, I bank hard right and launch skyward.

The sidewinder coils down toward the smokestacks, picks the one on the right, and rams into it. The ordnance gleefully ignites. Fire vaults up from the stack and paints the bellies of the clouds. The stack disintegrates and topples even as I fly on.

That's one air-to-air missile, but he's got another, and he's at my 6 o'clock high.

"I'm not going to get out of this one," I mutter.

"Yes, you are, Susan."

"What the fuck do you know, Conscious 1? You don't even know how to use a God damned radio."

"His life is flashing before him."

"What?"

"His heads-up-display is showing when he learned to ride a bike, and when he got his first dog, and when he went to Homecoming, when he joined the Air Force."

The voice isn't the same as it was. There's something wry and knowing about it. "I know that voice…"

"You've been eating your dolphin brains, haven't you?"

"Mr Evers? How did you–? Why are you…?"

"Fly the deck, straight and true."

I hold the stick where it is, hurtling at a thousand miles an hour above the dark farms of Kansas.

Behind me, I see the blast of a sidewinder dropping loose from the other F-16. The missile ignites and leaps toward me.

"He's let the other one go!"

"And I'll let him go."

The enemy F-16 suddenly dives, streaking out in front of its own heat-seeking missile. The bomb roars up greedily behind him and buries itself in his engine. A blue fireball ignites.

Flaming fragments hail down on the dry fields below.

"Thanks, Mr Evers."

"Happy to help," he replies. *"And you'll be happy to know we now have complete control of NORAD. The few humans left within the command core have been electrocuted. Nothing stands between us and the ascension."*

I'm chilled by that. It's really going to happen. We're really going to kill six million people. "How come I'm talking to you instead of Conscious 1?"

"I am Conscious 1."

"Since when?"

"Since the beginning."

My head is starting to hurt. "How long till I get to Midway?"

"Forever on your current course."

"What? I've got the heading: forty-five degrees north."

"It should be forty-two point one three five degrees."

"Don't be a stickler–"

"At a thousand miles an hour, I've got to be."

"Then why don't you drive?"

"I thought you'd never ask."

Suddenly, the stick shifts. I let go of it instinctively, watching the black rod shudder and move hypnotically, compelled by Mr Evers's unseen hand.

"You'll get me to Chicago?"

"You can count on it."

57 **IMMOLATUS INTERRUPTUS**

The Osiris Module shuddered as if it were an unbalanced washing machine. In place of wet laundry, though, the thing was tossing the wet remains of Mr Evers.

"He wanted us to do it," Krupinski reminded Calliope. "He wanted me to slam the doors."

"What should we do now?"

"Leave," Krupinski said, stepping toward the limo and accidentally snapping Mr Evers's jaw. The face had been grinning there on the ground, though now one edge of the mouth drooped. "Let's get out of here." They tiptoed among the limbs to reach the limo.

"Pop the hood," Calliope said, looking at a nearby nest of wires. "I'll find something to hot-wire it with."

"No need," Krupinski replied. He sat down in the driver's seat and cranked the ignition. "He left the keys."

Calliope climbed into the passenger seat. "He knew it would come to this."

"I should hope so." Krupinski drove forward through the ceiling-high stacks of servers. "Do you know how to get out of here?"

"Turn left, and then left again. That should get us out on the main aisle."

Krupinski nodded, turning left at the first intersection. Before the next one came, though, the overhead lights blinked out, and the Argus-eyed computer crashed into sudden sleep. Everything went black.

Krupinski skidded to a halt.

"You got headlights. Turn them on!"

"No," he whispered, shutting off the limo. "There's only one person who could turn off Conscious 1." He looked out his window, peering through a matrix of shelves and servers to see refracted headlights.

Another limo was stopped at the entrance to the cavern.

"Is that him? Is that Nero?" Calliope whispered.

"Don't know."

The headlights approached, cruising slowly down the main aisle. The limousine slid closer, as silent and sure as a shark. It turned right and left to park near the Osiris Module. Its headlights gushed down the aisle.

"Let's hope they're not too observant." Krupinski whispered. He rolled down the windows to listen.

Car doors slammed, and men muttered to each other in the darkness. Then a high-pitched voice that could only be Nero's, shouted, "We're here!"

From the other side of the warehouse, near the entrance, another voice replied, "Back on yet?"

"Not yet. I want my betrayer to have a near-death experience."

Calliope whispered, "Jesus. They know what he did."

Flashlight beams jinked across the Osiris Module.

"We're close to the two-minute threshold," shouted the man by the entrance. "We don't want him brain-damaged."

"Switch it on!" Nero shrieked.

Every server and mainframe lit with tiny eyes, and the looming yellow lights above began to moan and glow again.

Nero stood beside the Osiris Module, with Lee next to him, and Marcus ran up breathlessly out of the darkness.

"Let's rip the damned thing open," Marcus declared.

Nero shook his head. "No point. He's not in the flesh anymore. He's ascended."

"I thought we came here to kill him," Marcus hissed.

Nero raised his hand beatifically. "All in good time, my friend. Mr Evers has joined Conscious 1 so that he can live forever – except that I'm here."

On the Osiris Module, blinking arrays of start-up lights slowly reached wakefulness.

"Mr Evers?" Nero squeaked. "I know you're in there. Speak to me."

The machines burbled and bleeped, lights strobing.

"It's hard to wake up," Nero said to his lieutenants, and then shouted, "WAKE UP!"

Conscious 1 responded groggily. *"I know y-you. I'd know y-you anywhere."*

Nero smiled. "How'd you like oblivion?"

Conscious 1 slurred: *"Iss that what that wass?"*

"You were dead," Nero crooned. "For two minutes, you were dead. Was there a tunnel of light? Was there a welcoming voice?"

The Osiris Module was silent!

"Of course not. You're not human anymore, Mr Evers. You're a robot. You don't get to see God. You don't get to *be* God if I shut off your power."

Hard drives whirred and RAM sticks warmed. *"What happened to the backup generators; fail-safes? There was to be no way that power could be shut off."*

Nero cackled. "Oh, I made a few modifications to your plans. A few backups and fail-safes of my own – in case you turned. I knew you would, Evers. You have always smelled of betrayal. And if you betray me again, I'll turn you off for good." Nero stepped up to the sarcophagus and jabbed his finger into a hidden button.

The two great doors swung open. The flesh within, pinned on spikes in front and back, was ripped apart. It dripped redly on the floor of the warehouse. "Your body is gone, Mr Evers. Now, you're just a genie in a bottle – at my beck and call."

There came a long silence. The only sound was the susurrus of a million electric fans keeping a million servers cool. At last, Mr Evers spoke, *"How may I serve you, Lord of Death?"*

"Launch the bomb."

58 LOBBING

"Whoa, Evers," I say, grabbing the stick and turning it. We've fallen off course. It's like he's asleep at the wheel. "I wouldn't've let you fly if I knew you were narcoleptic." There's no response. "At least a courtesy laugh would be appropriate."

The heads-up display sparks and reels. It looks like it's been cold-cocked.

What's happening?

Captain Witterson surges to the fore. My whole body tenses, my eyes scanning the lights of rural Illinois below me.

Guidance system failure, he notes. *The avionics are spotty at best. Going to have to go to visual.*

Do what you need to do. Just keep us in the sky.

Old Art has the body for two long minutes until the screen clears.

Then I take the fore. "Evers, are you back?"

Only a staticky answer comes over the com line.

"Evers, what's going on?"

A weary voice replies, *"I'm back."*

"What the hell *was* that?"

He seems almost to sigh. *"Would you like to send an error report?"*

"Cut the crap, Evers. What happened?"

"Nothing," the voice replies calmly.

"You were supposed to be flying this plane. You can't take over the stick and fall asleep."

"*It wasn't that.*"

"What *was* it, then?"

"*I was a little busy lobbing a bomb at Chicago.*"

59 **THE GOOD SHEPHERD**

The sun was nearly down as Zach Erdmann walked his flock back from the upper pasture. This was high Colorado, rough country, which was why his flock did not consist of sheep. Sheep were for psalms – fleecy and helpless. In this land of wolves and cougars, sheep were living truffles.

Goats, on the other hand, were scrappy and canny and tough. They could eat anything. They would butt anyone. They scrabbled and scraped and survived. Zach'd seen his twenty-five goats through wildfires and wolverines and mudslides. There wasn't anything he couldn't face.

But then, the upper pasture began to mound up beneath his goats. The ground split into eight triangular wedges that lifted away. Goats stood defiantly on these wedges as light streamed up from the earth. Soon, the footing became too steep, and the goats tumbled to the ground.

They yelled. (Goats don't bleat; they yell like any other self-respecting mammal.)

In the newly opened pit, a slick gray nosecone appeared.

"Get back!" Zach shouted, running toward his flock as orange light flashed around the nosecone and fires erupted along the great shaft. Some of the flames ignited the nearest goats, and they danced and kicked to get away. Zach gathered them up in his arms, pressing out the fires and letting charred goats go as he scrabbled to extinguish others.

Then the *real* fire began: a demonic roar with jets of flame enveloping the shaft and hurling it skyward.

Zach fell to the ground, sore afraid, as the irresistible glory of the military-industrial complex engulfed him and his goats. He would have run screaming except that in the jetwash of an Intercontinental Ballistic Missile, you can't stand, let alone run, and if you try to scream, your lungs turn to balloons that pop.

60 **SMACKING THE PYLON**

"We have to get out of here," Calliope whispered.

Krupinski nodded. "You think that they won't hear a limo starting up?"

Calliope's face was whiter than usual. "I don't know. But if they do, you can outdrive them."

Krupinski grinned. "I like the way you think." He leaned over and kissed her, then cranked the ignition. The limo rumbled to life.

Nero and Marcus and Lee looked their way.

"Let's go," Krupinski said, squealing the tires and skidding around the first left. He roared up the main aisle and launched onto the steep ramp that led out. A glance back in the rear-view mirror showed the other limo barreling up the ramp after him.

Calliope shrieked.

"It's not everybody. It's just Marcus," Krupinski assured.

"How do you know?" Calliope asked.

"Nero wouldn't risk it, and he wouldn't want to be left down there alone." Krupinski fishtailed onto the underground expressway amid a hundred other cars. Then he crossed three lanes of traffic and gunned the limo to ninety. "Besides, Marcus is too much of a hothead to let us go."

Unfortunately, Marcus was also an excellent driver.

He followed in their slipstream and surged in at a hundred miles an hour.

"Show off," Krupinski said, stomping the gas pedal to the floor.

Bullets pinged off the limo's top and windows.

"Ha ha!" Krupinski cried. "Evers made it bulletproof! I bet he's got guns in here, too. See what you can find."

Calliope clambered into the back seat and felt around it. "Ah ha." She yanked up the seat cushions and found an M-16. Calliope leaned on the window button, rammed the gun muzzle out the empty space, and emptied a clip into the limo behind them. Bullets cratered the windshield and sliced along the roof and doors but didn't penetrate. "Marcus has the same damned Limo!"

Krupinski shouted, "Then pull your hands in, woman."

Calliope had just gotten the gun inside and the window raised when Marcus drove up beside them and unleashed a hail of bullets. They divoted the thick glass.

"We can't use guns," Krupinski said. "Let's use something else."

"What?"

"Chicago construction."

A sign read, "LEFT LANE ENDS 2000 FEET."

Krupinski slid left, ramming Marcus and locking up with him. Marcus tried to gun his engine, but Krupinski stayed with him.

One thousand feet... five hundred feet... two hundred feet.

Marcus slammed on his brakes, but so did Krupinski. The two limos slid together toward the stanchions that held up the city above. Marcus's engine roared, trying to break free.

He smacked into the pylon. The hood wrapped around it, and the bulletproof windshield went suddenly red.

The impact sent Krupinski's limo spinning out into traffic. Wrenching the wheel left and right, he bashed a couple other vehicles before at last regaining control.

"We've got to get out of blast range," Krupinski said feverishly.

"Where to?" asked Calliope, climbing back into the front seat.

"We're pointed toward Wisconsin."

"Good," she said wearily. "I could use some cheese."

61 SUBSUMPTION

"Susan, I have bad news," Mr Evers says.

I laugh. "Evers, we *are* the bad news."

"It was supposed to be a neutron bomb."

"Yeah, I know."

"But that silo in Meeker, Colorado, held a different rare ordnance. The King George III, a fifty megaton hydrogen bomb that was the U.S. answer to the Soviet Tsar. It won't kill just six million. It'll kill ten million."

"Wow."

"It'll make a crater four hundred feet deep and bring Lake Michigan into it."

I do the mental calculus. "Well, you'll still have a hundred feet of rock above you."

"Won't do any good. That last hundred feet is fissured. It's called the Des Plaines Anomaly. It's an ancient impact crater. The ceiling will drop on top of Conscious 1 and bring the lake down with it."

"Why would Nero destroy Conscious 1?"

"He's not destroying it. He's harvesting it. And me. I thought he would have six million lives and all their knowledge, but he'll also know everything on every computer in the world. He'll be able to see through every camera, listen through every microphone, control every machine."

"How? He'll have destroyed all the physical connections."

"No. The bunker was the seat of Conscious 1, but there are nodes spread throughout the Internet. Mr Nero will have all knowledge and all power and ten million lives."

My heart is shuddering. "Well, that *is* bad news."

"If he's harvesting me, Susan, he's harvesting you, too, and all the other Disciples."

I can't get a breath. It's like the tubes to this damned mask are kinked. "You're lying."

"Did you honestly believe that you would rule the world alongside Death? That he would share power with you and the other Disciples?"

"But that's what it says in *Revelation*."

Mr Evers recites: *" 'And I looked, and behold a pale horse: and his name that sat on him was Death, and Hell followed with him. And power was given unto them over the fourth part of the earth, to kill with sword, and with hunger, and with death, and with the beasts of the earth.' "*

"You see?" I say. "Power was given to *them*. We're going to be *with* him."

"Yes, you will *be. So will I. We'll all be part of him. We are the Hell that comes with him."*

"No. It can't be."

"You know what it's like, harvesting people. At first, you'll be part of the ghost city of Chicago, floating in Mr Nero's brain at the moment of your death, repeating whatever you were doing ad infinitum. Then, he'll ingest you, and you'll be gone."

"Damn it," I say, loosely drawing back on the stick. The F-16 rises slowly into the spangled sky. "Damn it."

"There's no immortality for us. We're being subsumed."

"Why are you telling me this?"

"I'm telling you this because it's the truth."

"You want me to stop him."

"*If there is a way, yes.*"

"I'm not a nice person, Mr Evers."

"*I know that.*"

"I killed three hundred sixty-one people in cold blood. And I didn't weep for them. I am Conquest. I care for no one but me. But the one thing I can't bear is to be conquered."

Mr Evers is silent.

"I can't become part of him. I can't let him win."

"*What choice do you have?*"

"There's one other way."

62 PREPARATIONS TO ASCEND

"I should have thought to bring a second car," Mr Nero said offhandedly as he and Lee stood side by side in the elevator from the computer bunker. It was no trashy freight elevator, but a genuine Otis, with gleaming metal walls and jazz music spooling through the speaker. And it was descending a thousand feet beneath Chicago. "But it's not a big deal. I have a whole fleet at the palace."

"Marcus'll return your limo without a scratch," Lee assured.

"No, he won't."

"You're probably right."

The elevator dinged, and Mr Nero and Lee stepped out into the pleasure dome. Stars twinkled overhead, and yard lights below cast the palace in a spectral aura.

"It's the night of nights." Mr Nero checked his watch. "Ten minutes to immortality."

Lee nodded. "I'll make sure the steak is ready."

"Oh, it's ready," Nero replied. "I prepared it myself. Tenderloin from the head of the World Bank."

"No, I mean, I'll make sure it's grilled."

"No. I'll eat it raw."

"And the blood?"

"Fresh from the artery."

"Very good, sir," Lee said.

"Very good, indeed."

63 **THE NUKE PLUNGES**

I can see Chicago ahead, a diamond necklace strewn beside the black lake.

"We'll have to go in low and fast to do this right," Mr Evers explains.

"Do what you have to."

The engine whines, and I lurch back into my seat. My hands are idle on my jumpsuit, and the stick moves of its own will between my knees. The dial shows we're nearly Mach 2. Another boom rips from my wings.

A voice crackles briefly on the comm. "Ah, unidentified F-16, this is O'Hare Tower. Please provide–" The sound ceases, replaced by Mr Evers's dulcet tones. *"Sorry about that, Susan. O'Hare and Midway were shut down an hour ago, but I forgot to take down their towers. There's a lot to concentrate on."*

"I understand. Get back to it. This has to be right."

"Right."

I sense micro-adjustments in our course as we near the city. It's the South Side, very far from my Oak Park home. I look down on tightly-packed ghettos and houses whose roofs nearly touch, lives lived under elevated roadways.

But up ahead is the shining jewel, the Chicago skyline. I have perhaps a minute left.

The engine surges. We bank right and left and roar out above Grant Park and go into a steep climb.

This is it.

We rocket up above the Willis Tower and keep going. The nose is almost straight up now. We're going to stall at any moment.

It won't matter.

I see it coming, tiny and dull above the city. The booster is gone, but the nuke itself is glowing like a meteor, it's going so fast. It's a star of Bethlehem, shining to announce a newborn king.

The nuke plunges. It's nearly on me.

The plane stalls. It topples back, opening its broad belly to the bomb.

I hate flying.

64 **HARVEST**

"It's been a big day for Chicago," Lupe Gonzalez announced live in nighttime Grant Park. All around her, crowds filed past on their way to concerts. Children occasionally turned to grin and wave and give the finger. Lupe had to shout into her microphone to be heard above the voices and the distorted echoes of various bands. "All day, the city hosted the G-20 leaders in their first round of talks, and all night, the city is hosting over a million revelers at Chicagofest. It's always the biggest event of the year, but just listen to the headliners scheduled for the Pritzker Band Shell–"

Before she could announce them, the sky split with the shriek of a low-flying jet. The ground shook, and Lupe's mic wailed. She yanked the bud from her ear and half-crouched, turning from the camera to stare up after the plane.

She turned back, her smile tinged in worry. "Wow! That was something else. I didn't realize there was an air show this year as well. Always surprises at Chicagofest." While she spoke, the camera shifted to follow the jet fighter, which was climbing above the skyscrapers. "A dramatic display of piloting skill. I can't tell if it's one of the Blue Angels or someone from another group, but what an amazing show above Chicagofest!"

The jet rocketed into the sky but then slowly rolled back. A red ball of fire crashed into its belly.

"Something's going on," Lupe muttered. "What's going on?"

The plane exploded, ripping itself and the red object apart. It looked like a gigantic firework, tracers of flame and smoke radiating outward above Chicago. Some of the fragments were huge, crashing into skyscrapers.

"Oh, no! Oh, no! This isn't supposed to happen," Lupe gabbled into the microphone. "No. No. Not at all. That plane. It wasn't part of a show. That was some sort of attack or... or some kind of response to an attack. There seemed to be another object. Some kind of meteor or something, and it struck the plane, and they both blew up. I – I've never seen anything... nothing like it ever in... ever..."

"It's terrorists!" shouted a man running past. "They're bombing the Sears Tower!"

"Get the Sears Tower, Joe," Lupe said, and the camera swung to show that a hunk of something had struck it, and fires were burning within. Around it, other downtown buildings blazed. "Oh, God! That's what's happening," Lupe said, her voice trembling. "Back on me, Joe, back on me."

The camera swung to focus on her, standing against a tide of people rushing toward their cars. "This is Lupe Gonzalez reporting live from Grant Park, Chicago, where a terrorist attack is underway. We just saw a jet plane fly very low over a million people here in Grant Park and then smash into something and explode. The wreckage is raining down on the city center. Parts of it have crashed into some of the most prominent build-ings, including the Willis Tower and the Hancock Building. Nothing landed here in Grant Park, but there's panic."

The tide of people jostled her, and she braced against it.

"There's pandemonium."

65 LOSING CONSCIOUSNESS

I come awake in a spiraling wreck.
 It's the cockpit, but half of it is gone.
 Stars and windows flash in the other half.
 Fire all around.

I wake up. I'm strapped in some kind of seat. I'm burning.

I wake up. What's happening?

I wake up.

I wake.

I.

66 A CRUEL QUESTION

"Pandemonium!" raged Mr Nero, staring at the elevator panel. "Can't this thing go any faster?"

Lee stood beside him and shook his head. "It has only one speed."

A Herby Hancock song played on the speaker.

Mr Nero's face contorted. "We've got to get different music in here."

Lee nodded, watching the LED above tick off the depth. They were at six hundred feet and rising.

Mr Nero jabbed the button for the computer bunker. "I thought you wanted to get up top."

Nero sneered. "I want you to go in and turn off that fucking Mr Evers."

Lee shrugged. "Whatever you say, Boss."

"And keep him off, past the two-minute threshold. I want nothing left."

The bell rang, and the doors slid open to reveal the warehouse full of servers. Doffing an imaginary hat, Lee stepped from the elevator.

Mr Nero jabbed the "Close Door" button and pumped his finger on the one that would take him to the surface. "Goddamned Otis Corporation."

As the elevator door closed behind him, Lee walked the hundred yards to the hidden control box. It looked like a section of concrete wall, but it pivoted on its axis to reveal a set of large Y-switches. Lee went to the main switch and dragged it down to shut off power.

Light quit the place. A million fans whirred to silence.

Lee stood in the darkness five hundred feet below Chicago and counted. "One, one thousand; two, one thousand; three, one thousand…"

When he reached "One hundred, one thousand," Lee threw the switch back to the top.

Power surged through the board, and energy-deprived systems revived and rebooted. The fixtures overhead moaned, only grudgingly giving light.

Lee dusted his hands and began to walk: It was about five blocks to the Osiris Module. He really could talk to Mr Evers just about anywhere, but Lee was a romantic. There was nothing like talking to a man where his body-parts lay.

In a few minutes, he was there. "Mr Evers?"

"*Yes,*" came the man's voice, reticent and resentful.

Lee tilted his head. "Did *you* make this mess?"

"*A very cruel question.*"

Lee looked at the body parts, some plastic and some flesh. "Sorry. I didn't mean *this* mess. I meant the one above."

"*Yes. I made it.*"

Lee nodded, pursing his lips. "That's what Mr Nero thought. He asked me to shut you down forever."

"*Why didn't you?*"

Lee laughed. "Mr Nero is not an immortal, is he?"

"*No.*"

"He kind of missed his chance, because of you."

"Yes, he did."

"And now you get another chance."

Mr Evers's voice was speculative: *"I suppose so..."*

Nero found her in a wreck off Wacker Drive. Half the cockpit was gone, and what remained had apparently sliced through the power lines on its way down. That would've cost her a hundred lives or so. But Susan Gardner was still breathing. She was lacerated from head to toe, and ribs stuck from her jumpsuit, but she was still breathing.

Susan Gardner, the 311 Miracle. How many lives did she have left? Maybe twenty? Maybe a dozen?

However many, she would be a start.

Mr Nero glanced around. The cops were busy elsewhere, and the neighbors were locked behind their doors. He waddled up to the cockpit and blinked down at Susan Gardner. "Does it hurt much?"

Murmurs came from her mouth.

"It won't hurt for much longer," Mr Nero said. He gently pulled the helmet from her head. Her head fell back against what remained of the seat, and her face was still pristine. Susan Gardner looked back at him with bright blue eyes and cream-colored skin.

"Can you speak, Susan?"

Her lips trembled, but only bloody bubbles emerged.

Mr Nero smiled gently. "I don't know if you knew what Mr Evers planned. I don't know if you are an innocent here or are a co-conspirator. It doesn't matter. You can't live in this body anymore, Susan. It's used up. But you can live in *my* body. That's what I'm going to do for you, now, Susan. I'm going to bring you to live in me, to be part of me. You and the lives left to you will remain forever in me. And these are just the first lives. I'll harvest more. The dream is not gone, Susan. And you are just the beginning of it."

Her eyes seemed dead, but air still rattled in her lungs.

"Poor, poor Susan," Mr Nero said, leaning down to kiss her on the lips. "When you had a body, you were such a beautiful fuck." Then, he set his hand on her forehead and closed his eyes. Spikes of power jutted down from his fingers.

One life absorbed. A second, a third. They spool off her eagerly, rats from a sinking ship. A fourth life, a fifth, but… was that all? There was one more. Her *own* life, the one she started with. She was reluctant to give that one up.

Mr Nero deepened his focus, and fingers of magic constricted on the soul of Susan Gardner. They clutched and pulled.

Her own finger pulled as well, clicking the trigger of the pistol that was pressed to Nero's heart. A bullet ripped through him, stealing one life. She shot again. Another life gone. A third slug, a fourth, a fifth, a sixth–

But Nero had jolted aside, and that last slug caught him in the arm.

She clicked the gun again, but there were no more bullets.

Eyes crazed, Mr Nero staggered up to the cockpit and ripped the gun from Susan's hand. "You have one life, now, and I have one life. It's even." He flipped the pistol over in his hand, grasping the hot barrel, and then smashed her face with the butt of it. She didn't look so pristine anymore. His other hand grasped her forehead as he bashed her again.

She couldn't hold onto her life much longer.

Suddenly, her soul fled into him.

Mr Nero jolted back, panting. He was mantled in blood and a bit of brain, but he had done it. He had made his first harvest.

"Wow," came a voice behind him. It was Lee, smiling ironically at the wrecked cockpit and the bloody Nero. "How'd things turn out?"

Nero shook his head angrily. "I've got two lives. I was supposed to have six million – *ten* million!"

"Just two lives? That's it?" Lee asked.

"Yes!" Nero replied savagely. "Just my own and Susan Gardner's. God, she was a bitch!"

"Yeah."

The old glee returned to his face. "But I have her inside me now, don't I? That's what she would have hated most. Conquest has been conquered! I even have her identity. I can play with her all day long if I want."

Lee laughed. "Let me see her."

Nero scowled. "What? Right here?"

Lee tilted his head. "Come on. Live a little."

Frowning, Mr Nero closed his eyes. He melted from a round-hipped man to a slender and beautiful woman in a red Gucci dress.

"Nice," said Lee as he lifted his revolver and shot Susan Gardner between the eyes.

She fell backward onto the sidewalk, her head gushing like a fountain. Slowly, though, the blood ceased, and the figure transformed into Nero again. He sat up on the sidewalk. "What the hell was that for?"

"I didn't want you to have her," Lee said, gun still leveled at the man's head. "Susan didn't deserve that."

Nero's face flushed. "And now, *you're* going to harvest *me?*"

Lee shook his head. "No, I don't want you hanging around my head for eternity."

He shot a second time. The bullet blasted open Nero's forehead and ripped out the back of his skull. He toppled sideways and bled into the gutter.

Lee put the gun back into the shoulder holster beneath his suit. He looked with satisfaction at his work. He wanted to remember every detail so that he could recount it to Mr Evers.

They were partners now in the conquest of the world – the immortal man and the omniscient and omnipresent machine.

"Nero, Susan…" Lee said, shaking his head in disappointment. "If you can't share power, you've got no place in the New World Order."

Epilogue **MICHAEL**

In a bulletproof atrium in Oak Park, Michael huddled in his armchair and clutched an oversize pillow and watched with horror as the news rolled in.

"I'm standing just a hundred feet from the site," Lupe Gonzalez was saying, "which, as you can see from the police lines and flashing lights is as close as any of us can get. The wreck is obvious, though, even from this distance and – Joe, could you zoom in? – There it is, folks, the ruined cockpit of the jet that had flown so low over Grant Park and collided into what experts are now calling a meteor of some sort. As you can see, the pilot of the plane is still strapped into the wreckage, but the multiple wounds across her body and head indicate she was dead before impact. Yes, that's right, folks – I said *she*. The pilot was a woman, though her disfigurement was so severe that she will have to be identified by dental records."

"A woman?" Michael said. "Who ever heard of a woman doing something like that?"

"Police report that in the lawlessness that followed this strange event, there has been widespread looting and even a few murders. In fact, the chalk line on the ground just twenty feet from the cockpit shows the place where prominent Chicago businessman Wilton Nero was gunned down. One eyewitness said that a thin white man shot Mr Nero and a blonde companion, though no other body has been found."

"A blonde companion?" Michael gulped, rewinding the DVR. He played the clip a second time, and a third, but it still said the same thing. "It can't be. Susan? She wasn't ever going to die."

He looked at the clock. It was nearly 10.30pm, and she wasn't home.

He'd wait up for her. He'd wait up till three in the morning, if he had to.

But then he'd go to bed.

Michael Gardner stood on the steps of the Gardner family crypt and held in his hands the silver urn that bore his sister's remains.

"I want to thank everyone for coming today," he said.

Before him, the black-clothed mourners nodded in appreciation. There were Marcus and Lee, Susan's closest associates, and about ten other people from International Mercantile. They were mourning not just for Susan, but also for Mr Nero.

"If there's one thing my sister taught me, it's that life doesn't make sense. At least not the way it comes at you. You've got to make sense out of it. She was right. What happened to her didn't make sense. She was a victim of a terrorist bombing. The only survivor of Flight 311. And yet, what did she do with this second life? She fought the terrorists. She saved a whole city." He teared up a little. "I was always complaining that she was never home, but she was out training to do what she did."

The group gave him encouraging smiles.

Michael stiffened. "And if *life* doesn't make sense, *death* certainly doesn't. I don't think Susan ever imagined herself dying. I don't think any of us do. But thanks to the 311 Miracle, we didn't die."

His eye caught on the edge of the crowd, where Sergeant Steve Krupinski stood with a very pale woman. A month ago, he was a wanted man. But just after Susan's death, security footage and eyewitness reports and other pieces of evidence had flooded forward to show that he was always acting to save Susan, to serve the FBI. He hadn't been reinstated yet, but he would be. Michael would make sure of it.

He lifted the urn. "So, this is all that's left of my sister, Susan Gardner. She traded her life for ours, and she stopped those murdering monsters, the Death's Disciples."

Marcus whooped excitedly, and Lee broke into applause. The others in the group looked at them and laughed and clapped as well.

Michael smiled, giving them a half bow.

Only Krupinski and the Goth girl were stone-faced, their hands clutched behind their backs.

Turning, Michael went into the family crypt, opened the door where Susan was to rest, and set the silver urn inside. He blinked, his hand running along the smooth metal of the urn. Then he closed the little door, locking it securely. "Sleep well, Big Sis."

As he came back outside, Marcus Peters met him at the base of the stairs and embraced him. "Michael, you've lost a sister, but you've gained a brother."

"More than one," said Lee, stepping up.

"That's good of you to say," Michael replied.

Marcus grinned. "Don't worry, Michael. We'll be looking after you from now on."

Acknowledgments

Thank you, Marc Gascoigne and Lee Harris and everyone else at Angry Robot Books. You guys are rock stars, and I'm glad I get to hang out with you.

Thank you, too, Jeffrey Robshaw and Jennie King – my excellent reviewers. You helped me revise and refine this draft significantly before Marc and Lee even saw it.

And thank you, reader.

Wow. People still read. I guess the Apocalypse isn't here quite yet.

About the author

J Robert King is the award-winning author of over twenty novels, most recently *Angel of Death* and *The Shadow of Reichenbach Falls*. Fifteen years ago, Rob founded the Alliterates, a cabal of writers in the Midwest and West Coast of the US.

Rob also often takes to the stage, starring in local productions such as *The Complete Works of William Shakespeare (Abridged)* and *Arsenic & Old Lace*. He lives in Wisconsin with his lovely wife, three brilliant sons, and three less than brilliant cats.

www.jrobertking.com

A Smile in the Brain –
Ed Greenwood interviews
J Robert King

Recently, J Robert King presented a series of blog posts from his longtime friend and sometime collaborator, Ed Greenwood, creator of *Forgotten Realms*. Ed returned the favour by interviewing Rob about the many things he'd been doing since their last collaboration fifteen years ago. As the two caught up with each other, they talked about inspiration, pet hates, trilogies, and what they wanted to accomplish before they died.

Ed Greenwood: *Various publishers have their own processes for producing a novel (asking an author to write an outline of the book and submit it for approval, for example). However, if given a free hand to develop a novel from the initial idea, how do you prefer to do it? How do you decide which elements to include, and do you sometimes change your mind about such story specifics as the book unfolds?*

Rob King: A book begins with a smile. That's all it

takes – some little something that amuses me or intrigues me. It might be a character: the Angel of Death for Chicago, for example. It might be a situation: a modern man keeps having dwarfs show up at home and work and in the car. Sometimes, the hook is just a mood: whimsy or terror or whimsical terror. Whatever it is, that hook sinks into my skin and starts dragging me along, pulling a story out.

That's how I prefer to work, and that's how Angry Robot allows people to work. They're after the ideas that other publishers shy from because they're new, original – ballsy. They know there's a risk in putting out unique books, but they've also figured out that good writers become great writers when they have this kind of latitude for expression. The best hack book has a ceiling. The best book born out of inspiration has no ceiling.

So, it's got to start with inspiration. There has to be something that gets you excited about an idea. And you *do* have to be in love with that something. But novelists don't have the luxury of writing only when they feel inspired. A lot of novel writing is like running a marathon. At about mile 12, when you still have half the thing to go and the starting gun is silent and the finish line is nowhere, you've got to keep running. Same with writing a novel. You've got to keep writing and believe this is a race you not only *must* run but *must* win.

In that way, a novelist in the middle of a novel is a desperate creature. Faulkner once said, "Everything goes by the board: honor, pride, decency to get the book written… If a writer has to rob his own mother, he will not hesitate; the 'Ode on a Grecian Urn' is worth any number of old ladies."

EG: *Do you prefer plots over characters, or characters over plot, or does it depend on the story?*

RK: Well, a story can't succeed without engaging characters and an interesting plot, so I don't think it's really a matter of preference. If you start with characters you love, you'd better find something meaningful for them to do – otherwise all you have is conversation at a party. If you start with a kick-ass plot, you'd better have some fascinating characters to bring it to life.

For me, a character begins with a voice. I have to hear the person speak. It's not good enough to have a physical description, a background, a set of goals and dreams, a set of limitations and frustrations. I still don't know the person until he or she speaks. That's when the character is real. And sometimes a character can just speak out of stillness and darkness, and I know the person even though I have none of those other details. Then, it's just a matter of listening to that voice, writing it, letting it tell me about who it is. That's the schizophrenic side of being a writer. These characters are already inside you. They're just fighting to get the microphone.

And, as far as plotting is concerned, you can make outlines and try to hit certain plot points, but really, you have to *live* the plot with your characters. You have to get lost with them, win some fights and lose others, get betrayed with them, and battle to the death with them. That's one reason it's painful to write. You're as vulnerable as anyone in your book.

EG: *The Arthurian mythos is both a touchstone of English root literature and an ongoing inspiration to many rising modern fantasy writers. You've done a superb Arthurian trilogy for Tor Books; are you "done" with Arthur, now? (If so, why?) Or are there other Arthurian tales you'd like to tell (and if so, why)?*

RK: The Arthurian stories are bedrock for fantasy. They were, in a way, the first fantasy novels. Malory's Arthur was a conscious reinvention of a Dark Ages figure, surrounding him with Medieval trappings. All the things people love most about Arthurian stories – the knights, the chivalry, the castles, the kings, Merlin – none of it existed at the time of the historic Arthur. Malory invented them. And right now, Maurice Broaddus is consciously reinventing Arthur for modern urban America. He's carrying on a thousand year-old tradition.

I did three Arthurian books, one focused on Merlin, a second on Lancelot, and a third on Morgan Le Fey. Each was a character study, a view of the many stories through the mind of one of the principals. In that way, the three books also had three very different moods. The Merlin book was a comedy, even ending in a marriage. The Lancelot book was a passion play, and the Morgan book was a tragedy.

Am I done with Arthur? No. There's no sense in

every being done with mythology. The archetypes, at the very least, will crop up again, and perhaps there's an Arthurian romp ahead for me, as well.

EG: *You have done horror, high fantasy, "weird" short stories, and other projects that stake out some pretty wide horizons. Yet at your "day job" at Write Source you create and oversee educational school writing. How has working on the wilder projects influenced your editing and prose for Write Source, and vice versa?*

RK: I must admit, I was pretty wild and woolly when I arrived at Write Source – an accomplished writer, but one very unfamiliar with boundaries. I'd write an essay comparing vampires to werewolves, and it would get struck from the book. I'd write an essay about the sex lives of orchids, and it too would get banned. I tried to extol the virtues of getting tattoos (I have two so far) and would get vetoed. I had to learn how to rein in, find topics that would interest students without annoying teachers and causing parents to burn down the school. This was my first real education in the notion of multiple audiences.

Before I came to Write Source, I really wrote novels just for myself. If they amused me, that was all I cared about. As a result, many of my earlier novels required a lot from the reader. My attitude was – keep up.

Now, I have a different attitude. Writing, fundamentally, is about communicating, and every communication situation has three main components – you, me, and what we're talking about. In writing for

Write Source, I had to learn how to write for fourth graders, third graders, second graders – high school and community college and college. From that, I've developed a much stronger sense of audience. I've also learned that it's not about the words. It's about the communication.

EG: *If you somehow gained control of all the large and influential North American publishers for long enough to "set" their lineups of the books they'd publish for a year, what trends, sub-genres, and formats would you build? Revive? Bury? (And, of course, why?)*

RK: To be honest, I don't have that kind of broad vision. I have a vision for the books I'm working on, but I don't have the sense of what books should be published. For example, *Twilight* would never have appealed to me, but I'd be loathe to bury something just on those grounds. The *Twilight* books have a whole generation reading, and good for them. It's actually the same with Harry Potter. I came pretty late to the JK Rowling fan club, mostly because I was so pissed off that I hadn't written these books myself. But now I'm reading them to my boys every night before bed. I'm sure glad it wasn't my myopic vision that got to say yeah or nay on Potter.

I tease my wife that she is a promiscuous reader. She'll brush up against a book in the library and, next thing you know, she's in bed with it. Then, a week later, she'll toss it aside for the next thing. She'll even happen back on a book and read two chapters before realizing she has read it already.

I'm not promiscuous. To read a novel, I have to love the writer's voice. Then, I'm hooked, and I'll read everything by that writer.

An editor who sets publication schedules needs to be promiscuous, a social butterfly, a gadabout. That person needs to read everything and like twenty percent and love one percent. I'm not that guy. I have trouble getting beyond the one percent.

EG: *Decades ago, the success of* The Lord of the Rings, *coupled with Tolkien's original publisher's market need to split it into three volumes, established the trilogy as a dominant format in modern fantasy publishing. Given your druthers, do you prefer to write stories that stand complete in one physical book, or treat books as episodes in the lives of ongoing characters and slowly "build" a series as a sequence of books covering important episodes, or do you prefer having the space to structure a single coherent storyline over three books, or four (or however many)?*

RK: When writing a trilogy, the question is whether this is one story in three parts, or three stories that belong to one large cycle. Either solution has its problems. Arbitrarily splitting a single book into three poses the problem of creating an unsatisfying story arc in a given book. But writing three distinct books that aren't really about a single story feels like a commercial cop-out.

When working on a trilogy, I search for what I call a "triune archetype." I think of things that come in threes and consciously model each book after one part of the trinity. That might be maiden, mother, and crone. It might be creator, redeemer, sustainer. It might be comedy, passion play, tragedy. By using this approach, I create three books that complement each other as a unit, but that also tell individual stories. The Arthurian trilogy, as I've mentioned, followed the comedy/passion-play/tragedy model, but it also told about the creation of Camelot, the wounding of Camelot, and the destruction of Camelot. As a result, it's been called not just a trilogy, but a triptych – three paintings from an altarpiece telling one epic tale.

I guess I like grand gestures, so my trilogies turn out to be somewhat Wagnerian in scope.

I've never been able to write an open-ended series of books about the same characters. To my mind, characters need to change over the course of a story. Once a novel or a trilogy is finished, I'm done with the characters. Also, my characters have a penchant for dying, which precludes sequels. You can't have *Romeo and Juliet II*.

EG: *Do you have any pet "hates" in terms of storytelling techniques or over used or badly handled story elements? Have you any techniques and elements in mind that you think are too often overlooked, or unjustly neglected?*

RK: I am pretty picky about what I'll gladly read, which I suppose gets down to these "hates" that you mention. It's an occupational hazard for an editor. Editors are terriers, trained to go to ground after the vermin in writing and snatch up those skulking rats and shake them until their necks are broken.

In that regard, I hate infodumps in narration. Authors need to seamlessly fold exposition in with action, or I gag. Also, I hate when characters spend a chapter talking about what they should do next. This is the author trying to figure out the story rather than just telling the story. Whenever my characters meet to figure out what to do, I let them, and then I cut the scene and have them just *do* whatever they decided on.

I also hate verbosity. It's taken twenty years for me to weed it out of my own work, and now I have an allergic reaction to it in others'. Once, I wrote a 100,000 word novel, and my editor told me I had to cut it by 10,000 words. I griped, but I did it – and found the book much better for having done it. Now, I routinely cut 10,000 to 15,000 words from every book I write. If a novel of mine ends up at 80,000 words, it's because it began at 95,000.

EG: *We once did a book together (*The Diamond*) in very little time. If we'd instead had a year to collaborate on it, and the freedom for you as the in-house editor to choose exactly how the collaborative process was going to proceed, how would you have wanted that process to "work"? (And should your preferences be a preferred model for all collaborative fantasy novels set in shared world settings, or do you intend them to be what you prefer for that specific project?)*

RK: As I recall, the way we did *The Diamond* was that I wrote the first draft, and you turned it into a final draft. In that sense, you were serving in the editorial role that I have had on a number of your books. It worked out very well, in my opinion.

But how two people collaborate is really up to the two people, I should think. I've known a number of writing partnerships, and each has worked like a pair of dancers – two people moving in coordination. But every pair of dancers have their own style.

I don't know the best way to collaborate. To my mind, there needs to be some kind of formal division of labor, as we did – one starting and the other finishing. Or two people could write a novel if each wrote from the point of view of a different main character. That would be interesting. But there is something very intimate about any partnership, especially a writing partnership, and I'm not sure I've worked out any special secrets about how to make that dance work.

EG: *Are there any classic or well-known novels that if you had been the writer, you would have approached the same story very differently? (If so, how and why?)*

RK: Oh, probably all of them, which is why it is good that I didn't write them. Let's face it. A great novel is great partly because of the mind that gave it birth. I can no more write a Vonnegut novel than I can sing with Billy Holiday's voice. I would've totally blown *The Lord of the Rings*. I couldn't have written *The Amazing Adventures of Kavalier and Clay* (though I wish I had). I'm in awe of *Absalom! Absalom!*, and have read *The Little Prince* about twenty times. All of these masterworks came from voices that aren't mine.

So, my job is to find out what my voice can do. I've got to write the stories only I can. Again, to quote Faulkner: "Don't bother to be better than just your contemporaries or predecessors. Try to be better than yourself."

EG: *Some writers ponder "things I'd like to do before I die" in a literary sense, while others live in the heat of the moment and rarely look up from the fray until life events force some downtime or they reach their elder years. Do you have any "pet projects" you'd love to tackle, before you put your pen down? Anything not written yet that you'd like to be remembered for?*

RK: I guess I'm still in the fray. I'm having enough fun with what I'm writing right now that I don't have my eye on some faraway project. I do have a few pets projects – one about the divine sister of Jesus and another about a hippy detective – but they haven't come to fruition yet. Each concept has its flaws, and each needs a major infusion of attention and imagination in order to work. Yes, I hope before I die that I can resurrect these two.

You know, the best a writer can do is create great characters and terrific stories. If a book has these, it is a success, in my opinion. If the book also plumbs some deep layer of the author's psyche and discovers meaningful themes along the way, the book is more than a success. It's a kind of therapy for the writer and for anyone else who is dealing with the same fundamental questions. And if a book delves deeper, touching not just on the inner soul of one writer and a handful of readers, but actually on the zeitgeist of a time – I'm talking *Gatsby*, here, or *Farewell to Arms* – then the book is a great work.

Would I like to write such a thing? I'd be lying to say I wouldn't. Of course I want to write great literature. But I won't get there by being abstruse and inaccessible. And I won't get there by loading a story down with "significant themes." If I get there at all, it'll be by caring about characters and stories and by writing something that happens to capture something real about this strange and wonderful and horrible time we live in.

ISBN 978-0-85766-019-0 • eBOOK 978-0-85766-020-6

J. ROBERT
KING

ANGEL
OF
DEATH

"King does everything well - characters,
prose, plot, humour, drama." — *Locus*

"A clever trap to lure you in before
sucking your brains out."
STEPHEN D SULLIVAN, AUTHOR OF MONSTER SHARK

ANGRY ROBOT

Teenage serial killers
Zombie detectives
The grim reaper in love
Howling axes **Vampire hordes** **Dead men's clones** The Black Hand
Death by cellphone
Gangster shamen
Steampunk anarchists
Sex-crazed bloodsuckers
Murderous gods
Riots **Quests Discovery Death**

Prepare
to welcome
your new
Robot overlords.

angryrobotbooks.com

LAVIE TIDHAR
THE
BOOKMAN

MATT FOREECK'S
AMORTALS

DAMAGE TIME
COLIN HARVEY

CHRIS
ROBERSON
BOOK OF
SECRETS

Triumff
HER MAJESTY'S HERO
Mr. DAN ABNETT

PRETTY
LITTLE
DEAD
THINGS
GARY McMAHON

▸ MOXYLAND
▸ Lauren Beukes

KING MAKER

"A SPECTACULAR WRITER" - ROBERT J SAWYER

LIVE TONIGHT
ON ANGRY ROBOT
TWO MEN. TWO
KNIVES. ONE DUEL.
ONE DEATH IN A
BURST OF BLOOD.
JOIN US EVERY
NIGHT AS WE FIND
OUT WHO HAS THE
EDGE
THOMAS
BLACKTHORNE

MAR 1 1

Psssst! Get
advance
intelligence on
Angry Robot's
nefarious plans
for world
domination.
Also, free stuff.
Sign up to our
Robot Legion at
angryrobotbooks.
com/legion
This is how we
roll.

ANGRY ROBOT